No Accident

Bennett Vignettes—Book One
A Historical Series of Enduring Romance
By Jennifer M. Seest

Cover Photography:
Unveiling of Monument to Confederate Soldiers and Sailors
Courtesy "The Maryland Historical Society"
201 West Monument Street, Baltimore, Maryland 21201
www.MDHS.org
Used with permission.

Portrait of Jennifer M. Seest
Courtesy "Suzanna Hand Photography"
Saint Mary's, Georgia 31558
my.homewithGod.com/photosbyhand
Used with permission.

All Scripture is quoted from the **King James Version** of the Holy Bible.

Copyright © 2003 by Jennifer M. Seest.

NO ACCIDENT
By Mrs. Jennifer M. Seest

Printed in the United States of America.

ISBN: 1-594672-25-3

All Rights Reserved. No portion of this book may be reproduced or transmitted in any form without the written permission of the author.

Published by Xulon Press
www.XulonPress.com

Xulon Press books are available in bookstores everywhere, and on the Web at www.XulonPress.com

Dedication

This book is dedicated to all of my sisters…by blood, by marriage, and by salvation, you are so precious to me. And special thanks to my sisters—Joann, Katie, Mom Bass, and Debbie—who helped me so much with proofreading and constructive criticism as well as well-timed praise.

And thank you, Daniel, for all your patience through early mornings, late nights, and leftovers as I worked on this project! You are my best friend on earth and definitely the inspiration for all the romance and fun banter between the characters in this my first book. *I love you!*

And I must take time to thank the LORD for allowing me to follow this desire of my heart. *You are my Saviour, my joy, my song, my all. Thank You for the trials. Though they sometimes seem like "accidents", I know they serve to draw me closer to You.*

Contents

1	Angels Watching	9
2	Doctor's Orders	14
3	Getting Settled	21
4	Good Morning	25
5	Testimonies	30
6	Growing In Love	39
7	Back to Church	47
8	Sunday Afternoon	54
9	Jessie's Elixir	60
10	Picnic at the Waterfront	68
11	Letters From Home	74
12	Christmas Carol	79
13	Behold, The Lamb of God!	90
14	New Year, 1889	99
15	Celia	105
16	Unequally Yoked	114
17	The Dye House Picnic	124
18	My Own Fault	132
19	Reunion	138
20	"God Be With You..."	146
21	Above All We Ask or Think	153
22	Arrangements	164
23	The Montague Farm	170
24	Honoring Parents	179
25	Justified	185
26	Vows	195
27	Charleston	202
28	Baptism in Baltimore	210
29	Back to Work	216
30	Uncle Wesley	222
31	Aunt Lavinia's Gift	229
32	The Trying of Your Faith	238
33	Recovery	243
34	Honest Communication	251
35	Happy Birthday, Charlie	263
36	Giving Thanks	271
37	Blessing Upon Blessing	279
38	God's Gift	287
	Epilogue	291

Preface

The inspiration for this book came as I was driving home after picking my son up from school in late April of 2003. A large truck pulled out in front of our vehicle, and we very nearly had an accident. Then it dawned on me, *"There are no accidents with God in control."* Before I reached our home, which is a mere five miles from where the "close call" occurred, I had the title, main characters, and story outline for this book!

How we deal with life's trials is so vitally important. It is my heart's desire to share with my readers—whether there are ten or ten million of you—that the Bible does have the answers for how to cope with our trials. Though the characters in this book are entirely fictional, their troubles are very real. My purpose in writing is to share in an interesting way some of the answers I have found in God's Word to the questions all of us have at one time or another.

But sanctify the Lord God in your hearts:
and be ready always to give an answer
to every man that asketh you
a reason of the hope that is in you
with meekness and fear....
I Peter 3:1

Acknowledgements

Hymns:
1. *Behold, The Lamb of God!*
George Frederick Handel (1685-1759).
2. *Doxology*
Thomas Ken, (1637-1711), Written 1674.
3. *My Plea*
J.L. Baker.
4. *O Holy Night*
Placide Clappeau, 1847; Translated from French to English by John S. Dwight (1812-1893).
5. *Rejoice, Ye Pure in Heart*
Edward H. Plumptre (1821-1891), Written 1865.
6. *Steal Away*
African-American spiritual, Dated pre-1860's.
7. *Thy Word is Like a Garden, Lord*
Edwin Hodder (1837-1904), *The New Sunday School Hymn Book*, 1863.

Text:
1. *Justified*, the sermon by "Pastor Crosby" in Chapter 25, is quoted directly from the author's pastor, Pastor Samuel Crosby, from a sermon preached Wednesday May 13th, 2003 at Coastal Baptist Church in St. Mary's, Georgia.
Used with his permission.
2. The *wedding vow excerpts* in Chapter 26 were from the author's own wedding, as given by Pastor Clarence Helms, November 1995 at New Testament Baptist Church in Floral City, Florida
Used with his permission.
3. *Grampa's Recipe for Bread Pudding* in Chapter 8 is the author's own concoction, and it is delicious, with or without the raisins!

Chapter One

Angels Watching

**Baltimore, Maryland
November 22, 1888**

The elevator never seemed to want to go down swiftly enough for Carol, so once again she opted for the stairwell. Although her office was in one of the tallest buildings in the city, the eight-floor climb did not seem so very formidable. Walking was much to be preferred to taking that modern, infernal contraption called an elevator! She fairly flew down the stairs, her gloved hand lightly touching the handrail just in case of a misstep.

As she made her way out into the late autumn sunlight the usual after-work-hours' sense of *freedom* filled her. *"What a blessing this job has been, Lord,"* she whispered softly, merging into the crowd moving to their various destinations along the city's sidewalk. She was headed toward one of Baltimore's beautiful parks for a moment of solitude before going home to her room third floor back at the boarding house.

When Carol's father was seriously injured in a farming accident, she knew that her secretarial skills could be the means of pulling her family through financially. Every Friday her paycheck was tithed, money set aside for her room and board, and every penny extra was sent back home to the small town in the Carolinas that Carol called home.

The Lord was an integral part of Carol's and her family's lives. They truly believed God alone had brought her father, William Montague, through the Civil War in one piece. William returned from the war to his childhood sweetheart, and he and his darling Emily had a home filled with love and laughter. Their three children—Carol being the oldest, then Caleb, and lastly Celia—were truly William and Emily's pride and joy. Caleb, nineteen, was still back home, helping their father keep up the farm as best he could. Seventeen year old Celia was about to graduate and hoped to use her teaching certificate by teaching at the local school. But twenty year old Carol headed to the nearest big city north of their hometown. She thought it best to use her secretarial training there, going far away from hearth and home. The thriving metropolis she chose was Baltimore, which had also survived the War Between the States, though strongly divided. The first bloodshed of the war had happened right there in Baltimore in fact. Then there was the devastating fire of 1873 that swept through much of the city, and the strong people of Baltimore came back better than ever from that terrible trial as well.

Baltimore's history was fascinating to Carol, coming from a small town; but she didn't have much time for study. The Monument to Confederate Soldiers and Sailors was not far from her boarding house, and it seemed a daily acknowledgment that the city of Baltimore believed there was heavenly intervention in the War Between the States as well. The strong angel towering over, yet gently guiding, the war-worn soldier.... It still touched her heart every time she saw it.

She was still picturing the guardian angel in her mind's eye as she stepped off the curb to cross Lexington. Normally in control, she froze in her tracks as she heard and then saw the horse and buggy bearing down from her left! With a scream she turned, trying frantically to regain the curb; but it was too late.

"*Good God*, what have I done?" cried the man at the reins. With one swift motion he was down from his buggy and looking into the bluest eyes he'd ever beheld. "Miss, are you okay?"

Carol was shaken, muddied, and embarrassed; but it wasn't until she attempted to stand that she realized she was also injured from her tumble and the collision. She seemed unable to put any weight at all on the injured leg.

Too embarrassed to face the man kneeling beside her, she looked at her lap as she replied, "I'm so sorry, sir. It was so clumsy and thoughtless of me...entirely my fault."

The man raised a brow, smiled, then went back to the task at hand: helping this lady and finding out who she was. He thought to himself, *"She's obviously no city girl, or she'd have never taken the blame for the collision. Yet her dress, hat, and gloves are comely enough, even though they're now speckled with mud from the accident."*

After these observations, he garnered his thoughts enough to introduce himself properly. "My name is Charles Bennett, Miss. Please, call me 'Charlie'. Is there anything I can do for your present relief? May I take you to a doctor in my buggy perhaps?"

"Oh! I do hope I won't be needing a physician, Mr. Bennett! I couldn't possibly...that is.... Could you please just give me a ride to my boarding house?" It was the first thing she thought of, yet it was simply unthinkable to inconvenience this stranger, so obviously a gentleman, in such a fashion. "Forgive me. I should not have presumed—"

"Don't give it another thought, Miss...Miss?"

A crowd was beginning to gather, the traffic having come to a standstill; and drivers and horses alike were becoming irritable. "Enough with the pleasantries, will ya?" cried out a particularly bothersome driver of a local mail wagon. Without any further ado, Charlie lifted Carol in his arms and placed her gently in the covered buggy.

Though tall for a woman at nearly five-foot-nine, she seemed light to the young man. His arms lingered about her a moment longer than needed upon setting her down, as he awaited her reply. Carol blushed, then averting her eyes again she said softly, "'Carol'. My name is Carol Montague, sir."

He climbed into the carriage as quickly as possible, and in no time they were moving down Lexington at a steady pace. Charlie noticed Carol's embarrassment; but he also knew that if she didn't unlace her shoe quickly, it could swell to the point of having to cut the leather boot off.

11

"Miss Montague, try to unlace and remove your shoe. Chivalry would demand I do it for you; but considering the recent complaints, I do not believe the traffic behind us would deem that wise."

She giggled, joining in the humor at the surly mailman's expense. Charlie rather liked the sound of her laughter, not raucous or artificial like he had heard from ladies at work. It was totally unrehearsed, fully heartfelt. "So, where are we headed?"

"Oh, well, Mr. Bennett...."

Turning to face her he gently corrected, *"Charlie...?"*

Again, the bubbling laughter caught his ear as well as effecting his heart is a strange, new way. "Yes, 'Charlie', I...you must have been on your way somewhere when I so rudely interrupted your mission! Surely if you just put me off at the corner of—"

"Forgive me, m'lady, but in the condition you are presently in I cannot as a gentleman 'put you off' to be walking anywhere. May I take control of the situation? My dear Carol, had I been driving the General a bit more slowly, the accident could have been completely prevented. Allow me to take full responsibility, and thus to take you to our family physician for treatment for which I will gladly pay. Please tell me you can agree to this without further dispute?"

It was her turn to raise an eyebrow and smile, for he made it sound like the epitome of ungratefulness for her not to accept his offer. He caught the look and chuckled, "Miss Montague, I do believe I may have met my match in autonomous thinking! Now, try to relax. Here, let me draw this driving robe about you. Whether from the cold or fright, you're still trembling; and this chilled November evening is doing nothing to warm you."

Carol's eyes softened at the stranger's kindness. It seemed like forever since she had been so well cared for, though she had only left her father's house in late spring. There was always so much work to be done that Carol had hardly taken the time to develop any friendships whatsoever. She had gone on through the days hardly thinking of the little kindnesses her family bestowed on one another daily, as her mother would say, *"in honor, preferring one another"*.

Carol listened as the handsome stranger tried to put her at ease with his steady banter about the weather, his buggy, and his hometown of Baltimore. She glanced at his clean-shaven profile, thankful for the lack of the current-fashioned facial hair. His hair was short, parted down the middle with waves and a stray curl here and there from the recent upset. He had smiling brown eyes and a rather broad, boyish face, which turned to look her way as he was talking and noticed her attentiveness. It was as he gestured that she noticed he wore a rather large ruby ring on his left hand. More than likely married, the sudden realization seemed a pity to Carol, though she did not wish to analyze her feelings about that discovery.

Just then he drew up his horse, the General, beside a neat, white-clapboard house with a sign out front: "Doctor Nehemiah A. Whittle, Apothecary".

"Here we are! Let me just check and see if he's in." Charlie hopped gingerly from the buggy and with long strides reached the door in no time.

His knock was answered by a nurse in neatly starched uniform, apron, and cap. After a brief word, she went back inside as Charlie returned to the buggy. "Nurse Whittle is Dr. Whittle's daughter-in-law. She's bringing a wheelchair."

"Oh, Mr. Bennett, certainly I am in no need of such a contraption! I can—", and as she attempted to stand to prove her point, she proved *his* by toppling sideways towards him. She thought she couldn't possibly have embarrassed herself further, but as she blushed crimson she knew otherwise. The throbbing in her right ankle was nothing to the throbbing of her heart though, as once again Charlie Bennett caught her close to him and carried her up the walk to where the nurse met him with the wheeled chair. Placing her gently down yet again, he smiled at her blush and confusion, brushing an escaped wavy strand of hair out of her face before allowing her to be wheeled away.

Chapter Two

Doctor's Orders

Doctor Whittle was short of stature, a good foot shorter than Charlie. His white handlebar mustache seemed to suit him however, along with his tousled white fringe of hair and wire-rimmed glasses perched atop his balding head.

"Well, young Charlie, you've rescued yourself a fair damsel! You say you're at fault for the injuries she has sustained?"

Charlie grinned like a schoolboy at the old family friend, fingering his bowler hat anxiously. "Yes, sir. The General and I ran her down on Lexington." Then realizing anew the gravity of the situation, he questioned, "I'm prepared to take full responsibility. How bad is her injury, sir?"

The good doctor sat down at his desk, adjusted his glasses, and wrote a few notes; then he pushed his glasses back up on his head and turned serious eyes to Charlie. "I know it could have been worse, but it does appear to be a fracture. She's going to have to stay off that leg for a good bit if she hopes to heal fully. You say you are taking full responsibility. Are you prepared for what that kind of responsibility entails? What do you know of her? of her housing? her job? her family?"

Charlie began pacing the small office. "Next to nothing, sir, but her name and that she lives in a boarding house here in town." It occurred to Charlie that unless she had the pleasure of being in a first floor room, her place of residence was out of the question. He raised concerned eyes to Dr. Whittle, who appeared to be examining Charlie as closely as he had the young lady in the other room. "What would you suggest, sir?"

The doctor's pale blue eyes sparkled as he smiled at Charlie's sincere concern. "I would suggest a week's bed rest in quiet surroundings, followed by several more weeks with a cast for recuperation. And, Charlie," he paused, holding the young man's attention, "she'll need a good deal of patience and prayer. My intuition tells me she's of a self-reliant turn of mind; and being cooped up, even for her own well-being, will not be easy for her."

Dr. Whittle had prayed for young Charlie Bennett's salvation since the day he brought Charlie into the world. The wise old physician knew that one of the curses of financial independence was a lack of dependence on the Lord, and he began to hope that perhaps this young woman would be the winning of the wealthy young man's soul.

"Take her to your family's home, Charlie, or maybe your Aunt Lavinia's. Get her settled in and send for her things, then contact her place of work to inform them of her condition. 'Tis a great responsibility, my boy."

"Yes, sir," Charlie spoke firmly almost as a vow, looking into the doctor's old eyes. "I'll see that she's well taken care of. And thank you, sir. Thank you very much."

Charlie shook Dr. Whittle's hand, then walked to the front room where Carol sat in a wheelchair waiting, her injured foot now adorned with a double splint wrapped in gauze. He braced himself for the battle he knew awaited him in convincing this young lady of her need of aid, of his need to *supply* the aid.

As he knelt before the wheeled chair, he took one of her hands in his own as he explained the situation Dr. Whittle presented them with. He watched her eyes, so transparent to her thoughts and worries, as they expressed her concern about her job, her being a burden to him, and something else....

"But, Mr. Bennett, I *cannot* lose my place. I'm only a stenographer, but I make money that my family *needs* right now...to *live* on!" She looked over his shoulder, out the window at the darkened street glowing with recently lit streetlamps. *"How can I explain?"* she thought desperately, even then knowing that there was nothing she could do. Everything he'd suggested made perfect sense, but until she returned to her job, there would be precious little income for her family. And how could this obviously affluent young man possibly hope to understand that kind of obligation, that kind of need?

Her eyes went down to her hand in her lap, then to her other hand in his strong, warm grasp. With an air of determination she looked into his eyes. "Well, Charlie Bennett, *the Lord giveth, and the Lord taketh away; blessed be the name of the Lord.* I will do as you wish and trust God will take care of me and my family."

The doctor, who from his place in the doorway heard as her soft voice quoted Scripture, smiled and offered a silent prayer that this young girl would indeed be the saving of Charlie Bennett, even if they did only meet "by accident".

※

As the buggy pulled into the circular drive before the Bennett House, Carol caught her breath. They had ridden in silence from the doctor's office, both thinking at runaway horse speed of what must be done before retiring for the night. The lanterns lit the portico of Charlie's home with warmth and welcome, and a distinguished-looking liveried servant came out upon their arrival.

"Mistah Charles!" spoke the mahogany-hued servant with the low, smooth tones of his people, "we've been *that* concerned for you, sir! And who is this here with you?" His large, inquisitive eyes searched Carol's face kindly.

"This is Miss Carol Montague, Lucas. We...um...met by accident this afternoon. I've only come to inform mother of where I'm headed. I hope to catch Aunt Lavinia at home."

"Oh, Mistah Charles, your Aunt Lavinia's *here*, havin' tea with your mothah! Do you both wish to come inside and speak with them?"

Charlie was already climbing down from the buggy distractedly. "Indeed, Lucas! That *is* a coincidence! Could you remain here with this young lady while I go in and speak with them both briefly?"

As Charlie dashed into the house, Lucas stood at attention beside the buggy muttering, "Ain't no *coincidence*, Mistah

Charles, 'tis the hand of the good Lord, that's what."

Carol smiled in the semi-darkness, for despite her pain and inconvenience, to hear from another child of God that the Lord may have a purpose in all she'd been through gave her a heartfelt sense of joy. She leaned toward Lucas from her comfortable place in the buggy.

"You know Him, too, do you, Mr. Lucas?" Carol asked the butler softly.

He turned, giving her a beaming smile in the near darkness. "Yes'm. I shore do."

In only a very few moments Charlie, closely followed by two of the most refined women Carol had ever beheld, came striding from the house. "Carol, this is my mother Laura Bennett and my Aunt Lavinia Sutherland. Mother, this is Miss Carol Montague."

Pleasantries were exchanged before Charlie got back to the order of business. "Carol, my aunt said she would gladly take you in tomorrow morning if you could stay here this one evening. Would that be agreeable to you?" His face held such concern that she could not refuse him, especially as his aunt and mother stepped forward to encourage her.

Lavinia spoke up first. "I am ever so sorry, Miss Montague, but our guest rooms are on the second floor! I will rectify this tonight so that you can have a first floor room for your recovery." Carol nodded, trying to take it all in; but just as quickly Lavinia prepared to take her leave. "Lucas? Please see to my carriage. Goodbye, Laura! A pleasure chatting with you, as always!" In a blur of sparkles, fur coat, and feathers, she was on her way home.

"Goodbye, Lavinia dear! Goodbye!" Charlie's mother called out. As she finished waving her handkerchief, she turned back to the girl in the buggy. "Miss Montague, you are *most* welcome. My son has explained what happened, and I want you to know that you are our guest. Charlie, can you carry her inside? She and I both need to get in before we catch a chill." She turned and walked to the front door, a picturesque silhouette in the open doorway. Charlie didn't hesitate, but unceremoniously scooped Carol up in his arms again, smiling down at her in the lamplight as he stepped inside.

The mansion was indeed as beautiful inside as out, with

statuaries, chandeliers, and the finest furnishings of wood, brocade, and marble that Carol had ever seen. But she was a bit distracted by Charlie's nearness, his face in profile just inches from her own. His coat smelled of lavender and sunshine and a hint of aftershave.

Trying to divert her thoughts from Charlie, she turned her head and noticed that there were crystal vases with multitudes of dried flower arrangements all along the way, from the foyer to the lovely room that was to be her abode for the night. There was a large window in the room that was to be hers, but it was curtained as night had already fallen. A garden had been brought inside however, with more dried arrangements, pale pink rosebud paper on the walls, matching pink rosebud chintz curtains and spread, and white eyelet trimmings here and there. It looked nothing like the rest of the house she had seen. The bedroom appeared to be very cozy and old fashioned, *homey* in fact.

Two maids came in to attend Carol after Charlie and his mother left. They gently removed her muddied suit, remaining boot, and petticoats, then gave her a sponge bath with rosewater—the sweet fragrance reminded Carol of her childhood. The younger of the servants, Jessie, helped her into a soft chenille robe just her size, that in its mauve hues seemed to go with the room. It smelled of lavender...like Charlie's coat! Carol smiled at the thought as Jessie brushed her hair then neatly braided it and the other servant, Beatrix, busied herself with a tray for "Missy Carol", as they had already taken to calling their new charge.

As the patient sipped a soothing cup of chamomile tea there came a knock on the door, and Charlie and his mother entered. Charlie's mother didn't seem to be as sparkling and showy as Aunt Lavinia somehow. She was still quite refined, but in a more retiring way.

"How are you, my dear? Oh, but I can see you've gotten some of your color back. Jessie, Beatrix, thank you so much for tending to our young friend." The smiling servants removed the empty tray and basket of muddied clothing and bowed out of the room graciously.

Mrs. Bennett sat on the edge of the bed and let her eyes roam about the room before turning back to Carol. "This was my mother's room for many years. She's been gone since just after the war, but we kept it just as it was."

Carol could tell that Mrs. Bennett was picturing her mother in the room, and she held her peace so as not to interrupt the precious memories. Then Mrs. Bennett turned misty eyes to her and placed a soft, warm hand on Carol's cheek. "I do hope you'll recover quickly, my dear, but know that you're most welcome for as long as it takes for you to heal." Next she reached into the desk beside the bed and pulled out stationery. "Feel free to use this and the pen and ink here on the desktop to write a letter to your parents. I can have Lucas post it first thing. And if there is anything else you need," she said, reaching deeper into the drawer and touching something that brought a smile. She pulled out a small but ornate silver bell. "Just ring this, and someone will attend you."

Mrs. Bennett stood then and walked discreetly over to the door so that Charlie could say goodnight; but as he looked into Carol's eyes, he was at a total loss for words.

"Miss Montague...Carol, if you would be so kind as to give me your address, I can go fetch your clothes and other personal belongings from your room and bring them back here." That seemed to break into her dreamy thoughts and cause her to start.

"Oh, Charlie...that is, there are things I need from my room, but I have no wish to burden you further...." With very little argument however, Carol gave him directions and the key to her room at the Bailey Boarding House on Harrington Street. With a feather soft kiss of her hand, he was gone.

∽∾

Much prayer went up on Charlie Bennett's behalf that evening. *"Lord,"* Laura Bennett took a moment to pray before she went to greet her husband as he arrived home late from the bank, *"do have Your will and way in this situation. Heal this poor child, and please let her somehow bring my Charlie closer to Thee. He needs You so. In Jesus' name I ask, amen."*

"And, Father, about Charlie," Doc Whittle prayed in his matter-of-fact manner, *"please touch his heart with his need for*

You. I can't help but think this girl...but You know best. Thy will be done."

"Dear Father in Heaven, what a blessed place You have brought me to! Thank You, thank You so much for taking such good care of me. A moment later, and I would have stepped out in front of that mail carrier!" Carol giggled, then winced as she moved her leg under the light coverlet. *"Please, Father, work this out so that my family need not suffer for my clumsiness. And please, bless Charlie Bennett and his family for their great kindness to me. In Jesus' precious name, amen."*

Chapter Three

Getting Settled

Charlie reined in the General in front of Bailey's Boarding House. He frowned at the attempt to reconcile the thought of the girl he rescued to this place as her "home". To say it was "unpleasant" would have been an understatement. Charlie didn't even feel entirely safe after dark in this section of town, much less did he want to think of Carol living there. He spoke to the General while climbing down from the buggy. "Well, she won't be living there anymore if I can do anything about the situation; or at least until she's healed, and then maybe I can help her find more suitable housing. 'Be right back, old fella."

Charlie confidently climbed the steps and rang the bell. The door was answered by a harried woman with disheveled hair, but wearing a clean work dress and apron.

"I'm terrible sorry, sir," she said, promptly identifying him as a gentleman by his attire, "but we ain't got n'more rooms to let."

"Pardon me, but I've come to collect Miss Montague's things. She's been in an accident, and I—"

The woman's face went pale as death. "No, *please God*, not Miss Carol!" She broke into loud wails and hand wavings and tears before Charlie had a chance to correct her misguided assumption.

"She's okay, ma'am! She's just off her feet for a few days. She is well, I assure you. I've only come to get her things from her room, if you'd be so kind as to direct me."

The woman wiped her eyes and nose on the corner of her apron, then smiled at the man for his kindness. "I'm that glad she's all right, sir! I'm that glad! Here, follow me. She's third floor, back."

The woman let him in, giving him a glimpse of a dimly-lit, worn parlor where sat from all appearances many of the boarders. They were indeed a varied lot from the glance Charlie gained in passing. Then he had to pay close attention to the narrow staircase up which the woman was leading him. At the third floor she guided him down the hall and to the right, where he saw an aged but clean door. Amazingly enough the whole boarding house seemed quite clean, though sparsely furnished. It was just old and rather stale from the sweat and smoke of the boarders.

She lit a candle with her oil lamp and handed it to him as he pulled out the key to let himself in.

If he had been shocked at the boarding house, he was even more so by the appearance of her room. Though a bit chilled from being unused all day, it was clean and bright, with newly white-washed walls, a white iron bed in the corner with two cheerfully colored patchwork quilts adorning it, a small table with a hurricane lamp, doily, and leather-bound book sitting beside the bed. There was a small chest of drawers with a daguerreotype of a family at the beach...two parents and three young adults from the looks of it; and, yes, one of the young people was Carol! He noticed that there was only one small window in the room that opened to the rear of the boarding house's lot; but there were pink muslin curtains pinned and draped appealingly at either side, and a paper shade for privacy.

Charlie felt as though he had stepped into another world, a change of scenery and mood in the same building that reminded him of how his grandmother's room stood out from the rest of his parents' home.

Not one to be sentimental when there was work to be done, he found the carpet bag under the bed as Carol had directed and quickly filled it with the items in and on the dresser and small chest of drawers. He asked the woman, still standing and sniffling at the door, "Is the furniture hers, or is this a furnished apartment?"

"Furnished, sir, but them's her linens and such. Let me strip the bed and fold 'em up for ya." And the woman did so quickly and efficiently, also removing the bit of muslin curtains, shaking off the tiniest bit of dust, and folding them neatly for Charlie.

"If Miss Montague is needin' a place when she's better, you just keep me in the know. I'll try to get this room she's cleaned up so nice back for her. She's been such a good boarder. She's all paid up for the month, but if she won't be back for a while," she paused, digging in a deep pocket in her work dress, "I'll send next week's rent back to her. I understand her folks is needin' it." Charlie handed her the key Carol had given him, and the woman tucked it in the same pocket she'd pulled the money from. She looked up at the handsome young man then, smiling. "You tell Miss Carol Meg Bailey is wishin' her the best, will ya?"

Charlie smiled at the woman, a bit taken aback by her profuse kindness. "I will indeed, ma'am. And thank you." He made a final search of the tiny room and carried the bundles out the door, down the stairs, and outside to where the General stood guard, patiently awaiting his master.

Charlie placed the carpet bag and linens beside him on the seat, the very seat Carol herself had graced but a short while earlier in the day.

What a fascinating woman this stranger is! Charlie was not a praying man, though his boyhood days were filled with memorized prayers and quotes and poems. Still, it occurred to him that Miss Carol Montague had kept him from his destination that afternoon, which was to be a visit to the local pub. Although he was no more a drinking man than a praying one, the other tellers at his father's bank, which several months ago had become his place of employment, had goaded and chided him about being a "Momma's Boy" and needing to step out and "be a man". They'd repeatedly invited him to O'Malley's Pub on Twenty-Sixth and Vineyard, but Charlie had never seriously considered it...until that day. He was bored with his routine, and for that reason alone he found himself headed down Lexington full speed ahead when he literally ran into Carol. *What a coincidence!*

The patient had already fallen asleep when he returned home, so Charlie turned her things over to Jessie and went to his father's study. His mother was just standing to leave as he knocked on the open door.

"Father, Mother? Are you turning in now?"

His mother approached him. "Yes, Charlie, dear. I was headed up just this minute. Were you able to retrieve all of Miss Montague's belongings?"

He described the trip to them in detail, his mother returning with him to join him on the davenport. His father sat at his desk, tapping his fingers lightly together as he listened. There was a moment of silence when Charlie finished his story, each dwelling on their own thoughts for a while.

"Had your mother not already brought me up to date on the situation, I would have presumed she was a shyster after your money, Charles." Charlie sat up to interrupt, but his father raised his hand a fraction to still him. "No, Son, I do not think that of the girl's motives, truly. Again, your mother has been sharing with me almost since you left to get her things. The girl—'Carol' is it?—sounds quite refined and genteel, perhaps a girl from a good family, but of reduced circumstances. Nevertheless, you must consider our family's reputation, our position in this great city, before you allow your heart to become involved with her...if it hasn't become so already...?"

Charlie stood quickly to his feet, and his mother prayed a quick, silent prayer for her precious son. He ran a hand through his hair before turning and answering. "Father, I will be completely honest with you. This woman is different from any other young woman of my acquaintance. It's more than her attractive appearance, which you will doubtless notice when you meet her. She seems strong and independent, but I...I long to protect her, too, somehow. I just can't put a finger on it. But I will be cautious, Father. Of that I can assure you."

"Thank you, Son. I appreciate your discretion in this matter. Now, I believe we all need some rest. Laura, I will be up in a few minutes; just let me finish this correspondence. Goodnight, Charlie my boy. Pleasant dreams."

Chapter Four

Good Morning

The next day dawned with its softest, rosy hues; and Charlie was taking his coffee on the veranda, albeit enjoying the warmth of his jacket that shut out the nippy November morning air. His mother joined him with her cup of tea.

"How are you this morning, dear? Did you sleep well?" she queried, wrapping her fingers around the teacup for added warmth.

"Okay, Mum, and yourself?" he asked politely, looking at his beautiful mother. She was dressed in pale green dress with a soft, ivory-hued wool morning jacket, gently fingering the pearls at her neck. Laura Bennett was such an elegant lady, a true pleasure to look upon, even at what her son thought of as the advanced age of forty-two.

Charlie was proud of his mother. She had lived through the War Between the States in a state divided, but her father believed in 'the Cause'—the rights of statehood. Then her beloved father died in battle, a brave officer under General Stonewall Jackson. When the war came to a close and times were still difficult financially, she stood her ground, a young woman defending her already failing mother and their home. Along came a gentleman from upstate New York with Christian principles, one who instead of wanting to evict Charlie's mother and grandmother from the family property they could no longer afford, desired to fix the house up and spend time getting to know the ladies who called it home. That man was of course Charlie's father, Benjamin Charles Bennett; and before long he had won the fair Laura and taken the house in hand, restoring it and improving on its pre-war state. Charlie was born nine months to the day after their wedding in December of 1866, on a beautiful September evening in 1867. At present their son was twenty-one years old, confident that he was ready to enter the world of finance with his father's blessing.

"You seem far away, Charlie. Where are you?" his mother asked, placing her emptied china teacup on its saucer before setting both aside.

"Forgive me, Mother. I was wool gathering. How is our patient this morning?"

Mrs. Bennett smiled contentedly. "She was still sleeping last I heard from Jessie and Beatrix, but they're both hovering about. They've special ordered an enticing tray of delicacies for the dear girl!" She laughed softly remembering Jessie's eager expressions in the kitchen earlier. "Charlie, do you think Miss Montague would be more comfortable staying here with us than going to Wesley and Lavinia's?"

Charlie had thought that for propriety's sake it would be best for Carol to stay with Aunt Lavinia, but in all actuality the two ladies had little in common. Wesley and Lavinia Sutherland were high society, and thoroughly enjoyed being so. He just didn't see Carol as being as comfortable with them as in his parents' less ostentatious home.

"It's up to you, Mother. She could be a companion for you, or rather *you* for *her* in her present state. I believe you two will get along famously." He paused, weighing his words before he spoke again. "She knows God, Mother. She quotes the Bible like it's everyday phraseology for her." Somehow that knowledge disturbed him, and he found himself frowning a bit. His mother caught the fleeting look, too, but didn't comment. "Yes, you and Carol decide what's best. I need to get ready for work, but I'll stop in and see if she's awake before I leave." That said, he stood, offered his mother his arm, and the two walked into their beautiful home.

A Historical Novel of Enduring Romance....

❧❧

From the way the servants were scurrying in and out of the guestroom, Charlie knew Carol was awake. He knocked.

"Yes? Come in," called the now familiar voice. Carol was sitting up in bed with the "tray of delicacies" before her; but he didn't seem to be able to get past her eyes and her beautiful hair, which was down and fell to the blanket across her lap in waves of chestnut-colored satin. His gaze brought the pink to her cheeks again as she lowered her eyes to her plate, still awaiting his greeting. "Good morning, Charlie."

It took a moment before he realized he was staring. "Pray, forgive me, Carol. I'm not a school boy to be gawking at you. It's just...your hair.... I'm not used to—"

She had forgotten Jessie had taken it down and brushed it out before giving her the breakfast tray. Carol understood Charlie's embarrassment completely. It was not socially acceptable for a woman to have her hair down in front of a man unless he was a near relative. She agilely gathered her hair in her hands, wound it round and round, and secured it with a tortoiseshell comb from the bedside stand.

"Forgive *me*, Charlie," she said softly, feeling terribly shy in his presence.

He ran his fingers through his well-groomed hair, and the ruby ring flashed brilliantly, teasing Carol with its possible significance. Looking at the ring rather than his eyes, she asked a bit haltingly, "Does your wife live here also, Mr. Bennett?"

She would have been pleased at his reaction had she been looking at his face, but she still focused on the ring on his left hand. "No. That is, I'm not married." He watched her eyes as they rose to his from his ring. "Oh, you noticed my ring. It was my grandfather's, but it is a trifle snug for my right hand. Would you like to see it?" He carefully removed the ring and held it out.

Knowing it was from his grandfather rather than his wife made the ring a fascination for Carol, for it was a truly stunning piece of jewelry. She reached tentatively for it as it sparkled and winked at her in the morning sunlight filtering in through the window.

"It's very beautiful. Forgive me if I sounded forward just then, I just...." He was coming to delight in her flushed cheeks, to look forward even to her blushing. But this time he graciously saved her from further explanation and reddening.

"No need to explain. I would have wondered the same had you been wearing a ring on *your* left hand." Then as an afterthought, "You're not, are you? Engaged or married, I mean?" He couldn't help but join her as she began bubbling over with relieved and joyous laughter, shaking her head with the negative answer he so wanted to see just then.

"No, Charlie. There is no man in my life but my father and my brother Caleb." Then they both paused, smiling at nothing in particular while she sat and he stood and the world went on about them. Wanting to say something brilliant but at a loss for words, Charlie walked about the room picking up his grandmother's brushes and hand mirror distractedly, pushing back the curtain a trifle further to look out on his mother's frost-glistening gardens.

"Please, don't let me keep you from your meal, Carol."

She chuckled again as she picked up her silver fork and pushed around a large blackberry. "Yes, I would not want to disappoint Jessie by not doing justice to this delicious meal! Fresh fruit, tea, a biscuit as light as ever I've tasted, and...what is this?" She spooned the white substance in the delicate bowl before her. "I don't believe it's grits after all. I have no butter, salt, and pepper, and the consistency's all wrong."

Charlie grinned. "No, indeed, my fair Southern belle! That is creamed wheat...more of a northern breakfast cereal. So what do you think? Do you like it?"

"I do! It's quite good with the fruit and sugar and cream. It just shocked me a little, as I was expecting something else. Truly, this is the finest breakfast I've had since arriving in Baltimore."

"Where are you from? I saw your family photograph in your room...here it is. Is this beach near your home, or was this taken while you were on vacation?"

"That is not far from our farm, though we don't visit often. Mother loves the ocean. This was taken the summer before last. Things were finally starting to look up for Poppa, then the accident happened at spring planting this past year. He was kicked by a mule, one he'd just purchased. The wound became infected, though he would have had great difficulty tilling and planting with broken ribs anyhow. My brother Caleb has really taken over the farm this year for all practical purposes."

Caleb seemed to look back at Charlie from the picture, looking like a happy and contented young man. Such a burden he had now resting upon his young shoulders.

Realizing the time, Charlie took out his pocket watch then looked apologetically at the invalid. "May we continue this conversation later? Duty calls, and I'm off to my 'cage'! That's what I refer to the teller stall as. We tellers find it apt," he concluded with a wide grin.

He headed for the door, but before he reached the doorway Carol said, "I will be praying for you today, Charlie Bennett. God be with you till we meet again!"

Charlie slowed his departure and turned as she spoke, memorizing the picture of her there. Then impulsively he blew her a kiss and left before he could see her reaction to his display of affection.

Placing her hand to her lips, she whispered once more, "*God, please be with him till we meet again....*"

Chapter Five

Testimonies

Laura Bennett was just headed to visit Carol when she heard the tinkling of the little bell. With a grin, she entered.

"Good morning, Carol. Did you sleep well?"

"Quite well, thank you," she answered. Carol really hadn't expected Mrs. Bennett to be the one answering her summons, and it took her a bit off guard.

"I'm sure it took a lot of courage to work up to ringing the bell," Charlie's mother said with a wry grin. "What did you need, dear?"

The younger woman gave her hostess a truly grateful smile. "If you would please have this letter posted? It is to my employer, Mr. Waterman, explaining my situation. And this letter also. It is for my parents in South Carolina." She handed the letters to Mrs. Bennett, fully expecting that to end their time together for the present. But Mrs. Bennett took the letters to the hall where Beatrix stood silently waiting, then Laura Bennett came back and sat down in a chair beside the bed.

Looking at the foot of her patient's bed, she asked, "Is that contraption my husband sent in helping keep the pressure off of your leg and foot? It looks like a tiny tent!"

"Oh!" Carol exclaimed, smiling in pleasant surprise. "I didn't know it was *his* doing! What a thoughtful gesture. Yes, it has been much more comfortable actually. Even the slight weight of the coverlet was uncomfortable before. Do thank him for me, won't you?"

"Why don't you thank me yourself, young lady?" Mr. Bennett asked, standing in the doorway. Even from the small portion of conversation he had overheard, Mr. Bennett could sense something of the difference in her Charlie and his wife had mentioned. Did his son suspect it was the difference of the kindred heart of a believer? He could only hope Charlie had that depth of perception, that spiritual "sixth sense". None of these thoughts registered on his face though as he approached, smiling and examining the leg-sized pup tent to which they were referring.

"It is a rather practical little thing, isn't it? I saw the physicians using them at the beginning of the war, when such things still were available for ones comfort." The memory disturbed him, so he changed subjects gently. "It's a pleasure to make your acquaintance, Miss Montague. I'm Charlie's father, Ben...yes, 'Ben Bennett'. Hardly original."

In her most prim and proper voice, Carol parried, "Quite to the contrary, Mr. Bennett; for you are indeed the first 'Ben Bennett' I've ever met!" The trio laughed together pleasantly, then Ben pulled up a chair beside his wife.

"Our son Charlie said you 'know God', Miss Montague. Is that so?"

Not sure where her host stood on this eternally important issue, she measured her words carefully. "Yes, sir. I have come to know Jesus as my Saviour and Friend through salvation." Ben and Laura Bennett exchanged glances at her simplistic boldness. It was music to their ears. Each reaching a hand out toward her, Carol was relieved that she had not offended them. "Do you both know Him, too?" she asked in quiet anticipation.

Both parents beamed. "Oh, *yes*, Carol!" they said over one another, each telling their testimony and filling in where the other paused. Carol had tears of joy on her cheeks before they both finished. Then rather abruptly, Mr. Bennett stood to his feet; and with a kiss on his wife's cheek, he bid the ladies farewell.

"Laura, take good care of our young guest," he said as he walked out of the room headed for his office at the bank.

"Would you mind telling me of your salvation experience,

Carol?" Mrs. Bennett asked gently.

Carol proceeded to tell of her independent childhood—always in control, always on the go. "Then when my father was injured this past spring, it was as though my whole world fell apart. But Mother's didn't. And even Father's didn't in his severely weakened state. But I was terrified, confused.

"It was then that Momma took me aside and explained her peace, her *contentment* in the midst of that very real trial. It was *the Lord* Who gave her peace. She rested in Him, gave all her trials to Him, knowing He would take care of us all because He *loved* us...enough to die for us.

"I had heard the sermons, but I just never really put it all together and accepted Him by faith until that moment. He cared. God Himself cared about Momma, about Poppa. God Himself loved *me*! She prayed with me right then in the kitchen, and when I took Poppa his tea I shared with him what Jesus had just done for me."

Carol paused, looking out the window a moment before going on. "I don't know what took me so long, but I'm so thankful that God is *'longsuffering to usward'*."

"Amen, child; amen." Mrs. Bennett stood then. She wanted to share Charlie's spiritual need with this dear girl, but she wasn't even sure herself what his actual condition *was*. She thought it best for the two to discuss this, knowing with Carol's spiritual-mindedness it would indeed come up in conversation eventually. So she let the moment pass.

They talked on a bit longer, then Mrs. Bennett brought up the housing situation. "So you see, you would really be no burden at all if you wish to stay here instead of going on to Lavinia's. My sister has a lovely home of course, even larger and far more grand than ours. But I would rather keep you here, selfish as I am!"

Carol shook her head, "No, Mrs. Bennett, I cannot even for a moment concede that you are selfishly motivated!" Both ladies giggled, then Carol went on. "And, 'yes', I would love to stay right here for as long as you'll have me." She hadn't meant to sound quite so contented, and she couldn't help blushing at her own forwardness.

Mrs. Bennett smiled serenely though and bent to place a kiss on the girl's forehead. "Then you may just be here for a very, *very* long while," she said softly. "I'll go let Lavinia know of our change in plans, then I'll get you a book from the library. What are your interests? Poetry? Novels? Botany? Travel?"

"I do enjoy Jane Austen's works, but right now I think...history. Yes, I'd enjoy reading some of your state and local history if you have it."

"We do indeed! Maryland history, coming right up."

Meanwhile, Carol picked up the book that had been brought from her room at the boarding house, a beautiful copy of the Psalms and Proverbs her parents had sent with her when she left. It was her dearest treasure.

She turned to Psalm 37:23 and 24, reading the verses aloud. *"'The steps of a good man are ordered by the LORD: and He delighteth in his way. Though he fall, he shall not be utterly cast down: for the LORD upholdeth him with His hand.'"* She smiled, looking up as she continued in prayer. *"Indeed, Father, though I fell, You have sustained me and provided for me in such a way as I could never imagine...what is the phrase Poppa used to use? 'Exceeding abundantly above all we ask or think'! Yes, this family has been such a blessing, but I know that this is all Your doing. Thank You again, Father. Thank You so much."*

☙❧

It was early afternoon before Charlie saw his father. Ben was never aloof with his son, but neither did he want there to be envy among the other employees toward Charlie's position as son of the bank president. He motioned to Charlie from across the room, letting him know that he wished to speak with him; and Charlie finished with the patron he was assisting before pulling down the blind and stepping out of his booth. He removed his visor and ran his fingers through his hair before stepping into his father's office.

"Hello, Father. How are you?" Charlie asked a trifle nervously.

"I'm fine, Son. I just wanted to talk with you for a moment about a most serious matter." He directed Charlie to a leather chair, then leaned comfortably on the mahogany desk. He wasn't quite sure where to begin, but rather than waste time, he jumped right in.

"Charlie, I've tried to be a good father to you in all things, but I believe I've been lacking in the most important. Do you know to what I refer?"

To his credit, Charlie *did* know. "Yes, Father. You're disappointed that I haven't been as interested in spiritual things as you and mother have taught me to be." Charlie could see that he was correct in assuming his father wished to speak of spiritual things. He felt as though his father's gaze was willing him to go on, and he took a deep breath even as his mind scrambled for an adequate defense. "I go to church with you, I even give of my paycheck. I'm no angel, but I've never been immoral or done anything...illegal." He stopped then, and looked up into his father's eyes, and the tears he saw there broke his heart. Father and son had never been demonstrative, but Charlie got up and went to his father. "Pray for me. Just...just pray for me."

"I will, Son. I will *continue* to pray for you to come to know Jesus personally, as Saviour." Ben Bennett had never talked much of spiritual things with his family...with anyone. It gave him a strange feeling to do so, a feeling of peace somehow. He took out a monogrammed handkerchief and wiped his eyes and blew his nose, then walked around behind his desk.

"Thank you for your honesty, Charlie. Don't ever forget that your mother and I love you and want what is best for you, in all things. I'm sorry it has taken this long for me to express, but after the talk your mother and I had with Miss Montague this morning—"

Charlie looked up quickly, "You went in to meet her?"

"I think it was no accident that you ran into her yesterday, Charlie."

Charlie was disappointed at his father's answer, thinking he still thought her to be a fortune hunter playing a charade of some kind. Mr. Bennett went on though. "I think God's hand is on that girl, and that somehow instead of our helping *her,* God is working through her to help *us.*"

Both men pondered this a moment, then Charlie broke the

silence. "I need to get back in there, Father, but...thank you." He put his visor back on and walked thoughtfully back to his booth. The other tellers noticed that the usually cheerful Charlie was being very grave, though he smiled at the patrons readily enough. They determined to help him lighten up by taking him to the pub after work, but he disappeared too quickly after closing.

※

Mrs. Bennett couldn't resist teasing her son when he came home that evening. "Hello, Charlie! Would you care to join me on the veranda? It warmed up quite nicely this afternoon." Charlie paused on his mission: heading straight for Carol's room. He turned politely to face his mother, but when he saw the grin on her face, he suspected her motives.

"Mother of mine, you can see right through me!" Giving her a playful kiss on the cheek, he proceeded to Carol's room. He was disappointed however when he reached it and she was not there. Her book and picture were still there though, so he knew she had not moved to Aunt Lavinia's.

"Mother?" he called, starting when he heard her giggle right behind him.

"Well, I *tried* to get you to come out on the veranda with me, but maybe you'd rather be out there with Carol?" With that said, she smiled as he walked purposefully out of the room.

He found their houseguest reclining on a bench facing the late-blooming roses, an unnoticed book in her lap. Her smile when she saw him made his heart skip a beat.

"Well, Miss Montague, how did you come to be out here instead of resting as per Doc Whittle's orders?" He stood there, his arms across his chest, looking down with mock severity.

Giggling unrepentantly, she looked boldly up at him. "Your *mother* thought it would be okay, and Lucas brought me out here not quite an hour ago. So it's them you have to blame, not me, Mr. Bennett!" Giggling a bit more, she motioned to a chair. It was a bit too far away from her for Charlie's liking though, so he moved it to her side.

It didn't seem possible for him to care so much after such a short acquaintance...barely twenty-four hours! But as they spoke of pleasantries and how each had spent their day, their comfortable relationship seemed as natural as an old married couple.

Her hair in the late afternoon sun seemed almost auburn, and although she had it attractively arranged, his mind's eye still pictured how long and beautiful it was down. Her skin was flawless except for a smattering of freckles across her nose. Her eyes, the first feature he had noticed when they had met, were a sparkling blue fringed with curly, dark lashes. He recognized the dress she wore as one he'd brought from her rooms the night before, a pale yellow day dress with pin tucks at the bodice and small puffed sleeves. For a moment he wished he were an artist, so he could paint her as she looked then.

"Why, Charlie Bennett, I don't believe you heard a *word* I just said!" This woke him from his artistic reverie.

"I'm afraid you're right, Miss Montague. Pray forgive me. I would tell you that I was overwhelmed by your beauty, but I'm afraid it would pamper your vanity!" With a quick intake of breath, she gave his hand a playful swat, but he caught her hand and held it close. "Please, go back to what you were saying."

She began again, telling him of the book she was reading, of the history of Maryland, her coming to statehood, her strong division of sympathies in the War Between the States; then Carol stopped abruptly as she noticed Charlie watching her lips. Her sudden silence brought his attention back to her eyes, and he could see her confusion.

"Carol, would it be...." He leaned nearer to kiss the lips he found so alluring, but before his lips touched hers he heard approaching footsteps. His whole being longed for that kiss, but he stood abruptly and walked over to examine a nearby rose bush as his mother approached.

Carol was flustered and more than a little confused, but she covered her emotions as best she could and talked with Charlie's mother. Mrs. Bennett couldn't help but sense something was amiss, and she felt it might be best to begin to chaperone the two more carefully.

"Charlie, I had a thought. Do you think that Dr. Whittle could loan us a wheelchair for Carol? I'm certain he has extras, and that would help so much with her getting about."

Although that *would* be more practical, Charlie wasn't quite ready to give up his one last opportunity of service. There was no explaining that to the ladies awaiting his answer however.

"Yes, that would be more convenient. Could you use the telephone to ring his office, and if that's okay with him I'll go pick it up before dinner?"

"Oh yes, that would be perfect, dear."

Carol looked at them with amazement. "You mean, you have one of Bell's machines right in your home? I mean, I'd heard that some people had done so, but...." She blushed, feeling like a gauche country girl. But Mrs. Bennett would not have her feel that way for long.

"Yes, dear," she said placing a finger beneath Carol's chin to raise her eyes from her lap. "We just got one a few months ago. Father wanted one to keep in contact with the office. It's in the little room off the foyer." Then turning back to Charlie, "I shall go ring his office now. And if Miss Montague is ready to return to her room to freshen up for the evening, would you be willing to attend her, dear?"

Charlie looked as though his mother had given him a gift. She smiled lovingly as she walked away from the two who were gathering Carol's things for the move back to her room.

As soon as his mother had reentered the house, Charlie knew it was time to explain. "I feel as though I should account for my actions earlier, Carol; and I would if I could. Although it may shock you to hear it so soon, I must declare that my intentions are completely honorable. Would it be acceptable if I began courting you, Miss Montague?"

"Oh, Charlie, have some mercy! We hardly know one another!" But he knelt before her, stopping her from further argument.

"You are different than anyone I've ever met, Carol. Not just outwardly, but inwardly, spiritually. I don't know much about you, but I know this: you already hold my heart in your hands. Please allow me the privilege of courting you, Carol. Will you?" He remained still, his hands clasped and resting on one knee.

Looking deeply into her eyes, he saw the answer, then her smile and nod sealed it. "I wanted to kiss you earlier, Miss Montague. May I do so now?"

"N-no, Charlie," she stuttered nervously. "Not yet. It has long been my heart's desire not to share a kiss with a man unless he is the one I'm to marry." She saw the incredulous look on his face, but went on. "No, I'm not teasing you. I just would not want to kiss someone, then him marry someone else someday. If I saw him and his wife one day, I couldn't help but think *'I kissed her husband!'*; and personally, I don't want that kind of guilt. So I decided as a young girl that I would not allow a man to kiss me until I knew he was to be my husband."

Charlie still had a look of slight disbelief on his face, but he actually respected this standard, however high it seemed to him. "Thank you for telling me, Carol. I can't say that I agree with this standard you've set for yourself, but I will honor it to please you. Agreed?"

Carol smiled sweetly and answered, "Agreed." Charlie reached out a hand for a handshake to finalize the "deal", but when she placed her hand in his he bent over chivalrously and kissed it. Then he stood to his feet, brushing the leaves from his trousers.

"Come, let me take you to your room." Once again she found herself in Charlie's strong arms, and she felt quite safe there. As he placed her on the little rolling chair before the dressing table, he turned the chair slowly, so she could see in the mirror to ready herself for dinner. He looked over her head at their reflection, then placed one more kiss on her soft, wavy hair.

"I shall miss the honor of carrying you about. Though I know the wheeled chair will be more convenient, I will envy it its usefulness. Until dinner," he said quietly, then he strode from the room to do his mother's bidding.

Chapter Six

Growing In Love

Monck's Corner, South Carolina
November 30th, 1888

"Poppa, look! It's a letter from our Carol!" Mrs. Montague waved the letter gleefully as she stepped up on the porch to join her husband, then sat in the wooden porch rocker next to him.

"Well, Momma, open it up and let's see what our girl has written." Mrs. Montague read while Mr. Montague rocked and looked thoughtfully out at the newly-harvested fields.

Dear Momma & Poppa~

You will be glad to know that I am well. It is needful that I update you on a certain happening that took place yester-eve. As I was leaving the office, I was involved in a small accident. Charlie Bennett, the driver, has been most kind, bringing me to his family physician and then to his parents' home to recuperate. I have a fracture of the bone in the lower portion of my left leg, but the doctor believes it will heal if given the proper care and time.

I am currently staying with the Bennett family. Charlie's parents are both Christians, and I'm almost certain Charlie is as well. He has been a perfect gentleman; and although I hope my stay here to be of short duration for their sakes and yours, I am quite sure I shall enjoy every minute of it.

She went on to describe the room, the servants, and the view of the garden she had from her bed, then concluded with:

The money enclosed is back payment for my room for the remainder of the month of November since I always pay in advance. Once my leg is healed I can find another room easily enough, I'm sure. And please do not worry, for indeed I am in better care than I have been since arriving in the beautiful city of Baltimore.
   Please give Caleb and Celia my love, as well as your own dear selves. I remain most sincerely yours~
                                    Carolina Anne Montague

Mrs. Montague folded the letter and carefully placed it back in the envelope. The stationery was simple, but of fine quality; and Mrs. Montague thought she smelled a hint of lavender.
"Well then, Poppa, it would seem our oldest girl has found herself on an adventure." She tried to keep her mood light, but she couldn't help but be concerned for Carol's injury and continued state of mind. Poppa was pondering the news in silence, but Momma wished for him to share his thoughts. "What are you thinking, William Montague? I *must* know."
"Only that our Carol is no longer a child. In fact her twenty-first birthday is less than a month away. I have peace knowing that the Lord is with her there just as He is with us here. Why, what are *you* thinking, Em?"
"That it might be best to send Celia up there to be with her sister once Carol's up and around again. Maybe by boarding together they can pool their resources and have a better room, not to mention one another's good company." She played with a stitch on her apron pocket, then after some moments of receiving no response, gave him another verbal nudge. "Well?"
Mr. Montague stood and walked across the porch, then leaned on the porch railing. "I think you're worrying, but I also

think your idea has merit. Why don't we talk with Celia about it tonight and see if the idea appeals to her as well."

Emily Montague walked to her husband's side and put her arm around his waist. He was still a bit thin, but doing much better with every passing week. "Yes, dear. And thank you for reminding me not to worry...reminding me Who is in control." She stood on tiptoe and kissed his grizzled cheek, then walked back in the house to finish making dinner.

※※

Baltimore, Maryland
The Bennett House

With the wheelchair, which had a leg extension to keep her injured leg elevated, Carol regained much of her independence. Mrs. Bennett had told her to feel free to explore the entire first floor if she wished, and she gladly did so.

It was late November, and Carol and Charlie grew more to be kindred hearts with each passing day. He brought her flowers, read her the paper, even wheeled her outside after carefully bundling her up from the cold. Mrs. Bennett had seen that Carol had but three dresses in her wardrobe, so she went through her mother's things and had several dresses remade and updated for Carol. A favorite was a navy blue gabardine suit which Carol planned to wear to church once she received permission from Dr. Whittle that it was safe for her to put weight on her injured leg once again. The cast on her lower leg and ankle was uncomfortable and awkward, but if it allowed her to begin walking soon it was welcomed.

Carol had ventured into the front sitting room and adjoining music room once before, but she had not been able to get close enough to actually play the piano she'd seen there. That afternoon however, Mrs. Bennett spotted her as she wheeled into the front rooms. She cleared her throat so as not to frighten the girl.

"Oh, hello, Mrs. Bennett. I thought you were still out. How was your luncheon?"

"Quite delicious, thank you; and it was so nice to visit and catch up a bit with Lavinia and our friends from the Garden Club." She walked past Carol and sat down at the piano, lifting its cover quietly.

"Shall I?" Mrs. Bennett asked almost mischievously, her hands poised above the keys. With Carol's giggling affirmative, Charlie's mother began to play a work by Chopin that was both familiar and beloved to Carol. When she ended her nearly flawless performance, Carol's enraptured face was all the applause she desired.

"Mrs. Bennett, that was unforgettably beautiful. Thank you."

Casually beginning another simpler piece, she asked, "Do you play, Miss Montague?"

"I do, but I haven't had the opportunity since I moved here to Baltimore. My mother has a small pianoforte in our parlor. She gives music lessons to the neighbor children; in fact, my secretarial training was in exchange for those lessons from our neighbor two farms south of us. But anyhow, Mother taught all three of us children to play."

Mrs. Bennett gave a few modulated chords signaling the finish of the piece, then stood. "Do you think I could help you over to the bench so you can play, my dear?" Lending a shoulder, Mrs. Bennett aided Carol in the few steps to the bench. Fortunately, her right foot, needed for the pedals, was not the one in the cast.

"Have you some music I may play?" she asked eagerly. She began to play a beautiful classical piece that was her father's favorite, then went on to play another sonata, then a few of her favorite hymns by Charles Wesley.

Carol was in the middle of *Love Divine, All Loves Excelling* when Charlie came in from work. He stood in the hallway listening, wondering when the last time was he'd heard his mother play. As he walked quietly toward the music room, he saw the two ladies dearest to his heart sitting there; but it was Carol who was seated at the piano. From her place behind and slightly to the left of Carol, Mrs. Bennett saw Charlie approach and raised a hand to still him.

Carol finished, then turned to look at Mrs. Bennett. Seeing that her focus was toward the sitting room, she turned to see

Charlie standing there. "Hello, Charlie," she said quietly, looking more like a naughty child "caught in the act" than the woman he admired whom he just discovered had a wonderful talent.

"I'll ring for tea, shall I?" Charlie's mother said, knowing that neither would answer nor likely even heard. Charlie came and sat on the bench beside Carol as his mother left the room, his eyes filled with wonder at this new discovery.

"Carol, why didn't you *tell* me you could play?" he asked quietly.

"You never asked," she said with that bit of coyness Charlie loved. His eyes went down to her lips, a signal she had come to know as Charlie's desiring a kiss. But although she yearned to kiss him just as badly, she stuck with her convictions, turned her head, and began to play a minuet, giggling all the way through it. When she reached the end, however, he took her by the shoulders and turned her to face him.

"Please don't tease me, Carol. It has taken all my self-control to adhere to our agreement."

"Forgive me, Charlie. I thought laughter would be better than tears, and it hurts me to withhold this expression of love from you, it really does."

"My darling girl," he said, his voice softening at her sweet honesty, "it will make the giving all the sweeter when I *do* receive that first kiss from you."

Her nearness was more than he could bear, and he dropped his hands from her shoulders and stood quietly. "I do hope that you have learned your lesson not to toy with my affections," he said good-naturedly, walking to the window and plucking an ivory-hued rose from the flower arrangement. By the time he brought it to her, she had regained her composure.

"Quite to the contrary, Mr. Bennett. I thought what you said then was a rather wonderful reward for my piety!" And with that Charlie couldn't help but throw his head back and laugh wholeheartedly. Mrs. Bennett came in with tea as Carol tucked the rose into her hair.

Charlie helped Carol back into her wheeled chair as Mrs. Bennett poured out tea for the three of them, then addressed them while stirring her steaming cup.

"So, Son, what do you think of Miss Montague's hidden talent? Shall we pull out the Christmas carols since the holiday is fast approaching?"

"Oh yes, let's!" Charlie walked over to a small, wooden filing cabinet and pulled out the folder marked "Carols". The word caught his attention. "This folder says it's *yours*! See, your name is even on the tab." To his surprise, she answered quite seriously.

"Actually, Charlie, I was named for the season, as well as for my home state. My full name is 'Carolina Anne', but I was born near Christmas and given the nickname 'Carol'." She giggled at both Bennetts' surprised looks. "I shall be twenty-one this year, an *adult*," Carol said with a put-on childish voice, belying her age. But the other two in the room were busily thinking of what they should do for her birthday, as well as what they should do for this dear girl for Christmas.

"When *is* your birthday, Carol?" Charlie asked, passing his cup to his mother for a refill.

Rather than say the elusive remark that came to mind, she behaved and answered, "The twenty-fourth," but Charlie didn't miss the sparkle in her eye that gave away her first intent. He chose to let it pass this time though.

"Really? Mine is the twenty-fourth of September! I just turned twenty-one myself. That is rather a milestone. What shall we do for her, Mum?"

"What would you have done had you been home, dear?" Mrs. Bennett asked thoughtfully.

Carol's eyes shone as she thought of Christmas at home. "Oh, it was so close to Jesus' birthday that we usually just had a cake and a quiet evening with family. One year we went caroling to the neighboring farms afterward! Usually though with the early evenings we would light the candles in the parlor and sing for an hour or so while different ones of us played. One year I remember distinctly, Poppa even played a made-up, simple tune on the pianoforte as a gift to me."

They all smiled at the shared memory. "What a wonderful family you must have, Carol. I do hope we have the pleasure of meeting them one day." Mrs. Bennett caught the look that passed from Charlie to Carol and busied herself with the tray.

"Well, your father is late again, Charlie. Why don't you take Carol into the gardens? I had Lucas trim back the bushes so that you could maneuver the path more easily in her chair. How does that sound?"

"*Delightful*, Mum. Thank you so much for thinking of that." Charlie kissed his mother's cheek before wheeling Carol out of the room. He got a shawl and a lap rug for Carol before going outside; it was sunset and quite cold, even in the protection of the garden. They could both see their breath as they strolled, and the lights from the house and the neighbors' houses twinkled at them through the trees along the path.

"Charlie, this makes me think of the hymn *Thy Word is Like a Garden, Lord.* Do you know it?" Charlie surprised her by singing the first verse with his clear, tenor voice. She joined him with a high harmony:

> *Thy Word is like a garden, Lord,*
> *With flowers bright and fair;*
> *And every one who seeks may pluck*
> *A lovely cluster there.*
> *Thy Word is like a deep, deep mine;*
> *And jewels rich and rare*
> *Are hidden in its mighty depths*
> *For every searcher there.*

"How beautiful! God's Word is so very precious to me, Charlie. I find verses each time I read it that touch me with the beauty of flowers and the treasure of jewels, don't you?"

Charlie hesitated a bit too long, but answered, "Yes, I suppose His Word is a wonderful thing. But just now I'm enjoying your company so well that I don't especially wish to discuss the ethereal. Is that acceptable to you, my dear?"

She knew he meant it as a compliment, but it came across as spiritually insensitive, almost as though he didn't know the joy of reading God's Word, of a relationship with Him. She started to ask about his spiritual condition, but he had heard his father's carriage arrive and had turned the wheelchair back toward the house. Her mind still troubled, she put off the question until later; but the opportunity did not present itself again that evening.

Chapter Seven

Back to Church

Although Carol had come to think she knew Charlie well and could even grow to love him, she began to seriously question his spiritual condition. Not just the incident in the garden, but several times since he had casually evaded her spiritual questions and comments. Carol's parents had always been a wonderful example to her of how blessed a marriage was when founded on the Lord instead of mere physical attraction or other surface commonalities. She had seen it with Charlie's parents as well, for although they may have been cumbered with the cares of this world due to their financial status, she knew their testimonies and love for one another. But what of their son?

Dr. Whittle had approved Carol's leaving the house occasionally, specifically to attend church. She was so excited, not having visited the Bennetts' church as yet, and still not feeling a part of the church near her boarding house room where she had been attending before the accident.

The Sunday following Thanksgiving was to be her first Sunday back in church, so she rose early to make preparation. Jessie had taken to "doin' Missy Carol's hair", and she did an exceptionally beautiful job for the occasion.

"Jessie," Carol asked while the servant was putting the finishing touches on Carol's coiffeur, "Where do you and your family attend church?"

Jessie beamed. "Over to the First Colored Baptist Church on

to the other side of town. It's a fine church, a fine church."

Jessie gave Carol's hair a final pat, then stood back, arms akimbo, inspecting her work. "You's all excited 'bout goin' to the Bennetts' church this mornin'. You'll be lookin' mighty fine for the occasion, Missy Carol!" With that vote of confidence she left Carol to finish her preparations.

Carol's one hat went perfectly with the navy gabardine suit, but she didn't want to put it on until after breakfast. So laying aside her woolen shawl, gloves, and hat, she made her way into her wheelchair and into the dining room precisely on time.

The gentlemen stood as she came in, Charlie coming around to help her get situated. Then Mr. Bennett prayed. *"Lord, for what we are about to receive may we show ourselves to be truly grateful. In Jesus' name, amen.* It looks as though Venetia has outdone herself with this breakfast! I for one shall make every attempt to do it justice."

Charlie rose with his parents to head to the buffet, but first he picked up Carol's plate for her. He bent low to whisper in her ear, "*These* are *grits* we're having today," then walked to the buffet chuckling. They were indeed grits, and fried fish, scrambled eggs, biscuits, and fresh fruit. Knowing something of her appetite, he got her a little bit of everything but the fruit, which he got extra of for her. Meanwhile his parents were telling her about the families in the church.

"And the Hursts attend there, and the Collins family. Oh, and you know Dr. Whittle. He currently has three generations of family attending the church. Charlie, you remember Albert, Dr. Whittle's grandson from Philadelphia? He has come down to stay with his grandfather. He's looking for a job and taking a few classes at the university, I hear."

"Albert? Oh, that's great, Mother! He always was a good egg when he came to visit. When did he arrive?"

"Just this past Tuesday, in time for Thanksgiving with his Baltimore relatives most likely. Ben, I wonder if you could use him at the bank. I know he needs a job, and the Whittles have been such good friends through the years."

"Yes, Father, and one of the tellers left this week; so we've all been working ourselves ragged trying to make up for the loss of manpower."

"I'll have to look into that. Now, I don't know about you three, but I'm finished and almost ready to leave!" Mr. Bennett pushed away from the table, most unceremoniously patting his full tummy. He received the reaction he wanted with an "Oh, Ben!" from his wife and giggles from the young folks, then he headed back upstairs for his hat, gloves, and coat.

Though she had been out in the garden numerous times since arriving at the house over a week ago, Carol was filled with excitement as Charlie helped her into the carriage for the ride to the church. This part of the city was a great deal more attractive than the parts she had lived and worked in. There were trees lining the street, and although they were bare of foliage due to the season, she could picture how beautiful they would look when spring arrived once more.

When the carriage pulled up beside the church building, Charlie's father got out first. He helped his wife down, then took the wheeled chair from the attendant and readied it for Carol. Charlie handed her down from the carriage, and with her long skirts one wouldn't have even known she had a cast on except for the chair and all the special attention. Charlie wheeled her around to the side entrance, bringing her in barely ten feet from his family's usual seat.

Mr. and Mrs. Bennett had already been spotted by Dr. Whittle, who brought his grandson over to meet Charlie and Carol.

"You're looking fine, Miss Montague! Charlie, make certain she doesn't get overly tired. This is her first excursion, and we don't need her to have a setback. Charlie, you know my grandson Albert. Albert, this is Miss Carol Montague." The grandfather stepped back as Albert leaned into the pew to shake hands with both young people.

"Charlie, it's good to see you again! And this is the young lady you...ahem...*ran into* some time back? How do you do, Miss Montague? You look lovely this morning."

Albert was a little shorter than Charlie, but broader of build. He had sandy blonde hair and deep dimples that gave him a boyish look. Carol smiled at the two men as they got reacquainted quickly and quietly, but her eyes were also taking in the beauty of the building. The high, open-beam ceiling drew the eyes heavenward, and the pipe organ playing softly in the background truly set the tone for a worship service. Mr. and Mrs. Bennett sat at one end of the pew, Charlie and Carol at the other. There were three pews across with aisles dividing, four rows in front of them, and numerous rows behind. The morning sunlight was filtering through the stained glass windows on either side, giving the whole of the auditorium a rich, purplish cast.

When the choir filed in wearing their cream-colored robes, the church stood to their feet and sang the *Doxology*:

Praise God, from Whom all blessings flow!
Praise Him all creatures here below.
Praise Him above, ye heavenly host;
Praise Father, Son, and Holy Ghost. Amen

Charlie held the hymnal for them as they sang, and their voices blended together so beautifully that it nearly brought tears to Carol's eyes. *"Surely I've misjudged him, Lord,"* she prayed in her heart with the opening prayer. *"For indeed, how could he sing Your praise so beautifully and not know You?"*

The pastor, the Reverend Miles H. Lehman, welcomed the guests most cordially, smiling over his spectacles as he looked at the different ones from the pulpit. Then after two more hymns and a beautiful offertory, there was special music; and of all things surprising, it was a duet by Albert and a man Carol discovered later was his uncle! They sang a very new but powerfully inspiring hymn entitled *Rejoice, Ye Pure in Heart*.

Rejoice ye pure in heart;
Rejoice, give thanks, and sing;
Your glorious banner wave on high,
The cross of Christ your King.
Rejoice, rejoice, rejoice, give thanks and sing!

Bright youth and snow crowned age,
Strong men and maidens meek,

Raise high your free, exultant song,
God's wondrous praises speak.
Rejoice, rejoice, rejoice, give thanks and sing!

With all the angel choirs,
With all the saints of earth,
Pour out the strains of joy and bliss,
True rapture, noblest mirth.
Rejoice, rejoice, rejoice, give thanks and sing!

With voice as full and strong
As ocean's surging praise,
Send forth the hymns our fathers loved,
The psalms of ancient days.
Rejoice, rejoice, rejoice, give thanks and sing!

Yes, on through life's long path,
Still chanting as ye go;
From youth to age, by night and day,
In gladness and in woe.
Rejoice, rejoice, rejoice, give thanks and sing!

At last the march shall end;
The wearied ones shall rest;
The pilgrims find their heavenly Home,
Jerusalem the blessed.
Rejoice, rejoice, rejoice, give thanks and sing!

Praise Him Who reigns on high,
The Lord Whom we adore,
The Father, Son and Holy Ghost,
One God forevermore.
Rejoice, rejoice, rejoice, give thanks and sing!

※

After the service, which appropriately enough for the season was entitled "The Thankful Heart", the family stood to file out the side door with Carol. There were several people who wished to meet her first however, so she was on her feet a bit longer than desired. Just as she thought they could leave, Charlie spotted someone he needed to talk with and left her side. Mr. and Mrs. Bennett were right there, and they saw her look of disappointment as Charlie walked away. Albert was just coming over to bid the family farewell, and he noticed the look in her eyes also.

"Miss Montague, how did you like the service?" he asked, taking her arm to assist her to her wheelchair that stood just outside the door.

"Oh, Mr. Whittle, it was wonderful. And your song! The melody is still in my heart, and probably will remain so for some time. *'Rejoice! Rejoice! Rejoice, give thanks, and sing!'*" She looked up at him and smiled sweetly as he saw her seated and comfortable.

"Do you like music, Miss Montague? It seems to me that Charlie was in the boys' choir when I came here as a lad, and as I recall his mother has musical talents as well, do you not, Mrs. Bennett?" He received a smiling nod in reply. "Carol, you must be truly enjoying your stay with the family. Well, I must find Grandfather! Have a wonderful afternoon, Miss Montague, Mr. and Mrs. Bennett," and with a tip of his hat he was gone.

Mr. Bennett had handed Carol back into the carriage before Charlie got back to them. "Forgive me, but I wanted to talk with Mr. Perkins about joining the choir." He was as excited as a schoolboy all the way home, and he failed to notice the other passengers' lack of comment until just as the carriage pulled in their drive. "Well, *I'm* excited about it!" he concluded, opening the door to help the others out almost before the carriage had come to a stop.

"We're all happy for your decision, Son," his mother said as he helped her down. "We're just a little weary from all the excitement over Carol's first outing. Do forgive our temporary lack of enthusiasm."

"Oh, of course," he said, taking special care to help Carol down gently. "I guess I should have talked with Mr. Perkins later and helped Carol instead of leaving her care to you, Father."

"Actually, I had assistance," Mr. Bennett said as he joined

the group outside the carriage. His voice was a study in nonchalance as he said, "Albert Whittle was there to help."

He saw Charlie slow his pace for just a moment. The younger man then opened the doors for the ladies and, looking a bit perturbed, glanced up as he uttered the monosyllable, "Oh?"

Chapter Eight

Sunday Afternoon

Sunday afternoons in the Bennett mansion were usually quiet ones, and this was no exception. All the servants had the day off as soon as breakfast was cleared and cleaned up, so it was also the day Mrs. Bennett prepared the noon and evening meals herself. She changed into a day dress after church and headed for the kitchen; and Charlie was already there ahead of her, jacket off, sleeves rolled up, and apron folded neatly in half and tied at his waist.

"Oh, Charlie, you don't need to help me today! Go spend some time with Carol, dear."

"Actually, Mum," he said, tying her apron for her, "when she saw me headed in here and asked what I was up to, she said she wanted to help, too." Mrs. Bennett shook her head with a smile. "She'll be in here in a few minutes."

"Here I am!" Carol announced, hobbling in from the dining room. Charlie gave her an apron, tied it for her, and sat her down at the butcher block table, handing her a sharp knife and some vegetables for salad.

"Then 'here you go', Chef Carol! Make a nice torn lettuce salad. I'm working on the salad dressing right now, and Mother is making gravy for the pot roast. Looks to me like a delicious meal in the works."

"Well, it's not like I couldn't *smell* how delicious it was going to be when we walked in after church! The whole house was filled with the aroma. Oh, Mrs. Bennett, are there any sunflower seeds?"

"Sunflower seeds? Umm…yes, here they are. What did you need them for?"

Carol giggled. "Actually, the salad! They're *delicious* in this kind of salad, as are raisins."

With that comment she had the attention of both Bennetts in the kitchen, who simultaneously said, "*Raisins*?", causing Carol no end of merriment.

"Yes, I'm serious! You have to try it!"

When the table was set and the food laid out on the buffet, Charlie gave thanks; then the Bennetts headed to the buffet table, Charlie again taking Carol's plate as well. When Mr. Bennett paused while dishing up his salad and picked out a raisin, then two, holding them up and asking incredulously, "Raisins in the vegetable salad?", he was met with laughter bubbling up from Mrs. Bennett, Charlie, and even an exasperated Carol. They all tried the salad with Charlie's dressing, and they unanimously declared it to be delicious, as were the roast, potatoes, caramelized onions, carrots, and biscuits.

As they cleared away the dinner plates, Charlie brought out a serving dish and a crystal gravy boat. "I made a bread pudding with vanilla sauce for dessert, but there aren't as many raisins in it as usual…'must have run short because of the salad." He served up the bread pudding and vanilla sauce for each of them before he sat down.

"Oh, Charlie, this is scrumptious!" Carol declared. "What is the recipe?"

Charlie rose quickly and headed back into the kitchen, calling over his shoulder, "Just a second," then "Yes, here it is," bringing a well-worn recipe card to Carol.

Bread Pudding

4 slices day old bread, cubed
2 T butter
1/4 cup packed brown sugar
1/4 cup granulated sugar
1 t cinnamon

1 t nutmeg
1/2 cup soaked raisins
==========
4 eggs, slightly beaten
1/3 cup granulated sugar
1 t vanilla extract
2 cups milk, scalded
Dash of salt

*Stoke oven to medium heat
*Melt butter in 2 quart shallow pan. Remove from oven.
*Place bread cubes in pan.
*Sprinkle bread with sugars, cinnamon, nutmeg & raisins.
*In medium mixing bowl, combine eggs, sugar, vanilla, and salt. Slowly add milk. Pour over bread cubes.
*Place pan in larger pan, adding approximately 1 inch of water to the outer pan.
*Bake until knife inserted between center and edge comes out clean, approximately 1 hour.

<u>*Vanilla Sauce, optional:*</u>
2 cups water
2/3 cup granulated sugar
2 T cornstarch, dissolved in 1/4 cup cold water

*In medium pot, heat all ingredients to boiling, stirring constantly, until thickened.
*Remove from heat.
*Add 2 T vanilla extract and 2 T butter. Stir until blended.

After a taste, she declared it to be the best she'd ever had. "Whose recipe is this?"

Mrs. Bennett answered with pride, "It was my father's recipe actually. He enjoyed making desserts especially, though I don't recall him making anything else in the kitchen."

"I don't know, Mum. As I recall from your stories, he could make a *mess* in the kitchen, when he made *this*!" All four enjoyed that word picture immensely. When they'd finished dessert, they rose as one to clear the table and help with the dishes and kitchen clean up.

What a comfortable scene of domesticity they all made as Charlie washed the dishes, Carol and Mr. Bennett dried, and Mrs.

Bennett put them away in the cabinetry and pantries.

"Mother, I always thought having a sister would get me out of K.P. duty." For that, he received a stinging wet-towel rebuke on his legs. "*Ow!*"

"Serves you right, Charlie Bennett!" his mother said, completely justifying Carol's quick and effective response.

When all was cleaned, dried, and put away, the four contented people retired to the sitting room. Before long, Mr. Bennett could be heard snoring from his place on the settee. Mrs. Bennett looked apologetically at the young couple, then woke Mr. Bennett and walked with him upstairs.

"Oh, Charlie, you have such a wonderful family. Do you know how blessed you are to have such a close relationship with your parents?"

"Indeed I do," Charlie said in all seriousness. "I've seen those who were not similarly blessed. It's my guess you were, though. Am I right? And that you have an equally satisfying relationship with your siblings?"

"Oh yes! The five of us have always been very close, and we three children became like best friends with our parents as we got older. Many a night Momma and I have sat up 'til the wee hours just talking, 'solving the world's problems' she called it." Then Carol grew pensive as she thought of the family she loved and missed. Charlie understood the cause of her sudden quiet mood, and he picked up her hand and kissed it.

"You know what it is to be loved, and to love in return. That's a beautiful gift, Carol."

"It is that, but that is not the *greatest* love." Charlie continued holding her hand, playing with her fingers, as she went on. "*Greater love hath no man than this, that a man lay down his life for his friend.* That's the kind of love I found when I met Jesus." Charlie paused in his caresses, and she withdrew her hand. "Charlie, do you know that kind of love?"

He was framing an answer when the doorbell sounded, and looking rather relieved he stood to answer it. "Albert! Doc Whittle! Welcome. Do come in, won't you?"

Doctor Whittle twisted his moustache as he entered, saying, "We thought we'd come check on the patient. There you are,

Miss Montague. Not too fatigued after this morning's outing, are you?" he asked, doing everything he could not to reach out for her wrist and take her pulse. "You do look a bit flushed, my dear."

"Hello, Doctor. Hello, Mr. Whittle." Seeing the good doctor's concern, she added, "I'm feeling fine, thank you. And I wouldn't have missed that service for all the crab legs in Baltimore!" They all chuckled at her metaphor as they took their seats.

"Please call me 'Albert', Miss Montague, won't you?"

"If you will in turn call me 'Carol'," she said, smiling candidly at the fair-haired young man.

There was a slightly uncomfortable moment of silence, then Doctor Whittle spoke. "Have you received a letter from your parents yet, Carol?"

"No, but I do hope to very soon! I wrote them a little over a week ago, the day after the accident actually. I'm sure they've received my letter by now."

Albert was looking around the room when he spotted the piano through the archway. "Charlie, do you play?"

"Nothing worth listening to, I'm afraid. But Mother does, as does Carol."

"Do you, Carol?" Albert asked excitedly. "Would you mind playing something for us now? Or are you too tired?"

In answer Carol rose to her feet, all three men standing in deference, and Charlie took her arm and helped her to the piano. She played two classical pieces she had memorized, then Charlie placed some sheet music before her.

"Here, play this," he said quietly in her ear. "It's one of my favorites!" And she began to play *Tales from Vienna Woods* with great talent and feeling. All three men applauded her efforts when she finished, and Charlie led her carefully back to her wheelchair. "You need to elevate your leg and rest."

"Yes, yes, we need to be leaving anyhow," Doctor Whittle said, rising slowly to his feet.

"Oh, must you?" Carol asked kindly.

"Yes, I'm afraid we must," said Albert. Doctor Whittle gave the patient's hand a whiskery kiss, then made his way to the door to shake Charlie's hand. "Thank you, Carol, for a most enjoyable afternoon," Albert said quietly, then stooped and followed his grandfather's example, kissing Carol's hand. "God bless you," he said, a warm look in his eyes. Then he walked away.

After seeing the men off in their carriage, Charlie returned to find Carol making her way out of the sitting room. "I am a bit tired, Charlie. Do you mind if I go to my room and rest a while?"

Charlie wheeled her to her doorway, then bent over and kissed her cheek. "Sweet dreams, Carolina," he whispered, then walked back into the sitting room for a bit of reading.

Meanwhile, out in the carriage Albert and his grandfather sat in comfortable silence. Eventually, Dr. Whittle spoke. "She's a lovely young woman, isn't she, Albert?"

Albert's face reddened that his grandfather had so clearly read his mind. "Yes, sir, she is that. Are she and Charlie courting, sir? Do you know?"

Dr. Whittle smiled as he handled the reins expertly in the Sunday afternoon traffic. "I'm not sure, Albert; but I would think so from his expressions and attentiveness today in his home and at church." He knew better than to inquire, "Why do you ask?", as the answer was written clearly on his grandson's fair face.

"Well, if you ever hear tell that they *aren't* courting, could you let me know?" Albert's grandfather was glad to hear the contented playfulness in his grandson's voice, and he patted him on the shoulders.

"I will that, my boy! I will indeed!"

Chapter Nine

Jessie's Elixir

Monday the third of December 1888 never dawned. It just seemed to seep its way into being with a steel grey sky and, for Carol, a bad cold. Jessie had already brought her a dose of her "home remedy elixir" and a pile of clean, soft handkerchiefs, as well as a steaming kettle for the fireplace to humidify the air. She was shaking her head in empathy when Charlie peeked in to say good morning.

"Whatever's the matter, Jessie?" he asked, smiling at the dark look Jessie gave him.

"Missy Carol is feelin' poorly, and it's as though the sun has gone out of my whole world! Even sick as she is, she's got the sweetest temper I evah did see, and I don't mean maybe." Charlie's smile faded as he caught sight of the red-nosed, puffy-eyed Carol sitting there, propped up with pillows, sipping Jessie's curative tea.

She smiled a tired smile, but when she said "Good morning" her voice was completely unrecognizable! Charlie rushed across the room to her side.

"Oh, my darling, you sound *terrible*! What can I do to help?"

The patient looked sleepily about her at all the trimmings and trappings Jessie had brought, and she shrugged her shoulders. "Jessie has me pretty thoroughly ensconced with every healing agent imaginable, and then one or two I've never heard of before." Carol began to laugh at her own silly joke, but the intake of breath brought on a spasm of coughing that left her all the more tired and breathless.

"Are you sure this is just a cold and not something more serious like pneumonia, Carol? Should we call in Dr. Whittle?"

Carol shook her head no. "If I'm not decidedly better by the time you get home from work, we'll consider it then. Right now, I just want to go back to sleep." She finished the last of the tea; then snuggling down in the blankets and rolling over with her back to him, she prepared to go back to sleep. "I hope you have a good day though, Charlie. God be with you...."

Just that quickly she had drifted off. Charlie was leaning over her to gently move her hair from her face when he noticed that it was down. He carefully placed his hand under her head, bringing the long tresses out from around the pillows.

"This will be in a terrible tangle if it's not braided," he said quietly to himself. He deftly brushed it out and braided it, then tied it off with the nearest thing he could find—one of the multitudinous handkerchiefs. He laid the braid on the pillow, then kissed her cheek. A soft sigh escaped her as she slept, and Charlie once again felt in his heart that she was the loveliest woman he had ever known. He kissed his fingertip and touched her nose, then walked out of the room as quietly as possible.

"I wonder what Jessie *puts* in that tea of hers anyhow?" he said to himself, chuckling all the way out the door on his way to the bank.

෴

Carol didn't awaken until nearly lunch time. She was feeling much better if her appetite was any sign. Jessie came in when she heard Carol stirring. "How you feelin' *now* Missy?"

Swinging her feet over the side of the bed and stretching, she gave a contented smile to Jessie's satisfaction. "Oh, Jessie, I feel like I could eat everything we had for breakfast, dinner, and supper yesterday! What was *in* that tea anyhow?"

Jessie busied herself polishing an imaginary speck on the bed stand. "Oh, now don't you go makin' Jessie give away her secret recipe! But know that it was prepared with love and ministered with a prayer for your healin'."

It was then that both ladies noticed that Carol's hair had been braided. "Jessie?"

"No, not me! Best as I can tell, Mister Charles done did it before he left for the office, being as it was done braided when I come in to check on you aftah he left for work. He's that fond of you, I reckon he didn't want it gettin' all tangled in yo' sleep. He's a thoughtful one, that boy," Jessie said lovingly, then looked out the corner of her eye to watch Carol's reaction. She smiled smugly at what she saw, then fluffed up Carol's pillows and eased her back under the covers.

"I know you think you's all better, but take it easy for t'day, Missy. The Missuz was that worried about you, I 'bout had to chase her out the door for her to go to her meetin' this mornin'! 'I takes care of Charlie when he gots the flu, I can take care of your girl, Missuz B!' An she knowed I would, too. I'll be back with a tray fit for...well, fittin' for *you*, Missy Carol!"

"Thank you so much, Jessie, especially for praying for me." She glanced around the room, enjoying anew its beauty and comfort. Just as Jessie reached the doorway though, Carol asked, "By the way, was that you I heard singing when I woke up?"

Jessie turned her great brown eyes to Carol. "I never meant to disturb you, Missy! Did I wake you up with my caterwaulin'?" she asked, bringing a hand to her cheek. But Carol laughed good-naturedly.

"I would *hardly* call what I heard 'caterwauling', Jessie! But I wasn't familiar with the song. Could you sing it for me again?"

Jessie stole back to Carol's bedside and said quietly, "It's just an old Negro spiritual my mama taught me, and her mama before her," she said as introduction, then looking off toward the window, she began to sing in her rich contralto voice:

> *Steal away, steal away, steal away to Jesus!*
> *Steal away, steal away home!*
> *I ain't got long to stay here.*

> *My Lord, He calls me,*
> *He calls me by the thunder;*
> *The trumpet sounds within-a my soul!*
> *I ain't got long to stay here.*

Steal away, steal away, steal away to Jesus!
Steal away, steal away home!
I ain't got long to stay here.

Green trees are bending,
Po' sinner stand a-trembling!
The trumpet sounds within-a my soul!
I ain't got long to stay here.

Steal away, steal away, steal away to Jesus!
Steal away, steal away home!
I ain't got long to stay here.

Both women sat in silence, the words and ambiance of the song touching their very souls. After a few moments, Carol reached out and grasped Jessie's hand firmly.

"Thank you." It was all she could say, but the joy and tear filled eyes she looked on Jessie with warmed that woman's heart. Jessie patted her and silently went out to get another "tray full of delicacies" from Venetia in the kitchen for her sweet, sweet Missy Carol.

⋙⋘

Monday at the bank was an interesting one for Charlie. Albert came in at ten-thirty just as a light snow had begun to fall, an overcoat covering his suit and tie for the job interview. The men smiled a greeting across the lobby as Albert entered a side office for the interview, and he came out an hour later just as Charlie was closing down his booth for his lunch break.

"Care to join me for lunch, Albert?" Charlie asked as they left the bank together.

Albert chuckled, "I need to calm down some before I eat, but yes, that'd be great! I don't know, I still get nervous taking tests and such; and I wasn't expecting that mathematics examination this morning."

Charlie nodded, "Guess I should have warned you, hunh? Yes, that's a very important part of the job, and being able to do your ciphering quickly and without a single mistake.... I can see where you'd be off your feed for a while!" Charlie turned in at a small café not quite a block from the bank. "This is my usual lunch spot. How about a cup of java?"

"'Sounds great!" The two attractive young men drew more than one lady's attention as they came in, but neither of them noticed. They placed their orders, then the pair began reminiscing about the times they were together during boyhood.

"I told Carol that I remembered your being in the boys' choir, but I didn't specify *which* memory," Albert said mischievously.

"Thanks, Friend!" Charlie answered, chuckling as he remembered the situation Albert was referring to. "As it was though, you were just as much to blame for that little mishap as I was! What was it, 'My uncle *needs* a frog in his garden, but I don't have big enough pockets to hold him!' Is that or is that not historically accurate?"

Both men continued chuckling as they pictured the twitching choir robe, then the terrified escapee frog jumping as fast as he could down the steps from the choir loft. Albert asked, "Did they ever trace the incident back to you?"

"Thankfully, no. Mr. Perkins merely stated that he did not want that *ever* to happen again, and we all agreed heartily. 'Good thing for you, hunh?"

"I thought for sure you would tell on me, good friend though you were!" Albert shook his head, still smiling. "But as I recall, it was the guilt for *not* getting caught that brought me to the place of salvation. Strange, isn't it? But my young heart was that grieved over that sin."

"*Sin*? You call that 'sin'? That was just a little childhood prank, Albert! Surely God wouldn't condemn someone for *that*."

Albert looked across at Charlie, seeing him for the first time as a man who may not even know God's plan of salvation. He had not considered that, but he didn't want to break the camaraderie they had. He offered a quick, silent prayer before he went on.

"Charlie, what is it that *does* condemn us?"

This took Charlie a bit off guard, but as with Jesus, answering a question with a question really made one think.

"Well, our sin condemns us."

"That's *exactly* right, but let's take this a little further. You know as well as I do that the Bible says *'For all have sinned and come short of the glory of God'*. That 'our righteousness', the very *best* we can do, 'is as filthy rags'. That means to me that we are all condemned before we ever overtly commit a sin. We're *born* sinners."

Charlie had heard this kind of talk all his life, but this time it really seemed to come alive, to include him. 'All' included him! He shifted uncomfortably in his seat, but the food came just then and stopped the talk for a moment. Albert asked the blessing over the food. Charlie actually hoped for a moment his friend had been side-tracked, but he seemed to truly have a one track mind.

Albert took a sip of the hot beverage and went right on. "Just about everybody knows John 3:16. But verses seventeen and eighteen are a continuation of verse sixteen. *'For God sent not His Son into the world to condemn the world; but that the world through Him might be saved. He that believeth on Him is not condemned: but He that believeth not is condemned already, because he hath not believed in the name of the only begotten Son of God.'*"

Albert could see the Word of God registering in Charlie's mind, but was it registering in his heart? He looked at his childhood friend and asked, "Charlie, have you ever placed your faith in Jesus to cleanse you of your sin?"

Charlie looked down at his untouched plate. "I...of course I *believe* in Jesus. I've believed in Him all my life, Albert!" He pushed his plate away. "But that's not the same, is it?" he asked quietly, looking up at his friend, whose fair hair seemed to glow as the sunlight peeked through the clouds and shone through the frosty window behind him.

"No, my friend. You need to believe *on* Him. Put your faith in Jesus Christ as your Saviour from your sin. Make it personal...read verse sixteen as *'For God so loved* Charlie Bennett *that He gave His only begotten Son...'*."

If Albert hoped that his friend would make a decision for Christ right then, he was to be disappointed. Charlie shook his head slightly, then said, "I need to think some more about this,

Albert. But I will. I promise."

With a look at his pocket watch, Charlie offered Albert his untouched meal, paid for it, and headed back to the bank.

The people in the restaurant thought Albert gave thanks twice for his food, but in fact he was praying for his friend's soul, for Charlie Bennett to have a hunger for the things of God.

∽∽∽

Albert got the job at the bank, and although Charlie was designated to train him, or maybe *because*, Albert did not verbally witness to him throughout their time together the rest of the work week. In fact, Albert made certain that he showed his friend the respect due a superior, and that his good work would reflect Charlie's diligence in training. Nevertheless, Charlie was reminded several times a day of their lunch conversation Monday, and his heart was convicted as though Albert had spoken of it daily. By the time Friday evening rolled around, Albert could tell by Charlie's reserve that the Holy Spirit had indeed been working overtime.

Charlie was showing him the end of the week closing of the books when Albert finally introduced more personal matters. "So if everything balances, take your cash box to Mr. Simms, turn your book in to the accounting office, and you're done. Any questions?"

Albert raised an eyebrow and said, "None about work, sir." He looked at Charlie's tired eyes and, realizing he could not "be the Holy Spirit" for his friend said, "I was wondering however if you could answer a rather personal question." The men got their coats, hats, and galoshes from the cloak room, then headed out the employee entrance.

Charlie walked silently to his buggy, adjusted the reins and harness, then turned to his friend. "Can I offer you a ride home, so we can talk privately?" Albert nodded, climbing into the buggy. They were on their way through the busy work traffic before Charlie spoke again.

"If you were wanting to ask me something more about our conversation Monday, please don't. I value your friendship, and I appreciate your concern. I just haven't had the opportunity to really think things through."

Albert nodded, then cleared his throat. "Actually, I was going to ask you about your houseguest." Charlie kept his focus on the road, but Albert could see his jaw tighten before he answered.

"Oh?"

"Yes," Albert went on carefully. "I was wondering if the two of you, that is, if you have an understanding."

"Yes, I am courting Carol officially and care for her deeply, Albert." Charlie glanced toward Albert as he spoke, and the moment's eye contact told Albert everything he needed to know. There was no animosity in his friend's eyes or words however, and Albert smiled.

"She seems like a fine young lady, Charlie. I wish you both all the best." It occurred to Albert that if Charlie didn't get his heart right with God, a permanent relationship could not take place between him and Carol, a believer. But he also did not think after just revealing his interest in her that he should be the one to bring this up. He quickly changed the subject to a safer topic, and the two enjoyed a relaxing chat all the way to Albert's grandfather's home.

"Thanks for the ride, Charlie! Hopefully I'll have my own buggy soon, though I don't know that I could afford the upkeep right now. Have a good rest tomorrow, and see you Sunday!" He shook Charlie's hand then hopped down out of the buggy, walking down the path to the house.

Charlie watched him safely to the front door, smiling as Albert turned back and waved after unlocking the latch. Finally he clicked for the General to proceed, then said quietly, "Thank *you*, my friend."

Chapter Ten

Picnic at the Waterfront

Charlie had it in mind to take Carol to the waterfront on Saturday; so he asked Jessie, Beatrix, and Venetia to help him put together a picnic basket. Everything was made ready when he walked casually out to the garden to find Carol. She sat in her chair on one of the paths, sketching the scene before her with remarkable accuracy. The corner of the garden held a small gazebo, and the magnificent live oaks towering above it made it look diminutive. She romanticized the scene a bit with some wildlife, but the lighting and season were very accurate. Charlie didn't want to disturb or frighten her into making an error, so he held as still as possible until she turned around.

"Charlie!" she gasped, "You totally caught me off guard!"

He saw that she was putting away her paper and pencils and quickly replied. "I didn't want to disturb your drawing. This is excellent, Carol! Really good!" He took the sketchbook from her hands and asked with his eyes if he could look again, and she nodded her concurrence.

As he turned the pages, he realized that this was not the first of her drawings since she came to his family home. There were portraits of each of the servants, each family member, and several beautiful scenes of the house. He turned back to the one of himself, studying it a bit. "Is this really how I look to you?"

Carol giggled. "One seldom recognizes oneself in a portrait, Charlie. I'm sorry."

He closed the book and handed it back to her. "Quite to the contrary, I had no idea I was so incredibly handsome!"

"*You*, Charlie Bennett, are incorrigible! What *am* I going to do with you?"

"How about joining me for a picnic lunch at the waterfront, sweet lady?" He bowed playfully, then with a flourish added, "Your carriage awaits!"

Carol was so surprised that she hardly knew what to do first. She excused herself to the retiring room, then came out and got her coat, hat, and gloves out of her room before joining him in the foyer. The excitement put a blush in her cheeks and a twinkle in her eyes that made her absolutely beautiful, and Charlie paused as he offered her his arm.

"I know we joke a lot, but, Carolina, you are a very attractive lady." She looked directly into his eyes and quietly thanked him for his compliment, then the two headed out the door.

Charlie tucked a lap quilt around Carol, checking to make sure the basket was secure before he hopped in the buggy and clicked to the General. It was not that cold in the sunshine, and there was plenty of that to be had. Charlie told her a bit about the different buildings they passed, but he saw that Carol was simply enjoying being out in the sunshine and fresh air. They heard a group of carolers singing on the corner, and shoppers were coming and going from every store along the way.

Carol put a gloved hand in the crook of his arm to pull his attention to an adorable child staring at a Christmas display in a toy store window, and Charlie didn't mind in the least when she neglected to pull her hand away. She began humming a cheerful tune, and they made their way to the park with Carol's songs and the clip-clop of the General's hooves for accompaniment.

Charlie pulled the buggy up to a hitching post and tied the General, loosening his bridle and placing a bag of oats around his strong neck. Then he helped Carol down from the buggy and picked up the basket and blanket. They walked across the shell and stone pathways until they found a sunny spot in the grass, then Charlie spread out the blanket for Carol.

"I do believe Jessie and Venetia have once again outdone themselves! *Look* at this food! Fit for a king!" Carol wasn't especially hungry, but watching the boyish excitement on Charlie's face made her smile and giggle with every succulent "find" in the picnic basket.

He drew out a small cluster of grapes and held one out to put in Carol's mouth; but when she leaned in to take it, he couldn't resist pulling it back out of her reach. She gave him a pout that tugged at his heart.

"Oh, you mustn't ever do that to me, for I could never say no to that kind of cuteness!" Charlie clutched his heart and held the grape back out for her, but rather than be duped again, she grabbed his hand, then bit into the grape. "Alas, my heart is broken, for I have lost her trust!" he said in high melodrama between chuckles.

Carol, still with his hand in her clasp, drew it to her lips once more and kissed his fingertip. Instantly sobered, Charlie touched her cheek with the back of his hand; then his stomach growled. "We need to bless this feast," he said, taking her hand in his. *"Dear Father God, I thank You for this day, for this food, and for this company. May Your blessing be upon us. Amen."*

"Charlie, do you think we're supposed to eat *all* of this?" Just then Charlie stopped loading plates long enough to unwrap two cups and a bottle of cherry cider. "Might I make a toast?" Carol requested as Charlie poured. "I drink a toast from me to thee! May we never disagree. If we do, phooey on you, here's to *me*!" Carol took a long sip, half choking amidst the giggles. She leaned back, resting on one of her arms so that she could have her injured leg comfortably positioned in front of her. Charlie sat with his legs crossed, the breeze blowing his hair into a mass of curls. He paused as he noticed Carol looking at him as he wolfed down the fried chicken and cornbread.

"Forgive my lack of manners, but this is *so* good!" Then he chomped down on another chicken leg without ceremony.

Carol smiled. "Actually, I wasn't thinking critical thoughts of your eating habits, Charles! I was just thinking how I'd like to sketch you just like that...with your hair wind blown and the sun on your face."

"The *true* Charles Bennett? Well, don't forget the shine of the chicken juices at the corner of my ravenous mouth!" Charlie went on eating, Carol studying him silently as she ate.

As the meal drew slowly to a close, Carol gathered the things and placed them back into the basket, wiping her mouth and hands on the linen napkin and sipping the last of her cherry cider. "That, sir, was delicious! Thank you! And thank Jessie and Beatrix and Cook and whoever else had their hand in spoiling us rotten with this outing."

Charlie smiled contentedly back at her. "You're welcome." He'd been thinking about so many things just then, so many questions. "Carol, do you feel up to walking a bit or would you rather sit here to talk?"

"Actually, may we stay here? With church tomorrow I don't want to do too much," she said, smoothing her skirts and removing her hat, laying it on the blanket between them. "What did you want to talk about?"

"Well, hypothetically speaking, if we were to one day, say, marry...how many children would you want?"

"'Hypothetically speaking'?" she asked, her countenance amazingly casual. "As many as the Lord would bless me and my husband with. I dearly love children."

"I know...that is, I've seen your reaction to the children at church and even the ones we passed on the way here. I imagined you'd want a large family." Charlie grew quiet, looking down at his folded hands in his lap. "What if you were to...to fall in love with someone who could not give you children? Would you still marry him?"

Charlie's eyes mirrored his heart, reflecting the pain of not knowing for whatever reason if he would be able to father children. There was no doubting the sincerity of Carol's answer though. "Oh, Charlie. When I marry, it will be for love of my husband, the man I want to be with for the rest of my life. If we can't have children, we could adopt. There are many children in orphanages who long for a Christian home and family. I'm sure I would be completely content with a house filled with adopted children if we in fact could not have our own." Then realizing what she had said, she added with a shy grin, "hypothetically speaking, of course."

Charlie nodded. "I guess I should explain. I suffered with a terribly high fever as a child. I had a younger sister who died from it. Mother told me a few years ago that Doctor Whittle had told her and Father that a high fever of that nature sometimes effected a person's heart, and also their ability to procreate. I just didn't want to proceed any further with our relationship if that was a...a hindrance."

"Not at all, Charlie," she said softly, placing her hand on his knee. He covered her hand quickly with his own, giving it a gentle squeeze. "I'm so sorry about the loss of your sister. What was her name?"

"'Lizzy'. I don't remember much about her as I was only six when the fever struck. But she was so full of energy. I still remember seeing her curls bouncing when she was chasing me." Charlie looked down at the pattern in the blanket to gather his thoughts, then he went on. Hypothetically speaking, would you want boys or girls?"

"*Yes*," was all she said, and they both laughed.

"How long have we known each other now, Carol?"

"Well, the accident happened on November twenty-second, and today is the eighth of December. We just passed our two week anniversary!"

"Two weeks? Is that really all it's been?" He paused, looking deeply into her eyes as he became aware of a warm tug on his heart. "I guess it's too soon then to tell you—"

She placed her hand over his lips gently. "Yes, it's too soon yet," she said, but her eyes spoke volumes. He kissed her hand softly, then she drew it away. In an attempt to lessen the tension, she added lightly, "Of course, if you should have any more hypothetical questions...."

Charlie laughed before he began his line of hypothetical questioning again, and the afternoon was spent in total fellowship of kindred hearts.

When it was time to go, Charlie helped Carol to her feet. As she stood before him with her hands still in his, he noticed that she was not but a few inches shorter than himself.

Noticing his expression, Carol asked, "What is *that* look for, Mr. Bennett?"

"If you must know," he said, tucking her hand in the crook of his arm as he walked her to the buggy, "I was just noticing how tall you are. You're nearly as tall as I am! Not that it bothers me. Not in the least. I was just thinking if I'd have hugged you just then how nicely you would fit in my arms." He saw the red cast to her cheeks and added, "You know, I really like you a lot, Carolina Montague."

Her eyes sparkled in appreciation as she replied, "And I rather like you, too, Charlie Bennett." Charlie retrieved the basket and blanket, re-bridled and untied the General, and they all headed home.

Chapter Eleven

Letters From Home

"Carol? You have a letter in today's post, dear!" Mrs. Bennett brought the letter out on the veranda where Carol had been napping in the sunshine. She reached out for the letter eagerly and opened it, reading it aloud.

> My Darling Daughter~
> Your father and I were so pleased that the Lord has taken such good care of you in our absence. Please thank the family who has taken you in for us, letting them know that we greatly appreciate their kindness to you.

Carol smiled at Mrs. Bennett, who had taken a seat in one of the rocking chairs.

> We have a suggestion for you if you do not think it too much trouble. We were wondering if it would be more convenient for you to share a room with Celia, as she was considering going to Baltimore to take a teaching position second term. With the two pooled incomes, you could have a much nicer room, not to mention the blessing of your sister's company! She is eagerly awaiting your reply before finalizing her plans for moving, as she does not wish to presume. Please

write and let us know if this idea meets with your approval, dear.

I am sending your birthday gifts and Christmas gifts this post, and I do hope they will arrive in time as the holy day is fast approaching! Please know that we will be thinking of and praying for you, for God's blessings on your birthday and His, my dear child.

We miss you more than words can say.

All my love~ Momma

Carol sat with the letter in her lap for some time, simply staring out into the sleeping gardens. "I hadn't really thought about leaving. Isn't that silly of me? I guess I've grown accustomed to being spoiled here." She laughed quietly as she folded her mother's letter, carefully placing it back in the envelope. "Mrs. Bennett, thank you again so much for your hospitality. I...I suppose it's because you are a Christian that I feel such a kinship to you. I've just felt so at *home* here, and I'm so grateful." Mrs. Bennett stood and walked to Carol's side.

"Carol, I don't believe it was just an accident that brought you here. I'll always believe the Lord Himself brought you into our home and lives." She bent and kissed Carol on the top of her head, then knelt beside her wheelchair. "Has Charlie mentioned that he had a sister?" Carol nodded as her eyes grew misty. "Then you have some idea of what a precious gift your presence has been to me. I like to think that our Lizzy would have been something like you had she grown to adulthood...tall, joyful, even gifted at the piano as you are. I have thanked God every day you've been here, did you know it?" Carol shook her head with a crooked, teary-eyed grin. "In Christ, you *are* a part of our family! I will have that consolation when you go traipsing off with that sister of yours someday in the not-so-distant future," she said with a chuckle. Then with a hand on Carol's cheek she added, "And you will always be welcome here, Carol. Always." Carol covered Mrs. Bennett's hand with her own, then looked at her with her heart in her eyes.

"Thank you so much, Mrs. Bennett," was all she could say.

≈≥≤

"Have you asked Carol to the Christmas Banquet yet, Charlie?" his father asked as they rode home together that evening. The bank employees had a very elegant Christmas ball and banquet each year, but this would be the first year Charlie would be attending as an employee instead of a family member.

"Great day! I'm glad you reminded me! It's on Christmas Eve, isn't it?" Charlie's father couldn't help but chuckle at his boy's excitement. Not ten years ago, he was this excited over toys he would receive. Now his eyes were sparkling over a certain young lady he hoped to share Christmas with.

Charlie had been so busy thinking about what to do to make her birthday and Christmas special that he'd completely forgotten about the banquet. He determined to ask her that very night.

"Son, have you thought any more about what we talked about the other day in my office?" Mr. Bennett asked, cutting into Charlie's thoughts.

"Well, sir, I've really been busy lately, but I haven't slacked off any in what I had already been doing. I have officially joined the choir, though I was too late to sing in the oratorio Christmas morning. Do you know that they're doing excerpts from Handel's *Messiah*? It should be beautiful!"

"Yes, I'm sure it will be."

Mr. Bennett was disappointed that Charlie seemed to be putting off any spiritual growth, but he was, after all, getting more involved in church. *"Perhaps,"* he thought, *"I was mistaken. Perhaps the boy is already a believer and just needs some spiritual maturity. Give him time...."*

≈≥≤

Carol was only too happy to agree to go to the Bank Christmas Banquet as Charlie's guest, but when he mentioned the ball she realized she may not have anything suitable to wear for such a formal occasion. When her Christmas package arrived just three days before Christmas, she never imagined it would hold the solution to her dilemma.

Untying the string and peeling aside the brown paper, she removed the lid of the box. Behind layers of tissue paper, she found the most beautiful gown she had ever beheld...a deep garnet velvet with fitted bodice, full skirt, and puffed sleeves. When she stood suddenly to her feet and held it up, something of weight fell to the floor amid the tissue, box, and paper. She looked down to see her mother's pearl brooch fixed on a bit of garnet ribbon. Reaching down to pick it up, she stood there smiling and crying alternately when Charlie's mother found her there.

"Oh, Carol! Isn't God *good*? You'll be the belle of the ball, my dear child!" Then Mrs. Bennett spotted the note in the bottom of the box. She handed it to Carol, who read:

My Darling Daughter~

Do not scold us for choosing such fine gifts, for your Father insisted upon them as much as I did. Caleb did a fine job managing the farm, and with some of the money left over from harvest we felt we needed to buy something extra special for our dear girl who sacrificed so much for us. I hope it brings you as much joy wearing it as it brought your Father, Celia, and me picking it out for you. May God bless you with another wonderful year, my beloved daughter. Happy Birthday, and a blessed Christmas, dear!

All my love ~ Momma

Carol held the dress up to her and carefully turned in a circle, her whole countenance glowing with pleasure. "And to think," she said, continuing her thoughts aloud for Mrs. Bennett to hear, "this was on its way before Charlie even asked me to the banquet! Mother said in her letter last week that she had mailed this package the same day she wrote!"

Beatrix peeked around the corner at the ladies, and Carol spotted her. "Oh, Beatrix, could you please take this to my room before I spoil it?" Beatrix took the gown in her capable hands, then in one smooth move picked up the wrappings in her other hand as Carol sat down looking at the brooch.

"You know, it's long been a tradition of mine to decorate in dark red and white at Christmas time...makes me think of the verse, *'Though your sins be as scarlet, they shall be as white as snow; though they be red like crimson, they shall be as wool'*. Momma remembered...or Poppa did, one." She looked at Mrs. Bennett's smiling face and answered, "Yes, Mrs. Bennett. God is very, *very* good. Always!"

Chapter Twelve

Christmas Carol

Christmas Eve had arrived, as had Carol's twenty-first birthday. When she rose with the dawn she headed for the music room, not to play, but simply because the windows faced the sunrise. She set the brake of her chair, then stood carefully and stepped to the piano bench to look over the music that had been there the night before. She still recalled her conversation with Charlie's mother....

"Carol, your playing, the pieces you've chosen, have seemed rather melancholy of late. I know that being apart from your family on special occasions is difficult, but is there something else effecting you? making you sad, my dear?"

Carol didn't even finish the piece she was playing for the tears that came to her eyes. Mrs. Bennett sat beside her on the bench and took out her handkerchief, handing it to Carol without a word.

"Mrs. Bennett, I believe you know me well enough to know I would never wish to hurt Charlie. He...I...."

Laying a gentle hand on the girl's flushed cheek, Mrs. Bennett gently said, "You love him."

Carol couldn't help but smile at the declaration. "Yes, ma'am, I do." But once again the cloud of worry crossed over her face as she said, "But should I? He doesn't seem to care about things of the Lord, at least he won't talk with me about Him, about his relationship with Him. Does he know the Lord?"

Mrs. Bennett's eyes locked on Carol's, and Carol could see the concern, the doubt, the love—to an even greater degree than that of her own love for Charlie, as only a mother can feel.

"I don't know, Carol. I hope so. I pray so." The women who loved Charlie Bennett shared a tearful embrace. "Let's pray for him, Carol. Right now." Both women bowed their heads and prayed for this dear one's soul, and for God's will to be done in this relationship between him and Carol.

She was brought out of her reverie quickly as Charlie entered the room. "Happy birthday, Carol." He stood in the sitting room looking at her with such an expression of love that her heart literally pained her, but she gave him a smile.

"Thank you, Charlie." He approached her then, and, seeing the traces of tears, pulled something from his pocket.

"I'm sorry you have to be away from your family on this special day, but I want to give you your gift early. Hopefully it will cheer you up." He handed her a crimson velvet box with a cream satin bow on it.

"It's too pretty to open!" she said smiling at the giver. She opened the box to discover a beautiful, sterling chain bracelet with a single charm on it, a heart! "Oh, Charlie, it's exquisite!"

"Wait, look!" Charlie turned the heart charm around to reveal an ornate initial...the letter "C". "I just wanted you to have a constant reminder that you have my heart, which is the real gift I'm giving you today. Happy birthday, Carolina." He fastened the bracelet on her wrist, then drawing her close he whispered into her ear, "I love you."

"Oh, Charlie...and I love you. I don't know when I started loving you, but I can tell you without any doubt that I do now, so very much."

A masculine voice startled the two apart. "Hmmm. 'Looks like someone got their birthday present early!" Mr. and Mrs. Bennett had just come down the stairs for breakfast when they heard voices in the music room. "Happy birthday, Carol."

Carol blushed crimson, but Charlie didn't seem to notice this time. He stood with her hand in his and smiled like a man in love. "Mother, Father, I have something I want to share with you both. I just told Carol that I love her, and we wanted you two to be the first we told."

"Well, I can't pretend that news is a surprise, but I *can* tell you that I'm very happy for you both." Mr. Bennett gave Charlie a hearty handshake, then beamed a handsome smile at Carol, still seated at the piano. Mrs. Bennett stepped forward then, and although Charlie in his enjoyment of the moment didn't notice anything amiss, Carol knew that last night's conversation still weighed heavily on her heart.

"May God bless your love for one another, my dears," Mrs. Bennett said softly, embracing Charlie, and Carol as she stood. Then the four of them went in to breakfast.

※

After yet another delectable meal, Mr. and Mrs. Bennett presented Carol with their gift for her birthday, a lovely silk shawl. It was cream with beautiful detailed embroidery, and there was a small purse to match. "Thank you both so much! I will not be able to fit through the doors to leave the house tonight, my head will be so big!" They all laughed merrily at the incongruous thought of their dear girl puffed up with pride, then Mrs. Bennett spoke up.

"Indeed, it may be *Charlie* whose head is puffed up, for he has yet to see you in your beautiful gown!"

"This is true," Charlie agreed amiably. "I only got a general description of this gown of yours. You're likely to drive me to distraction just coming in the room!"

And eight hours later, that is precisely what happened. Charlie was ready early and went to the sitting room to wait. He heard a rustling in the hall and stood, and when Carol came around the corner he was thoroughly distracted by her beauty.

The gown set off her fair skin to perfection, the garnet material being so dark that it nearly looked black in the candlelight. Her hair was drawn up in a pearl-studded comb and ornately braided, one carefully placed ringlet lying behind her left ear. She wore her mother's pearl brooch on the satin ribbon at her neck, and the bracelet Charlie had given her was still in place at her wrist. Carol stood there for so long that she grew embarrassed waiting for Charlie to say something, so she did an elegant pirouette, tilted her head to the right, and asked softly, "Well, how do I look?"

Charlie took her gloved hand and kissed it before replying, "Absolutely beautiful, Carolina Montague." Charlie was a very dashing picture himself in black tuxedo, snowy white collar and cuffs, and cranberry and white striped cravat, his top hat and gloves sitting on the settee. They were still standing there hand in hand when Charlie's mother and father came down the stairs.

"Oh, don't you two look handsome!" Mrs. Bennett said sincerely, herself a picture in hunter green taffeta. Charlie came forward and kissed his mother's cheek before returning to take Carol's arm.

"Shall we go?" he asked, and they gathered their coats, hats, and gloves and made their way to the awaiting carriage.

The four arrived a little early at the rented hall to make certain everything was in readiness. The chamber orchestra was just arriving, each taking out their instrument and tuning it for the evening's music. The banqueting tables were set off to each side, and every available space was adorned with evergreen boughs, candles, and cranberry ribbon. Charlie escorted Carol and his mother to the head table while Mr. Bennett walked around talking with different ones in charge of the banquet.

"It may be some time before everyone is here. Carol, why don't you sit down for a while?" Charlie pulled the chair out for her and turned it so that she was facing away from the table and could look around the room. Then he pulled his mother's chair out for her, checking the place card to be certain he had the right seat.

"It looks like Jennings has outdone himself this year, Mother. I do believe he begins planning these on Christmas Day for the following year!" He smiled at the ladies, then explained to Carol who Mr. Jennings was.

Mrs. Bennett excused herself and walked over to join her husband, and Charlie seated himself beside Carol.

"You hide your cast so well that I sometimes forget that you're wearing one. Do you think we could have one dance together tonight, or would that be overdoing it?"

Carol's eyes were glittering with excitement. "I think I will be fine actually, and if you're asking me for a waltz, I'm accepting!" She saw him look to her lips, which this once were shining with the slightest bit of lip rouge and gloss. His face was already so near her own she could smell his cologne; but he leaned closer still and whispered in her ear.

Carol giggled gleefully. "*No*, Charlie! Mistletoe does *not* deem our agreement 'null and void'!"

Charlie snapped his fingers good-naturedly. "You can't blame a man for trying! Oh, look! There's Albert!" Charlie stood to welcome Albert and the lady who was with him, whom Charlie couldn't help but notice seemed to fade in comparison to Carol's dark beauty. Albert shook Charlie's outstretched hand, then kissed Carol's hand before introducing his date for the evening.

"Miss Carol Montague, Mr. Charlie Bennett, this is my cousin, Meredith Atkins." Meredith was a good deal shorter than the other three, and was very fair of hair and complexion like her cousin. And her smile showed dimples that didn't even look real they were so deep! But it was when she spoke that Carol knew her to be a kindred spirit, for she had the slow, comfortable southern accent Carol herself possessed to a lesser degree.

"Do I detect a southern accent, Miss Atkins?" Carol asked as the men began a conversation.

"Yes, you do indeed, Miss Montague. I'm from South Carolina actually. I'm up here with my family visitin' for Christmas." Although her accent was very pronounced, her countenance was beautifully transparent; and Carol felt quite relaxed in her presence. "I'm so pleased to meet you. Albert told me about you, that you were southern, like me. And he also told me of another commonality, that you are in fact a Christian, Miss Montague!"

"Oh, please, call me 'Carol'. And, yes, I am glad to say I am indeed a Christian!"

"And won't you please call me 'Merrie'? It's what all the family calls me. Of course, I get no end of ribbing this time of year, with 'Merrie Christmas' being on everyone's lips!"

"Like I don't hear it with 'Christmas Carol'?" The ladies were laughing and exchanging stories when the gentlemen turned to help them to their feet, as the festivities were about to begin.

Mr. Bennett made some welcoming remarks, then escorted Mrs. Bennett to the middle of the ballroom, the orchestra playing a beautiful rendition of a Strauss waltz. The gentlemen then turned to the ladies.

"May I have this dance, Carolina?" Charlie asked, and the two made their way into the swirling, sparkling, crowd. "This cast will be helpful indeed if shuffling keeps you from stepping on my feet, Miss Montague."

Carol laughed up at him. "Charlie Bennett!" she said with mock-offense in her tone. "I'm having a hard enough time totin' this awkwardly heavy cast around without your making fun!"

"Well, you're doing a splendid job, my dear! And, may I add, I was right," Charlie added with a smug expression on his handsome face.

"About...?"

His look was no longer teasing as he answered, "You *do* fit perfectly in my arms." For some reason his partner barely noticed the weight of her cast for the rest of the waltz.

❧❧

Charlie asked his mother for a dance after the dinner was served, eaten, and cleared away. Mrs. Bennett was a very beautiful lady, and Mr. Bennett watched his wife even while talking with Carol at the table. Carol caught his adoring look and watched the dancing pair a moment before turning back to him.

"It's nice to see a couple besides my parents who are still so obviously in love after many years of marriage."

"Not so many years, Miss Montague, twenty-two years tonight actually."

"Oh, Mr. Bennett, happy anniversary! I was so caught up in my birthday that I completely forgot! Pray forgive me."

Mr. Bennett only chuckled, his gaze following his bride and their son around the room. "Not to worry, dear! Anniversaries are really only celebrated between two. I'm sure you understand. Charlie remembered, which meant a lot to Laura, of course."

"Of course," Carol replied quietly. Charlie was such a

thoughtful young man. She turned again to look at him, and through the crowd she caught a glimpse of his handsome face looking lovingly down at his mother. Something one of them had said had them both laughing as they moved in time to the beautiful music.

"I suppose this has become a sort of anniversary for you and Charlie, since you declared your feelings for one another this morning. I'm very happy for you both. I...I don't quite know how to tell you this, but I've often since the accident thought that the Lord allowed you to come into our lives. I think Charlie is the reason, not just his emotional heart, but his spiritual heart could very well be effected by your meeting. Do you know it?"

Carol turned to find Mr. Bennett looking at her, his warm, brown eyes looking like an older version of Charlie's. "Yes, Mr. Bennett. I hope with all my heart that our relationship will only strengthen his spiritual relationship with the Lord, and that if he does *not* know Christ as Saviour yet, that he soon will come to know Him."

As the song drew to a close, Mr. Bennett reached out and placed his hand over hers. "You are an answer to prayer, Miss Montague. Truly. Ah, here they come." Mr. Bennett stood to seat his wife, and Charlie came to Carol's side.

"Would you care to join me for the next dance, Miss Montague? Or perhaps for some punch?"

"Oh, punch, please!"

"Good! I've worked up a thirst trying to keep up with that lady!" Mrs. Bennett giggled, waving a gloved hand at her son while using her fan effectively with her other hand.

Carol stood to go with him to the punch table, skirting the dance floor as they made their way around the room. After picking up two crystal cups of punch, they stepped into an alcove beside a large window which was letting some deliciously cold winter air into the crowded ballroom. They sipped their punch with their backs to the window, watching the couples swirl past, enjoying the music and the cool air.

"Charlie, thank you for inviting me here tonight. This has been so enjoyable...I shall never forget my twenty-first birthday as long as I live!"

Charlie smiled, looking down at her as the breeze touched her slightly limp ringlet of hair. He reached out and took the ringlet in his hand, twirling it around his finger to restore its curl. "Good, but I still plan on reminding you every year of this wonderful night, and also trying to 'top it' every year hereafter." Carol turned to look at Charlie, her eyes sparkling like sapphires in the semi-darkness. "Yes, Miss Montague. I intend, 'Lord willing, to spend the rest of my life with you." The love he felt took his breath away.

"I love you, Charles Bennett, with all my heart." Carol turned to look at the width of the windowsill, then sat down comfortably, turning her bracelet around and looking at the heart. "I was tempted to kiss you on your handsome cheek just then, but I daresay you would have turned your face at the last moment!"

Charlie chuckled, holding his cup of punch with both hands as he looked distractedly at the remaining ruby-colored liquid. "You're beginning to read my mind." He smiled as they exchanged another eloquent look, then said softly, "And I love you, Carolina, with all my heart."

～

When the foursome arrived home shortly before midnight, Lucas was there to greet them, taking their coats and hats as they walked into the sitting room. Charlie guided Carol to the settee so she could put her feet up; then he and his father each took high back chairs while Mrs. Bennett made her way to the piano. She began to play Christmas carols, the words echoing in each listener's heart though no one was actually singing. *O Come, All Ye Faithful*, *Silent Night*, *The First Noel*.... Then Mrs. Bennett began playing and singing *O Holy Night*, and Carol walked over to the piano and harmonized with her.

O holy night! the stars are brightly shining!
It is the night of the dear Saviour's birth;
Long lay the world in sin and error pining,
'Til He appeared and the soul felt its worth.
A thrill of hope the weary world rejoices,

For yonder breaks a new and glorious morn;
Fall on your knees,
O hear the angel voices!
O night divine, O night when Christ was born!
O night, O holy night, O night divine!

Led by the light of faith serenely beaming,
With glowing hearts by His cradle we stand;
So led by light of a star so sweetly gleaming,
Here came the wise men from Orient land.
The King of kings thus lay in lowly manger,
In all our trials born to be our Friend;
He knows our need,
Our weakness is no stranger.
Behold your King! before Him lowly bend!
Behold your King! before Him lowly bend!

Truly He taught us to love one another;
His law is love and His gospel is peace;
Chains shall He break, for the slave is our brother,
And in His name all oppression shall cease!
Sweet hymns of joy in grateful chorus raise we,
Let all within us praise His holy name;
Christ is the Lord!
O praise His name forever!
His pow'r and glory evermore proclaim!
His pow'r and glory evermore proclaim!

Mr. Bennett and Charlie joined the ladies at the piano, and the four held hands as Mr. Bennett led in prayer.

"Dear Father in heaven, we thank Thee this night for sending Your only Son that night so long ago. We thank Thee, knowing that without Him, we would all be lost and undone. Father, help us to serve Thee better, to love Thee, and to love others with the love Thou hast so willingly shown us. I thank Thee for my bride, our precious son, and for this dear child of Thine who is with us this night. Please bless us and guide us, Father, to do that which is pleasing in Thy sight. In the name of Thy Son

Jesus we pray, amen."

Mr. and Mrs. Bennett excused themselves then, giving hugs to the two young people before making their way upstairs for the night. Charlie took Carol's hand and walked with her back to the settee.

"It has been a wonderful day, Carol, hasn't it?"

"Unforgettably wonderful, my love." She placed her hands in his, then smiled sleepily. "May I kiss your cheek, Charlie?" she asked quietly, and Charlie leaned forward. The kiss she gave was feather soft, but she giggled as she leaned back, then stood to her feet.

"What are you giggling about?" Charlie asked, coming to his feet as well.

"Well, if you must know, I was thinking you were going to turn your head!"

Charlie grinned. "It took everything in me *not* to do just that!" He stroked her cheek with the back of his finger. "Our first kiss will not be a stolen one though, Carolina." His dark eyes glittered as he looked into hers. "But would you have minded so much if I *had* turned my head?"

Carol raised an eyebrow, grinning coyly; but the late hour got the best of her, and she stifled a yawn. Charlie smiled. "I suppose we'll never know! Good night, my love, and happy birthday." He kissed his finger and touched the tip of her nose, then gently directed her to her room.

She laid a hand on the doorway and turned to look over her shoulder at him as he strode down the hall and climbed the stairs to his room. "Merry Christmas, Charlie," she whispered to his retreating back.

She went into her room where Jessie waited to assist her. "Oh, Missy Carol, you looks like this was the bes' night of your life! You looks just like one of Miz Bennett's roses, all blushin' an' pretty!"

Jessie guided her over to the dressing table and took her hair down, brushing the luxuriant length until it shone in the lamplight. Carol carefully removed the bit of ribbon that held her mother's brooch and placed it on the dressing table lovingly. She left Charlie's heart right where he had fastened it that morning.

"Jessie, it was the most wonderful day I've ever had!" she said as her faithful friend helped her out of her gown, petticoats, and corset and into her robe. Carol removed the shoe and stocking from her right foot and the large sock that was covering her cast, then walked to the pitcher and basin to wash her face and hands and wet a cloth for her feet. Jessie braided her hair for her, as had become the custom since Charlie had done so when she was ill; then the beloved servant pulled back the comforter and removed the bed-warmer. Carol removed her robe then, draping it over a chair beside her bed and enjoying the comfortable freedom of her shift.

"Thank you, dear friend," Carol said with a sigh as she slipped between the soft cotton sheets. "And a wonderful Christmas to you and yours."

Jessie patted her hand and turned the lamp down low. "Bless you, honey. Bless you."

Chapter Thirteen

Behold, The Lamb of God!

The church service Christmas morning was absolutely awe-inspiring. The excerpts from Handel's *Messiah* were beautifully presented, and when Pastor Lehman stood to give the message the Lord had laid on his heart, his eyes were glistening with tears.

"Thank you, choir, for those beautiful selections from Handel's inspiring oratorio." He then turned toward the main auditorium, placing his spectacles on his nose as he opened his Bible. "If you would please, turn in your Bibles to the Gospel of John, chapter one, beginning with verse six. Please stand with me for the reading of God's Word.

> 6. There was a man sent from God, whose name was John.
> 7. The same came for a witness, to bear witness of the Light, that all men through Him might believe.
> 8. He was not that Light, but was sent to bear witness of that Light.
> 9. That was the true Light, which lighteth every man that cometh into the world.
> 10. He was in the world, and the world was made by Him, and the world knew Him not.
> 11. He came unto His own, and His own received Him not.
> 12. But as many as received Him, to them gave He

power to become the sons of God, even to them that believe on His name:
13. Which were born, not of blood, nor of the will of the flesh, nor of the will of man, but of God.
14. And the Word was made flesh, and dwelt among us, (and we beheld His glory, the glory as of the only begotten of the Father,) full of grace and truth.
15. John bare witness of Him, and cried, saying, This was He of whom I spake, He that cometh after me is preferred before me: for He was before me.
16. And of His fulness have all we received, and grace for grace.
17. For the law was given by Moses, but grace and truth came by Jesus Christ.

"Now skip down if you would to verse twenty-nine.

29. The next day John seeth Jesus coming unto him, and saith, Behold the Lamb of God, which taketh away the sin of the world.
30. This is He of whom I said, After me cometh a man which is preferred before me: for He was before me.
31. And I knew Him not: but that He should be made manifest to Israel, therefore am I come baptizing with water.
32. And John bare record, saying, I saw the Spirit descending from heaven like a dove, and it abode upon Him.
33. And I knew Him not: but He that sent me to baptize with water, the same said unto me, Upon Whom thou shalt see the Spirit descending, and remaining on Him, the same is He which baptizeth with the Holy Ghost.
34. And I saw, and bare record that this is the Son of God.

"You may be seated. One of the songs the choir sang this morning is taken directly from this passage: *Behold the Lamb of*

God, which taketh away the sin of the world.

"This is not a traditional Christmas message that we just read, but when we think of Christ's birth, we remember that Jesus the Christ was born in a stable. There was no room for this King of kings but in the lowliest of places, a sleeping and feeding place for animals. Even a freshly cleansed stable with new hay...all cobwebs swept from the rafters, the dirt floor swept free of all dust and refuse...even a spotlessly clean stable would not be what I would consider an adequate place for a King to be born!"

Pastor Lehman paused, removing his glasses and placing them beside his open Bible on the pulpit. He leaned forward, looking at his congregation from the lofty height before continuing. "But a stable is the perfect place for a *lamb* to be born. The Lamb of God, which taketh away the sin of the world!

"We remember back in the Old Testament, the instruction for the Passover upon the exodus from Egyptian bondage, then the instruction for sacrifices in the tabernacle and then the temple. The sacrifice of a spotless, innocent lamb. John the Baptist here is telling the people of Israel, who knew firsthand about the sacrificial system, that Jesus was the embodiment of what the sacrificial lamb represents! For the blood of sheep did not wash their sin away. No, that was only a beautiful picture Jehovah gave His people of the perfect sacrifice that was to come! And just as the blood of the lamb applied to the doorposts brought freedom from the bondage of slavery to the Egyptians, the blood of the Lamb of God, Jesus Christ, brings about freedom from the bondage of sin and death when applied to our heart through faith in Him."

He closed his Bible then and looked down into the faces of his church family. "Each of you is infinitely precious to God. Though our righteousness is as filthy rags according to the prophet Isaiah, God Himself loved us enough to send His only begotten Son to be born in a stable, live a sinless life, and offer Himself as the sacrifice for our sin on the cross of Calvary.

"I would like to ask the choir and organist to repeat the performance of the song *Behold, the Lamb of God!* from *The Messiah.*"

As the choir sang this soul-stirring song once more, many

closed their eyes in prayer, seeking to focus on that Lamb of God and the sacrifice He made, beginning with His being born in a tiny stable in Bethlehem, and culminating in that ultimate sacrifice of His death on the cross. Carol didn't even notice the tears flowing unchecked until Charlie handed her his handkerchief. Glancing up at him, she couldn't read his expression; but if she were to guess she would think him angry for some reason. He looked back up as the pastor closed the service with prayer.

Albert and Merrie and a few other Atkins cousins came up and spoke with the Bennetts and Carol before they left. "May we come by for a short visit this afternoon perhaps?" Albert asked Charlie and his parents.

"That would be lovely, Albert!" Mrs. Bennett replied kindly.

"Yes, do come. I've something I'd like to discuss with you if I may. We'll see you later then," he said, offering Carol his arm as they left out the side door.

The carriage ride home was a quiet one, as most were that morning after the touching message. Charlie stared out the window unseeing, frowning at the cold but sunny day. When they were nearly home, he spoke.

"Please forgive me, but I just don't understand. I don't understand God at all! Why would He come, knowing what was going to happen? Why did He have to die?"

Mr. Bennett offered a quick prayer before answering his son's honest questions. "Son, the answer is in John 3:16. *'For God so loved....'* God the Father so loved us He gave His Son. God the Son so loved us He gave His life. We have yet to realize the full extent of the love of the Holy Spirit, as His work in our hearts and lives daily guides and protects us. But He came and He died because He so loved us."

Charlie ran his fingers through his hair as he raised his frustrated eyes to his father. The carriage stopped, and the four alighted, walking as one into the sitting room to continue the conversation. "But *why*, Father? Why did He love us so? Why did it have to be His blood? His death?"

"Son, if I knew the answer to that I would have the mind of God, and I do not. I do not know why blood is required to atone for sin, but that is what God told us in His Word. And not just any blood, but the sinless blood of Jesus the Christ, the Son of the living God! I don't know, Charlie. I wish I did." He ran his fingers through his hair much like his son had done, then stood and gazed out the window.

"But...not meaning to be disrespectful, but isn't that an awfully somber topic for a Christmas message?" He directed this question to the ladies.

"Yes, it is," his mother answered meekly. "It is a *very* somber message if one has never accepted Jesus as their sacrificial lamb." Charlie stood and walked over beside his father. "But Charlie," his mother continued, "when you know that He came to die for *you*, it's an immeasurably *joyful* message! Just think of how happy you were to tell us of your love for Carol, of her love for you! How many times multiplied is that love when it's between God and 'the world' that He so loved?"

"Yes, that makes sense. I still don't understand it all, but I...," he hesitated, turning to look into the eyes of the two women he loved, "I can understand being joyful over the *love* shown by His death." His father turned then, a tired look on his face.

"Let's go in to dinner now, shall we? I'm quite certain there is an exceptionally fine feast prepared." When they started into the room there were gifts beside each place setting, and Mrs. Bennett told Carol those were from the staff.

"Oh! May I please go to my room and bring out their gifts then?" she asked excitedly. Mrs. Bennett nodded, smiling broadly as Carol did her best despite the cast's impairment to dash to her room like a happy child.

When she came back into the dining room, she held papers rolled up and tied with different colored bits of ribbon and string. "I don't have any money with which to buy the gifts I would have liked to have given each of you," she said shyly to the family and staff who were all present. "So I have *made* you each something!" She read the names penciled on each of the scrolls, then went about the room passing them out.

Each servant unrolling the artwork she had created for them gasped and hugged her and showed each other and the family what she had made. Carol blushed profusely as she took her seat, but she was so pleased that they liked their gifts. She had made each of them a calligraphy Scripture verse framed with pen and ink scrollwork and flowers or wildlife at the corners. Jessie was in tears as she looked at hers, the words to *Steal Away* penned and a beautiful sketch of a bird in flight decorating the upper right hand corner. Each of them went around the table, giving hugs and pats and handshakes for the different gifts. As Carol opened her gift, she found a beautifully woven basket filled with small handmade soaps and ribbon roses and lined with a doily.

"How beautiful!" she exclaimed, examining the basket more closely. "What is it made of?"

"Pine needles, Missy Carol!" exclaimed Beatrix, and she pulled out a three-needled piece of pine straw that was nearly a foot long. "Them big old loblolly pines put out a needle I can braid and twist and make into all kinds of pretties like this here basket." Then she backed up and looked at Mr. Bennett as he unwrapped his gift. It was a beautiful, highly polished stone paperweight, and its base was another ornately woven pine straw masterpiece. Beatrix smiled broadly as he recognized her handiwork. Charlie had a similar paperweight, and Mrs. Bennett a basket much like Carol's.

The paper was cleared, gifts set aside, and course after course of delicious food and drink was brought out for their Christmas dinner.

"A blessed Christmas to all, and to all a good night! I do believe I'm ready for a nap!" Mr. Bennett was making his way to the doorway when Mrs. Bennett cleared her throat, stopping him. "Oh yes, I do believe we have a few more gifts to open in the other room, have we not?"

He led the way to the formal living room, which had a beautiful nativity scene decorating the mantle. Mr. Bennett went over to the Christmas tree which stood in between two large picture windows. Bending down with comical groans and moans, he began picking up presents. After Charlie helped Carol and his mother get situated, he came and joined his father in passing out the gifts. The three scrolls found there were conspicuously examined, passed back and forth between Mr. Bennett and Charlie. Then Charlie spotted their names penciled along the ribbons and gave his mother hers, placing his and his father's atop their ever-growing piles of gifts.

When all the gifts were passed out, Charlie seated himself as Mr. Bennett opened the family Bible and read from the book of Matthew, chapter two. The story of the gifts of the wise men brought the focus back where it should be, and after reading the passage he gave a prayer of thanksgiving for their precious family and friends who had bestowed these gifts upon them. Just as he finished praying, the doorbell sounded. Lucas announced that Aunt Lavinia had arrived.

Mrs. Bennett stood to greet her sister, hugging her on the threshold of the room. "Merry Christmas, Lavinia, dear! How are you?"

It was then that Carol realized Aunt Lavinia hadn't been to church, that she'd never seen her at the church to her knowledge.

"Oh, I'm fine, dear, just fine! I spent the morning with Wesley's family on the north side. I've only just come by to see if you've opened your gifts. Wesley sends his love...." She said this absent-mindedly, waving a gloved and be-jeweled hand in the general direction of their home.

Mr. Bennett greeted Lavinia warmly, placing a kiss on her powdered and rouged cheek. Charlie went to her and did the same, then she waved her hands motioning them back to their gifts. "You all have some work cut out for you!" she said, laughing merrily.

When the last bit of wrapping paper was tossed into the fire, Carol sat there on the couch with her hands at her cheeks. "I've never in my life had so many gifts as you all have given me yesterday and today! Thank you so much!" She stood and went from person to person giving hugs and words of thanks as the different ones retired to the sitting room. Then she reached Charlie. "Charlie, the book of watercolors is absolutely beautiful. I shall treasure it always." He took her hand and drew her over beside the window seat.

"And thank you for that beautiful drawing of the General. I have something else, but it is of a personal nature. I thought perhaps to wait until we were alone...."

He walked over and reached deep under the tree to a package hidden there, then brought it over and placed it in her lap.

Growing more and more curious, she unwrapped the gift in record time, and there she found a silver vanity set, mirror, comb, and brush, with the same ornate "C" engraved on each as was engraved on the heart Charlie gave her for her birthday.

"Why, Charlie, they're beautiful! But surely the watercolors book was enough?"

Charlie laughed, "Actually, the book was an afterthought...after I realized these might be too personal a gift to open in front of the rest of the family." He reached out and touched her hair, remembering that first morning after they'd met when he had seen it down. "If I had my way, you'd wear it down all the time," he said softly, noticing how the afternoon sun shone on the red highlights. "Anyhow," he said standing to his feet rather abruptly, "shall we join the others now?" Carol stood to her feet with Charlie's assistance, but looked back down at his collar when she saw the intensity of the love in his eyes.

"Please don't look at me like that, Charlie Bennett." He put a finger under her chin, raising her gaze to his eyes, but the tears he saw there moved him greatly.

"What is it, Carol? What brought these tears? Have I offended you?"

She sat back down in the window seat and took the handkerchief he offered. "Thank you," she said, handing it back to him folded; but he motioned for her to keep it.

"You never seem to have one when you need one," he said, lightening the mood. Then he repeated, "Now can you tell me what caused your tears?"

She twisted the handkerchief in her hands as she spoke. "The feelings I have for you, they're so strong. It's almost overwhelming for me. And when I see in your eyes that same passion, it's almost more than I can bear. I know we've spoken hypothetically, but—"

"But one day I hope to make you my bride, and we will be free before God and man to share our love with one another." He took her hand in his and placed a kiss in her palm. "Until then, I need to be more...more careful of my thoughts and feelings, considering how clearly they show in my eyes." He reached out and touched the heart charm as it dangled from its place on her wrist. "Forgive me, please?" he asked simply, his arms aching to hold her close, but his head wisely telling him to be patient.

She took a deep breath, then stood to her feet again. "Yes, Charlie. If you'll forgive me for anything I've done to cause those thoughts and feelings." He remained seated long enough to look up at her with the boyish grin she so adored.

"You've done nothing but been a perfect lady, Carolina. Just go on being your lovely self." Then he stood, offered his arm, and escorted her into the sitting room where they found the sisters talking in hushed tones while Mr. Bennett snored softly from the settee.

※※※

Charlie felt he'd discussed spiritual matters enough for the day; so when Albert, Merrie, and her sister Juliette arrived the afternoon and evening were spent playing dominos, snacking, and talking pleasantly. The other three young people didn't leave until nearly ten, and after the late night Christmas Eve, Charlie and Carol were both ready to retire when his parents headed up to their rooms.

"Charlie, thank you again for a most wonderful day. I shall enjoy wearing the cloak your parents gave me...so stylish and beautiful! And the monogrammed handkerchiefs you gave me that Aunt Lavinia gave *you* are both practical and...and *funny*!"

Charlie smiled back at her, putting his hands in his pockets to keep from reaching out and touching the wavy strand of hair that had escaped the snood she had put on that afternoon. It was the closest she'd come to wearing her hair down, and she looked absolutely beautiful to him.

Looking up at the arch over both their heads, he saw a strategically placed bit of mistletoe in the holly garland. His look drew Carol's attention upward, and she spotted it as well. With a soft sigh she kissed her fingertip and touched Charlie's lips, then folding her hands behind her back and said, "Perhaps next year, Mr. Bennett. Yes, perhaps next year. Merry Christmas, my love."

"Merry Christmas, Carolina; and God bless us, every one."

Chapter Fourteen

New Year, 1889

The year 1889 was welcomed in with an ice storm and several inches of wet snow. Having grown up in the coastal south where snow was such a rarity, Carol was thrilled with the winter wonderland. She asked Charlie at breakfast if they could go for a walk in the snow before it all melted.

"Sure! That sounds great. Umm…but what about your cast? I don't think we have galoshes that will fit over it, and we're supposed to keep it dry remember." The look of disappointment on Carol's face made his mind work overtime to find a solution. "No, wait. Go ahead and get your hooded cloak my parents got you for Christmas. I'll see what I can do." He wiped his mouth with his napkin and, excusing himself from the table, walked purposefully out of the room.

Mr. and Mrs. Bennett were as interested as Carol to see what he would come up with, so when she stood to get her things, they went out front to the portico to see what he was up to. Charlie was shoveling then salting a path in the slush, and his parents could see that the path headed for a bench midway between the house and the street. He wiped the snowy slush from the bench, then dried it a bit with his handkerchief before surveying the scene.

He didn't see his parents until he was nearly back to the portico. His boyish grin reminded them that he wasn't such a very big, grown up boy yet if he still so thoroughly enjoyed playing in the snow.

When Carol stepped outside, Charlie scooped her up unceremoniously and carefully carried her to the bench. He then proceeded back to the house and collected her satchel with her pencils and sketchbook. As he reached the door Jessie handed him a steaming mug of cocoa, and a blanket which she draped over his arm. Then back out to the bench he went.

As soon as Carol spotted her drawing utensils her smile grew into bubbling laughter. Charlie handed her the mug of cocoa, then the art supplies. Next he busied himself placing the blanket around her, making sure to keep the slush back from her skirts and feet. Finally, he stood with his hands on his hips and surveyed his work. Carol struck a pose for him, and he burst out laughing.

"We are a silly pair, are we not, Miss Montague?"

"Yes, we are that, Mr. Bennett! But here, there is room for you to sit and share some of this delicious cocoa with me! Come." She scooted over and patted the seat beside her, and he gladly joined her on the bench.

"Whew! I'm glad you warmed the seat up a bit! It's still wicked cold!" he said, and received a not-so-stern glare for a reprimand. They looked up at the portico and waved at Charlie's parents; but Mr. Bennett had an idea of his own, and the two walked back in the house shortly after they waved back.

"Oh, it's just beautiful when it snows and the sun comes out! Let me try to sketch a bit before it all melts away." She went to work, only drawing the shadows of the sparkling, pristine whiteness; but still she felt unable to do it justice. "Look how the ice coats every needle of that hemlock, Charlie. Isn't it lovely?"

Never taking his eyes from her face he answered, "Yes, very lovely indeed." Carol caught his compliment and smiled her thanks.

"Oh, Charlie, you're so very good to me. I really enjoy your company!" A shadow crossed her face as she remembered what she'd wanted to talk with him about. He noticed, and leaning forward asked her what was wrong.

"It's just that I'd love to go on like this forever, but I know that, well, Celia arrives next week; and I haven't even found a place for us! I need to contact Mr. Waterman about starting back at my job, too."

She looked at Charlie with her heart in her blue, blue eyes and said, "I've enjoyed being here more than you could possibly know. Your parents, the servants, the beautiful house and grounds...any of those are reason enough to miss being here. But add to that the convenience and pleasure of being able to see you several times a day, and...."

Charlie looked out at the snowy scene before finishing her thought for her. "And it just seems like part of you will be missing when you're so far away. Yes?"

"Yes," she answered as she looked at his handsome profile. Carol took another sip of cocoa, then handed the mug to Charlie. "Charlie, can you help me find a boarding house for Celia and me to live in?"

"Of course. I'd be glad to," Charlie said quietly as he sipped the melted whipped cream off the top of the cocoa. "Your sister is going to be teaching at the school, and your office is not so very far from there. Perhaps we should begin our search midway between the two?" He looked at Carol for confirmation of his brilliant strategy, but she was giggling. She reached into the pocket of her cloak and pulled out one of his handkerchiefs with which to wipe the last traces of whipped cream from the corner of his mouth.

"Oh, Charlie, I will miss you."

"Well, I'll miss you, too," he said casually as he drank the remaining cocoa. "But it isn't as though we'll be *that* far apart!" He put the cup down on the bench between them, then reached for her hand, looking at how small it looked with her fitted glove resting in his gloved hands. "It will just make courting you that much more of a challenge, m'dear!"

"Do you think it will be a problem if I continue attending your church? Your pastor has been such a blessing to me, but I wouldn't want to appear forward."

"I don't think that would be a problem at all. Please continue joining my family in our pew. Bring Celia, too, for there is ample room enough for her as well."

Carol laughed. "Actually, I was thinking about joining the

choir, so I wouldn't be sitting in the pews at all! I would think Celia would eventually join the church and sing in the choir as well. Celia has a beautiful singing voice." She looked up at Charlie as a cloud covered the sun. "Do you have any idea how very much I love you?"

"Yes, I believe I do. And I've never been so comfortable, so *at home* in anyone else's presence in my life." He kept her hand in his as he looked back out at the trees and the drive. "I really *like* you as well as loving you. I enjoy being with you, spending time with you, watching your reactions." The heart charm had worked its way from between her glove and her cloak and was making a tiny chiming sound as it swung back and forth, touching the button on the cuff of her sleeve. "And however far apart we are, you'll always have my heart."

"Thank you. You know, I haven't taken if off since you fastened it there. I will treasure it always, I promise."

The cloud moved on, and the full sunlight on the snow and icicles was brilliant. Charlie stood, collecting their things, and offered his arm. Carol draped the blanket over her arm and began the walk back to the house, then they both stopped as they heard the sound of approaching sleigh bells!

"Whoa, boys!" Mr. Bennett slowed the pair of black horses to a stop and grinned broadly. "Care to go for a ride? I know the snow is a bit slushy for the sleigh, so I just put the bells on the horses and hitched up the buggy. Charlie, go get your mother. Oh, there she comes! Come, Laura!" He offered a hand to help Carol up, then guided his wife up to the driver's seat beside himself; and when Charlie climbed in and all were settled, off they went!

"Oh, what a *treat* this is!" Carol said loudly enough for Mr. and Mrs. Bennett to hear from their place in the front seat. Mr. Bennett's driving skills put her totally at ease, and as she saw Mrs. Bennett tuck her arm in the crook of her husband's elbow, she took Charlie's arm comfortably.

"What a perfect day. We've been blessed with so many of them, but I try to never take them for granted." She snuggled in a bit closer to Charlie as they took to the open road on the edge of town, and the breeze picked up a bit. Charlie smiled down at her, then when he saw how pink her nose and cheeks had become from the cold and wind, he put a protective arm around her gently.

"Thank you," she whispered, and when he looked down at her he noticed she was looking at his mouth. Thinking he must still have a bit of a cocoa mustache, he licked his lips, then drew a gloved hand across them.

"Better?" he asked, but now she wasn't looking at him at all. "Carol?" She turned and looked up at him with a rather embarrassed grin.

"There was nothing on your lips. I just...."

"Oh," he said, then as light dawned on his face, he said, "Oh!" and smiled at her discomfiture. "Well, it is good to know that the feeling is mutual; but would it be better if we weren't quite so close?"

"I don't think even my blushing would keep me warm enough for long. I'll just behave myself and talk about something."

"Such as?" he asked, raising a brow and smiling hugely.

"Umm," she said, suddenly distracted by the scent of Charlie's aftershave. "How about...."

"How about what we need to get done today, like finding your new boarding house?" Charlie chuckled as he saw her "cold-water-in-the-face" expression.

"Yes, like that," she said quietly.

Seeking to keep a chummy air about him with the woman he loved closer than she'd ever been, Charlie went on with his monologue, trying to distract them both from their current closeness and their soon coming separation.

"Like I mentioned before, I think there may be a very suitable place for you both to board at a sort of halfway point between Waterman's and the school. It may be a bit nearer the school actually, but as she is your younger sister I didn't think you'd mind taking up the slack. It even has a nice-sized lot as I recall, a little kitchen garden and a nice place to sit out of doors when the weather's agreeable. You and Celia could have a nicely furnished room, putting up your pretty curtains and bedspreads and such...maybe with a bit of a sitting room for gentlemen callers?"

Carol didn't reply, and when he looked back down at her, her eyes were closed in sleep. He placed a kiss on her shining, sweet-smelling hair; then pulling her hood further down to keep her warm, he settled in and enjoyed the rest of the ride in thoughtful silence.

Chapter Fifteen

Celia

When Celia's train arrived at the station, Charlie and Carol were there to greet her. Celia was somewhat shorter than her sister, and her hair was a little darker; but there was definitely a strong family resemblance. Charlie sat in amazed silence as the two chattered nonstop from the depot to their newly-acquired rooms at the boarding house.

"Oh! Is this it? This looks *lovely* Carrie!" Celia smiled as Charlie helped her and Carol down from the carriage, then returned to collect her trunk.

"I say, you must have come with a good deal more trappings than your sister, Celia," he said, lugging the trunk to the doorway. "I'm just thankful these rooms are on the second floor instead of the third!"

"Oh, *dear*! Were you *really* on the third floor, sister? That must have been difficult. It's no small wonder you had to stay elsewhere after your accident."

"Indeed, and I shall need to be cautious even yet. Dr. Whittle only removed the cast the day before yesterday, and my leg is still a bit tender."

Arriving at the door, Carol pulled the key from her purse. "Well, here we are! Home, sweet home!" Carol, Beatrix, and Jessie had all been working hard on the room for two days, and it fairly shone in the afternoon sunshine coming in at the windows. There was a small table and chairs, a davenport, coffee table, and wing back chair, and the smallest of kitchens in the main room. This suite had its own bath, which was a tremendous blessing. The door to the bath and the door to the bedroom were down a short hallway to the right. There were two beautiful vases filled with dried flowers, and Celia couldn't help but walk from room to room talking of every detail. Charlie carried the trunk to the bedroom, carefully placing a note and a rose for Carol on her pillow before walking back out to join the ladies.

"I'm terribly sorry, but I need to get back to work. I took a late lunch break, but that hour is fast drawing to a close. Perhaps I may call tomorrow evening?" he asked, and Celia discreetly stepped out of the room for their farewells.

"Oh, Charlie, I miss you already!" she said with a tear escaping down her cheek. He pulled her close and kissed her forehead, then picking up his hat made his way to the door.

"If you ever need me, day or night, telephone me. There is a booth downstairs. I've left our home number in the note for you in your room." The sweet smile she gave drew him back into the room for one final hug goodbye, then he tipped his hat and departed. Celia came out when she heard the door close, note and rose in hand, and hugged her sister.

"I think, Sister, we have much to talk about...?" she queried, and received a giggling, tearful nod in response. Carol went to the kitchen and put the kettle on for tea, taking some cookies out of the box Jessie had given her that morning.

"To be sure, I've been spoiled until I am practically useless! I do hope I am not *too* much of a pampered child for our first few days together, until I become reacquainted with the mundane tasks of cooking and cleaning again!"

"Your Charlie is quite handsome! And it is quite obvious he is most fond of you. Is he as nice as he seems?"

"I would wish for you such a loving, attentive suitor," she said with a soft smile. "But there is one problem."

"What is that, Carrie?" she asked, placing teacups and the cookies on a little tray.

"It's difficult to explain, but I do not know for certain that Charlie is born again." Celia lifted sad eyes to her sister, then took her arm and sat down on the davenport while the water heated. "He is very moral. He attends a wonderful Bible-teaching church. Both his father and mother are Christians; I've heard their testimonies. But I still am unsure of Charlie's salvation. You'll pray with me for him, won't you, Celia?"

Hugging her close Celia vowed, "Every day 'til we *know* he knows the Saviour, Carrie. I promise."

⁂

The Bennett household was very quiet that evening. After dinner, the three retired to the sitting room, Mrs. Bennett going to the piano and playing a peaceful sonata. Charlie picked up the paper as his father had, but it couldn't hold his attention for more than a paragraph. His father's voice broke into his scattered thoughts.

"Why didn't you go over there this evening, son? You're obviously there in spirit."

"I'm sorry, Father. I'm not very good company tonight, am I? I just thought it would be best to let the ladies have time to get reacquainted. Believe me, it was a sacrifice!"

Mr. Bennett chuckled. Finishing the sonata, Mrs. Bennett came and sat down beside her son.

"I think that was very considerate, Charles. I don't know that I could have done the same! I miss the dear girl already, and if Jessie's expression when she got home after helping there this morning is any sign, I think the entire household is mourning her loss." She put her hand on Charlie's knee then and asked, "But she isn't lost to us *forever*, is she, dear? Or is that none of my concern?"

Charlie grinned at his mother. "No, Mum, I believe you have every right to know. Our relationship is leading in the direction of matrimony." Mr. Bennett peered over his paper and winked at his wife. "My only concern at present is how slowly I need to proceed. It seems we've known each other all our lives, but we only just met two months ago. What *is* the proper length of time for a courtship?"

"Well, that all depends on the couple, Charlie. Your father and I were only six months from the day we met to our wedding.

My parents however had a seven year engagement." Charlie stood to his feet so quickly that his mother couldn't help but laugh. "It was necessary in their situation, dear, but I'm not saying I recommend such a lengthy engagement! Now come back here and sit by me."

"But, *seven years*! I can hardly imagine it." His father's shaking newspaper caught his attention. He joined in with his father good naturedly, then added, "You've nothing to laugh about, Father! You only had a six month engagement!"

"True, but I accomplished much during those six months. Have you considered that you need a home for the two of you? You need to prepare a place for her, Charles. You have a lucrative position at the bank. With your degree, you could have one of the executive positions there one day. That's a promising future, but not if you're homeless! Correct me if I'm wrong, Laura, but do not ladies want a...a 'nest to feather' when they wed?"

"Yes, but, Ben, it doesn't have to be a mansion like I was blessed with through my family. A one bedroom cottage with a small garden would suffice two people in love who are just starting out, would it not?"

Mr. Bennett scratched his whiskery chin. "It would at that," he replied smiling. "But nonetheless, its something that must be established before the wedding, where you shall live. And Carol was reared on a farm, Charlie; so although she will likely be most willing to leave her job, she will expect to have household duties...maybe wanting a garden, some hens.... I don't *know* this, but she doesn't strike me as a woman who would be in the calling card, clubs, and bridge circles. She may even desire to live outside of town."

"Of course," added Mrs. Bennett taking up her crocheting, "you would be most welcome to live here until you start your family, wouldn't they, Mr. Bennett? There is more than ample room. Forgive me if I'm assuming too much, Ben, but I would so thoroughly enjoy having Carol here when you men are off at work every day."

"This is a possibility, if Carol would be interested. Nevertheless, it takes time to find out her preferences, then carry them out. Even with that easy option of bringing her here,

Charlie, you'd want to make changes in the rooms you took."

The conversation gave Charlie much to think about, but after some moments of silence he replied, "I suppose that first I need to actually *propose* though, yes?" The three smiled at one another's presumption. "I have much planning to do, a lot to think about." Rising and kissing his mother's cheek, he said his goodnights and headed up to his room.

❧❧

The next two weeks were very busy ones. Carol and Celia both returned home exhausted from work every day, though Celia was quickly growing to love her young pupils. Carol's secretarial work was quite repetitious, so the stories her younger sister shared every evening were a balm to her. Charlie came by every other evening after work. He didn't wish to impose however, so he never stayed for the evening meal unless specifically invited beforehand.

January the twenty-seventh saw both girls and Charlie in choir, and Mr. and Mrs. Bennett were so pleased. Charlie sang tenor, sitting next to Albert in the second to the last row of the choir loft. Though the girls sang different parts, both being the tallest in their section they were assigned to sit side by side in the third row. The four were also included in an *a cappella* octet which sang an occasional special arrangement in the services.

After church that first Sunday in choir Mr. and Mrs. Bennett invited the Montague sisters for Sunday dinner. Celia was thrilled to see the home her sister had spoken so highly of, and Carol felt as though she were going home. As they made their way up the drive, Celia looked out the window of the carriage at the beauty around her.

"Oh, Sister!" she said, drawing her attention away from Charlie for a moment, "It's simply breathtaking!" Lucas beamed at Carol as he helped her and the other ladies down from the carriage. When she first stepped in the door, Carol and Celia were arm in arm. "Oh, Mrs. Bennett, Mr. Bennett, what a lovely home you have."

Mr. Bennett replied, "Why, thank you, Celia. We're most

pleased to have you here." As Jessie and Lucas helped everyone with their coats, hats, and scarves, he went on, "Let's go directly to the dining room, for I do believe everything is in readiness!"

Carol held back as everyone entered and sneaked a quick hug from Jessie. "What are you doing here? It's your day off!"

"We slipped back quick soon as church was ovah. Ain't no way you'da kept me away when I heard my sweet Missy Carol was comin'! No, ma'am!"

Charlie caught their conversation; and after he'd seated the sisters, he took his place between them, leaning to whisper to Carol. "As soon as they heard you were being invited for dinner, they all asked one by one to work half-day today. I do believe there isn't a person in this household that hasn't missed you, Carolina."

After Mr. Bennett asked the blessing, course after course of delicious food was brought and placed before them. Neither Celia nor Carol had ever had Beef Wellington, and both were delighted with it.

When Jessie and Beatrix brought out apple crisp *ala' mode* and coffee, Carol grinned. "You remembered!" Apple crisp was her favorite, but especially with hot caramel and ice cream.

"Actually, Father remembered. I wouldn't give him too much credit though, as it's *his* favorite as well."

Mr. Bennett smiled at his son and the ladies, ate his dessert, then did his Sunday afternoon repeat performance of pushing away from the table with extreme effort and making his way slowly to the sitting room to read the newspaper with his eyes closed.

Mrs. Bennett took Celia's arm amiably and asked, "Miss Celia, do you enjoy the piano like your sister does?" She steered her gently to the music room, shooing Charlie and Carol out back to the veranda for some time alone. Despite their full stomachs, they nearly skipped out the door, grabbing coats off the hook on their way out.

"Oh, Charlie, I've missed everything about you! Your smile, your humor, your family, your home. Thank you so much for having Celia and me over today." She closed her eyes, turning her face up toward the warmth of the sunlight as they walked slowly down the paths of the garden.

"Better not walk that way long, Miss Montague, or you're liable to break your other leg."

Carol laughed and linked her arm with his. "And this time, your parents would think I'd done it on purpose!"

"No," Charlie said, his face a straight as a poker, "they'd doubtless think I tripped you!" Their laughter mingled, coming into the kitchen window and bringing contented smiles to three dear souls cleaning up from dinner.

"We've been so busy lately, Carol...too busy. I've missed you terribly."

"I've missed you, too, Charlie."

Charlie looked up at the clear blue sky, taking a deep breath before introducing the subject dearest to his heart. "Would you mind if I asked another hypothetical question?"

"Not at all," Carol said, though her heart skipped a beat in anticipation.

"If we were to marry, where would you want to live?"

"Oh, this one's easy! With *you*!" Carol laughed and ran on ahead to the gazebo.

"I'm serious now!" Charlie said as he took the steps to the gazebo in an easy bound. "Where would you want our home to be? You've got to have some kind of preference on this sort of thing, don't you?"

"What are my options?" she asked as she leaned over the railing, catching a twinkling glimpse of the sun through the trees overhead.

"Well, we could afford to purchase a home with a mortgage, or we could buy a small home on a bit of acreage and have our dream home built, or we could live here—" Her head turned so quickly at the mention of the last that he paused. "What?"

"Do you mean it? We could live here? With your parents? Do you think they would...that is...."

"Actually, Mother suggested it." Carol turned pale at this news, something he'd never seen her do. He stood there feeling rather helpless and asked again, "What? What is it?"

"You've spoken of this to your mother?"

"Well, yes, and Father as well. What is wrong?"

111

"I...I don't know. It's just that, well, we are not yet *engaged*, and I just feel, strange somehow, that you've discussed this with them." She turned back to Charlie before going on. "I don't know why. I mean, I love your parents dearly; and you and I have spoken hypothetically about marriage and children. I just...I didn't think...."

Charlie went and stood beside Carol at the railing, placing one hand over hers. "I'm sorry. I didn't mean to make you feel uncomfortable." Carol looked down at their hands, then noticed that Charlie looked weary somehow. His shoulders were slumped as he leaned on the railing, and his eyes had a haggard appearance when he turned to look at her. "I've sort of taken it on as a project of late, to figure out how to work things out so we can be married soon, and we won't have to spend so much time apart." He moved away then, and she suddenly felt cold. "I'm not ready to officially propose yet, Carolina, but if I could I'd marry you today. Does that make sense? I...I find myself *needing* you as well as loving you."

"*My God shall supply all your need, according to His riches—*"

He turned so quickly it startled Carol into silence. He gripped her upper arms firmly as he whispered fiercely, "Don't start quoting platitudes at me, Carol! Tell me how you *feel!*"

Looking up at him with a calmness she didn't feel in the least, she said quietly, "That *is* how I feel, Charlie. I place my feelings in God's hands, knowing that He in His love and provision will supply my need, whether that need be food, or clothing, or shelter, or a job...or a husband's love. But all in His good time."

He realized how tightly he was holding her and let her go, turning back to the railing. "I'm sorry for touching you in that manner. I'm not angry with you. I'm just so frustrated that everything seems to be moving so painfully slowly right now."

Carol placed her hand on the sleeve of his coat, saying softly, "You're not alone. I pray daily that the LORD will give me the patience I need in so many areas of my life, but most certainly in waiting for His timing in our relationship! Do you think I don't long to be back here with you? I don't really know what all the marriage relationship entails; but I know that my parents are very happy, and your parents are very happy. I want us to know that kind of happiness!" She paused, then added, "But in *God's* timing, Charlie. I truly believe we will be together as man and wife one day, but it must be in His perfect timing."

"I know that in my head, but it's convincing my heart that is so difficult right now."

"I understand, my love, I really do. It's much like every trial. We know with our head knowledge what we should do, sometimes even according to God's Word. But our heart...our feelings and desires just don't seem to want to line up like we know they should. It's a daily battle. But God will take care of us in this as well as every trial if we but ask...and trust...."

Charlie glanced at Carol, then looked back out in the garden. "This is a fine way to spend our first time alone together in weeks. Forgive me?"

Carol wished he could have continued on, assured her of his faith in the Lord, but he did not. With a sigh, she tucked her hand in his, answering, "Of course. Let's walk, shall we?"

Chapter Sixteen

Unequally Yoked

Week after week passed with much the same hectic schedule. Winter began melting into spring, but this year the bulbs peeking through the snow didn't bring Charlie joy as they always had since childhood. Their presence seemed to serve as a reminder that time was passing, yet he was no closer to gaining his heart's desire. And what made it worse to him was that Carol didn't seem to be suffering at all. Her beautiful countenance was serene every time they met. Charlie knew from the fit of his clothes that he was losing weight, but Carol seemed to be rosier and happier and even more beautiful than ever since her sister's arrival in Baltimore.

Albert couldn't help but notice his friend's distress, and he suspected the cause to be a spiritual battle. One morning at work he asked to join Charlie for lunch, and the two men made their way to the café around noon.

"Maybe this time I can do the food justice! Last time I came, I was a nervous wreck from the exam. Remember?"

"Yes, yes I do remember. But you haven't eaten here since?"

"Actually, I usually bring some leftovers in a sack lunch and eat in the break room." He looked over at Charlie, noticing for the first time the way Charlie's suit seemed to hang on him. "Come to think of it though, I don't recall seeing you *take* lunch breaks very often. Are you feeling well, Charlie?"

"I'm okay I guess. Just a little off my feed." Looking down at his chest and pulling at the material of his vest, he added, "I guess I have lost a little weight, hunh?"

"Yes, Friend, you have. Let's order, then we can talk." Both men ordered soup and sandwiches with iced tea to drink when the waitress came for their order.

After they gave their menus to her and she left, they began their conversation in earnest. "What's going on in that thick head of yours, Charlie Bennett?" Albert asked with a lightness he didn't feel.

"I just don't know, Albert. It's...it's as though Carol and I are getting further and further apart, not just physically or geographically, but—"

"Spiritually? Emotionally?"

"*Yes!* And I don't know what to do about it! It seems like the more I fret over it, the worse it becomes, but I just don't seem to be able to get a handle on this." He ran his fingers through his well-groomed hair, then reached for his tea when it came and took several great swallows before he caught the look in Albert's eyes. "What?"

"Well," Albert took a sip of tea then went on, "I rather think that the Lord is trying to work on your heart, but you're too busy to allow Him to. There is so much to our lives, so much that must be balanced and weighed as to the place...the *priority* if you will...which the different things in our lives should have. Carol is a fine girl, Charlie, but you and I both know that your relationship to the Lord *must* come first. Carol would want that as well." Albert didn't know quite what to do when Charlie didn't respond, so he gave him time to think.

After several quiet moments, Charlie voiced his thoughts. "You know, I told you I would think about what we discussed the first time you and I ate here, but I've allowed myself to become so all-consumed with courting and work that I really haven't."

Albert nodded. "But you do remember?"

"Of course. A *personal relationship* with God." His mind went back to the talk he had with Carol in his parents' garden. "Carol and I spoke of that some time back actually, about knowing what needs to be done, but...but not feeling like it, basically. Like with our trials."

Albert gave a bit of a laugh, "With *everything*. There's a constant battle going on in us. We know what we need to do, but getting our will in line with God's is no simple task. I think the Apostle Paul had a bit of a tongue twister on that very subject, *that which I would do, I do not*."

The food was brought to the table, and after a brief blessing, Albert was pleased to see his friend eating well. "But, Charlie, have you taken that first step with God? Have you received Jesus as your personal Saviour?"

Charlie finished chewing the huge bite of roast beef and provolone sandwich before wiping his mouth and answering. "Well, I do know I'm a sinner."

"You must be *born again* though, Charlie. You must be saved from your sin. Not by your own merit...."

"Yes, I remember what you said before, that the very best we can do is 'as filthy rags'. That's rather a tough line of reasoning."

"But that's where faith comes in, not 'reason'. Have you placed your faith in Christ's death on the cross, His sacrifice, to wash your sin away? Or are you just 'sorry for your sin' and trying to do good things to make up for it?" Albert could see the answer on Charlie's face, but his friend remained silent. "Oh, Charlie, with as much as I've prayed for you since our talk in December, I just *know* that one of these days you will come to understand all of this."

Not wanting his friend to close the doors of communication, Albert changed subjects after another lengthy silence. "By the way, are you taking Carol to the Bank Picnic at the Dye's Estate next weekend?" he asked, stuffing the last bite of sandwich in his mouth.

Charlie felt relief at the change in subject. "Actually, I was going to ask her tonight. I was invited to dinner with her and Celia. You know, come to think of it she may not feel she should go if Celia has to stay home. Do you have a date yet?"

Not willing for the world to tell Charlie that he had wanted to ask Carol if Charlie wasn't taking her, he wiped his mouth with his napkin and shook his head "no".

"Well, what do you think? You've seen Celia at church and in choir and such. I think you two would have a good time together. And you would be doing me a favor...."

Unable to turn down a request like that, Albert agreed. "I'll speak to her of it at choir practice Saturday afternoon. But if you need to let Carol know of my intent, feel free." Pushing back his chair, he added, "Well, I'm done! Let's head back to work, shall we?" This time Albert took the check, and the two left the café content, but thoughtful.

Albert could tell that he'd done too thorough a job in changing the subject. He could see by Charlie's expression that he was thinking of the picnic instead of anything of eternal value they had discussed previously. Albert told himself that God's Word does not return void though, and with a heart full of prayer he returned to work.

❧❦

When Charlie asked Carol to the picnic, she did mention Celia's being left alone; so Charlie quickly told her of Albert's intentions to ask Celia on Saturday. He saw her relieved expression, reminding himself to thank Albert again for his willingness to take Celia.

"It should be a very nice day for a picnic. Mid-March is beautiful out in the country, and the Dye Estate is an especially fine one. The Dye family give a company picnic every year for the bank employees. Mr. Franklin Dye Senior is one of the bank executive officers. I don't know if Father and Mother will be going this year though. I believe Mother had some other event scheduled with her Garden Club."

"It sounds lovely, Charlie. Thank you for inviting me, and for seeing to it that Celia could come." She looked down at her teacup as she replied, and Charlie grew restless again at her lack of enthusiasm. Celia came in then, however, putting a stop to all personal conversation.

❧❦

Albert approached Carol and Celia before choir practice Saturday. "Hello, ladies! It's good to see you both." Celia smiled sweetly, noticing that Albert, who usually seemed to only have eyes for her sister, had included her in the greeting.

Carol replied with her usual gracious smile, "Thank you, Albert. It's good to see you, too." Glancing past him, she added, "Is Charlie here yet?"

Albert successfully hid his disappointment, and with a smile replied in the affirmative. When Carol walked into the practice room and Celia began to follow, Albert stopped her. "Miss Montague, may I have a word with you?"

"Of course, Mr. Whittle." She had noticed that he and Carol always referred to one another by their first names, but she did not yet feel at liberty to do so. When he didn't correct her, she felt justified.

"The bank where Charlie and I are employed is having a company picnic in the country a week from today. Charlie is taking Carol, and I was wondering if you'd care to join me?"

Celia had noticed before what pale blue eyes Albert had, but they'd never been directed at her. Distracted into asking the first thing that came to mind, she asked simply, "Why?"

This was not at all the reply he expected, and it caught his attention as nothing else about Carol's sister had.

"'Why?' Well, because I don't have a date and thought you might enjoy it."

Celia wanted to pinch herself for her reply, but she really was surprised he'd asked. "Forgive me, Mr. Whittle. Yes, I would very much enjoy going to the picnic with you next Saturday." The smile he gave her was genuine, and it struck her how very handsome Albert Whittle was. "Will we be riding with Charlie and Carol?"

Albert surprised himself with his instantaneous answer. "No. There will be a procession of buggies out to the estate, so we do not need a chaperone, unless you'd be more comfortable...?"

"Actually, that sounds fine, Mr. Whittle."

"Won't you please call me 'Albert'?"

"Yes, Albert," she said, smiling beautifully.

As the two walked into the choir room, Albert said, "You don't really look that much like your sister, do you?"

"Actually, Carol takes after Poppa's side of the family. I take after Momma's."

Looking into Celia's eyes for the second time, he noticed that hers were as green as her sister's were blue. "Well, your parents certainly must be proud to have two such lovely Christian daughters."

"Thank you, Albert," she said, blushing slightly. "That was one of the nicest things anyone has ever said to me." That said, she turned to gather her music and went to find her place beside her sister.

※

Sunday morning there were at least four choir members who were more than slightly distracted, but from their outward attentiveness to the pastor, no one would have known. The choir special was breathtakingly beautiful, and Mr. and Mrs. Bennett shared smiles with Charlie and Carol after the choir was seated. Then Pastor Lehman stood, climbed the steps to the pulpit, and began to preach.

"Please turn in your Bibles to II Corinthians chapter six, and please stand for the reading of God's Word.

1. *We then, as workers together with Him, beseech you also that ye receive not the grace of God in vain.*
2. *(For He saith, I have heard thee in a time accepted, and in the day of salvation have I succoured thee: behold, now is the accepted time; behold, now is the day of salvation.)*
3. *Giving no offence in any thing, that the ministry be not blamed:*
4. *But in all things approving ourselves as the ministers of God, in much patience, in afflictions, in necessities, in distresses,*
5. *In stripes, in imprisonments, in tumults, in labours, in watchings, in fastings;*
6. *By pureness, by knowledge, by long suffering, by kindness, by the Holy Ghost, by love unfeigned,*
7. *By the word of truth, by the power of God, by the armour of righteousness on the right hand and on the left,*

8. *By honour and dishonour, by evil report and good report: as deceivers, and yet true;*
9. *As unknown, and yet well known; as dying, and, behold, we live; as chastened, and not killed;*
10. *As sorrowful, yet alway rejoicing; as poor, yet making many rich; as having nothing, and yet possessing all things.*
11. *O ye Corinthians, our mouth is open unto you, our heart is enlarged.*
12. *Ye are not straitened in us, but ye are straitened in your own bowels.*
13. *Now for a recompence in the same, (I speak as unto my children,) be ye also enlarged.*
14. *Be ye not unequally yoked together with unbelievers: for what fellowship hath righteousness with unrighteousness? and what communion hath light with darkness?*
15. *And what concord hath Christ with Belial? or what part hath he that believeth with an infidel?*
16. *And what agreement hath the temple of God with idols? for ye are the temple of the living God; as God hath said, I will dwell in them, and walk in them; and I will be their God, and they shall be my people.*
17. *Wherefore come out from among them, and be ye separate, saith the Lord, and touch not the unclean thing; and I will receive you.*
18. *And will be a Father unto you, and ye shall be my sons and daughters, saith the Lord Almighty.*

Pastor went on to preach on the Christian walk, but Carol, Albert, Celia, and Mr. and Mrs. Bennett all froze when they read verse fourteen. *"Be ye not unequally yoked together with unbelievers...."*

Mr. and Mrs. Bennett, Carol, and Celia had doubts, but Albert *knew* that Charlie was lost. Albert began to pray for his friend beside him from the moment the verse was read.

Mr. and Mrs. Bennett glanced at one another during the reading, then looked up at their son and his intended bride, wondering if their dating was even in accordance with Scripture. If their son did *not* know Christ as Saviour.... When they looked up at Carol, she had blanched, looking from the pastor to her Bible with a face so pale it startled them both. Tears filled Mrs. Bennett's eyes as she realized what pain the future held for her dear loved ones, yet if Charlie was *not* a Christian and never became one, his *eternal* future was far more bleak than the pain his separation from Carol would cause him. She reached out and took hold of her husband's hand for strength, then spent the rest of the service praying for their precious son.

"*Dear God,*" Carol prayed silently to her Lord, "*is this what You've been trying to tell me? Is this why You haven't given me any peace about our relationship these past weeks? I must be bold. I must know if he is Your child or not. Planning a future with him is out of the question if there is a possibility that we would be unequally yoked.*

"*Forgive me, Father. Please forgive me, for You know as well as I that he already has my heart. Ending our relationship will be...will be the greatest trial I've ever endured, Father. I need Your strength. I pray as though I know that he is not Your child, but even now I pray that he is...that he's just experiencing spiritual growing pains.*" She paused, looking out at the congregation, and when her eyes met Mr. Bennett's, a tear sparkled on his cheek. "*Oh, God, Charlie* doesn't *know You! They know it, too,*" she prayed, and it was all she could do to keep her tears in check until she reached the privacy of her and Celia's room.

❧❧

"Carrie, what are you going to do?" Celia asked, her sister's pain causing her own heart to break.

Carol blew her nose in one of Charlie's handkerchiefs, smiling at the bittersweet memory. "I must ask him point blank if he is a Christian, and if he is not, we must...we must...."

Carol clung to her sister as both girls wept. When the tears began to slow, Celia wiped her own tears with the apron she'd put on upon arriving home to fix their dinner. "Lie down a while, Carrie. I'll go make you a cup of tea." She helped Carol ease under the quilt; but when she came back a short while later with the hot cup of tea, her sister had drifted off into an exhausted slumber.

Albert came by after he'd eaten his dinner with his grandfather, who was also greatly concerned still about Charlie's spiritual condition. Albert knocked quietly as everything seemed quiet in the room, but Celia answered. He could see the evidence of tears on her face, and without a word he gave her his handkerchief and guided her to the wing back chair, kneeling before her on the shining wood floor. "How is she?"

That was all the sympathy Celia could take, and the tears flowed down her cheeks yet again. Albert took the handkerchief from her hand and dabbed at the tears, his heart greatly moved by the love this woman had for her sister. "How did you *know*?" she asked in hushed tones.

"Charlie has been a dear friend of mine since childhood. I never doubted his salvation until a few months ago."

"Do you know for sure? Is he lost?"

Unable to bring himself to say a word, Albert nodded mutely.

"Carol doesn't know for sure yet, she only suspects. I think it best to allow her to talk with him and hear from his own lips." Just thinking of the pain this would bring brought on a new onset of tears, and Albert stood to busy himself walking around the small room. Celia got control of her tears again and asked softly, "You care very much for my sister, do you not, Albert?"

Having this knowledge out in the open made Albert sigh in relief. "I *do* care for your sister, Celia. In fact, until yesterday I would have been eager for the chance to court her." He picked up the still warm cup of tea and brought it to Celia. "But the truth is, I've prayed so hard for Charlie's salvation that somehow courting her would be a betrayal...an action that said, however subtly, that I didn't believe he would ever accept Christ. I don't believe that, Celia. I don't know how long it will take, but I honestly believe Charlie will come to know Christ as Saviour; and when he does, your sister will still be waiting for him."

"Thank you, Albert. Thank you so much."

"Well, I'm not at all the martyr here," he said, barely hiding his embarrassment. "It's not just my friendship with Charlie that brought on my change of heart. It's not even the fact that I never really stood a chance with Carol." He smiled at the confusion showing in Celia's green, sparkling eyes. "It's that yesterday I discovered that I hoped I might stand a chance with her little sister."

When understanding dawned, the smile Celia gave him was like sunshine after rain; and Albert was glad he'd had the courage to speak so openly.

Chapter Seventeen

The Dye House Picnic

The buggies arrived almost simultaneously, and the men went to the door together. Carol answered it, a vision in her sapphire blue skirt and jacket. Charlie, remembering Albert's interest, glanced over at him, seeing that he, too, had noticed Carol's loveliness. Then Celia came around the corner with her wraps and hat, and the four were off.

After getting Celia settled into his grandfather's buggy, Albert climbed in. He took a moment first though to take in Celia's beauty.

"That color does you justice, Celia Montague. You look very pretty in green." Catching her blush before she looked away, he added, "*And* pink," to which Celia replied with an even deeper blush. Clicking to the horse to follow Charlie and Carol, he went on. "Aren't you going to say something about how dashing *I* look?"

This brought a ripple of laughter from Celia, which Albert found charming. However, it suited his current mood best to tease her further. "Are you saying then that my appearance is humorous, Miss Montague?"

She squelched her giggles long enough to see the grin on Albert's face; and smiling up at him as she opened her parasol, she replied, "I do believe, Mr. Whittle, that this will be a most enjoyable day!"

Charlie and Carol's conversation was very subdued. Carol's

mind was caught up in thinking how to go about asking Charlie of his salvation, and Charlie's was wondering now if she would say "yes" when he asked for her hand as he intended to that afternoon. His grandfather's ruby was burning a hole in his vest pocket, its new setting a beautiful swirling filigree in silver. He had the other setting melted and molded into a gold band for himself, to be put on at a date in the not-too-distant future. But Carol seemed so reserved, so distracted in his presence anymore. He wanted to tell her right then that he loved her, but he believed it best to *show* her somehow...to prove by his actions that his love was constant. He reached behind the buggy seat and pulled out a beautiful bouquet of roses, bluebells, and baby's breath.

"The very first blooms from Mother's roses. She wanted them to be for you." Carol held them close, smelling the rich fragrance as their heads swayed with the buggy's movement.

"Thank you so much, and please thank your mother also. How is she doing? I...I didn't get a chance to speak with her Sunday after the service."

Charlie chuckled, "As I recall, you didn't get a chance to speak with *anyone* after the service Sunday! You were out of the choir loft and had turned in your music before I ever had a chance to say goodbye!"

"I'm sorry. I wasn't avoiding you. I just...didn't feel well. I needed to get home and be alone for a while."

"That's what I figured, but when I went by later I saw Albert Whittle going in—" Charlie saw out of the corner of his eye how quickly Carol looked up at him. He hadn't meant to divulge his knowledge about that particular bit of information, but the truth was seeing Albert there ahead of him had hurt deeply.

"Now it's my turn to apologize. That was beneath me." Carol didn't reply to his apology, which he took in a bad light. Rather than allow himself to become angry however, he quickly changed the subject.

"It's beautiful out, isn't it? Not a bit like the day when I first ran into you. Seems like I thought you had a bad case of freckles, when in all actuality it was spatterings of mud!" He laughed alone, but he did see a small smile appear on Carol's lips. "Of course, if you *had* been freckled, I'd have loved every one of them, I'm sure." Carol was sitting too far over for him, but he reached his hand out to cover hers as it lay on the seat between them. "I love you, Carolina."

"I know...." When Carol didn't reply in kind, he glanced over to find her eyes filled with tears. "And I love you, too, Charlie, more and more every day." Charlie wanted so much to stop the buggy and talk with her, but they were merged into the picnic procession.

"Why are you crying then? Our love used to make us want to dance around the room like children. Now it makes you cry. And those don't look like happy tears, either. What have I done?"

She pulled his hand up to her lips and kissed it, then pressed her cheek against it. "Can we just enjoy our ride and the picnic? I promise I will talk with you about what is worrying me before you bring me home tonight. We have the whole wonderful day ahead of us. Let's pretend we haven't a care in the world." Carol knew she was putting off the inevitable, but she so wanted a day to remember with Charlie...a day she could treasure for however long it took....

"Agreed," he said, smiling as he used the same word he'd used when he'd told her he would stand by her standard of no kissing until their engagement. His smile broadened as he thought to himself, "*Lord willing, today will be that day!*"

The ground was a trifle too soggy from a recent rain to eat on a picnic blanket, so the Dyes had set up tents with table upon table of foods and beverages for them all to enjoy. Although Charlie remembered that Celia and Albert were there, he still suspected Albert's affections and tried to keep Carol to himself as much as possible. Little did he know how much Albert and Celia were enjoying themselves, yet praying for his friend and her sister throughout the day. The four did sit down together for lunch.

"Charlie, where are the beverages? I mean, I saw bottles of wine, but is there anything else?" Charlie and Albert rose to find some punch, and the girls were in immediate consultation.

"Carrie, have you spoken? Have you asked him yet?"

"No, Celia, I haven't. But I'm quite sure I already know the answer." Both girls sat in silence as they thought of what this knowledge meant. "Somehow, I believe with all my heart that

Charlie is God's best for me...for my husband..., but I know I have to wait until he's one of God's own." She looked with pleading eyes at her sister sharing, "I just want this one last day, Celia. To look back on and cherish. I don't know when he will accept Christ, but I'll wait, however long it takes...."

"Albert said almost those very same words. He said that he had wanted to court you, but that he knew that you'd wait for Charlie until his salvation."

Carol turned hurt eyes to her sister, saying, "Oh, Celia, I'm so sorry that he had feelings for me! I've only ever noticed Charlie's attention." She twisted her napkin around her fingers nervously. "I never meant to hurt him, nor to keep him from noticing what a dear *you* are."

"Well, actually, he never felt hurt by you. In fact, he said that it was his hope of courting *me* that helped him get over you." The girls gave one another a quick hug before Celia went on, "And I can't say that I'm sorry that his affections were so easily transferred, for I find Albert Whittle to be quite the most endearing man of my acquaintance."

Carol squeezed her sister's hand, her face wreathed in smiles. "I'm so happy for you! For you *both*! I will be praying for you, for the Lord's will in your relationship."

Just then the boys walked up with glasses of tea for each of them, and Charlie smiled in relief when he saw Carol's joyful expression. She never mentioned anything about their discussion at the meal, but the expressive looks that passed between Carol, Celia, and Albert were not lost on Charlie. They were, however, misinterpreted.

After the meal and a game of lawn golf, the group split up and went to sit on the blankets out on the edge of the gardens. Many of the other men were well on their way to becoming inebriated, carrying their bottles of wine and filling and emptying their glasses regularly. Carol would not have even taken a seat on the blanket except that a photographer had set up his camera for a quick group photograph. Charlie understood her discomfort and helped her to her feet as soon as the shot was taken. As it was, she refused to look at the camera with all the wine bottles scattered around the blanket.

Charlie directed them over to the Dyes' gazebo, a lovely little affair with a pair of large swings facing each other. The whole structure was covered with wisteria and climbing roses, the first of which was in full bloom. Carol leaned over the railing to smell the wisteria cluster nearest her, but she could see that it was time to talk with Charlie. He heard her sigh deeply, forlornly. Her back was to him, and he hesitatingly put his hand on her arm, turning her gently around to face him.

"What is *wrong* with us, Carol? I don't understand. I love you dearly, and I truly believe you still love me; but it's as though you're pulling away from me a little more every day." He ran his fingers nervously through his hair in that gesture Carol had come to know and love, but the hurt-filled eyes he raised to look at her with were more than her heart could take. Tears pooled in her eyes as she reached out to the railing for support.

"Charlie, I *do* love you, with all my heart. It's just that I don't...we don't.... I fear we're 'unequally yoked'!" She paused then, pulling her handkerchief out of her string purse at her wrist, but the voice Charlie answered her with sounded relieved somehow.

"Carol, I don't care about social standing or money or anything like that! You know my family; we're not prejudiced or proud. I would be most *honored* to marry you, darling!"

"Oh, Charlie, that is not what I'm referring to at all. I know that your family's social standing would not come between us, but I believe our *spiritual* standing does." Charlie's eyes darkened a moment with suppressed anger, but Carol went on. "Charlie, the Bible says that I as a Christian should only marry another Christian. I know that you are very moral and attend religious services, but that no more makes you a Christian than...than my sleeping in a barn would make me a horse!" She was gesticulating wildly with her frustrated hands, trying so hard to find the right words and failing miserably from the look of Charlie's confused expression. "Oh, I'm not saying this right at all."

Charlie chuckled nervously, then said, "No, you're not, but I do believe I understand what you're attempting to say. You're telling me, as Albert has told me several times now.... How did he put it? I need to place my faith in Jesus, not just believe He existed in history. I need to trust that His dying on the cross is the only thing that will gain admittance to heaven one day, not my works, my family, my morality.... That is what you're saying, yes?"

"Yes, Charlie! Have you done this? Have you asked the Lord to forgive you of your sins? Have you received Jesus as your Saviour?"

His hesitation gave him away yet again. "No, Carol, I have not." He could have told her that he had been thinking about it. He could have told her *why* he hadn't made that decision as yet. It wasn't so much that he thought his morality to be enough. The truth was, from everything Albert had shared with him and everything he could find when he searched the Scriptures, his morality was decidedly *not* enough. He just didn't think he had the time to concern himself over that, with his job, his goals, his dreams for the future.... Yet nearly every aspect of his future involved his marriage to Carol, and she was saying that she would not marry him if he wasn't a Christian! It was maddening. But he also knew that to make a decision like salvation, to admit one's sin and have a new way of life with Christ as Master, was not something he could do on a whim, even if it were only to please his beloved Carol.

Minutes passed in silence as each thought about the next step that must be taken. "Carol, I had every intention of asking you to marry me this afternoon; but I believe you would say 'no' if I asked you right now. Am I right?"

Carol's tears spilled down her cheeks as she twisted her handkerchief in her hands. "You are right. As much as I love you, not only do I believe we cannot be married, but I believe it best that we stop seeing each other, Charlie. I'm so sorry." She began to sob, and Charlie drew her to him in a gentle embrace, petting her hair and hushing her as though she were a frightened child. Her sobbing slowly ceased, and she drew away from him, turning to leave; but Charlie stopped her.

He turned her back to face him and took her chin in his hand. His eyes searched her face, memorizing every detail before looking deeply into her sapphire blue eyes.

"You need never worry about seeing me as someone else's husband, Carolina." As his eyes went to her lips, lips that would not deny him this farewell, he gave her the most gentle, lingering kiss imaginable until she was totally breathless. His arms encircled her waist and held her close, and their tears mingled as he pressed his cheek to her own. "Oh, my love, my dearest love," he whispered, but she was once again drawing away. She lifted her great, sad eyes to his, then turned and fled toward the house.

Charlie dropped weakly to the bench, his head in his hands as he wept; then he pulled the ring from his vest pocket and placed it on his little finger.

Albert and Celia were walking in the gardens when they caught sight of Carol. "Bring her to the buggy," was all Albert said, and Celia flew to her sister. As the two reached one another, Carol nearly fell into her sister's arms.

"We're taking you home, Carrie." Celia was holding back her own tears, but she determined to remain strong for Carol's sake. Placing an arm around her for support, Celia helped her sister to the carriage house where Albert was hitching up the horse. He helped the ladies into the buggy, feeling a bit disconcerted at how shaky Carol was.

Once seated, Carol leaned on the side of the buggy, still sniffling but more in control. Celia gave her a fresh handkerchief that was dampened with rosewater from a tiny bottle in her purse, and Carol held the cool cloth to her eyes and face. The fragrance reminded her that she'd left her roses from Charlie behind somewhere, but she knew there was no going back for them.

Albert and Celia spoke quietly, at some point realizing that Carol had fallen asleep from exhaustion. "Oh, Albert, I just wish someone could have been there for Charlie. If Carol is this distressed, I know Charlie must be in terrible shape."

Albert's look was thoughtful as he answered. "Yes, but perhaps the Lord can even use the pain Charlie is feeling to draw him to Himself. We just need to pray all the more fervently for Charlie, that he doesn't become hardened or bitter."

Albert glanced down at Celia, looking so small and fragile just then, but he also knew the strength of spirit both she and her sister possessed. "I'm so glad that you are here, Celia. God knew Carol would need you." He smiled down at her upturned face and added, "And I think perhaps He knew I needed you, too." She tucked her hand in the crook of his elbow as he held the reins, and the three continued silently back to the boarding house.

Chapter Eighteen

My Own Fault

Charlie had seen Carol leave with Celia and Albert, and in a way he felt relieved that she was being well-cared for. Still blind to any feelings but his own however, he felt more than a little jealousy at the thought of Albert consoling Carol.

"It's your own fault though," he said quietly to himself. He was thankful he hadn't told his parents of his intentions to propose to Carol that day, or their expectant faces when he returned home would have been more than he could bear. He was less than half an hour behind Albert's buggy on his way home, and he spent extra time brushing the General and cleaning the harness and buggy before going into the house.

When he heard piano music from the front door, he tried to come in quietly enough to go to his room without seeing his parents, but his father was in the sitting room and called him in.

"How was the—" Mr. Bennett stopped mid-sentence when he saw his son's face. Setting aside his paper, he stood, embracing Charlie as the younger man felt the tears burning his throat and eyes again.

Mrs. Bennett stopped her playing abruptly, making her way to the two men she so loved as quickly as possible. "Do you want to talk, Charlie?" his mother asked softy, the tears glistening on her lashes.

Charlie nodded, and the three sat down. "I...I asked Carol to marry me." To his astonishment, his parents did not react with surprise, even knowing from his response what her reply had been. "You *knew* she'd say 'no'? How? *Why?*"

"Oh, Charlie," Mr. Bennett said with a sigh, "we've prayed and prayed for you since before you were born. Prayed for your salvation, for your health, for your life's mate. But Pastor's sermon Sunday made it perfectly clear that...that if you were not yet a Christian, you could not marry Carol."

Charlie stood to his feet. "I'm close to coming to that point, but...but something's holding me back. Maybe it's my own pride." He walked over to the piano, running his hand across the smooth expanse of polished wood. "I wish now I had just bowed my head right then and prayed, but...."

Charlie's parents exchanged a pained look before Mr. Bennett added, "But you didn't."

Charlie nodded, then left the room as he felt angry tears coming. He stopped at the doorway, not looking back into the room, but saying, "Don't stop praying. Please don't." Then he fled upstairs to his room while his parents went to their knees at that very moment and continued in prayer for Charlie Bennett's soul.

❧❦

Charlie left the house early Sunday morning, riding the General fast and hard when he reached the edge of town. He couldn't bear going to church and seeing Carol, and he didn't feel it was right for him to be in the choir now that he had acknowledged his spiritual condition. This became a ritual for him every Sunday morning, to leave at dawn and ride until church was about over, then return to the house. He knew his parents were hurting over his actions, but it went on for months. Through spring and even the hottest parts of the summer, his Sunday morning routine remained the same.

During the week he worked as hard as ever at his job, but he spoke with no one of personal matters. He wouldn't even allow eye contact with Albert. In all actuality, he was quite angry with Albert, who from the glimpses he caught was maddeningly joyful over his current circumstances. Once again, Charlie blamed himself for allowing Albert the opportunity to court Carol, but it still made him angry.

It was the middle of autumn when Charlie saw Carol face to face again. He had intentionally stayed away from every place he felt he might see her, but he'd forgotten how close Westside Park was to her place of employment. After work one day, he took his buggy to the park, hitching it to a post and deciding to go walking for a while.

He patted the General on his strong neck and told him quietly, "You aren't the only one who needs exercise, old man," then he began a stroll about the park's perimeter. He was on the far side of the park when he spotted her, sitting on a bench, reading. Charlie slowed to a stop, debating whether he should speak to her or walk on, when she looked up and saw him standing there. His eyes slid closed at the feelings that flooded him upon seeing her, and he would have turned to leave had she not called his name. He slowly walked to her side where she now stood before the bench, her book set aside.

She held a hand out to him. "Hello."

He took her outstretched hand and bowed over it, then quickly released it and straightened to his full height. "Carolina. You're looking well." In fact, she looked more beautiful than ever, wearing a dress of the same reddish brown as her hair. Her skin seemed to glow in the late afternoon sun.

"Thank you." He was about to excuse himself when she went on, seeing his discomfort. "How...how are you doing?"

His brow shot up, his mind filling with sarcastic remarks; but the look on her face showed the same genuine concern as that of his parents. He looked down at the bowler hat in his hand before replying quietly, "Not very well actually. But thank you for asking." They stood there, so near each other, yet still seemingly miles apart.

"I was just waiting for Albert. We're having dinner together this evening. Would you care to—" With a quick, slashing gesture of his hand he cut her off before she could invite him to join her, her sister, and Albert for dinner.

He regained his composure before speaking, but she could still sense the anger in his voice. "I...sincerely hope you have an enjoyable evening. Goodnight." And with that he replaced his hat, tipped it, and was gone.

Albert walked up shortly after Carol had returned to the bench, having seen them from a distance and giving them time to talk. He was surprised to find Carol's eyes dry when she looked up at him.

"Well?"

"That didn't go well at all. There were a million things I wanted to say, things I've thought of in my prayers and daydreams that I would say to him when I saw him again. But pretty much all I could say was 'hello'."

He put out his arm to escort her to his grandfather's buggy, then the two were headed to the boarding house where Celia had dinner almost prepared. Charlie caught a glimpse of them climbing in a buggy as he was leaving the park, more certain than ever that he was a fool for leaving the door open for Albert to court Carol.

༄༅

Somehow Charlie made it through the first anniversary of meeting Carol. Next the holidays were upon them, every little thing bringing back memories of the previous year—every ice storm, every sprig of mistletoe, every carol. He stayed away from the Bank Christmas Banquet, certain he'd see Carol there with Albert celebrating Christmas and her twenty-second birthday together just as he had celebrated her twenty-first birthday with her the previous Christmas. He had no heart for festivities anyhow. It was a relief to see the final snowfall melting away, making way for the spring of 1890.

Another Sunday morning was upon him. The monotony of the past year's schedule was wearing on Charlie, but once again he rose with the dawn, saddled his horse, and went riding. When he reached the edge of town, he encouraged the General to gallop, but there was no releasing the tension Charlie felt building up inside himself.

The General had worked up a lather when his rider slowed him finally. The slower pace allowed Charlie to think more clearly—something he didn't necessarily wish to do, but what he *needed* all the same. He allowed himself to really think about his life, and it was blatantly clear to him that he was running, but not necessarily just from his pain over his lost love. There was another love wooing him, an infinitely stronger love than even his great love for Carol.

The Holy Spirit began bringing verses of God's love to Charlie's remembrance as he rode nearly another mile before stopping beside a large, lone oak. He dismounted, patted his horse's strong neck, and dropped the reins to allow the General to graze. Charlie went to sit under the tree, slowly lowering himself to the ground.

Toying with a stick, he looked up. *"God, can You hear me?"* His voice seemed to be caught and carried away by a breeze, but he went on. *"I know that Your Word says that if I regard iniquity in my heart, You won't hear me. But I want to do something about that."* He broke the stick in half, then put his arms on his knees, his face bowed down in prayer and grief.

"How long have You been waiting for me? waiting to show Your love for me? waiting for me to love You?" The tears began to come as he realized that he was spurning God's love all this time just as Carol had spurned his, yet his action to God was without just cause!

"Lord, You love me far more than I love Carol. You even died for me, which I'll never understand. But, God, I'm tired of running. I'm tired of disappointing my parents and You, Lord. I know it's too late for me and Carol; but, God, it's not too late for me and You.

"Please forgive me of my sin. Wash me clean with Your Son's precious blood. Help me to be the man You want me to be, in Jesus' name and for His sake and glory, amen."

He looked up, half expecting the whole earth to have changed during that prayer, and in a very real way, it had. The weight on his heart that he'd felt for so long was gone. Looking up, he offered the first of a lifetime of asides to his prayers, *"I'm sure we're both wondering what took me so long, right, Lord?"*

Mounting the General, Charlie rode swiftly home; only this time unlike the Sundays of the past year, he tied the faithful horse's reins to the hitching post and sought out his parents. They were not home from church yet, so he sat down in the sitting room to wait.

※※※

It was Palm Sunday, and the service was inspiring to say the least. After church, Mr. and Mrs. Bennett made their way to the front to speak with Carol and her sister. Carol hugged Mrs. Bennett tightly, then with eyes glowing with love she shook Mr. Bennett's hand. "How are you both?"

"Praising God for another day, my dear. This is such a special time of year, remembering Jesus' going willingly to Jerusalem to die on the cross for our sin."

She looked from one to the other of them before asking, "And how is Charlie?"

Mrs. Bennett looked to her husband to answer. "He's well physically, but about worn out from running I would guess. Keep praying." He saw the girls exchange glances, unable to frame a suitable reply.

"We have been and will continue to do so, sir," Albert said quietly as he came up then to escort the ladies home. Offering an arm to each, they walked away. Mr. and Mrs. Bennett walked in silence to their buggy.

"I miss her so much, Ben." Mrs. Bennett was long past tears, or so she thought.

"I know, dear. And I miss our son, too. I know we still live in the same house, but...."

"Yes, I know." Mrs. Bennett raised her parasol as Mr. Bennett unhitched the horse from the post, though from its blinking eyes and stance it had enjoyed its Sunday morning nap in the sunshine.

When they arrived home, they saw the General tied up out front and exchanged glances. Rather than dropping off Mrs. Bennett and taking the buggy to the carriage house, they tied up to the hitching post and went inside, where they found Charlie standing in the middle of the sitting room, beaming at them both.

"Mother, Father.... I'm *home*."

Chapter Nineteen

Reunion

Theirs was one of the sweetest reunions this side of heaven, and it was a long while before anyone had settled down enough to do anything but hug and talk. Eventually, the three of them realized how hungry they were. Mrs. Bennett headed to the kitchen to prepare a quick Sunday dinner while the men took the General and the horse and carriage around to the carriage house.

Throughout the meal Mrs. Bennett kept pausing to squeeze Charlie's hand, so dearly had she missed her relationship with her only living child. And now for him to know the Lord—God had been so good to them!

"Charlie, have you thought about telling Carol?" The way their son stiffened made Mr. Bennett sorry he had broached the subject, but his son recovered quite well.

"I've no doubt at all that she would be happy for me in my decision. But after thinking and praying about it while I was waiting for you to arrive home from church, I decided that it wouldn't be...fair...somehow. It would seem that her relationship with Albert is...has developed into...."

He couldn't bring himself to finish, but his parents both understood. "You see, I saw them together in a jewelry store last week, and I strongly suspect they were looking at rings." Charlie paused, then giving them both one of his boyish smiles, went on. "But I can honestly say I'm happy for them both. Sad for me and my thick-headed ways that ended my chances with her, but happy nonetheless for their sakes. Albert has always been a true Christian friend, and...well, I know there's not a finer woman in the world than Carolina Montague."

Charlie excused himself from the table and began clearing his plate, glass, and silverware, taking them into the kitchen. Mrs. Bennett whispered to her husband, "But, Ben, she *loved* Charlie, I'm sure of it!"

"Nevertheless, if Charlie has prayed about it...." The two gathered the remaining serving dishes and glasses and went to join Charlie in the kitchen.

&

Monday was one of the most challenging days of Charlie's Christian life, and it was especially difficult that he had to face it when spiritually only a day old. He prepared to eat crow after avoiding his friend for so many months...was it a year? Charlie approached Albert in the cloak room just before the work day was to begin, but he caught the tail-end of a conversation between Albert and another co-worker whom Charlie suspected to also be a believer.

"So, the end of your bachelor days is gettin' close, hunh? I'm really glad for you, Brother! Really glad!" The other man shook Albert's hand heartily, then turned to walk out of the cloak room. He had to turn a bit sideways to get past Charlie, who seemed frozen in his tracks.

Charlie had wanted to tell Albert of his salvation, but he just didn't think it was appropriate timing. Instead, he went forward, catching his old friend's eye as he hung up his jacket and placed his bowler hat on the shelf above it.

"Albert? I...I want to apologize for my behavior. I've been wrong to avoid you as I have, and I'm truly sorry." Albert looked as though he could have been knocked down with a flick of a finger, but with the same friendly smile as if they'd never gone a year without speaking, Albert shook Charlie's outstretched hand.

"Apology accepted, Charlie; and thank you." Before he could say anything more though, Charlie walked out of the cloak room and headed for his teller's booth. There was still a good ten minutes before the bank opened however, and Albert followed Charlie into the tiny room.

"Charlie, I wanted you to know that I'm getting married. I wanted you to be the best man, but since you...well...I ended up asking Caleb." Looking at Charlie's slumped form, Albert suspected he shouldn't have said anything, but he wanted Charlie to know that he still considered him one of his closest friends. After a moment, however, Charlie turned with a gentle smile.

"I'm happy for you, Albert. Truly." Charlie turned and began counting his cash drawer to make certain everything was in order before beginning his day. When he heard Albert close the door behind him however, he paused in his counting long enough to look up, praying, *"Oh, God, I didn't think it would be this hard. But thank You for getting me through this."*

※

"You say he spoke with you this morning?" Carol placed her hands on Albert's arm as he told the story to her and Celia that evening before dinner.

"Yes. He apologized for...for the way he's avoided me since...you know."

Carol stood up quickly and headed for the kitchen, then stopped suddenly, her skirts making a rushing sound as she spun around to ask him, "Do you think—"

"That occurred to me too...that perhaps.... But he would have *told* me. There's no reason for him not to tell me, not a one that I can think of." He looked to his fiancé, quietly asking, "Celia, should I not have said anything?"

To his surprise, both Montague women answered "No!" then giggled. Carol went on. "No, Albert, I'm glad to know that his heart is softening at least. He's been...so hard.... This just encourages me to pray all the more fervently for Mr. Charles Bennett!"

She went to the kitchen sink and washed her hands, then neatly tied her apron before putting the meal Celia had prepared for them on the table. Albert was a regular fixture for dinner, and the three of them had prayer each evening before he headed home. Carol gave her sister and Albert a few minutes alone each night, but always was there to chaperone.

"Now that you two are getting married next week, what are we going to do about our living situation, Sister?"

Celia looked to Albert, who answered, "We wanted to talk things over with you before finalizing our plans. I know you can't afford this apartment alone. Would you consider turning this suite over to us and taking a smaller apartment here? Or," Albert added, warming to the subject, "I've found a very nice cottage on Dogwood Circle. You would be most welcome. There's room enough with the upstairs and downstairs, and—"

"Oh, I think the cottage sounds wonderful for you! But not for me. I...I want to stay here. And with the new job you helped me find, Albert, I should be able to afford it if I'm careful with my other expenditures. I'll just sign the boarding agreement in my name only when I return from the wedding." She stopped in her meal preparations and looked around the small but homey room. "I know it's only a room; but, well, Charlie helped me find it and all. It's special to me." She smiled at the two loved ones sitting on the couch watching her. "Now, you two get back to your planning while I get supper on the table!"

⊷⊶

Mr. Bennett had been offered by the board the opportunity to promote his son, but he felt the timing hadn't been right. Now with his son's heart and attitude change in addition to the skill and dedication he'd shown on the job, Mr. Bennett knew the time had come.

The man who had held the comptroller's position for years was soon to retire, and Mr. Bennett called Charlie into his office to discuss the changes. He concluded with, "You'll have a lot of responsibility, Son, but I believe you're ready for the job. There is also the occasional entertaining of clients and other public relations work to be done. I have just such a need tonight, if you feel up to it after a long day in 'the cage', as you so aptly call it." Charlie chuckled, wondering how his father had heard the term.

"That would be fine. Mr. Jennings has more than earned his retirement, and I'd better jump right into the responsibilities. What does this 'entertaining' entail?"

"Well, this evening I need you to take Mr. Vanderhuff's daughter to dinner while he and I go over some important paperwork. The bank will cover the costs, and she needs to be treated to the very finest." He saw his son's expression...one of facing an unpleasant task. "Not to worry, Son! She's a lovely young lady, and I do believe if given a chance you might even *enjoy* your evening!" Both men chuckled, then Mr. Bennett went on. "Even though we're already down one man, I think you should leave early to dress for the evening."

"Albert's gone."

"Yes, Son. He left at noon in preparation for his trip to the Carolinas. His wedding is next week."

Charlie nodded, then recovering, asked, "What time do you need me back here?" After arranging a meeting time, Charlie went home, bathed, and dressed for the evening. He came down at a little before six and met his mother at the foot of the stairs.

"You look so handsome, Son!" she said proudly, kissing his smooth, clean-shaven cheek.

"Thank you, dear lady!" he said with a grin as he popped open his top hat and placed it on his head with aplomb. "I'd stay and chat, but I'm on assignment! Father has me baby-sitting a client's daughter this evening as part of my new responsibilities."

Taking his arm as he made his way to the door, his mother told him gently, "She may be a lovely young lady, Charlie. Don't underestimate the Lord. This may be His way of sending along someone even more suited for you." Charlie smiled down into his mother's concerned face, but she went on. "I love you, Son, and God loves you even more. Don't be surprised when He blesses you *'exceeding abundantly, above all we ask or think'*. Have a good evening."

He bent down and kissed her soft cheek, then went out into the sunset.

∽✢∾

Miss Victoria Vanderhuff was indeed a beautiful young

woman, but Charlie found himself comparing her with Carol. The obviously high-society Miss Vanderhuff seemed overdone somehow, her jet-black hair and pallid complexion were too strong a contrast for his taste, but she was nonetheless elegant. He asked if she had a preference in where to eat that evening.

"Oh, I've heard much of Stewart's...you know," she said, dramatically quoting an advertisement they had both seen, "'Stewart's Fine Dining—The Finest Food in Baltimore, with live piano music for our patrons' listening pleasure'. I'm sure that would be delightful!" Then as a considerate afterthought she added, "If that appeals to you...?"

"Of course, Miss Vanderhuff, that sounds fine."

"Please, call me 'Victoria'; and may I take the liberty of calling you by your first name, Mr. Bennett?"

"Of course, Victoria," he replied, and seeing her smile in the lamplight, he asked, "Did I miss something?"

"Well, it might help if I knew what your first name *was*!" They both laughed amicably as Charlie introduced himself, but she didn't call him by his nickname. She rather purred his given name, and although he was sure some men might find that voice alluring, Charlie didn't in the least. He continued downtown and hitched up the buggy at Stewart's, and the two walked in.

Although she realized it and had come to expect it, Charlie didn't realize that they were by far the handsomest couple in the room. The *maitre' d* made much of them as he took them to a secluded table for two, sheltered by potted palms and decorative pillars. There were countless candles lit and tiny decorative lamps at each table, and the look of the whole room was enchanting. Just as they were seated, the pianist began a new selection, drawing Charlie's attention; and he was distracted as he tried to make small talk with the woman of the world across from him.

When the waiter came for their beverage order, Charlie looked to Victoria for her preference. He was disappointed, but not surprised when she ordered a glass of wine for herself. He however ordered iced tea, drawing a condescending look from both the waiter and Victoria.

"Don't tell me you don't drink *wine*, Charles?" She raised a pencil-thin brow in a look of mock surprise before he answered.

"Actually, no, I do not." He didn't think she wanted to hear his Biblical reasons as to why not, so he very smoothly changed the subject. "How long has your family been in the Baltimore area, Victoria?" he asked, grinning to himself at how easily she was distracted by her favorite subject, *herself*.

When the waiter returned with their drinks and after Charlie finished ordering for them both, Victoria had begun a monologue of some of her accomplishments. In the midst of her discourse, he asked, "And do you play the piano?"

She feigned a blush as she said, "Actually, no. I never learned. I do appreciate listening to others play, however; and the young lady playing over there seems to be an *exceptional* pianist." Charlie followed her glance over his left shoulder, and turned to look into the eyes of Carolina Montague!

Somehow she managed never to miss a note, but her heart was beating so hard she was sure everyone in the room could hear it. *"It is Charlie!"* she thought, working with all her might to concentrate on the music before her. When he and the very beautiful lady he was with had come in, she had only caught a glimpse of his profile, but she had been almost certain it was Charlie. She was already an hour into her playing, and when she finished that piece she stood to her feet, walking as quickly as she could to the break room for a much-needed five minute respite.

He knew his actions could be misconstrued as rudeness, but when he heard the music stop, he interrupted Miss Vanderhuff. "Forgive me, but could you excuse me a moment? I won't be long." Before she could respond he had placed his napkin on the table and walked swiftly away, leaving a very confused lady sitting there sipping her wine.

Asking a waiter for directions, he made his way to the break room where he found Carol looking out the small window.

"Carol?"

The sound of his voice was more beautiful to her than any song she had played that evening. She turned around slowly as she saw him shortening the distance between them. He stopped but a few feet from her, taking in her beauty. She wore a simple but elegant gown of black taffeta, her only adornment being the pearl brooch from her mother pinned at the bodice and, yes, the bracelet he had given her. She wore her hair up in the same pearl-studded combs she had worn to the Christmas ball as well, and his heart turned over with love before he could remind himself that she was no longer his to admire.

"Hello, Charlie. It *is* good to see you!"

"You're looking lovely, as always, Carolina. Are you well?"

"Yes, I am, thank you. And you?"

"Aside from the shock seeing you has brought me, yes." He felt himself redden at his bluntness, but went on. "What are you *doing* here? I mean, besides the obvious. Did you get a permanent job here as pianist?"

"Yes! And it has been wonderful already. A bit tiring, but wonderful. I work a full day at Waterman's, then come here from six through ten every other evening. It's like getting paid to practice!"

"You're using your talent. That's good." He didn't know what else to say without being too effusive, but she seemed to accept his compliment. "Actually I've been wanting to speak with you—"

The *maitre' d* came in then and formally let Carol know her break time was nearly up. She smiled an apology to Charlie as she headed for the door. "Perhaps we can talk after the wedding. We leave first light on the train."

"Of course, of course. Yes, perhaps then." She stood there before him, looking more beautiful than he remembered, and he reached out for her hand and kissed it. His voice sounded wistful even to his own ears as he said, "Goodbye, Carolina." He took one last look, then walked swiftly from the room.

"Oh, Lord, I still love him so! Please, please draw Charlie to Yourself. And someday, if it be Your perfect will, reunite us."

When the *maitre' d* looked back at the break room door, Carol came out looking as elegant and composed as ever, walking confidently to the piano and playing the most beautiful music he'd ever heard. "*As well she should,*" he thought to himself smugly.

Chapter Twenty

"God Be With You..."

Charlie somehow made it through dinner without making any more *faux pas*. As they rose to leave Miss Vanderhuff held proudly to her handsome escort's arm, even as he looked one last time at Carol. She looked up at him, as she was between songs; then while still holding his gaze she began playing *Tales from Vienna Woods* from memory. She mouthed, "God be with you...."

"And with you," he whispered, Miss Vanderhuff turning to him in confusion since his sweetly spoken phrase had nothing to do with what she'd been talking about.

Charlie paid for the bill, carefully folding the receipt and placing it in his billfold. Then the two made their way from the sparkling excitement of the restaurant and into the soft lamplight of the streets.

Charlie tried to listen attentively as Victoria rambled on and on, but his heart was not in it. He was too busy praying silently for the Lord to give him strength for the next time he saw Carolina, presumably as Mrs. Albert Whittle.

When they arrived at the bank and Charlie turned Miss Vanderhuff over to her father's care, he breathed a mental sigh of relief. He waited in the outer office for his father, then the two headed home together.

"How did it go?" his father asked distractedly as he climbed into the still expensive-perfume-fragranced buggy.

"Honest opinion? I have never met a more self-absorbed

person. The evening would have been a complete waste had we not run into Carol." Knowing he had his father's undivided attention, he proceeded to tell him of the evening's events. Mr. Bennett could tell that Charlie was working hard to keep his feelings suppressed, and he smiled at his son sadly.

"Charlie, I'm *so* proud of you. I can't imagine how difficult that must have been for you, but you were a true Christian gentleman."

"Thank you, Father." He smiled in the semi-darkness. "Quite honestly, if Albert had been there this evening I do believe this true Christian gentleman would have decked him, good Christian friend though he is!" He chuckled a bit, the humor softening the blow to his heart slightly. The humorous frankness made his father all the more proud of his boy, and the two continued talking all the way home.

Mrs. Bennett stepped out on the portico with Lucas when she heard the horse and buggy pull up. The three came in while Lucas took the General around to the carriage house to settle him in for the night. When he caught a whiff of the expensive French perfume, he huffed, mumbling, "Missy Carol didn't never wear such a stink-oil, no suh!" The General snorted in agreement.

Charlie took off his hat and gloves, placing them on the table in the foyer as he joined his parents in the sitting room. He untied his cravat and removed his shoes, placing his stocking feet casually on the coffee table. Mr. Bennett retold the story of Charlie's evening while Charlie himself sat there, his fingers entwined and his eyes closed.

Mrs. Bennett wanted to commiserate with Charlie at first, but she knew that wouldn't help anything. The ticking of the mantle clock could be clearly heard as the two parents sat thinking and Charlie began snoring.

"He's exhausted, and understandably so. This has been such a difficult week, and I doubt next week will be any better with… with the wedding and all." He smiled as Charlie continued snoring quietly. "I'm so proud of him, Laura. So very proud." Then he cleared his throat a couple of times to wake his son before directing him to his room.

The lamp beside Charlie's bed was lit and the comforter

147

turned down, but as he went into his room and closed the door, he dropped to his knees beside his bed and prayed again for strength to endure what the coming days would bring forth. As he climbed into bed his last waking thought was of Carolina, playing his favorite song and mouthing, "God be with you...." He drifted off still fully clothed into a mercifully dreamless sleep.

༺༻

April 6th, 1890 was Charlie's first time back in church in over a year. As had been his routine, he rose with the dawn; but this being Resurrection Sunday, he went to the veranda to focus on that glorious dawn so many years ago.

After a long time in prayer, he joined his parents for a subdued but delicious breakfast, then readied for church. The three left together a short time later. Albert's and Carol's absence from the choir loft was conspicuous to Charlie when his family arrived. He noticed Celia's absence from the choir as well, realizing that she would of course be a part of the wedding party. Dr. Whittle was there, however, and Charlie determined to speak to him following the service.

Charlie found that the sermon and familiar old hymns all held new depth of meaning to him now that he was a child of God. The Wesley hymn, *Rejoice—the Lord is King!* truly touched his heart, strengthening him and allowing him to truly "lift up" his voice and rejoice with his whole being.

> *Rejoice, the Lord is King! Your Lord and King adore;*
> *Rejoice, give thanks, and sing, and triumph evermore;*
> *Lift up your heart, lift up your voice;*
> *Rejoice, again I say, rejoice!*
>
> *Jesus, the Savior, reigns, the God of truth and love;*
> *When He had purged our stains He took His seat above;*
> *Lift up your heart, lift up your voice;*
> *Rejoice, again I say, rejoice!*
>
> *His kingdom cannot fail, He rules o'er earth and heaven,*

The keys of death and hell are to our Jesus given;
Lift up your heart, lift up your voice;
Rejoice, again I say, rejoice!

He sits at God's right hand till all His foes submit,
And bow to His command, and fall beneath His feet:
Lift up your heart, lift up your voice;
Rejoice, again I say, rejoice!

He all His foes shall quell, shall all our sins destroy,
And every bosom swell with pure seraphic joy;
Lift up your heart, lift up your voice,
Rejoice, again I say, rejoice!

Rejoice in glorious hope! Jesus the Judge shall come,
And take His servants up to their eternal Home.
We soon shall hear th'archangel's voice;
The trump of God shall sound, rejoice!

Following that and a few other joy-based hymns of the resurrection, Pastor Lehman preached mostly from the book of Philippians rather than remaining in the traditional Resurrection Sunday passages; and Charlie truly felt prepared for the coming week. Immediately following the service, he went up and spoke to the pastor of his salvation.

"Oh, Charles, I'm so happy for you, my Brother, and for your parents! When do you wish to follow the Lord in believers' baptism and share you testimony with the church family? Would next Sunday work for you?"

Charlie thought a moment, then replied with a smile, "Yes, sir. Next Sunday will be fine. Thank you, sir!" Next he sought out Dr. Whittle.

"Good morning, Doc," he said smiling as he came upon the older gentleman gathering his things for his departure.

"Charlie, lad, it *is* good to see you!" Dr. Whittle had followed the story of Charlie's trials of the past year through his grandson, praying all the while for this young man he so dearly loved. "How are you this beautiful Easter morning?"

"I am well, sir, and yourself?"

He smiled broadly, "Excited to be going down for Albert's wedding this week! I—"

Not meaning to seem rude, but not wishing to remain on this particularly painful subject, Charlie chose to bring up what he came over to speak with the doctor about in the first place. "Sir, I wanted to tell you that you've been remiss in your responsibilities. I happen to know of a birth you missed just a week ago, and I thought you should be confronted for your dereliction of duty."

Doctor Whittle's eyes widened with surprise as he twisted his mustache. "Well, really, Charlie, I don't think—"

"I was born into the family of God, sir," Charlie said with quiet confidence; and the old doctor whooped for joy, grabbing Charlie in a powerful hug and drawing the attention of not a few church members still milling around the sanctuary.

"Oh, Charlie, that's.... Have you told Albert? Carol?"

"I tried, sir, but I...that is, with their getting married, I didn't...."

The short phrase whirled around in Doc Whittle's brain—*'Their getting married'?*" The whole situation became crystal clear in a moment, and he began scratching his whiskers as he worked his mind at a furious pace trying to decide what to do. "Charlie, I really think you should tell Miss Montague...*before* the wedding."

His heart was wrenched when he saw the struggle Charlie was going through as he answered, "But, sir, do you think that is...the right thing to do? I mean, Albert has been the best friend I've ever had...."

Doctor Whittle held up a soft, wrinkled hand. "Son, if there is a possibility that Carol is still in love with you, would it be fair to *her* to be bound in marriage to anyone else?" The light he saw in Charlie's eyes encouraged him to go on. "If she is God's best for you and you are God's best for her, I think the honorable thing to do is to let her know of your salvation and give her the choice. Don't you?"

"Well, *yes* sir, if you put it that way." Charlie reached out and shook the doctor's hand, the smile barely disguised on his handsome young face. "And *thank you*, sir!" And with that,

Charlie nearly ran from the church to find his parents waiting patiently in the carriage.

॰ঌ৸৽

"You're *what*?" His parents spoke simultaneously, and Charlie laughed out loud.

"At the suggestion of Doctor Whittle, I'm going down to tell Carol I still love her and hopefully break up her wedding to Albert." He shook his head, adding, "I don't understand it myself. Doctor Whittle's own grandson. But I suppose if you thought someone was marrying me who was in love with someone else, you'd want to...to be certain, too." His mother's eyes were filled with pain and confusion.

"Charlie, I don't want to discourage you, but we all know Carol to be a very caring, dedicated individual, capable of great love and even self-sacrifice. If she is committed to this relationship—"

"Then she will return to Baltimore as Mrs. Albert Whittle," Charlie finished for her with a calm he did not feel. Then he added, "But if she still loves me, I *must* know it. I must let her know that I am now qualified to be her husband before God. She must have the opportunity to decide for herself."

Mrs. Bennett wanted to weep when she thought of the pain this final rejection could cause; but somewhere in her heart of hearts, that glimmer of hope came back to life.

"Go to her, Son," was all his father said; and when they arrived at the house he ran inside and packed, then asked his father to take him to the train depot. A handsome smile stretched across his face when he found that a train would leave within the hour that would be passing through Monck's Corner, South Carolina on the following day. Gladly paying for the ticket, he and his father sat in comfortable silence as they waited.

When Charlie stood to make his way to the train, he turned to shake his father's hand. Mr. Bennett pulled him into a strong embrace, then unknowingly uttered the phrase that had been singing in Charlie's heart since Friday evening, "God be with you, Charlie."

Charlie turned to wave to his father as he climbed aboard, calling, "He *is*, Father. Come what may, He is with me *always*!"

Chapter Twenty-One

Surprises

When Mr. Bennett arrived home, the doctor's carriage was out in front of their house. Confident that it was a social call, he made his way in for the fellowship he always enjoyed in the good doctor's company.

When he opened the front door, he heard Laura cry, "*Oh, thank You, Lord*; there he is now!" She practically ran into his arms, crying and laughing and he thought well on her way to hysteria, then she took his arm and walked with him back into the sitting room where Dr. Whittle was standing.

"Doctor?" Mr. Bennett asked, his heart racing.

When he opened his mouth to speak, Mrs. Bennett took a seat as she excitedly said, "He has a bit of news for us, dear!" Both men smiled at her as she stated the obvious, then Doctor Whittle returned to his seat and spoke.

"You both know that my grandson Albert is marrying next week. I just wanted to come by and invite you to the wedding." Mrs. Bennett tried her best to scowl at him for his elusiveness; but she knew, too, how thrilling his round about way of telling her had been.

"We are very close to you, Doctor, and to Miss Montague of course. We just—" He paused to find the right words; but rather than prolong his agony, the good doctor finally explained.

"Yes, I know...coming down for her sister's wedding wouldn't mean quite so much." He sat there with a twinkle in his eyes, watching as the light dawned on Mr. Bennett's face.

"Her *sister's* wedding? You mean *Celia's*?"

"Well, now, I was under the impression that Celia was Carol's *only* sister. But yes, my friend. My grandson Albert is marrying *Celia* Montague, not Carol."

Mrs. Bennett sat there patting her palms on her knees before flinging herself into her husband's arms. Doctor Whittle stood, making his way to the door. "My offer stands. I would like very much to invite you to the wedding. And if my intuition serves me right, this could be a *very* important wedding for the two of you... very important indeed!"

Mr. and Mrs. Bennett had stood to their feet as he spoke, both of them coming forward now to give Dr. Whittle a warm embrace. "Charlie rebuked me for not being present at a birth last week. He then told me it was *his* birth, his *new birth*. I just thought it amazingly appropriate that in the very same conversation I was able to send him to make things right with Carol.... Almost like a 'new birth' gift, don't you think? Well, goodbye, dear friends. I should think you have some work and serious planning ahead of you!" He paused, then added, "And I'm so very glad Charlie's come to Christ. So very, very glad."

The good doctor took his hat, gloves, and walking stick from the entry table before letting himself out the front door.

Ben looked into his bride's eyes, the years dropping away in the joy of this news. "Oh, darling, do you think Doc is right? Do you think Charlie will bring Carol back as his bride?"

"I *do*, Benjamin. I really do. And I believe they'll want to come back here. Hadn't he mentioned they had decided that would be best for a while?"

"Yes, as I recall that is what he had mentioned." He smiled conspiratorially to his wife before saying, "Upstairs or down?"

"I should think upstairs. Charlie's room is large and has the bathroom right there in the suite. His rooms may be a bit masculine—"

"But then Carol can decorate to her heart's content. Yes, I think you're right. And Charlie's bed is larger than the one in your mother's room." Mrs. Bennett's cheeks turned pink as her eyes sparkled.

"Oh, Ben, I wish I could be there when he finds out his mistake!" The two walked to his office arm in arm, setting down on paper what needed to be done and when.

※

The clickity-clack of the train did its best to lull Charlie to sleep, but not having spent the money for a sleeper car, he was still upright. His eyes were closed, but his mind was far from resting. He prayed fervently for hours as the train wound its way southward along the coastline.

Monck's Corner was one of the last stops before Charleston, a city of renowned Southern hospitality which he had often wished to visit. Somehow his thoughts went from the city itself to seeing the city with Carol, and before he'd allow himself the privilege of dwelling on that subject he went back to praying, soon falling into a deep sleep.

He woke to the smell of coffee, looking about the orange-tinted passenger car in confusion before he recalled where he was. The sun was just about to peek over the horizon, and it looked like the beginning of a beautiful day if the brilliance of the sunrise was any sign.

The conductor told him they were about an hour and a half out of Monck's Corner, and Charlie stood and stretched a bit, walking to the tiny restroom before returning for a cup of the conductor's hot, strong coffee. He pulled his shaving kit from his suitcase, but the lack of hot water in the restroom prevented his getting a very good shave. He nicked himself twice, dotting the places with tissue, before returning to his seat to pray and wait.

There was a handsome looking couple across the car from him who must have come in from the sleeper car, and the man bore a strong resemblance to Albert. Charlie tried not to stare, but when the man had eye contact with him, he stood and walked over to where they were seated.

"Forgive my asking, I was wondering if you mightn't be related to a friend of mine. Do you know a young man by the name of Mr. Albert Whittle?"

The two exchanged a surprised glance with each other before

affirming, "We're his parents!" Charlie was elated to meet them, but he did know more than a moment of discomfort when it occurred to him that he was coming down to break up the wedding they were so eagerly traveling down to witness. He spoke kindly to them though, telling of his friendship with Albert, and his respect for him.

"You are his friend Charlie? Oh, it is wonderful to meet you! He has spoken so highly of you. So you know Miss Montague, his bride-to-be?"

Charlie nearly winced as he replied. "Yes, I do. She's...she's a lovely Christian lady." He didn't want to seem rude, but he couldn't bear the questions he knew would follow if he didn't excuse himself. The Whittles smiled and shook his hand though, Mr. Whittle adding in parting that perhaps they could both stay in the same hotel. Charlie went back to his seat feeling every inch a Judas, but praying for the rest of the trip that the Lord would still manage to work this whole situation "together for good".

As the train decelerated signaling its arrival at Monck's Corner, Charlie stood and gathered his things, then offered his assistance to the Whittles. The three were directed to one of the two hotels in town, and Albert had made reservations for his folks. Charlie also took a room, but after throwing his suitcase on the bed and washing his face, he hastened back down the stairs to find a horse and get directions to the Montagues' farm.

✑✐

"Carol, could you please pass the biscuits?" Caleb asked. Albert began to laugh good-naturedly.

"Goodness, Caleb, you are a growing man! Doesn't that make *four* for you?"

Caleb gave his soon to be brother-in-law a crooked grin as he buttered the biscuit carefully. "You're only grousing because you think it means less for *you*!" The whole table laughed at the boys' banter, which had gone on almost non-stop since the three arrived late Saturday evening. After everyone was finished, Mr. Montague kissed his wife, thanking her for the meal, and headed to the fields while the children and Mrs. Montague made short order of the cleanup.

"Hey, Albert, you want to come help me and Poppa in the fields today?" Caleb asked just to be a nuisance, but the hard work appealed to Albert just then. Sitting around the house talking with Celia would be nice, but....

Celia was looking out the kitchen window. "Momma, someone's coming. Were we expecting anyone?"

"My parents are arriving on the afternoon train, I believe; could it be them?" Albert joined her, pushing back the curtain a tad, but seeing the lone man on horseback he knew it wasn't his folks. As the man turned to come down the road toward the house, Albert recognized him. He turned to Carol with a huge grin and stated simply, "It's *Charlie!*"

❧❧

As Charlie brought his horse to a stop, he saw Carol come out the screen door. He tied the buckskin to the hitching post, then walked up the front porch steps to greet her. It occurred to him that Carol hadn't spoken a word; she just stood there waiting patiently as though she had somehow been expecting him. It was more than a little unnerving, but Charlie bent to kiss her outstretched hand before speaking.

"Hello, Carolina."

"Hello, Charlie." She walked over and took a seat in a porch rocker, looking up at him with a curious smile. "Why didn't you tell me you were coming down for the wedding when we talked at Stewart's last week?"

"I...I didn't know myself until yesterday afternoon actually. I need to speak with you about something. Carol, I'm a Christian." Carol stopped rocking and just sat there as though transfixed, then she put her face in her hands, the tears flowing so quickly they fell between her fingers.

Charlie knelt beside her, telling of his salvation experience, even taking the time to thank her for praying. He thought her tears were a bad sign however, that as his mother had said, having made the decision to marry Albert....

He pulled out a handkerchief and handed it to her, and the

smile he saw when she moved her hands encouraged him to go on. "I know why you're here, but won't you please reconsider?"

Smiling but confused, Carol finished drying her tears then asked, "Charlie Bennett, what *are* you talking about?"

Charlie ran frustrated fingers through his hair. "Your marriage! Your marriage to Albert!" to which Carol replied with uncontrollable laughter. Charlie turned, leaning on the porch railing. "I fail to see what is so confounded humorous about *that*."

Unable to allow him even a moment's further anxiety, she rose to stand beside him, answering softly, "Albert will be a bridegroom Friday, Charlie; but *Celia* will be his bride."

Charlie stood motionless, thinking himself in a dream. As he turned to look in Carol's sparkling blue eyes, he asked dumbly, "Not you?"

"*No*, Charlie."

Carol took Charlie's hand, leading him off the porch and out to a large swing beneath a great live oak on the edge of one of her father's fields.

"You're not...not in love with him then? I thought...I mean, when I'd seen you two together..., and then in the jewelers; and then when I heard of the wedding, I naturally presumed...." Carol sat down on the swing, leaving room for him to join her; but his mind was far too active for his body to sit still. "But you're not in love then?"

Her smile broadened as she tilted her head to the side. "Well, now, Charlie, I can't really say that." She reached her hand out to him, but he was a little too far away. "I am very much in love with someone actually. You'll never guess who...."

Charlie turned hope-filled eyes to her, grasping her hand as though it were a life-preserver, and he pressed a hard kiss into her palm. "Please tell me...."

"Actually, he's a...a *new* man.... In a very real sense I only met him today." She stood to her feet then since he would not join her on the swing. "Oh, Charlie, I never lost my love for you. I didn't really *try* to take my love for you from my heart. But there wasn't a day, hardly an hour, that went by that I didn't pray for your salvation." She placed a trembling hand over his heart, and he covered it with his own. "I had to wait until I knew Jesus was in your heart before I would allow myself to tell you again." Her eyes filled with happy tears as she looked up at Charlie. "I love you so."

He pulled her to him and held her close. "Oh, my darling...," he whispered in her ear, then he stepped back so quickly she swayed slightly.

Charlie looked down at his hand and slowly removed the ring from his little finger, where it had resided since her refusal over a year ago. Seeing the ruby in the new setting, tears of joy fill her eyes again as he dropped to one knee. "Ow!" muttered Charlie, connecting with an old acorn; and Carol giggled through her tears as he took her hands in his.

"Carolina Montague, from the day we met you have been in my heart. I love you more than I ever thought possible, and I want to spend the rest of my life with you. Will you be my wife?"

She bent slightly, placing her hand on his cheek, as she answered with all her heart. "I thought you'd never ask! Yes, my love! Oh, *yes*," and he slipped the ring on her finger.

Charlie stood to his feet, ignoring the leaves and grass on his trousers, and just stared at Carol—taking in her hair, her eyes, her gown. "I want to remember just how you look right now." His eyes went to her lips once more, then returned with a question in them to her eyes. "May I?"

"Oh, Charlie, *please* do." Charlie placed his hands on her cheeks and watched as Carol's eyes slid closed. With great control he kissed her lips ever so softly, then drew back to look at her upturned face. When her eyes opened and a sigh escaped her smiling lips, he knew without a doubt that there would never be another woman for him but Carolina Montague.

"When?"

"'When' what?" Carol asked from the haze of joy that had engulfed her.

"When will you be my wife? When can we be married?"

"Oh," she said, then walked over and sat on the swing. This time he joined her, resting one elbow on the back of the swing so he could look at her face.

"I mean, do you need a long engagement to prepare for a formal wedding? Do you wish to be married at our church in

Baltimore?" He touched a curl that had escaped her combs. "Or could we say our vows with your sister and Albert Friday?" He couldn't help but laugh as her eyes grew larger than any he'd ever seen. "Never mind! Never mind, that would be completely unfair. I understand. It takes time to arrange everything—"

"Well, actually as maid of honor I have a beautifully appropriate new gown to wear. We'd have to get the marriage license today though! And what about Albert and Celia? It is *their* special day. I don't think they should be forced to share it."

"But, if we got the license and all, we could have a small ceremony after theirs if your pastor agrees."

"And Poppa...don't forget, you need Poppa's permission!" It was Carol's turn to laugh at Charlie's huge eyes. She looked down at her ring, then glanced at Charlie. "This will make *two* daughters lost in one day instead of one! I mean, you'd better go ask him before we go to town for the license!"

Charlie was suddenly all business as he stood to his feet. "He's probably in the cow pasture," she said, pointing in the general direction. He turned to get his horse, then was back in two strides holding Carol like he'd never let her go. She half expected another kiss, but he had a job to do. Kissing his finger then touching the tip of her nose, Charlie strode to his horse, mounted, and headed out without another word; and Carol made her way to the house. She stopped abruptly on the porch as she saw four faces wreathed in smiles peering out the sitting room window! Caleb, Celia, Albert, and Mrs. Montague came running to the door as she entered, everyone hugging and laughing and crying and talking at once.

"Charlie got *saved*, and he's come all the way down here to ask me to marry him!"

"Praise *God*!"

"Oh, my darling girl! I've never seen you so happy!"

"The *nerve* of that guy, proposin' to my big sister before he ever even *met* the rest of the family!"

"Can we make it a double ceremony?" When those words crossed Celia's lips, the other four turned to stare. "I mean, if that's all right with *you*, Albert."

Albert grinned broadly. "I would like nothing better than to share our wedding day with your sister and my best friend." Celia smiled adoringly at her soon-to-be groom, then turned again to hug her sister. "Besides," Albert continued, "we can spend the rest of our lives reminding each other when our anniversary is coming up!"

"Yeah, and it'll sure save the folks a heap o' trouble marryin' ya both off at once instead of having to do the big shindig a second time! Too bad I don't have a sweetheart—" For that comment Caleb received two sisterly and one motherly swat on his strong, wide back, plus a hearty laugh from Albert.

"Well, I do have several lovely cousins who plan to be here for the wedding...." Then it was Albert's turn to be reprimanded. They all laughed as they turned and walked into the sitting room to discuss the plans. Mrs. Montague went to get cold tea for them all, bringing the tray full of mason jars and a plate of lemon cookies for the crew.

"Charlie is out talking with Poppa right now, but we'll need to head for town to procure a marriage license."

Mrs. Montague smiled at her ever "in charge" daughter who at the most romantic moment in her life was still remembering what needed to be done next. "It's a shame Charlie's parents can't be here. But even if we got a letter in today's post, they couldn't possibly get it in time to come."

"They could if we called them on a telephone in town!" Carol said, her eyes sparkling with joy over seeing Mr. and Mrs. Bennett again.

Just then they heard heavy footfalls on the front porch steps, and all turned as one to look as the front door opened. Mr. Montague came in alone, shut the door, took his hat off, and headed for the stairs. Carol stood to her feet and was inches from the entryway when her mischievous Poppa peeked around the corner with a big grin.

"Charlie's hitchin' up the wagon so you two can go get a license," he said, then hugged his daughter close. "'Course I said 'yes' to that question he asked me first!" He swung her around in a circle, then the two went into the sitting room to join the others.

Charlie wasn't long in hooking up the buggy, then he went in to join the awaiting crowd. There were no seats available; but

Caleb, who had been sitting beside his older sister on a sofa, stood to allow Charlie to sit there. Charlie reached out his hand to Caleb as they exchanged places.

"The name's Charles Bennett. Nice to meet you!" Caleb couldn't even feign a stern face, but gave Charlie a huge smile, a firm handshake, then a hug. Albert came over and joined the two standing there.

"Hello, Charlie—my friend, my brother in Christ, and soon to be my brother-in-law!" The two men hugged, and every heart in the room was touched by the friends' reunion. Mrs. Montague handed Charlie a mason jar of tea and a couple of cookies, then took some to her husband.

"So, what would you think of tying a double knot Friday?" Albert asked, going to stand behind Celia's chair.

"Do you really mean it?" asked Charlie, looking from Albert to Celia; then taking Carol's hand in his he asked, "Would it be all right then?"

"Celia brought it up actually," Albert said, smiling down at her upturned face. "We'd be most honored, Charlie."

Charlie looked down at his bowler hat as he turned it around in his hands. "Here I thought I was coming down here to stop a wedding, and I end up participating!" Everyone turned curious eyes at him as he and Carol laughed. "Well, I thought my best friend had gone and fallen in love with Carol!"

He went on to explain all the times he'd seen them together, then realized that it was usually the *three* of them. Except at the park and then more recently the jewelers, which had been the real clincher for Charlie. But Albert had wanted to surprise Celia, and had gotten Carol to help him choose the perfect ring. "And when I saw Carol at the restaurant Friday night and she mentioned the wedding, I naturally thought...." Charlie turned and looked straight at Carol. "But even that was no accident, for it was that evening that I came to the point of really giving my love for you over to the Lord."

"Oh, Charlie, there are no 'accidents' with God," Mrs. Montague said quietly. "'Incidents', yes, but not 'accidents'. If we go back as far as Mr. Montague's accident two years ago, that is what brought Carol to the point of knowing she needed the

Saviour! And had that 'accident' never taken place, Carol would have never left home."

Mr. Montague spoke up then, "*All things work together for good to them that love God, to them who are the called, according to His purpose.* Your both being at that street at just the right moment...I mean, our Carol is not clumsy or distracted easily. There is no reason why she shouldn't have stood there on the curb while your buggy passed right by. But God allowed all these things to work together for *good*, children." He looked down for a moment before adding, "There are times that things happen that we will never know in this lifetime *why* they took place. But God is faithful. Remember how He used this 'accident', and it could very well help you get through other trials of life with the childlike faith it takes.

"Now, I think Charlie and Carol need to take a trip to town to pick up somethin'. Before you go though, and before all the busyness of the weddings begins, can we take a moment and pray together as a family?" Mr. Montague knelt down beside his chair, and his wife, children, and future sons-in-law followed suite. Mr. Montague prayed first, then each prayed in turn around the room. When it was Charlie's turn, he could barely speak his heart was so full.

"*Dear Father in Heaven, thank You for saving me. Thank You for keeping me, for allowing me to be born to Christian parents and brought up in this great country. Thank You for my Christian friends who never stopped praying for me....*" His voice broke, but he went on, "*And thank You for working things together so that I was blessed with meeting Carolina and her family. Oh, God, You've blessed me more than I could ever ask or think...far more than I ever deserve. I'm so glad that I'm Your child now. Help me to do that which is pleasing in Your sight, and bless each of Your children here. In Jesus' precious name, amen.*"

Chapter Twenty-Two

Arrangements

The men helped the ladies to their feet, then all went around giving hugs and claps on the back until Carol remembered they had an appointment in town. Albert and Celia joined them in the wagon, each couple "chaperoning" the other.

"Oh, great day! Albert, I've been so caught up in the goings on that I neglected to tell you, I arrived on the same train as your parents! They were settling in at the hotel when I rode out. In fact, that's probably them coming there," he said, squinting in the sunlight as he looked down the road.

Albert laughed, adding, "I can't blame you for feeling you were distracted, Charlie!" He began waving his arms, then hopped down from the wagon as his parents' buggy pulled alongside. After hugging them both, he turned to introduce them to his bride-to-be. "Mother, Father, this is Miss Montague! Miss *Celia* Montague," he added, looking out the corner of his eye at Charlie. His parents missed the clarification and exchange as Albert helped Celia down from the wagon to stand alongside him and his parents.

"It's wonderful to finally meet you, Celia!" Mrs. Whittle said, hugging the girl close. Mr. Whittle kissed her cheek as he shook her hand, then looked at his son with a grin.

"She's every bit as lovely as you described in your letters, Son." Looking up at Charlie, he went on, "And we met your friend Charlie on the train, and this young lady must be Celia's sister. It's good to meet you," he said, tipping his hat.

Carol was the first to realize that the Whittles probably wished to go with Albert and Celia to meet her parents; but she also knew they needed to get their marriage license, and the two had been their chaperones.

After hearing their dilemma Mr. Whittle put in, "I don't think that should be a problem. You're going to town, then returning home in an open wagon? You should be okay. Just be sure to get back in time for supper!" Albert and his father helped Celia and Mrs. Whittle into their buggy, then the four headed back toward the farm.

Carol took Charlie's offered arm; then adjusting her parasol, they continued toward town at a leisurely pace.

"I can't believe this is happening," Charlie said, his voice still reflecting his wonder. "I never even *prayed* that we'd be able to marry so soon."

"Like the verse in Ephesians says, God has truly blessed us above all we asked or thought! But we've waited a long time in one way since we've known for over a year that we were meant for each other. Hypothetically speaking...."

Looking down into his fiancé's smiling face, Charlie bent over and kissed Carol hard on the lips. *"Charlie!"*

"It's no longer 'hypothetical', my love. You will be mine to have and to hold from Friday through the rest of our lives!" He grinned as his focus went back to the road. "Sorry I had to kiss you so suddenly. There have just been so many times I've wanted to do that, and now that I had the right—"

"Well, you're not quite *licensed* yet, don't forget!" Carol replied with a rather flustered half-grin.

Charlie laughed. "No, not yet! But we're about to rectify *that* problem as well!" He clicked at the horse to pick up the pace, eager to get the license taken care of and have something to eat.

"Carolina, I love you. And it was you who brought me to the place of realizing my need for Christ. I do believe my life is pretty much complete! I do want to know what His will is for us though...not just marriage, but beyond that. Where should we live? Is my position at the bank His perfect will? How soon should we begin adoption proceedings?"

"I think I'd like to be a bit selfish and have you to myself a while before we bring children into our home." Carol's smile turned thoughtful as she asked, "And are you completely certain you *can't* father children? What if Doctor Whittle was wrong about that?"

Charlie looked down at Carol lovingly. "We shall just pray that he was." After a brief pause he added, "And speaking of Dr. Whittle...he *knew* Celia was marrying Albert!"

"Of course he did, but...?"

"He tricked me into coming down here, presumably to break your engagement to Albert! Bless his heart. I will thank him profusely when I see him next! Oh, but he will be here for the wedding, will he not?"

"Yes, of course! He arrives Thursday if I'm not mistaken. So he's the one who sent you down after me? What a dear soul!" The two sat thinking of the whiskered matchmaker a moment longer before Carol spoke again. "Charlie, can we call your parents so that they know of the wedding? I don't know if they could make it down, but they should at the very least be invited."

"What a wonderful idea! If I remember correctly there was a telephone in the lobby of my hotel. We can ring them from there." Thinking of appearances, Charlie quickly changed his plan. "No, I shall call them when I return to town this evening. It would not be best for your reputation to be anywhere near that hotel with me."

The grip on his arm tightened as she said softly, "I'm so glad you thought of that, Charlie. Thank you."

"You're welcome," he replied soberly. After a moment of companionable silence, he asked, "Where shall we go on our honeymoon when I *am* licensed?" As was his goal, her cheeks turned red again, then he added with a little more seriousness, "Or shall we just head back to Baltimore? Actually, I was supposed to be baptized Sunday."

"Oh, Charlie, how wonderful! Do you think we could head back to Baltimore for that, then honeymoon 'officially' at another time?"

"If you mean spend our wedding night in a Pullman car, no, definitely not!" He turned to look at his fiancé, though due to the ever growing traffic on the road he could only caress her with his eyes. "I shall arrange to take a room in the other hotel...see if they have a honeymoon suite. Don't mention where we will be staying to anyone though. I don't trust that brother of yours not to kidnap you and hold you for ransom."

"Oh, dear! Don't even mention such a thing, because Caleb would be apt to try it! He'd say the ransom was for a good cause though, I'm sure." The two laughed, then pulled up in front of the courthouse. After filling out the necessary paperwork, they headed to the church and the pastor's study, knocking on the outer door. They were admitted by his wife, who served as secretary.

"Carol! Hello! It's good to see you, dear. And who would this gentleman be?"

"This is Mr. Charles Bennett, Miss Gloria," adding with a blush, "my fiancé!" Miss Gloria beamed at the two before escorting them to her husband's office door. She knocked quietly, then peeked in.

"Honey, it's Miss *Carol* Montague and *her fiancé* to see you." Knowing what his reaction would be, she stepped aside to allow the two to enter, then closed the door behind them.

Pastor Crosby stood, leaning over his desk to shake hands with the two of them. He sat down, staring at them with a look of amazement.

"Well, Carol, leave it to you to surprise everyone like this! Can you please tell me a bit of what happened...how this came about so suddenly?" The two looked at one another, but Charlie told the story, wanting the pastor to get to know him. He also went on with his personal testimony, then concluded with his proposal and Celia and Albert's suggestion of a double ceremony.

"Do you think that would be acceptable, sir?"

Pastor remained silent as he rubbed his clean-shaven chin thoughtfully, but a teasing grin was already peeking out. "The only thing that ever prevents me from performing a marriage ceremony is if one or both of the parties are unsaved or living like they are, Mr. Bennett. As you have clearly shared with me that you are a child of God, and I already know Carol's testimony, I would be most honored to preside over your marriage ceremony."

He went over the schedule Celia and Albert had agreed upon when they spoke with him Sunday afternoon, then prayed with them before they rose to leave.

"Pastor, would you and Miss Gloria care to join us for lunch?" Carol asked before leaving.

"Oh, no, Carol. We've already eaten. Thank you for the invite, though! You have a place in mind?"

Carol grinned up at Charlie. "Actually, I was going to take him to Pete's Fish House. They're still in business, yes?"

"Yes, indeed! God bless you both, and I'll see you Wednesday night."

They were out in the sunshine again before Charlie asked, "Wednesday night? I thought the wedding wasn't until Friday?"

"Oh, it is. Pastor was referring to the prayer meeting we have on Wednesday evenings. It's really a family time, bringing our burdens and blessings and requests before the Lord. Pastor gives a brief challenge, too. Kind of a condensed version of Sunday services. I've missed it in the city."

"It sounds like a good idea, though I don't suppose it would attract those who don't know the Lord in the first place. Sunday is more than enough for them! Ask me, I know." He smiled as Carol directed him to the restaurant. "You know, yesterday was the first Sunday that I actually was glad to be in church. I'd missed it by skipping out all that time I was in rebellion, but it was more than that. Every hymn, every verse...they came alive for me, Carol! It was amazing."

"You forget, I was a lost church-goer myself, Charlie. I know those same feelings. It is amazing, isn't it?"

The two walked into the cool shade of the restaurant, sitting at a wooden booth with a kerosene lamp on the table. "Not exactly Stewart's, I know!" Charlie reached his hand across the table, taking hers in his tender hold. "But I'd rather sit by an open fire with you than endure another meal at Stewart's with Miss Vanderhuff!" He went on to tell of the evening, Carol shaking her head and laughing at intervals.

"You'll never know how distressed I was when I realized you were there with her. I don't know her personally, but I was afraid—"

"That I'd taken leave of my senses?"

"No!" Carol laughed, "No, but that perhaps you were dating her. How was I to know that you were there on 'business'? And you looked so incredibly handsome in your tuxedo."

"You noticed!" She slapped his hand playfully before he added, "And you in your taffeta gown with your mother's pin and my bracelet for adornment. You were breathtaking, Carol. Heartbreakingly beautiful."

The waiter came for their order then, and the two enjoyed the rest of the meal talking of her hometown and some of its other charming features. When they left the restaurant they decided to walk up and down main street looking at the half dozen shops a bit, and Carol spotted something in one of the store windows that drew her attention.

"May I step in here? I'll only be a moment." Charlie stayed outside when he saw from the window display that she had entered a ladies' clothier. He waited patiently until Carol came out with a hatbox in her arms and a smile on her face.

"I had the dress, new gloves, and shoes since I was in the wedding anyhow. I just found the most darling hat to wear, with a long, lovely veil!"

Charlie shook his head. "I wouldn't have cared if you'd have chosen to wear a snood." Seeing her look of disappointment, he added affectionately, "But I will just have to wait to see your hair down again *after* the ceremony." This brought the pink back to her cheeks and the smile to her lips.

Charlie helped Carol into the wagon, placing her hatbox behind them. She opened her parasol, and the two made their way back home.

Chapter Twenty-Three

The Montague Farm

Charlie enjoyed the camaraderie between the family members of the Montague household. Carol's mother reminded him of his own mother in many ways, yet in appearance she was almost her perfect opposite. She was somewhat shorter than Carol, more like Celia; and her coloring was high contrast with her dark brown hair streaked with white at the temples. She was almost gaunt, yet she had deep dimples when she smiled, which was often.

Mr. Montague, like Carol and Caleb, tended to look mischievous with his large eyes and ready smile. His hair was parted down the middle like Charlie's own, and he sported a well-groomed mustache. Mr. and Mrs. Montague both seemed to be quiet, though in fact they were only enjoying watching their children and their soon-to-be children by marriage interact. But being part of this family gathering made Charlie long to call his own parents, that they might join him. After all, he was all they had left, and he really believed that they needed to be there for such a momentous occasion.

After dinner and cleanup, the group in its entirety decided to go for a sunset stroll in the orchard. Caleb changed his mind as the group paired off so quickly, heading for the barn to do some chores.

Mr. and Mrs. Montague walked beside Carol and Charlie as they skirted the edge of the trees, while the Whittles walked down one of the rows between the trees. Mr. Montague spoke first.

"Charlie, I don't know you very well, but it would be my guess that you've been rather quiet this evening." Not wanting to put him on the spot, he turned to his daughter and asked, "Am I right, dear?"

"Yes, Poppa. You don't think we've overwhelmed him with our family banter, do you?"

Charlie grinned, patting her hand at the crook of his arm. "You can't frighten me off that easily!" The four laughed before he went on. "No, I was just thinking of my parents...how much they would enjoy being here."

Mrs. Montague's voice was filled with sympathy as she joined in. "Of course, Charlie. And you are their only child. Did the two of you call while you were in town today? Are they going to be able to come?"

"Actually, no, we didn't call yet. Charlie was going to call when he got in this evening." She looked up into his face, seeing from his expression as he looked at the sunset sky that he needed to contact them right away. "Charlie, why don't you head back to town and call. I know that you need to talk to them, and you doubtless need your rest as well. You couldn't have gotten a very good night's sleep on the train."

The excitement of the day and the discomfort of the previous night caught up with him in a moment, and he stifled a yawn, then chuckled as Mrs. Montague said, "If you think you can make it back without falling out of the saddle!"

"I should be good for the trip back to town, but I do think it would be wise for me to call it an evening." He reached out and shook Mr. Montague's hand firmly, then bent to kiss Mrs. Montague on the cheek.

"I'll walk you back to get your horse," Carol added, telling her parents, "I'll join you all in a few minutes in the sitting room?"

"Yes, dear. Have a good evening, Mr. Bennett."

"Yes, goodnight, Charlie!" Mr. Montague was already quite fond of Charlie, perhaps because of all the prayer that had gone up on the young man's behalf. As he and his wife walked hand in hand several paces behind Charlie and Carol, he brought his wife's hand up for a kiss. "We've been so blessed, Emily. So very blessed." The two continued on praising the Lord together for all He had done in their family.

When Charlie and Carol reached the barn, they found that Caleb had already saddled up Charlie's horse. "I'm not sayin' 'here's yer hat, what's yer hurry?' I just thought you might not want to mess with saddlin' him up if it got to be late." Charlie couldn't help but smile as he clapped the younger man on the shoulder.

"I didn't take it wrongly in the least. I *would* take it wrongly though if you saddle him up for me Friday...after the wedding!" The three of them laughed. "I'll need a *two-seater* then, Caleb. Thank you for this. It was thoughtful. Have a good evening."

"Yeah, I'll be wishin' you the same. Reckon I'll have to see your face first light tomorrow, too, though, hunh?"

Carol and Charlie both looked over their shoulder at Caleb, their faces so similar in their raised-eyebrow expression that Caleb had to laugh. "Goodnight!"

The last glow of sunset was almost gone and the moon was giving her reflected light as they walked Charlie's horse to the front of the house. They could see Mr. and Mrs. Montague through the sitting room windows, lighting extra lamps for the group that would be making its way in shortly.

Charlie turned to Carol in the moonlit darkness, then looked up at the stars. He took her hand in his before he spoke. "I can't believe today actually happened, Carolina. I keep expecting to awaken on the train—"

"Oh, Charlie," Carol let go of his hand and put her arm around his back as he stood there beside her. "If you do wake up and find it was all a dream, just remember that I love you. When you come to declare yourself, I'll say 'yes' again and again!" He pulled her close, nestling his face in the softness of her hair.

"Thank you for that. And thank the Lord for His obvious blessing on us."

Carol looked up at him as he moved to leave. "Could I have a kiss on the cheek?"

Even in the moonlight he could see the mischievous smile she had on her face, and his mind went back to the Christmas after they first met. "Do you trust me?"

"Well, I win either way!" she said with such an adorable cockiness in her voice that Charlie hugged her close with his free arm and kissed her soundly on the cheek.

"Goodnight, Miss Montague! Pleasant dreams!" With the reins still in his hand he took hold of the saddle horn and mounted his horse, smiling down at her as she held her hand to her cheek. "I love you!"

Carol hugged herself in the darkness, still grinning until the sound of Charlie's galloping horse faded in the distance. Caleb found her on his way back to the house, teasing, "If anyone had ever told me my level-headed big sister would go plum silly for a fella one day, I'd of never believed it!" Then he offered her his arm, the two entering the brightly lit house together.

෴

Charlie returned the horse to the stable, then inquired about using the buckskin the rest of the week. He headed for the second hotel in town then to make the reservation for Friday evening. They didn't have a special honeymoon suite, but the manager took him to show him one of the rooms, and it was quite attractively decorated. Charlie requested a few extras, then put down a deposit, securing the room. When he reached his own hotel, he went directly to the telephone booth in the lobby.

Charlie was pleased that the 'phone was picked up right away, but disappointed that it was Lucas and not his mother or father. "Where are they, Lucas?"

Mr. and Mrs. Bennett had informed the servants of the situation, and Lucas found it infernally difficult not to give his congratulations. "Oh, they's at a dinnah party. They be home 'bout ten or 'leven, I 'magine."

As dearly as he loved this man who had been a part of his family since before he was born, Charlie didn't think it right to leave a message about his forthcoming marriage. With a slightly heavy heart he answered, "Oh. Well, could you tell them I called and really need to get in touch with them? It's very important." He gave Lucas the number for the hotel telephone in the lobby, then added, "and I'm sure someone would get the message to me. Otherwise, I'll be calling tomorrow morning before Father leaves for work."

"That sounds fine, Mr. Charles, just fine. I'll tell 'em. Mhmm, goodnight!"

"Goodnight, Lucas, and thank you." He put down the receiver and walked out of the booth, another person stepping in right behind him. Walking upstairs to his room, he went about his evening routine, ending with what was fast becoming a new part of his routine: kneeling beside his bed in prayer.

"Father, please work things together that my parents can come to Carolina's and my wedding. I do not have peace about their not being present. I wish to honor my parents who have sought to honor You all their lives. Please help me contact them if it be Your will. In Jesus' name, amen." Charlie climbed into bed then and was asleep before he had time to worry.

✌︎

Charlie's ride to the Montague farm Tuesday morning was with a heavy heart. He had tried again to contact his parents by telephone, but met with disappointment as he had accidentally slept late. Usually Mrs. Bennett hadn't left the house before nine, but a very monotone sounding Jessie had stated that his mother had just left to go shopping. Charlie debated calling his father at the office, but decided to wait until the evening once again.

It was a very easy ride from town to the farm once Charlie gave his concerns to the Lord. He heard a church bell and men's voices singing in beautiful harmony at one point, and a little while later he rode by a simple sign stating that it was the entrance to a monastery. He enjoyed the occasional shade as the live oaks made a canopy over the road. When he came out of the last patch of coolness, he encouraged his horse to a comfortable gallop the rest of the way. Even so, he didn't arrive at the farm until nearly ten o'clock.

"Oh, good, here he comes!" Celia had been sitting on the porch with Carol as she waited, and they were both becoming anxious. She stood, giving Carol some privacy in her morning greeting of her fiancé as she walked in the house and let the group know of Charlie's arrival.

Charlie threw his right leg over the saddle and slid to the ground, then walked up on the porch where Carol stood. He held his hat in his hand as he made his apology.

"I'm so sorry, I overslept. But better late than—" She stopped him mid-sentence with a huge hug, then blushing despite herself, she took his hand as they took the buckskin to the barn.

"Well, maybe I'm not so sorry if I get *that* kind of reward for my tardiness!" He laughed, then apologized again. "I never got to talk with my parents, Carol. I tried last night and again this morning." The coolness of the barn and the sweet smell of hay and oats filled the silence as they both tried to think what to do.

"When is the very latest they could be told and still make it in time? Thursday?" Charlie nodded. "But it's only Tuesday, Charlie. Still, I'll make it a matter of prayer."

She watched him remove the saddle and bridle and toss in some hay, then after she carried over a bucket of water the two sat down on a rough-hewn bench to talk. "Charlie, do you think... that is, if we can't get hold of them, I really think we should postpone the wedding. You're thinking that, too. I can tell by your eyes."

He looked down at their hands, their fingers entwined. "I'm their only child, Carol. It just—"

"Wouldn't be right. I know." She looked down at her ruby ring, then turned a beautiful, smiling face to Charlie. "I'm willing to wait, Charlie. I am. I know we've waited almost a year and a half—"

"One year, four months, and...."

She began to laugh but found Charlie's face very near her own. Placing her hand behind his neck, she gently pulled him forward for a kiss. He kept a tight rein on his emotions, loving that she had initiated this very welcomed kiss. His heart was racing when she pulled away, and he saw that she was surprised by her own depth of feeling. "Thank you for that, Carolina. But we need to go join the others."

With a breathless voice that matched his own, she consented. They stood, still hand in hand, and walked back to the house.

Caleb came forward first, grinning as he took Charlie's hat. "Welcome back," he said, then handed him something.

"What's this? A hat? I have a hat!" Charlie grimaced as he saw Caleb's expression. "That bad, hunh?"

"Well, old man, let's just say...yes! That bad!" Caleb took the narrow-brimmed cowboy hat from Charlie, put it on his brother-in-law-to-be, and molded the brim a bit. "There! What do you think?"

"I think if you're happier with it, I'm happy!" Charlie took the hat off, hanging it carefully on the hat rack with the six or seven others that hung there. "Your sister never said anything about my bowler hat...?"

Carol smiled innocently up at him, little lights of mischief dancing in her eyes. "No, I never did, did I?"

"Well, before you hurt my feelings, let's go in and talk with everyone!" The three of them made their way to the kitchen table where the majority of the family was talking. Albert stood and shook Charlie's hand as he came in, then smiled a knowing smile.

"He gave it to you, hunh?"

"'Fraid so."

Albert laughed. "Don't feel bad. He got me one, too."

The whole group laughed as Charlie, Carol, Caleb, and Albert took a seat, then Charlie asked, "Where are the fathers?"

Caleb answered, "Poppa and Mr. Whittle were out surveying the fields. Momma, Mrs. Whittle, and Celia have been making baked goods since before sun up—bread and pound cake from the smell of it. I've been quizzing Albert for the last hour or so, and now I guess I can start in on you!"

"Ask away! I've nothing to hide." Caleb actually wanted to know the men's testimonies, how they had met his sisters, how they knew one another. He wasn't being the nuisance he made out like he was being, and Charlie greatly appreciated that Caleb wanted to know his brothers-in-law better.

After he'd finished his line of questioning, he smiled diffidently. "'Sorry I was so inquisitive. It's just that, I never had a brother, and now to get two in one week...I'm just really enjoying this." He shared his testimony then, having been saved at church as a seven year old boy, the same day as Celia in fact.

Charlie smiled. "I never had a brother either, Caleb. You have an older brother though, don't you, Albert?"

"I sure do! He's married and living up in Philadelphia with his wife and their two children."

"I envy you both your testimonies, Brothers. If I had been saved as a young boy as each of you were, I'd have never gone through the past year. Carol and I could have been celebrating our first anniversary soon! I had every intention of proposing at the Dye House Picnic, and instead I went home—"

Carol, who had stood during the conversation and gone to help the other ladies, went to stand across the table from Charlie. "Oh, please let's not think about that. The Lord has brought us together now. The Lord drew you to Himself. I'm content with that...more than content."

"Of course, forgive me. I suppose...no, I *know* that the Lord used that rejection to eventually bring me to the point of salvation." He looked at his two new brothers. "Well, shall we go see if the fathers need us to give them a hand?"

Mrs. Montague turned, wiping her brow with the back of her hand. "Actually, it's goin' on lunch time. When you find them, could you bring them back to the house to wash up for lunch?"

"Yes, ma'am. I'd be glad to." The three young men exited through the back door, and the girls wiped off the table and began setting it for lunch.

Mrs. Whittle's heart was touched by the conversation she'd just heard from the boys. "Do you realize how blessed we are, Emily, to have three such boys in our families now? God has been so good to us, hasn't He."

"Momma," Celia asked sweetly, "would you mind telling Mrs. Whittle about you and Poppa's story? I've always loved hearing that."

Mrs. Montague went on to describe her childhood a little, then the young man she'd met in secondary school. He had gone off to war, barely old enough but eager to enlist when the War Between the States broke out. "He asked me to wait for him... said he knew he'd be back, that the Lord had given him a peace about it. I often wonder how many 'close calls' the Lord protected my William from to bring him home in one piece. But

He did, and we married the week he got back. Times were more than difficult...for everyone; but the Lord blessed us with good crops, then with our Carolina, Caleb, and Celia."

At some point during Mrs. Montague's story, Mrs. Whittle's hands grew still; and as the story drew to a close her eyes filled with tears. "What is it, Mary?"

She pulled a handkerchief from her pocket before sitting down and sharing, the other three ladies seating themselves to hear the story as well. "It's just that...my Lawrence was in the War...fighting for the Union. Our men could have faced each other in battle, Emily! And Albert was born after the war, though our oldest came just before it began. God protected both of our husbands. Our children, marrying this Friday, would have never been born had God not protected William and Lawrence."

This realization amazed them all, and they reached out to one another, holding hands as the precious mothers prayed a sweet prayer of thanksgiving and rededication of their beloved children.

Chapter Twenty-Four

Honoring Parents

The Bennett House
Baltimore, Maryland

"What do you think?" Mrs. Bennett stepped aside so her husband could inspect her handiwork. She had arranged Charlie's furniture a trifle differently, adding a matching wardrobe for Carol's things and a bedside stand and lamp for the other side of the bed. There were at least three vases ready for flowers, but other than the essentials the room was undecorated. Mr. Bennett nodded his approval.

"Well, I'm not sure how you managed to keep from adding quilts and hooked rugs and doilies, but I'm proud of you. It looks perfect. Now, are you packed and ready to go? The train leaves in an hour and a half."

"Oh, yes! I do believe I have packed that bag over and over again in my mind over the past day and a half. I'm so excited I can hardly stand it!" As they walked hand in hand to their rooms to finish their preparations for the trip she asked, "But are you sure we shouldn't call Charlie and let him know we're coming?"

"It'll be good for him to be surprised for a change." He laughed. "I don't know how he didn't trick Jessie into saying something this morning. She told me when I got home at noon that he'd called again. I'm glad she didn't have to lie to keep our plans a secret."

"I don't think she could have, so the Lord worked that out for us all." Throwing a few last things in their bags, they went to the door, hugging and shaking hands with the servants on the way out. "We should be back Saturday morning, and if Charlie still wants to be baptized Sunday, they'll be home Saturday night! Goodbye!"

Jessie stood in the doorway after everyone else had gone back to their duties. "They're comin' home, Lord! They're comin' *home*!"

⚜

"I'm going home, Carol. We'll probably have to postpone our wedding. I'm so sorry."

After another unsuccessful call to his home Wednesday morning, Charlie had ridden posthaste to the farm to tell Carol. Caleb hitched up the wagon, then he, Albert and Celia, and Carol all went back to see Charlie off on the morning train. Hardly a word could be spoken on the trip back into town, and it was a slightly bruised and very dusty group that stood on the platform watching the southbound train pulling in.

"I got my ticket. The train heading north from Charleston will be here within the hour. If all goes well, we may make it back here in time. I don't see how, but maybe we can all come back on the train tomorrow." Putting his ticket into his billfold, he started when Carol cried out.

"Charlie, *look*!" Charlie turned just in time to be caught in a huge bear hug from his father and mother.

⚜

After changing his ticket over to tickets for two to Charleston Friday, then from Charleston to Baltimore Saturday, Charlie walked back over to the excited group. Carol and his mother were still arm in arm, sparkling tears of joy still glistening on both dear ones' cheeks.

Charlie took Albert aside while the others were talking. "Do you have a place to stay for the first night of your honeymoon, Albert? I'd made reservations at the Crescent, but I've changed my mind...'heading down to Charleston since the wedding is in the morning. What do you think? Shall I change the room I have reserved to your name?"

"Actually, that sounds great, Charlie! Thanks!"

The group walked *en masse* to the hotel where Charlie had a room, checking his parents in and letting them rest a while and freshen up after their overnight trip. Carol hugged both parents close before giving them directions and telling them goodbye, already eager to see them again out at the farm.

The wagon ride back to the farm was a much more pleasant, slow-paced one. Caleb drove while the four lovebirds sat in the back with some tarps and feed sacks for cushions, the buckskin tethered to the rear of the wagon.

"I'm so glad you didn't have to go home, Charlie," Celia said amiably.

"Not half so glad as I am, dear sister!" Carol added, reaching out for Charlie's hand. Charlie told them he had felt so many different extremes of emotion over the past week that he felt he could eat a table-full and sleep until the wedding!

All four of them laughed, and laughed all the harder when Caleb added, "Now you know how I feel every day of my life!"

When they pulled in at the farm, Mrs. Montague and Mrs. Whittle were on the front porch. Both jumped to their feet, Mrs. Montague letting out a joyful holler when she caught sight of Charlie. "Praise the Lord!" was all she would say over and over again, so thankful for the many ways the Lord had intervened on her oldest daughter's and son-in-law's behalf.

Suddenly she stopped praising long enough to say, "Caleb, go dress me another chicken! We don't have enough for eleven mouths...'specially since one of 'em's yours!" Caleb laughed all the way to the chicken coop. "Anyone thirsty?" she asked, leading the way indoors to enjoy mason jars filled with strawberry lemonade.

Carol and Charlie were holding hands on the settee hours later when most of the household was napping or rocking on the front porch. "Carolina, I have something...." He reached into his pocket and pulled out something small and shiny. "I had it made from the old setting from Grandfather's ring. I thought we might could use it for my wedding band."

"It's beautiful, Charlie! So simple and perfect. Yes, I think that's a lovely idea. Does it fit?" She placed it on his finger easily, then took it back off, putting it temporarily on her thumb.

"They matched the size of the original ring. It's funny," he added thoughtfully, "all those months I kept it in my bedside stand. I never forgot about it, though it's amazing to me that I had the forethought to bring it when I left Sunday. Either 'forethought' or 'presumption', I'm not sure which!"

Carol looked down at her left hand, her ring on her third finger and Charlie's gold band on her thumb. "I would call it 'faith' I think, Charles." She looked up at him with such admiration in her eyes that Charlie reached out to kiss her cheek. She moved, catching him full on the lips in a lingering, sweet kiss. Charlie couldn't help but chuckle at her smug look, as she folded her hands in her lap and started talking again. She forgot what she was saying though when she heard the Bennetts' carriage pull up out front.

Charlie and Carol both helped with the introductions. Having both seen Carol's family photograph she had in her room when she stayed with them, Mr. and Mrs. Bennett only felt like they were 'meeting' Albert's parents.

"That's good though," Albert replied. "We've got about thirty aunts, uncles, and cousins coming in tomorrow!" The whole group laughed before Albert added, "And, Carol, Meredith and her family are coming."

"Oh, I'm so excited to see her again! I don't believe I've seen her since last Christmas, do you know it? When your grandfather had Celia and I over for the family Christmas festivities. That was so thoughtful."

The group walked around the homestead. Mr. and Mrs. Whittle and Albert and Celia politely left the group after a while and returned to the house, giving the four parents time to get to know one another better.

Mrs. Bennett and Carol were arm in arm again when Mrs. Bennett took something out of her tapestry purse. Unwrapping it, she revealed two handsomely ornate sterling silver tussie mussies. "I thought they could hold your and Celia's wedding bouquets,"

Mrs. Bennett said with quiet excitement. "I wish I could have brought fresh flowers from my garden, but they'd never have withstood the trip."

Carol hugged her soon-to-be mother-in-law's arm close. "I shall just have to wait and see your beautiful flowers when we come to visit!" This brought the roses to her cheeks, but they came to full bloom when Mrs. Bennett added for Charlie's hearing also that they had his rooms prepared.

"If that is what the two of you still want, that is...?" Carol looked up at Charlie, who was walking at her other side. He nodded his consent, then Carol stopped the procession to hug his mother close. Charlie mouthed his sincere thanks as his mother looked over Carol's shoulder in her embrace. "I'm really being selfish, wanting to keep the two of you close for as long as I can!"

Mrs. Montague joined in, arm in arm with Caleb. "Hopefully Caleb will bring home a bride someday! The upstairs will seem half-empty until he does. Not saying," she added with a chuckle, "that I want it to be real soon, mind you, Son!"

"I know, Momma. I know!"

The group went in and had an early supper of roast chicken, spring peas, mashed potatoes, and biscuits, washing it all down with mason jars of Mrs. Montague's delicious iced tea. Albert, Celia, and Caleb sat at a make-shift table in the sitting room to give the group of eight more room at the main table.

Mr. Bennett ate his fill, then wiping his mouth and patting his stomach turned to his son with a grin. "I think we'd better keep Carol out of the kitchen if she cooks anything like her Momma. Otherwise, we'll all be buying larger-sized wardrobes in a matter of months!"

Mrs. Montague smiled sweetly, then stood. "Actually, one of my wedding gifts for each of the girls is a recipe file with some of our family recipes. It's a good thing I had them ready for their hope chests a long time ago, or Carolina would have been short-changed! Mary, if you have any you'd like to add, or you, Laura...?" She handed each of them some blank recipe cards, then handed Carol her recipe file, receiving a kiss of thanks in return. "I'm so glad you and Celia will both be living in Baltimore. It will be so much easier an adjustment for you that way."

Mrs. Bennett smiled, replying, "And easier for *me*! Though I do believe when they have their first argument, we'll be apt to side with Carol!" Everyone laughed again, even Charlie.

"Thank you for the warning, Mother!" He laughed some more, drawing her hand up for a kiss. "Now, on a more serious note, don't we need to be getting back into town for church tonight?" At that reminder, the family rose as one to make short order of the cleanup.

Mr. and Mrs. Bennett offered Carol and Charlie a ride, and Celia and Albert rode with his parents. The Montagues, Caleb driving, were not far behind. They went to the hotel first to freshen up and get their Bibles. Carol and Celia waited in the lobby, looking around the large room.

"Where are you two going on your honeymoon, Carol?" Unable to prevent a blush, Carol told her of their plans to go to Charleston for their wedding night, then head home Saturday for Charlie's baptism Sunday. "Oh, I do wish Albert and I could be there for his baptism!"

"Has Albert told you of his plans?"

"Yes, and actually, he made the mistake of telling me over dinner...in front of Caleb! He told me that Charlie had given him his reservation for the Crescent. The look on Caleb's face told Albert immediately of his mistake, but then he calmly told Caleb 'what goes around comes around, Brother! Just remember, you'll be the bridegroom one day!' That seemed to squelch Caleb's schemes." Both sisters laughed, but they were still more than a tad concerned that Caleb might still try something.

The Bennetts then the Whittles came down to the lobby, and the group walked over to the church where the girls' brother and parents were already seated.

Chapter Twenty-Five

Justified

"Open your Bibles if you would to Romans chapter four. Let's stand together and read verse twenty-five.

"*Who was delivered for our offences*—that's talking about the Lord Jesus Christ, of course. *Who was delivered for our offences, and was raised again for our justification.*

"Now go on to the beginning of chapter five. *Therefore being justified by faith, we have peace with God through our Lord Jesus Christ: By Whom also we have access by faith into this grace wherein we stand, and rejoice in hope of the glory of God.* Now, read it again. *Who was delivered for our offences....*

"Jesus Christ was delivered for our offences, and was raised again for our justification. *Therefore being justified by faith, we have peace with God through our Lord Jesus Christ.*

"Let's pray. *Father, help us tonight as we look into these Scriptures for a few moments. Teach us and lead us into Thy truth. We'll thank You and praise You, in Jesus' name, amen.*

"Thank you, you may be seated.

"I preach on this quite a bit, but I'm gonna do it again tonight. Justification. Justification means 'remission of sins and absolution from guilt and punishment, or an act of free grace by which God pardons the sinner and accepts him as righteous on account of the atonement of Jesus Christ'. To justify means 'to pardon and clear from guilt, to absolve or acquit from guilt and merited punishment'. I wish you'd get that in your mind, it's *merited* punishment. That means we deserve it. 'And accept as righteous on account of the merits of the Saviour or by the application of Christ's atonement to the offender.'

"Justified. What does it mean to be justified? It's a legal term and means that 'God declares men to be made righteous'...to be *made* righteous. Look in Romans four with me, verses five and six. *But to him that worketh not, but believeth on Him that justifieth the ungodly, his faith is counted for righteousness. Even as David also describeth the blessedness of the man, unto whom God imputeth righteousness without works.....*

"The Bible says in II Corinthians 5:21, *For He hath made Him to be sin for us*—talking about Jesus Christ—*Who knew no sin; that we might be made the righteousness of God in Him.* God justifies us *freely*; we're made righteous. We're not righteous of ourselves, but we're *made* righteous, hallelujah! We're wicked and undeserving and defiled, corrupted. And we deserve the worst. And yet God justifies us by the free merit of His grace through the Lord Jesus Christ.

"If you could just see this, you'd be shoutin' hallelujah! There you are or there I am, standing in my sin, degraded before God, and all my righteousness as filthy rags. I'm standing before God a beggar, dirty, defiled, unkempt, unclean, headed strait out into the devil's hell, what I deserve! And God Almighty looks at me...and there's His darling Son, standin' there in my place—pure, undefiled, holy. He's all that I need to be, and I'm all that I ought not to be. And God says, 'If you place your faith in My Son, I'm gonna take Him and put His righteousness on you. You're gonna be *just like* My Son Jesus Christ. I'm gonna make you righteous.'

"Now you say, 'Preacher, I don't deserve that!' Well, I don't either! None of us deserves that, we didn't work for it.

"Look at the Scriptures again.... *For him that worketh not, but believeth on Him that justifieth the ungodly, his faith is counted for righteousness.* God can declare us justified when we by faith trust Him through His Son, because Christ has met the debt of our sin and has totally satisfied God the Father.

"I John 2:2 says, *And He is the propitiation for our sins: and not for ours only, but also for the sins of the whole world.* Jesus

Christ is the propitiation...that's a big word. It simply means 'Jesus Christ met the just demands of the Law'. God is satisfied with His death on Calvary. God said the debt's been paid in full. Every sinner that comes to Jesus Christ and places his faith in His atoning work, God said, hallelujah, 'I'm gonna make you righteous; I'm gonna *justify* you!'

"Oh my! Don't you see? I'm tellin' you right now...better loose this tie a bit. I'm a firm believer in the fact that some folk don't know what I'm talkin' about, because if they did, they'd be shoutin' the victory! Folks, *we've been made righteous*! We've been justified by the Christ of Calvary! Not because we deserve it, but because God has done that for us!

"Why should we enter into His gates with thanksgiving? Why should we come into the house of God with praise? Why should we give God the glory? Why should we always be lifting our hands and our heart and our voice to God, singing His praise? Because, *thank God*, He's justified us when we deserve hell!

"God has declared us righteous! You say, 'Preacher, do you think anything's been brought up by the devil before God about you?' Well I'm gonna tell you somethin', Brother William Montague, what do you reckon the devil's gonna say to God Almighty about God the Son? He ain't got *nothin'* to say about Him, has he? He can't say anything about God the Son because He's pure and holy and undefiled; and I tell you that because of the justification of God Almighty, I stand right there with Him! And *you* stand right there with Him, and *you* stand right there with Him, because God has made us justified through salvation!

"Next I want us to look at the *need* for justification. Why would a person need to be justified? Well, look at Romans chapter five and verse six and you'll see the first reason. The reason I need to be justified is because I was ungodly!

"*For when we were yet without strength, in due time Christ died for the ungodly.* We needed to be justified because we were ungodly. Second, because it says we were yet without strength. And then we need to be justified because down in verse eight it says *But God commendeth his love toward us, in that, while we were yet sinners, Christ died for us.*

"We needed to be justified because we were sinners and

ungodly, and not only that but down in verse ten you'll find out we need to be justified because we were the enemies of God!

"For if, when we were enemies, we were reconciled to God by the death of His Son, much more, being reconciled, we shall be saved by His life. Thank God! Mankind outside of Jesus Christ—unsaved—needs to be justified because we're ungodly, we're without strength, we're sinners, we're enemies of God, and we cannot be justified any other way! Mankind needs to be justified because we're lost, wicked, and undone.

"My wife and I were comin' home from somewhere yesterday, and we were talking about a situation. I don't understand all this, I don't claim to. But the truth is, modern man does not want to accept this message! It's a strange thing to me that they wouldn't, strange because it's the only message of hope that they have. It's only through the meritorious death of Jesus Christ that we can be justified, that we can be saved! And yet mankind doesn't want to receive that. He wants somethin' easier. He wants someone to tell him that he's doin' pretty good; someone to tickle his ears and say, 'You'll be all right! God loves everybody, don't worry about it. Just have a big time and it'll be all right.' It *won't* be all right! But modern mankind doesn't want the Truth it seems like. And yet they must understand they're ungodly. If a man doesn't understand they're ungodly and lost, how are they ever gonna be saved?

"We *need* to be justified because we're ungodly. I don't know how to explain this, to say this to get you to fully understand it. You see, I realize that in myself tonight, if somehow, and God won't do this.... If my understanding of the Bible is correct, this is the only thing God *cannot* do. But if God could take me and separate me from the righteousness of Jesus Christ tonight, you know that I'd still be just as ungodly as I ever was? If He separated me from the righteousness of Jesus Christ, I've got none of my own, folks! I have none of my own.

"When I go before God Almighty, I stand in the righteousness of Jesus Christ, hallelujah! I go before the Throne, and God accepts me because I appear in the righteousness of Jesus my blessed Lord! God sees me like that, and I've been made righteous because God Almighty did it! And He's pleased with it, by the way.

"Now, let me give you this real quickly. *How* am I justified? *Meritoriously* I'm justified by His death. Look at Romans 3:24. The Bible says, *Being justified freely by his grace through the redemption that is in Christ Jesus....*

"I've been sayin' this ever since I started this lesson tonight. We've been justified meritoriously by the death of Jesus Christ. The merit of Jesus Christ warrants my being justified tonight!

"*Instrumentally*, I'm justified by faith in Jesus Christ! Look back over in chapter five. *Therefore being justified by faith, we have peace with God through our Lord Jesus Christ: By Whom also we have access by faith into this grace wherein we stand, and rejoice in hope of the glory of God.* God dealt with my heart, and by faith I put my trust in Him. God says now that I've put my faith in Him, I'm justified by Him. This is my plea. I've got nothin' to offer God. Oh, listen! It's *Him*; it's Him, folks. By faith in Him I'm justified.

"And then *evidently*. You say, 'What do you mean by that?' I mean, by the *evidence*. How are we justified? By works. Look over at James 2:24, and I know you'll need to see this. The *evidence* of our salvation, the evidence of our justification shows up in our works!

"James 2:24, *Ye see then how that by works a man is justified, and not by faith only.* Our works show the world that we're saved, that we're justified.

"I told someone the other night right here in this church, I said, 'Look, the only way I can tell if a person is saved is by what I see in their life. I can't see their heart. I'm not God. What I *can* see is what they do with their life. When a person displays a bad attitude, a cross spirit, an ungodly personage about them, I see the signs that they're not saved, because they're not showing forth the works of God.'

"But let me tell you again, folks, we are justified *meritoriously* by His death, we're justified *instrumentally* by faith in Him, and the *evidence* of our justification is our works. But I want you to know before I get off that point, that we are justified *totally* through *grace*. Ephesians 2:8 and 9 *For by grace are ye saved through faith; and that not of yourselves: it is the gift of God: Not of works, lest any man should boast.*

"And that leads me to the next thing, how *completely* we're justified. In Acts chapter thirteen, how justified am I? How completely am I justified? I get tickled just thinking about this. Acts 13:39, I'm justified *fully*. *And by Him all that believe are justified from all things, from which ye could not be justified by the law of Moses.*

"Oh listen, isn't that wonderful that we're justified fully by the blessed Son of God?

"And in Romans 3:24, I'm justified *freely*! *Being justified freely by His grace through the redemption that is in Christ Jesus....* Hallelujah! Aren't you glad it's grace? Aren't you glad tonight that justification does not depend on what you and I can do? It depends totally on Him.

"I hear the world say, 'Oh, you Christians! You believe you can get saved and live any way you want to and still go to heaven.' Well, they're *right*. I can drink all the liquor I want. I can carouse all I want. I say this because, when I got saved, God changed my *want to*. I can drink all I want, which is *none* because I don't have a desire for that anymore.

"Oh listen, friends, I believe I'm saved by grace plus or minus nothin'. I'm not going to *do* anything or *refrain* from doin' anything to deserve it. I'm just gonna glory in it, and try to live for God and do the best I can for Jesus Christ. But I know it's by *grace*. It's not by what I ever could do.

"When I stand before God yonder in heaven, I'm not gonna have somethin' in my hand to say, 'Here, Lord, look here what I've done to get to heaven!' I'm gonna say, 'Hallelujah, I ain't got a thing, Lord! I tell ya back yonder in '69, thank God You came by and convicted me of my sin, and I placed my faith in Jesus Christ; and You *justified* me because Jesus Christ died on Calvary, was buried, and rose again! And You said You made me righteous!' So if I don't get to heaven, it's because God didn't keep His Word, because I've been justified! *Freely* from all things! *Fully*, thank God!

"Look at the *Results* of being justified, Romans 8:33, *Who shall lay any thing to the charge of God's elect? It is God that justifieth.* Who in the world is going to accuse us? Who can condemn us? What is the result of our being justified? We're *free from condemnation*! Nobody, nothing can condemn us before God Almighty, because He has made us righteous through the Lord Jesus Christ! Amen!

"Being free from condemnation brings me into *Peace*! Romans 5:1. Look at it. *Therefore being justified by faith, we have peace with God through our Lord Jesus Christ*. I tell you, I may not have a lot of worldly goods; but I have peace with my heavenly Father! We're not at enmity anymore! I'm not His enemy anymore! Thank God, He made me righteous, and I'm one of His tonight because He's justified me, hallelujah! Thank God, I have peace!

"Oh, and He promises me *Happiness*! Look over in Psalm 32:2. *Blessed is the man unto whom the LORD imputeth not iniquity, and in whose spirit there is no guile*. Are you listening to me? We're *blessed*! We've been promised happiness.

"Then not only that, but being justified entitles me an *inheritance*. Look over in Titus chapter three and verse seven, *That being justified by his grace, we should be made heirs according to the hope of eternal life*.

"Do you know we've been promised an inheritance? In John 14:1 through 3, we've been promised a *Home*. We're promised *crowns* in various places in Scripture. We're promised an inheritance reserved in heaven for us in I Peter 1:4 and 5, one that's incorruptible, undefiled, fadeth not away, reserved in heaven for us! I don't know which of those words I like best, but I tell you, it's incorruptible, that means it won't perish or rot! I like the word undefiled because that means no one's messed with it; hallelujah, it's mine! It's clean and pure and belongs to me. It won't fade away! And I think the last word is my favorite, it's 'reserved in heaven for me'!

"Do you know that being justified by faith through the Lord Jesus Christ that yonder in heaven there's an inheritance that's got my name on it? You can't mess with it, the devil can't mess with it, God's reserved it yonder in heaven for me, and thank God it's gonna be there when I get Home! It's my inheritance, not because I deserve it, but because I've been made righteous. An inheritance you don't have to work for, it's just given to you."

"And then because I've been justified, it *prevents me from boasting*. Look back with me at Romans 33:27, *Where is boasting then? It is excluded. By what law? of works? Nay: but by the law of faith.*

"And back to Ephesians 2:8 and 9, *For by grace are ye saved through faith; and that not of yourselves: it is the gift of God: Not of works, lest any man should boast.*

"Where is boasting? How can we boast? We have *nothing* to boast of but the Lord Jesus!

"'Well, I just tell ya, I'm *somethin'*!' No, you're not! And I'm not either! Boasting's excluded! We have nothing to boast of. But we have Jesus Christ. Let me tell you something tonight in case I don't get to tell you again this side of eternity. Make much of Jesus Christ! He's the One.

"Oh listen, I hear a lot of talk and songs that don't glorify the Lord, that don't say a thing of any eternal value. Make much of Jesus, folks. He's the One that's worthy! He's the One that's done it all! Make much of Him.

"And then lastly, what's the *result* of justification? It secures me *Glory*. Look in Romans 8:30, *Moreover whom He did predestinate, them He also called: and whom He called, them He also justified: and whom He justified, them He also glorified.*

Hallelujah, I tell you, it secures me Glory. (Just an aside for all you folks who don't speak with a southern dialect? That word 'Glory' is synonymous with 'Heaven', amen?) The result of justification is our heavenly Home!

"I'm gonna sing this song in closing, though my voice is scratched up with allergies....

Should I at the gates of heaven appear
To answer the challenge "What claim hast thou here?
What hast thou to offer, yea, what is thy plea?"
With blessed assurance my answer would be:
"All that I have is Jesus! All that I claim is Jesus!
All that I want, all that I need,
All that I plead is Jesus!"

Of all earthly treasures nothing I've brought,

No great deeds of merit have I ever wrought.
Tho' vile and unworthy as mortal could be,
I've nothing to offer but this is my plea:
"All that I have is Jesus! All that I claim is Jesus!
All that I want, all that I need,
All that I plead is Jesus!"

My sins, they are many; my virtues are few.
The blood of my Saviour will carry me through!
When Christ in my place died on Calvary's tree,
Hallelujah! That opened God's heaven to me!
"All that I have is Jesus! All that I claim is Jesus!
All that I want, all that I need,
All that I plead is Jesus!"

"I hope that's your plea, and I hope that you rejoice in your justification tonight. Let's pray together."

※

Charlie could hardly say a word as he left. He felt like his head was reeling from all the spiritual knowledge packed into that one "lesson", as Pastor had called it. He shook the pastor's hand as he left with the rest of the group, thanking him for the sermon.

When he walked with Carol out to the wagon where she would be riding home with the family, he smiled at her. She was respecting his thoughtful spirit, knowing how the sermon had touched his heart.

"Thank you, Carol. I know we both wanted to talk since you're going home now; and I won't see you for nearly ten hours!" She smiled as she listened to him ciphering his way through another conversation. "But that sermon...."

"Yes, I know. I remember his teaching us as children that justified meant *'just-as-if-I'd never sinned'*. Isn't that beautiful?" Seeing that the group was heading out in their different directions, and Caleb was waiting patiently to drive her, her folks, and Celia home, she gave Charlie a quick kiss on the cheek and a beautiful smile. He helped her into the wagon before waving them off down the moonlit road.

"I love you, Carolina Montague. But you'll be 'Carolina Bennett' forty-eight hours from now! Thank You, Lord." With that prayer in his heart, Charlie walked down to the hotel to spend some time with his parents before retiring.

Chapter Twenty-Six

Vows

Thursday was spent preparing food for the dinner following the rehearsal as well as for the wedding breakfast, and putting the finishing touches on the traditional fruit and nut cake that would serve as wedding cake for both couples. There was a reception hall at the church to be decorated, and Carol and Celia insisted on filling both the reception area and the church with as many flowers as they could find. Rather than waiting for the evening to rehearse, the wedding party met together after meeting the train bringing in the last of the guests.

Charlie laughed as he saw more and more of Albert's family arriving. "How many hotel rooms filled with Whittles is that now, Albert?"

"Well, there are Whittles, but there are also Atkinses and Dodges! Yes, I think that brings the hotel room count to about eighteen…nearly every room in the hotel!"

"You're right. I think they only have twenty-five or maybe thirty rooms total." Carol walked over to Charlie then, directing his glance to Caleb as he stood talking with the new arrivals… specifically, Merrie Atkins. Charlie quietly got Albert's attention. "Yes sir, there it goes…she's getting married, and now she has nothing better to do than to marry off every other available friend and family member of her acquaintance!"

He earned a pout for that one, and Albert discreetly left to find Celia, as the group was heading for the church next to rehearse the ceremony. Carol turned to join the rest of the group *en route* to the church. Charlie caught up, then matched Carol's steps stride for stride; but she wouldn't look at him.

"You have to talk with me *some* time, Carolina. Even if it's only to tell me I'm incorrigible." He saw enough of a grin to jump in front of her and walk backward a few paces before she stopped. "Is this going to be our first quarrel?"

"Oh, Charlie. You—"

"I'm sorry if what I said embarrassed you. I know you meant well. I just didn't want Caleb to catch your look and back off because of it."

"Oh dear, really? Was I that obvious?"

Charlie looked down at his new hat, which he held in his hands, before asking, "How long of a courtship do you think they'll have?"

"Well, I thought now that they've met they could write one another, and…oh, Charlie!" This time she swatted him with her fan before beginning to laugh at her own thoughts and actions. "I think *I'm* the one that needs to apologize. Will you forgive me?"

Charlie scratched his chin in mock thoughtfulness before stating, "But if I forgive you here and now, we can't kiss and make up!" That of course earned him another swat, then the two walked arm in arm together the rest of the way to the church.

※※

"Albert Whittle and Celia Montague, and Charles Bennett and Carolina Montague, have come to me expressing their desire and their conviction that it is God's will to become husbands and wives." It was ten o'clock, the morning of Friday, April the eleventh, eighteen-hundred ninety.

Charlie looked down at Carol, a vision in pale blue silk taffeta at his side. He could still see the color of her beautiful eyes through the filmy veil, but as he took her hand he could feel her trembling. He looked back down at her, then winked, knowing that her cheeks would be bright pink under the veil, but feeling her relax somewhat.

"Marriage is a very sacred institution. For a marriage to be truly happy, Christ must be Lord of each marriage partner and the home. In the Bible, we see that God compares marriage to the relationship between Himself and the church. Ephesians 5:22 through 33 states:

> 22 *Wives, submit yourselves unto your own husbands, as unto the Lord.*
> 23 *For the husband is the head of the wife, even as Christ is the head of the church: and He is the Saviour of the body.*
> 24 *Therefore as the church is subject unto Christ, so let the wives be to their own husbands in every thing.*
> 25 *Husbands, love your wives, even as Christ also loved the church, and gave Himself for it;*
> 26 *That He might sanctify and cleanse it with the washing of water by the Word,*
> 27 *That He might present it to Himself a glorious church, not having spot, or wrinkle, or any such thing; but that it should be holy and without blemish.*
> 28 *So ought men to love their wives as their own bodies. He that loveth his wife loveth himself.*
> 29 *For no man ever yet hated his own flesh; but nourisheth and cherisheth it, even as the Lord the church:*
> 30 *For we are members of His body, of His flesh, and of His bones.*
> 31 *For this cause shall a man leave his father and mother, and shall be joined unto his wife, and they two shall be one flesh.*
> 32 *This is a great mystery: but I speak concerning Christ and the church.*
> 33 *Nevertheless let every one of you in particular so love his wife even as himself; and the wife see that she reverence her husband.*

"Thus as Christ is the head of the church, so Albert is to be the head of Celia, and Charles is to be the head of Carolina.

"Albert, Charlie, this is your wedding day. You are about to become a husband with all the privileges and responsibilities involved. Pray that God will help you to become the kind of husband you should be. You are to lead your family in serving Christ. You are to love your wife as Christ loves His Bride, the Church.

"Celia, Carol, this is a very special day for you young ladies. This is your wedding day. You are to become a wife, a help meet for your husband. You are to follow his leadership as the Church follows Christ.

"Albert and Celia, Charlie and Carol, as a minister of the Gospel, your pastor, and your friend, I wish you the very best of God's blessings for the days and years to follow."

Pastor Crosby went through the vows for Albert and Celia first, but Charlie and Carol were already facing one another holding hands. When the pastor came to stand before them and said their names, Charlie felt Carol jump a little she was so lost in thought.

"Charles, will you have this woman to be your wedded wife? Will you love her, honor and keep her in sickness as in health, in poverty as in wealth, and forsaking all others keep thee only unto her so long as you both shall live, do you so promise?"

Never taking his eyes from his bride's veiled face, he vowed, "I do."

"Carolina, will you have this man to be your wedded husband? Will you love him, honor and obey him in sickness as in health, in poverty as in wealth, and forsaking all others keep thee only unto him so long as you both shall live, do you so promise?"

He could see her smile as she vowed, "I do," giving his hands a gentle squeeze.

"Charlie, please repeat after me the following words: *I, Charles Bennett....*"

Carol had given Charlie her ruby to be used as her wedding ring, and he kissed it before placing it on her finger. She likewise kissed the gold band that was to go on his finger. "Charlie, I too love you...with a love as beautiful and never-ending as the circle of this ring.... By placing this ring on your finger...in the presence of these witnesses and in the sight of God...I take you to be my beloved husband... vowing that I will be a faithful wife to you...until death shall part us."

Pastor Crosby had both couples kneel, laying hands on Albert and Celia, then Charlie and Carol as he prayed God's blessing and guidance on their lives together. When the men helped their brides to their feet, Pastor Crosby finished the ceremony, first pronouncing Albert and Celia husband and wife and allowing them to seal their vows with a kiss, then turning to Charlie and Carol. Albert and Celia turned as well to watch.

"Forasmuch then as you, Charlie, and you, Carol, have offered yourselves to each other, believing it is God's will for you to become one flesh, and believing that God has led you to this place; as a pastor, and by the power vested in me by the state of South Carolina, I now pronounce you husband and wife." Charlie wasn't totally certain until afterwards if Pastor paused there on purpose, but then with a huge grin he finished with, "You may kiss your bride, Charlie!"

He lifted her veil, draping it carefully over her adorable hat, then he leaned to kiss his bride. Though it wasn't planned, the whole church having heard of the ordeal surrounding their uniting, before they came apart the sanctuary was filled with applause, even Albert and Celia clapping as huge tears of joy fell down Celia's cheeks.

Directing the two couples to face the audience, Pastor concluded the ceremony with, "I introduce you to Mr. and Mrs. Albert Whittle, and Mr. and Mrs. Charles Bennett!"

Before walking back down the aisle, the couples turned to embrace one another, then went down to the front row, each hugging two sets of parents. Laura Bennett couldn't say a word, she just smiled and hugged and cried. Mrs. Montague was much the same, then after their children all walked down the aisle, the parents came out and hugged and clapped one another on the back, all agreeing it was a most beautiful wedding.

When they reached the reception hall, they had a few brief moments before the receiving line started. A photographer took each couple's picture, then took a photo of the two couples together. Charlie and Albert went to get a quick cup of punch for themselves and the brides, but when they got back the receiving line was well under way.

Shortly after the cake-cutting ceremony, Mr. and Mrs. Montague came to hug Carol. "Charlie said the two of you would need to be leaving shortly." Mr. Montague beamed at his oldest daughter. "There's nothing more to say, only I hope and pray that you will live in God's blessings, being as happily married as your mother and I." Mrs. Montague walked arm in arm with Carol to the retiring room to freshen up.

"What is it, Mother?"

"I never talked with you about what...about tonight. I talked with Celia about it last Saturday night, but of course...."

"Did your mother speak with you?"

"No, but...well, it can be rather frightening at moments." Mrs. Montague blushed as she saw her daughter's eyes widen. "But your husband loves you as your father loves me; and I know that he will be gentle, treating your love as the treasure it is." She cupped her daughter's face in her hands as she added, "Remember this though, in time this part of your marriage will bring pleasure to you both. Don't settle for endurance. This is a blessed coming together, blessed by God. Sometimes your coming together will bring the blessing of children, but sometimes it will bring the physical blessing of mutual pleasure. Sometimes it will bring the joy of knowing you brought pleasure to your spouse. Either way, enjoy this very precious time with your husband, on your honeymoon and all your married life. There, now that I've fatally embarrassed you...."

Hugging her mother in her strong young arms, Carol whispered, "No, Mother. I'm glad you told me."

As they joined the others out in the reception hall, Celia hugged her sister. "We're coming back here after we see you off, but I think just about everyone is going down to the train. We won't be able to talk then, so I'll just say that we shall have much to discuss when we all get home to Baltimore!" Hugging her close again, Celia whispered, "God be with you, Carrie!"

"And with you, Celia! Come to the Bennetts' home when you all get settled in! I'll be there...well, I'm a *Bennett* now, so of course I'll be there! I think we may stay at the apartment Saturday night though."

"How romantic! That always was a cozy place. Now run

along, Charlie is looking for you!"

Looking around the room, Carol spotted Charlie standing by the tables talking with one of the wedding guests. He looked so refined and handsome; then Carol caught a slight movement as he reached out, took a small sandwich, and tucked it into his the pocket of his tuxedo! Carol couldn't help but laugh.

"It's a good thing I didn't plan on changing *him!"* Carol said to herself with a grin.

Chapter Twenty-Seven

Charleston

Charlie and Carol waved farewell to the wedding guests who had come to the depot to see them off. Letting down the window, Charlie even leaned out and waved, Carol blowing kisses to her precious family. As the train pulled away, he left the window open to let in the country air. Carol's veil was billowing, so she carefully removed her hat and hat pins, placing them gently into her hat box.

"How long a trip is it to Charleston, Charlie? Oh, how wonderful! We're going to *your town*, Charlie! *Charles*ton!"

Charlie chuckled. "I hadn't even thought of that actually! I just have always wanted to see Charleston." Pulling his pocket watch from his vest, he went on. "We should arrive around four o'clock. I have wired ahead for a carriage to take us to the waterfront, then to a hotel not far from there.

"Did you know that I had made reservations at the hotel in Monck's Corner? Not the one I'd been staying in, but the other? When I realized that we only had one night before our train ride back for my baptism, I wanted to make sure we got to see a little bit of Charleston at least." His eyes wandered over her beautiful gown, her hair, her hands. He reached out and took her left hand, placing a kiss in her palm. "You gave me this hand today, Carolina," he whispered, all his heart in his voice.

"I gave you my heart long ago though."

"One year, three months, and eighteen days ago. Yes, I gave

mine to you then, too." He touched the little silver heart on her bracelet, memories of those early days filling him with longing.

"I think it's funny that you remember to the day...probably to the hour though you spare me that recitation!"

Charlie laughed. "That's what happens when you marry someone who does ciphering all day long." He looked down at her lovingly. "You don't mind so much, do you?"

"I would have it no other way." Thankful for the private room, however cramped, they pulled the shades and spent much of the rest of the trip to Charleston taking pleasure in one another's company after their many months apart.

✥

"Oh, Charlie! Do you know where this takes me back to? What it reminds me of?"

Charlie grinned. "Our waterfront picnic! I hoped it would. I believe from the map this is called 'White Point Gardens'. It's a beautiful spot. Perhaps we can come out here for a stroll tomorrow before the train leaves. Unless of course you'd like to stop now...?"

"No...no, I'd just as soon go to the hotel, Charlie." He couldn't believe the look he saw in her eyes.

"Why, Mrs. Bennett, I do believe you said that without even blushing!" After a short pause he added, "Oops, I spoke too soon," and joyed over his wife's blushes as he drew her close to his side.

The azaleas and irises were in bloom all around the city, but Charlie wanted to come back and see the many crepe myrtles blooming. The driver pulled up at the Red Lion Inn, giving the bell hop their trunk and accepting Charlie's payment and generous tip with an air of utmost dignity. Charlie stopped at the front desk, signing them in and getting the key, before they made their way to their room. The bell hop opened the door for them, placed their trunk down, and made his way out quietly, Charlie barely remembering to give him a tip. Then they were alone.

Carol walked over to the window, which looked out on a tiny, formal garden. The stone walk and lush foliage were charming, and she motioned for Charlie to come stand beside her. They stood there looking out on the beautiful garden for a full minute, then Charlie turned to his wife of several hours. "Are you hungry? There is a small restaurant right next door."

"No, I actually was able to eat quite a bit at the reception. This fruit basket looks like it will be tempting later though." Charlie was glad he had thought to have the fruit basket placed in their room.

"May we pray together now, Carol? I know that we would not be here tonight had the Lord not intervened again and again in our lives. I want us to pray that the Lord would always have His hand of blessing on us, and for us to always seek to know and do His will." Looking adoringly into her husband's eyes, Carol nodded; and the two knelt beside a wing back chair, each pouring out a heart of thanksgiving to their Savior and Creator.

Charlie helped Carol to her feet, then stepped over to pull down the window shade. When he turned, he saw Carol taking out her hairpins, her hair tumbling in a silken mass of waves and curl over one shoulder. Removing his jacket and loosening his tie, he put out his hand to Carol.

"Come, Carolina. Come to me, my precious, heaven-sent bride!"

෴

Carol woke up slowly, seeing the early morning light coming in around the shade at the window. Charlie was still asleep, snuggled up behind her as they both lay on their sides. *"Momma always called this 'nestling like spoons', saying how very comfortable it was. I definitely agree!"* Trying to carefully move Charlie's arm without waking him, but needing very much to take care of her needs, she lifted his arm slowly. A light sleeper, Charlie snuggled in all the closer.

"Charlie? Charlie, I need to get up," she whispered, quietly giggling. Charlie just tightened his hold around her.

"What *for?*" he asked, his voice low and gravelly from sleep.

She turned in his arms to face him. "Must I ask your permission to take care of my personal needs first thing in the morning?" He let her go, squinting at her with a crooked grin.

"I'm sorry, I just thought we were so comfortable!" Carol still took the time to lean over and kiss him on the cheek before climbing out of bed and going to the necessary room, taking care of her now very urgent need.

When she saw the tub, it looked so inviting that she started the water and poured bath soap in. She piled her hair on top of her head, securing it with hairpins. After hanging her robe on the hook on the back of the door, she climbed into the luxuriously warm, fragrant, bubbly water. She pulled the curtain most of the way across, but still she was glad to be neck-deep in bubbles when Charlie came in in his pajama bottoms and slippers. He went to the sink and brushed his teeth, then sat on a stool next to the tub and just looked at her, bringing the first blush of the day.

"Good morning, Mrs. Bennett! And how are you this fine spring day?"

"Oh, feeling quite pampered and cherished actually. And yourself?" Her eyes were drawn to his bare chest, then back up to his face. Charlie grinned.

"I'm feeling rather fascinated...discovering more and more about my beloved wife." He caught her staring at his chin and cheeks next, then realized the cause. "You've never seen me with whiskers, have you?" She shook her head 'no'. "May I kiss you before I shave?" With a giggle, Carol nodded, then with upturned face welcomed his good morning kiss. Instead of lingering, he gave her little kisses on her cheek and neck, but she went deeper under the bubbles.

"That *tickles*! They're all prickly! I thought they'd be softer somehow, like Poppa's mustache."

He walked to the sink and pulled out his shaving mug and razor, working up a good lather after dampening the brush with hot water. "Actually, it takes a while before whiskers start feeling soft. But I was of the impression for some reason that you didn't like facial hair...?"

She giggled, taking the sea sponge and scrubbing her arms and legs. "You're exactly right. I've always liked that you were clean shaven."

"Good. Then shaving twice a day will be worth it if it pleases my lovely wife."

"Do you really have to shave two times every day?"

"Only if I want you to kiss me in the evenings, too. So, *yes*, I most certainly do! It's not a problem really. It doesn't take long."

"And I love the smell of your aftershave!" She said this almost without thinking; but of course he caught it, and loved her all the more for it.

"Do you? I never thought you noticed!"

"That's one of the first things I noticed when we met. When you picked me up to put me in the buggy you smelled so good. Then I remember smelling that same fragrance when we danced at the Christmas Banquet. And on the New Year's Day buggy ride in the snow...."

"Yes, we were rather close that day. Then you fell asleep as I recall. I hope my aftershave doesn't always have that effect on you, darling!" He wiped his face with the towel that had been around his neck, then applied his aftershave. Coming over to the tub again, he bent over and kissed her.

"Mm...that's nice."

Charlie kissed her once more, then headed for the door. "You'll probably want to get out soon, you're about out of bubbles." He peeked around the open door with a raised eyebrow and a very crooked grin.

"*Charlie!*"

☙❧

Charlie was fully dressed when Carol came out in her shift, holding her corset. "Time to learn something *new*, dear. Can you help me fasten my corset?" He came over to her, looking at the stiff piece of clothing in her hand.

"Good heavens, Carolina! This doesn't look in the least comfortable. How's it go?" He helped her pull it over her head, settling on her waist and hips, then she directed him to pull the ties as tightly as he could and fasten them. There was very little discomfort when he proclaimed the job finished, and Carol laughed.

"Well, at least I'll be able to have Jessie or Beatrix help me when we get home. I suppose I can look big as a cow for a day or two!" She put on two lightweight petticoats before going over to find her dress.

"I don't see you as looking any less beautiful than you looked yesterday or any other day I've ever seen you. In fact, you look *more* beautiful...maybe because I know you aren't uncomfortable, but maybe because you're *mine* now! I have you and will hold you 'till death shall part us'."

Carol was pulling her dress from the wardrobe when she felt Charlie's arms go around her waist. "How am I ever going to get us to the train on time if I keep wanting to kiss you every time I look at you?" Charlie and Carol both smiled as she pulled her gown over her head, arranging the skirt while Charlie buttoned up the back. He paused to kiss her neck before fastening the top buttons. "I love you, Carol."

With another kiss, Carol pulled out her combs and brush and went to work. Charlie sat down on the edge of the bed, just watching with fascination as she so quickly and deftly brushed and twisted and braided her hair, fastening it with her combs and hairpins before turning for inspection.

"Well? How do I look?"

"Carolina Bennett, you look ravishing!" He offered her his arm, grabbing his hat before heading out for breakfast. "I don't know about you, but I feel half starved. Let's eat a good breakfast, then get a carriage to take us the long way to the train." He pulled his pocket watch from his vest pocket. "It's eight-thirty now. The train leaves at ten-fifteen."

They went to the restaurant next door Charlie had seen the night before, ordering cocoa for him and hot tea for her to start out with. Then came crescent rolls and peach jam and fresh strawberries for Carol, and rib eye steak and eggs and two biscuits for Charlie. They held hands across the table after they both had finished their meals.

"Charlie, I had an idea I wanted to ask you about. I know that we will be living at your parents' home for a while, but could we spend one more night alone before going home?"

"What did you have in mind?"

"Actually, my rooms at the boarding house. Albert and Celia moved everything but her suitcases for the wedding to their cottage week before last, and I was going to keep the apartment. I was just thinking that—"

"As long as it's paid for, we may as well have one more night of honeymooning?"

"Yes, if that's all right with you?"

Charlie kissed her hand before whispering, "But aren't those beds rather small?"

Carol blushed crimson before replying. "Mine is a double bed, Celia's is a twin. If the double isn't big enough, we can push the two together, I suppose."

"That sounds good to me." The waiter came with their check before Charlie could embarrass her further. Charlie paid the check, and the two walked out into the sunshine-filled Carolina morning.

"The carriage is supposed to be here for us at nine-thirty. We'll have to hurry to get our trunk ready to go." The two made short order of packing their things, then the bellhop came to cart the trunk to the lobby and into the waiting carriage. Charlie helped Carol in, asking the driver if they'd make it on time to the train if they went back by White Point Gardens. The driver told him it wouldn't be a problem as long as they drove through and didn't plan to get out and walk, to which Charlie agreed before climbing in beside his wife.

Charlie told Carol what the driver had said. "We have to come back here someday, Carolina. I'd like to spend a week or two here. Would you like that?"

"Oh, *yes*! Maybe for a 'second honeymoon' for our first anniversary! I'd love it. But then, I'll just love being wherever you are. That sounds sappy-sweet, but I mean it. I really enjoy spending time with you, Mr. Bennett."

She snuggled up to his side as his arm went around her, and they came together in a kiss that distracted them both to the point that they were halfway through the White Point Gardens before they realized it! Giggling, then looking out the window at the giant oaks, the shell-strewn walkways, and the beautiful rivers converging at the point, the two enjoyed the garden's beauty until the carriage turned up King Street headed for the depot.

Carol waved at the passing scenery, whispering, "We'll be back someday, 'Lord willing!" Then with a sigh of blissful contentment, she snuggled back up against Charlie's side for the rest of the ride.

Chapter Twenty-Eight

Baptism in Baltimore

The long train ride back to Baltimore went by fairly quickly for the newly-married best friends. The two passed the time with their quiet, flirtatious banter and many hours of Bible reading and discussion. Charlie found God's Word to be a constant source of delight as well as instruction. He had learned many of the verses during childhood, but as with the sermons and hymns, each verse came alive with meaning.

"Who's your favorite Bible character, Carol?"

"*Jesus*," she answered with a sweet smile. "And then I would have to say David in the Old Testament and the disciple John in the New. Who would yours be?"

"Well, I was always rather fond of Peter. He just seemed so...*human*, always putting his foot in his mouth...talking when he should be listening. Rather like me."

"I don't think of you as being like Peter. Let me see. Who would you *want* to be like?"

"Jesus. But other than Him, the Apostle Paul...or Stephen. A bold witness of the Gospel."

Carol looked at her husband through different eyes. "Charlie, do you think perhaps the Lord may call you into full-time service someday?"

His brow furrowed in thought. "I've never really considered that. I would definitely be open to it. What would you think of being a pastor's or missionary's wife someday?"

"To be honest, I hadn't really thought about it either, though I've always wanted to serve the Lord any way I could. This is definitely something we need to make a matter of prayer." The two held hands and prayed together right then and there, acknowledging as a couple the Lord's right to direct their paths as He saw fit.

When they got off the train it was well after dark, and by the time they finally reached the boarding house after hiring a carriage, they were both exhausted. It didn't help matters that the matron followed them upstairs.

"This is a *respectable* place I run here, Miss Montague! It simply isn't acceptable to have male callers at this hour of the night!" Carol smiled sweetly at her accuser, knowing how it must look to her.

"Mrs. Sykes, this is my *husband*, Charlie Bennett. We are just arrived back from our honeymoon and would like very much to get some sleep."

"Gracious me, I'm so sorry! Oh, and congratulations!" She nodded, her hair curlers moving in time, then beat a hasty retreat back down the stairs.

"That would have been hysterically funny if we weren't both so tired." Charlie opened the door and carried their trunk in, Carol coming in behind him and closing the door quietly. They went back to the bedroom after a shared glass of cold water, removing enough clothing to sleep comfortably and falling asleep almost as soon as their heads touched the pillows.

&

"Good morning, darling." Carol smiled as she kissed her still groggy husband, then made her way to the bathroom. Charlie stayed in bed, still smiling when Carol came back in minutes later. Climbing back in the small bed beside her husband, she lay on her side looking at his profile. "I love you."

"I love *you*." Carol leaned over to kiss him, not expecting the strong embrace she was met with. "You are most desirable, my love." Taking her face in his hands, he looked into her eyes many moments before his eyes traveled down to her lips. "Your love was worth waiting for, not just your passion, but your sweet spirit." She sighed deeply as he kissed her again. "What's wrong?"

"I'm enjoying this Solomon's Song reenactment as much as you are, but if we don't get ready soon, we'll be late for your baptism!"

Charlie grinned, kissing her once more before saying, "Point well taken. I'm getting ready now!"

Charlie had nearly forgotten that they didn't have a ride to church, so he went downstairs to telephone his parents. He asked them if they could leave a little early for church, picking them up on the way. Mr. and Mrs. Bennett were ready early, so they left within the quarter-hour.

When he got back upstairs, Carol was dressed and fixing a quick bite to eat in the tiny kitchen. She and Charlie came together for a final kiss before being in public again. "Charlie, do you think we kiss too much?"

"That's an interesting question. If we kissed every time we *wanted* to kiss, I think that might be too much. But we can't do that, so *no*, I don't think we kiss too much." Charlie laughed, leading her to the davenport to eat while they waited for his parents' arrival. After a brief prayer of thanks for the food, they resumed their conversation.

"I know that right now our relationship seems a little heavy on the physical side, but it will balance out in time. We're *newlyweds*, Carolina." He touched her hair with the back of his fingers, smiling at how the sunlight made it shine.

With a gentle smile he continued. "One never really thinks of their parents as being romantic, but my mother lost a baby through miscarriage when I was eighteen. I doubt Mother and Father had planned to or were trying to have another child; but of course they were thrilled when they found out about him, then crushed when they lost him. All that to say, there is no age limit on physical attraction. Think about it, Abraham and Sarah had their son Isaac at a *very* old age."

"So, you think you'll still want to kiss me when I'm ninety?"

"Do you think you'll still *want* me to?" They both laughed, then Charlie went on. "Actually, I've always figured that is why our vision goes first...no, wait! I mean it! When we're both ninety, I'll still be picturing you as my beautiful bride. You'll still be able to envision me as your handsome groom."

"When you put it *that* way, it's a lovely thought." Peering out the window, she added, "Oh, here are your parents!" They both giggled as they stuffed the last of their breakfast in their mouths. "Get your carpet bag with your change of clothes. I've got the Bible." The two grabbed their hats and headed downstairs, meeting his parents before they got out of the buggy.

The baptismal service was beautiful, and Pastor Lehman's explanation of the significance of baptism made it all the more meaningful for Charlie and all who knew him. Pastor shared, "Baptism is not what saves, or Jesus would never have been baptized! Jesus did not need *saving* as the Saviour. But He was baptized to be identified as 'set apart'. This is why we go through this simple but profound step in our Christian life, to be identified with Christ, to be 'set apart' from the world as a believer."

Although there were several new Christians being baptized that day, Charlie was the only one who had been a member of the church before salvation, and Pastor emphasized this. "Charlie, you joined the church through statement of faith as a child. Did that save you? No. You were 'baptized' then, though without faith in a manner of speaking you just 'got wet' since you were not yet a believer. Did getting baptized save you? No. Church membership, baptism, good deeds...none of these 'save' us. Only by placing our faith in Jesus Christ the righteous, in His finished work on the cross, can we be saved."

When Charlie was in the baptismal pool, Pastor asked him again before baptizing him, "Charlie, have you placed your faith in Jesus Christ, the Holy Son of God, to forgive you of your sin? Then, Charlie, upon your profession of faith, I baptize you now, my brother, in the name of the Father, the Son, the Holy Spirit—JEHOVAH. Buried in the likeness of His death...raised in the likeness of His glorious resurrection!"

Charlie and Carol joined his parents for lunch after church, then the four of them went upstairs to see their new "home".

"Oh, Mother, it's *perfect*! Thank you so much for getting this done for us!" Carol walked around, looking out the window at the gardens, smelling the flowers in the vases throughout the room.

"When can we bring our trunk over?" she said finally, her hands clasped together. Mrs. Bennett went to her sweet daughter-in-law and embraced her.

"How about we take naps first, then send the men folk over. You and I can do another walk through then, and you can decide what decorating changes you'd like to make."

"Oh! But, this is Charlie's room! Surely—"

Charlie cut in, "It's *our* room until we build or find a home that would be more suitable. If you wish to paint or re-paper the walls, have at it!" Carol looked around the room again, taking in the color scheme carefully.

"Actually, I like the shades of green used in here. It's a very relaxing room. I think with my quilts it will add just enough 'femininity' for my liking."

Mr. Bennett couldn't squelch a big, noisy yawn; and smiling rather sheepishly, he led his wife from the room, closing the door behind them.

"We're *home*." Charlie went to stand behind his bride, who was still gazing out the window at the gardens. He reached for her hair, taking the hairpins out and watching it fall in shining profusion. Expecting to see his eyes lit with passion, Carol was surprised when she turned to find her husband's eyes misted with unshed tears. She touched his cheek gently, waiting for him to share his heart.

"Oh, Carolina, I never allowed myself to dream we'd be here one day...standing together in this room as man and wife." He took her hand, leading her to the small loveseat by another large picture window. "I remember when you first came, after the accident. I wanted to kiss you that day in the garden, that first day when I got home from work. I thought when I kissed you that first time...when we said goodbye at the picnic.... I thought that kiss would have to last me the rest of my life. Then when I proposed, what, a week ago tomorrow? That kiss was so perfect...so sweet." He leaned forward for another kiss. "Remembering back just a week ago, I still thought you were about to marry Albert! I was rushing around in here getting things together for the trip. Just a week ago...."

Carol snuggled close to his side on the loveseat, her hand resting on his chest. "It seems so strange, yet so wonderful! I never doubted that you would be saved one day; but as weeks turned to months and you didn't make a decision for the Lord, I began to wonder if I'd be an old woman before you finally got your heart right, then proposed!" He was so quiet she thought he may have gone to sleep. "Charlie, are you ready to go to bed and take a nap?"

She felt rather than heard her husband chuckle. "Well, *yes* and *no*...."

Chapter Twenty-Nine

Back To Work

Baltimore, Maryland
April 13th, 1890

When Charlie and his father got back from getting their trunk and personal items from the rooms at the boarding house, the two Mrs. Bennetts were in the music room playing the piano. Charlie's mother went on playing when the men came in, but Carol came to meet them at the door.

"It's nearly dark! I was getting worried," she said, clinging to Charlie's arm after he set down the trunk. His father laid the pile of folded bed linens and doilies on top of the trunk before joining the rest of the family in the sitting room.

"I think all your pretties will make your rooms upstairs look just right." Mr. Bennett couldn't help grinning at the lovebirds on the settee, Carol still holding tightly to Charlie's arm as he talked about the work the two had gotten done.

"We'll need to head back after work tomorrow and do a final cleanup, but I really think—"

"'After work'? Are you really going to work tomorrow?"

Charlie understood her disappointment. "I'm sorry, darling, but it can't be helped. I may be able to take a long weekend next weekend and have a bit more of a honeymoon, but I really cannot afford to be away from the office more than the week I've already taken. You understand, don't you?"

Looking down into her pleading blue eyes, he knew she understood but didn't want to say goodbye even for that short time after so little time together. "You can decorate the room tomorrow, plus you'll need to spend time with Jessie and Beatrix and the rest. From what Father said, it was all they could do to shoo them away for their day off today!" Charlie put his arm around his wife, planting a kiss on her temple. "What's for supper? I'm so hungry the leather of the trunk handles looked like beef jerky!" Mrs. Bennett came in from the piano laughing at her son's comment.

"You don't *appear* to be wasting away, dear! But we made up some sandwiches and pretzels...." She'd no more mentioned the food when Charlie started to get up, making them all laugh as they followed him to the dining room for supper.

⸙

Charlie and his father hauled their things upstairs, but they didn't opt to unpack until morning. "Thank you, Father. We're turning in now. I'll see you in the morning. You're leaving at the usual time?"

"Of course, Son. Goodnight. Goodnight, Carol! Welcome home." When Mr. Bennett left with the lamp, they were amazed at how bright the room still seemed with the moonlight coming in at the windows. Carol leaned over the back of the loveseat to look out on the garden.

"Oh, Charlie, it *is* a full moon! Can we go outside and walk in the garden?" Wanting to remind her of work in the morning but unable to bring himself to do so, Charlie took her arm and guided her downstairs. The lamps were low, but the couple was able to make their way out onto the veranda without additional lighting.

"Look! The lightning bugs are out! Let's catch one!" She darted from green glow to green glow, giggling and catching her skirts in the bushes occasionally, but having a wonderful time. At some point it went from her chasing lightning bugs to Charlie chasing her, and eventually one was caught. Falling down on a small patch of grass they laughed until the tears were flowing, then Charlie pulled her to him, kissing her with an ardor he had only just days before discovered he possessed. Helping her back to her feet, he kissed her once more before the two strolled about the garden paths arm in arm.

"Do you know, if the Lord works with us as He did with your parents, I could already be with child, Charlie?"

He hesitated a bit before asking, "Do you not remember...."

"Of course, darling, but it's still *possible* if He so wills. I know we wanted to wait, and in a way I still do. But the thought of sharing in the creation of a tiny soul...." She stopped, then stepping in front of him on the path she went on. "I will be content if He chooses otherwise, truly I will. I just...I don't know...I guess all of our romancing keeps me thinking of what the end result could be. I'm sorry, that's not very amorous though.'

Charlie traced her lips with his finger. "If I could see your face more clearly, I'd say you're turning pink, Mrs. Bennett." He reached for her and held her close. "Believe me, I hope and pray that the Lord will bless us with children, Carolina. Many, many children. But I also hope we can balance parenthood, marriage, work, and our Christianity in a way that pleases Him." He held her there for several minutes, enjoying the gentle breeze and the night sounds as he gently stroked his wife's hair and back. "Now, I suggest we return to the privacy of our rooms."

"Yes, Charlie."

೭ೀ౨

Mr. Bennett noticed how tired and somber Charlie was on their ride to work the next morning. Charlie couldn't help but grin though when his father asked if he was well.

"I'm fine, Father, just rather worn out from the emotional ups and downs of the past week. Do you know, a week ago right now I still didn't know that Albert was marrying Celia rather than Carol? I was still on the train!"

"Amazing, isn't it? God has truly wrought a wonderful work in your life. And is married life all that you hoped it would be?"

"Much, much more than I hoped for. Carol is...she is more than I ever dreamed a wife would be. She's my dearest friend besides the Lord, and the fact that she knows Him too makes our relationship all the more perfect. I can't imagine the emptiness I would feel had I not been saved though, you know it? There is so much more to us than physical. We enjoy one another spiritually, mentally, emotionally.... I understand a little of what you meant now when you taught me a spouse was to be a 'completer'. That's the perfect word for what we share."

Mr. Bennett grinned. "I'm so glad for you, for both of you." He remembered his honeymoon so many years before, and the two of them silently shared very similar thoughts and prayers for their spouses the rest of the way to work. There was much to be done when the men arrived at the bank, and very little time for personal reflection was available to either of them for the rest of the day.

This also ended up being the case for their brides. Carol was just getting out of bed when Charlie left; and when a knock came at the door and Jessie entered grinning and clasping her hands together in front of her, Carol leaped from the bed to hug her friend. "Oh, Missy Carol! You look so beautiful! I done forgot what a beautiful girl you was! But you prob'ly prettier for bein' loved now. Heav'n-blessed love makes every woman more beautiful!"

Carol didn't know how to ask, so she blurted out, "Jessie, are you expecting?"

Jessie nearly turned inside out smiling. "Well, thank the good Lord I'm not fatt'nin' up all over like I did with my Jacob! Yes, this wee one is due in late summer."

"'Jacob'? You have a child already?"

"Me an' George, we been married since shortly after you lef' in '89. I don't know as you've ever met my George. He works as a blacksmith in town...hopes to have his own shop someday. He's a Christian, Missy Carol, don't you worry none! He's a good man, and a good father to our boy."

She smoothed the material of her skirt, emphasizing the slight roundness evidencing the coming child. "I'm so happy, and I can't wait for God to bless you and Mistah Charles with young'n's." She went about the room tidying things as she talked, never sitting still as she spoke.

Carol changed into a fresh shift, then began adding the layers that made up her daily attire. Jessie helped with the corset, pulling the strings so tight that Carol lost her breath for a moment. "You want I should loosen this a bit, Missy?"

"Oh, no...no, I just need to get used to it again is all. Charlie did the tightening the past two days, and I guess just that quickly I've grown accustomed to the freedom!"

The two laughed together as Carol sat before the mirror, taking the braid from her hair and brushing it out before Jessie began arranging it. "I've missed having you do my hair, Jessie. You make me look and feel like a princess when you're done braiding and weaving my hair into one of your masterpieces!" Then going back to the subject dearest to her heart, she began asking Jessie some questions about Jacob and her pregnancy with him. Jessie answered honestly and openly, sharing in her almost poetic speech the joy she felt carrying and giving birth to her son.

"An' he looks jus' like me! I wanted him to look like my George, but it wasn't to be. He gots these big old eyes and high cheekbones like his Momma! Mind you, he gots his Poppa's appetite!" She paused a minute with Carol's hair before asking, "Shall I start prayin' for a little one for you right away, Missy Carol?"

Carol's eyes slid closed as she smiled, then looking into her friend's eyes in the mirror's reflection, she replied, "Yes, please, Jessie." She saw her friend look up before she began praying. It surprised Carol at first, used to bowing and closing her eyes, but it was just as natural as could be for Jessie to pray this way.

"Father, this child of Yours wants a baby. Please bless her and Your son Charlie with a child in Your good time. In Jesus' name, amen." She went right on braiding and pinning, and Carol sat there looking at her with a totally new appreciation.

"Thank you, Jessie." She smiled at her dear sister, then it dawned on her, "Oh *dear*! I completely forgot about work! I need to get ready and go to the office if only to turn in my resignation...oh, but I'll probably need to give two weeks' notice. I wonder if Charlie would mind if I kept my job piano playing at Stewart's until they can find someone else?"

Jessie helped her dress, getting her some fruit to eat in the carriage on the way to Waterman's. Her supervisor was completely understanding, and when he heard who her husband was, and more importantly, her father-in-law, he most willingly let her go without serving her two weeks training a replacement. She decided to go in to Stewart's that evening since she was scheduled, then discuss the future of her job there with Charlie.

Chapter Thirty

Uncle Wesley

Carol found that she needed to work the two weeks at Stewart's since they could not find a replacement on such short notice, but she really didn't mind the work at all. She and Charlie were both able to get Friday off, and first light found them traveling to the train, only this time with the nation's capital as their destination. Carol had never been, and it had been years since Charlie had the pleasure of touring the great city. The trip southwest to Alexandria, then riding in a hansom cab to the capital itself, filled Carol with excitement. The two had luncheon at a quaint little restaurant not far from the grassy stretch of the mall, then they set out on foot.

"Do you want to go up the Washington Monument?"

"Not really, do you?" The huge eyes she raised to his told him not to push the point. "May we walk down toward the Capitol? It must be huge to look so large from this far away!"

"It is. I was only twelve or thirteen when I came with my parents, but I recall thinking it went on for seemingly blocks and blocks."

The two enjoyed walking around the Capitol, the mall, and even heading over for a look at the White House before going in search of a hotel. They stayed at a bed and breakfast Friday night, and after a delicious morning meal of hotcakes, fresh fruit, whipped cream, cocoa, and juice, they made reservations for a second night. They slept well after a day of touring the

Smithsonian and several statues and parks.

When Sunday came they headed into the first church they found, a large church with pillars and stained glass windows much like theirs in Baltimore. But although the architecture was beautiful, the preaching was more of a political speech than Bible; and the two were ready to head home.

"I believe Albert and your sister were getting back from their honeymoon today. Perhaps we can go visit them if we don't get in too late."

"That would be wonderful! I've missed Celia so much."

"I'm just still thankful it's not *Albert* you've been missing!" They laughed together, but both were exhausted. When they climbed aboard the train they took a private compartment, relaxing and quickly falling asleep as the train raced toward home.

When they reached the last stop before Baltimore, Charlie telephoned home to let his parents know when they'd be arriving. Lucas answered.

"Mistah Charles, your Momma's at your Aunt Lavinia's. Your Uncle Wesley, he done had a stroke last night. You want I should pick you up and take you straight over there?"

"Yes, Lucas, that would be ideal. Thank you." Carol could see by Charlie's expression that he had received bad news, and he was quick to explain.

"Is Lavinia's husband a Christian, Charles?" She had suspected as much, but the look on Charlie's face made it perfectly clear that he was not a believer.

"He's always been aloof from our family because of our religious affiliations. Father and Mother have never tried to force their religion on Uncle Wesley, but I think sometimes the Holy Spirit is so evident in some people's lives that those who don't know Him are scared off...usually under the guise of one imaginary offense or another."

"What about Lavinia? I've never seen her at our church, but does she know Christ as Saviour?"

"I don't know, Carol. She always has been close to Mother of course, and very affectionate and giving. She may have been saved as a child though, I don't know."

"Well then, let's both pray for each of them as though they're *not* saved." She looked into her husband's concern-filled eyes, getting his full attention before adding, "Charlie, this could be your first real opportunity to be a bold but loving witness for our Saviour." Charlie nodded, then pulled his Bible from their carpet bag. The two poured over salvation verses until the train pulled into the station.

❧❧

Mrs. Bennett was there at her sister's front door when the carriage arrived. "I'm *so* glad you're home. Come." She led the way through the beautiful mansion to her sister and brother-in-law's suite. Carol's eyes grew larger and larger as she glanced about, seeing room after room filled with priceless, beautiful treasures.

They could hear Lavinia's voice from the doorway, grief filling every syllable. "Lavinia, dear," Laura interrupted gently, "Charles and his wife are here." Lavinia turned red, swollen eyes to them, then turned back in silence to her husband's seemingly lifeless form. Mrs. Bennett reached out her hand, helping Lavinia to her feet. "Come, Sister, you need to eat something and refresh yourself. I can't nurse both of you, dearest." Lavinia stood slowly, glancing back at her husband before heading to the door on her sister's arm. Charlie and Carol approached the bedside hand in hand.

"Uncle Wesley? It's Charlie. I...I don't know if you can hear me, but just in case you can, I'm going to share something very important with you." He nearly shouted for joy when his uncle's eyes opened, one in a droopy squint. Stark fear was evident in Uncle Wesley's expression, and he reached out for Charlie's hand.

"Uncle Wesley, I'd like to share my testimony with you. Would that be okay?" With the slightest nod from the head on the pillow, Charlie began his story.

"Do you see this lovely lady beside me? This is my wife, Uncle Wesley. Her name is Carolina." One side of Wesley's mouth went up in what looked more like a grimace than a smile, but Carol reached out and place her hand over his and Charlie's clasped ones for a moment before Charlie went on. "I don't know if you and Aunt Lavinia knew about all of this, but even though I've attended church all my life, I was not a Christian. I did all the things Christians do. I didn't do the things Christians didn't do. But I had never placed my faith in Jesus to take my sins away. And this lady here wouldn't marry me until I did. I spent a full year running from the Lord, separated from Carol, even missing the fellowship with my parents because of my refusal to repent and turn to the Lord."

Charlie's voice grew softer when he saw tears begin to fall down his uncle's cheek. "Three weeks ago today, I asked the Lord to forgive me of my sin and received Him into my heart and life. And He *did*! He forgave me of my sin, restored my fellowship with Himself, with my parents, and with Carol as well." He let go of his uncle's hand then, placing it back on the blanket; and he opened his Bible and began to read verses from the book of Romans.

"Romans 3:10 says *As it is written. There is none righteous, no, not one.* Not me, not Carol, not you, Uncle Wesley. No one who has ever lived on this earth is righteous but Jesus Christ, the only begotten Son of God.

"Romans 3:23 tells us *For all have sinned, and come short of the glory of God.* Not only are we *not righteous* we're *sinners.* Every one of us.

"Romans 5:8, *But God commendeth His love toward us, in that while we were yet sinners, Christ died for us.* Even though He knew we were all sinners, He showed His love for us by dying on the cross to save us from our sins.

"Romans 6:23, *For the wages of sin is death, but the gift of God is eternal life through Jesus Christ our Lord.* All we receive as wages for our sin-filled life is death, but if we accept the gift of God provided through Jesus' death on the cross, we receive everlasting life!

"Romans 10:13, *For whosoever shall call upon the name of the Lord shall be saved.* That's anyone. I called on Him to save me three weeks ago, *and He did*, Uncle Wesley.

"Romans 10:9 and 10, *That if thou shalt confess with thy mouth the Lord Jesus, and shalt believe in thine heart that God* hath raised Him from the dead, thou shalt be saved. For with the heart man believeth unto righteousness; and with the mouth confession is made unto salvation."

Aunt Lavinia and Mrs. Bennett were standing in the doorway when Charlie handed his Bible to Carol. He had no idea how many of the verses they had heard, but he went on as though he'd never seen them.

"Uncle Wesley, would you like to receive Christ as your Saviour?" When he nodded, more strongly even than before, Lavinia gasped, running from the room. It was not easy as Wesley Sutherland had lost his ability to speak, but Charlie prayed, then shared with Uncle Wesley that he could simply *think* a prayer. Charlie would pray a few words, then pause for his uncle to pray them in his heart. Tears began flowing down Charlie's cheeks unchecked as he saw his uncle's lips moving ever so slightly in what was likely the first prayer of his life.

When they finished praying, Uncle Wesley's eyes opened again, and the grimace smile returned, looking more beautiful than Charlie or Carol could have ever imagined. Charlie hugged his uncle, then Carol stepped forward to read a favorite passage.

"John fourteen, verses one through six:

1. *Let not your heart be troubled: ye believe in God, believe also in Me.*
2. *In My Father's house are many mansions: if it were not so, I would have told you. I go to prepare a place for you.*
3. *And if I go and prepare a place for you, I will come again, and receive you unto Myself; that where I am, there ye may be also.*
4. *And whither I go ye know, and the way ye know.*
5. *Thomas saith unto Him, Lord, we know not whither Thou goest; and how can we know the way?*
6. *Jesus saith unto him, I am the way, the truth, and the life: no man cometh unto the Father, but by Me.*

When it was time to go, Charlie and Carol kissed Uncle Wesley's cheek. "We will be back tomorrow, Uncle Wesley; and we'll be praying for your healing. Would you like us to open the curtains so you can watch the sunset? It looks like a beauty."

Wesley nodded, then looked to the door in search of his wife. "We'll send her to you, sir, as soon as we get downstairs. Goodnight, sir, and...and *God bless you*!" Carol turned and waved from her place at her husband's side, then the two walked silently but with light hearts down the stairs. They found Lavinia and Charlie's mother in conference in the sitting room.

"Do you need us to stay a while?" Charlie asked quietly, but the look and voice with which his aunt turned on him startled him like little had in his young life.

"I think you have done *quite* enough already, Charles Bennett. How *dare* you talk of sin to a dying man, your own *uncle*? I always thought you were a loving, respectful young man, but then you go in and *preach* your self-righteous drivel at the side of your only uncle's death bed?" She buried her face in her handkerchief then, and Mrs. Bennett turned sad eyes to her son, expecting him to leave.

With a quiet but firm voice, Charlie said respectfully, "Aunt Lavinia, I've loved you all my life; but it would be a strange kind of love if I never shared with you or my uncle what was most important in my life...and yours. This may seem presumptuous, but I believe if you go upstairs, you'll find Uncle Wesley to have more joy than he's ever had, though he has a difficult time expressing it. He accepted Jesus as his Saviour just now." Lavinia looked up from her handkerchief then, her eyes confused and still flashing fire, but she held her peace. "Goodbye, Aunt Lavinia. Mother, will you be coming home later?"

"No, dear, but I will see you tomorrow." She stood up and hugged her son, squeezing him so tightly that Charlie thought his heart would burst with love for his dear mother. She turned her smiling, tearful eyes to her daughter then, hugging her close and whispering, "Just *pray*...."

Lucas still stood with the carriage when they came out into the moonlit night. Charlie could see from his expression that he was concerned, and he shared a quick praise about his uncle's coming to Christ. Lucas clapped his big hands together, looking up to heaven with a heart-felt *"Thank You, Jesus!"* before he handed Miss Carol and Charlie into the carriage for the ride home.

Chapter Thirty-One

Aunt Lavinia's Gift

Mr. Bennett was waiting for his son and daughter when they returned home. When they told him of his brother-in-law's coming to Christ, he patted his fingertips together thoughtfully.

"Now we need to pray for Lavinia's soul. She's always been so self-sufficient. Sometimes the hardest part of getting someone to the point of salvation is getting them to see their lost condition, their need."

Charlie pondered this before adding, "Yes, and I know from my own experience that accepting that free gift of salvation is part of the challenge for someone who has always been on the 'giving end'. There is no estimating the worth of salvation, but when a rich man...or woman...is faced with the fact that we can't earn it or buy it.... That makes for a difficult impediment indeed.

The three spent time in prayer before retiring, and Charlie went to the kitchen for some fruit, bread, and cheese for himself and Carol, as they had missed supper.

"Oh, Charlie, thank you so much. I'm totally famished here!" She reached for the strawberries, popping one in her mouth so quickly that Charlie began to chuckle. "Could you please help me out of this corset? I feel so uncomfortable."

Lifting her heavy gown and draping it on a chair, he reached to untie the strings of her corset. "I must be getting better at tying then!" He laughed as her hand went to her heart when he removed the corset.

"Thank you! I just feel so tired and achy. All this travel must not agree with me." She climbed into bed then, but not before grabbing the plate full of food from her husband. "Mm...come try this bread with a slice of cheese. It's delicious!" Not one to be shy about eating, Charlie joined his wife until every crumb was devoured.

"That hit the spot. Now, Mrs. Bennett, are you ready for sleep, or would you mind another session of ardent kissing?"

"Could you just hold me? I'm feeling rather worn out. Here, snuggle up behind me and we can sleep like spoons."

"Head to toe?"

Carol couldn't help laughing. "*'Head to toe'*? No, I mean like when you place spoons together and they kind of, I don't know, 'nestle'...? Oh, just remind me never to let you put the silver away!" She giggled a bit more before reaching to turn down the lamp. "Goodnight, my love."

"Goodnight."

≈≈≈

Wesley Sutherland went Home to be with the LORD sometime during the night. Mrs. Bennett sent word to Ben and Charlie and Carol the next morning, and when she came home at noon for some much needed rest, she shared in detail of what had taken place after the young couple had left.

"Oh, Carol, it was so incredibly poignant. Lavinia is lost, in every way now that her dear husband Wesley is gone. She was able to get control of her emotions before going up to see him after you two left, but he was smiling that twisted grimace of a smile as he stared out the window behind us. I asked him about his salvation experience at one point. He looked directly into my eyes and nodded with perfect understanding apparently, then he turned to gaze out the window again.

"Poor Lavinia had fallen asleep in the chair by his bed just before midnight; and I began to sing to him, some of the dear old familiar hymns of our Home in Heaven, which Wesley in all his unchurched years had never heard. He fell asleep around one and never woke up. The physician they called in said he must have had a second stroke which took him in his sleep."

Carol smiled through her tears. "But to be absent from the body is to be present with the Lord, and Uncle Wesley is *Home* now, Mother!" The two embraced, but Carol straightened rather suddenly. "Forgive me, I...I'm just feeling a little achy. But now we need to be praying for your dear sister."

It occurred to Laura Bennett what the cause of her daughter's discomfort could be, but she tucked the thought aside as the two joined in prayer for her sister's salvation.

✥

Mrs. Bennett returned to the Sutherland Mansion to help in the preparations for the funeral and burial. Lavinia was absolutely worthless with grief, and Laura suspected the Holy Spirit's working on her heart. Still, she never brought up the salvation verses they'd heard Charlie share with Wesley Sunday night. Finally it came time to decide where the funeral was to be held.

"Do you think your pastor would allow the service to be held at your church, Sister?"

"Yes, I think he would be most willing to hold the funeral there. Do you wish for him to speak?"

"Perhaps. Yes, I think Wesley would want that." Lavinia's eyes were still filled with confusion, but as the week went on, she grew more at peace.

At the funeral Saturday, Charlie, Carol, Albert, and Celia sang an *a cappella* quartet arrangement of Newton's *Amazing Grace*, and Lavinia's eyes never left her nephew's face.

When everyone was giving their condolences at the Sutherland mansion that evening, Lavinia wept quietly, but she spent time with each guest. When she finally worked up the courage to talk with her nephew, he was more than willing to step into a more private room.

"Oh, Charlie, can you ever forgive me for the way I spoke to you Sunday night? I was so very wrong...."

Charlie drew her close to his chest, patting her beautiful snowy-white crown of hair affectionately. "Aunt Lavinia, how could I *not* forgive you when the Lord has forgiven *me* of so much?"

She pulled back, looking up at her nephew's handsome face. "Oh, Charles, bless you! And bless that beautiful bride of yours! You know, I have a wedding gift for you. I just picked it out this week, so in a way I feel like Wesley helped me pick it out for you. He never much cared what I bought while he was living, always let me spoil or neglect you as I so chose. Here, come and see what I've found."

The two walked from the hall through the large mahogany doors opening into his uncle's library and study. There on the desk were three beautifully bound books. "This is *Strong's Exhaustive Concordance of the Bible*. I thought you might wish to add it to your collection. And here is a wonderful atlas that has been in Wesley's collection for years that I think you will enjoy. And this," she handed a much smaller book to him, "is a book on being a homemaker. Our mother gave it to me when we married before the war, then I loaned it to Laura to read. I think Carolina will find it very interesting, even entertaining in places!" She looked at her only nephew as he stood there still looking at the concordance. "Are you pleased then?"

"Yes! They're *wonderful*, Aunt Lavinia. I'm sorry I didn't say so right away, I was just so distracted. This is a wonderful book, a superb study aid. And I'm sure I'll enjoy the atlas and Carol will enjoy the homemaking book as well. Thank you so much." He hugged his aunt then, noticing not for the first time how different she was from his mother.

She reached out her hand, sparkling with diamond rings and bracelet, and patted his cheek. "Bless you, Charlie Bennett! You're a dear boy." She turned to return to the last of her guests before adding, "I'll see you at church tomorrow. Don't be late!"

Charlie's eyes closed in a quick prayer as he answered with a smile, "I'll be there!"

Charlie was so excited to see his aunt at church the next morning that he failed to notice how pale his wife was looking. The four siblings-in-law were in the choir all together for the first time in many months, and Charlie's heart felt quite full. When he watched his aunt make her way to the front during the invitation he nearly shouted for joy. He didn't mean to look down from the loft, as the choir always sang a quiet invitational hymn; but when he saw movement at his mother's side, he knew Lavinia was coming to the Lord.

Pastor quietly motioned for Laura Bennett to come up to counsel her sister, taking her into an alcove for privacy. At the close of the service, Pastor Lehman mentioned a soul coming to the Lord, then dismissed with a prayer of blessing for all those there and those who were unable to come.

When the final "amen" was said and the organ music began playing as everyone gathered their things, Charlie's heart nearly stopped as he saw his wife drop to the floor, her sister easing her down as gently as she could.

❧❧

Mr. Bennett told his wife of Carol's fainting at the close of the service as soon as she reached the carriage.

"Ben, I think she may be expecting!" she said excitedly. Her husband's expression went from worry to extreme joy in an instant.

"But, how did you know this?"

"She hasn't really been complaining, but she did mention feeling achy when I hugged her last week. It occurred to me then, but with the funeral and all I never had a chance to speak with her. I hope the doctor discovers this right away so they won't be so worried."

Mr. Bennett grinned. "He'll probably do a pregnancy test first, and when the rabbit dies, leave with a smile!" He hugged his wife close to his side in the buggy, then encouraged the horse to pick up the pace.

Doctor Whittle was carrying his bag downstairs when the Bennetts arrived home. Their son was pacing the floor nervously. Doctor Whittle set down his bag, then began methodically rolling down his sleeves.

"I have a test I need to run at the office right away, but I'm almost certain I know what caused Carol's illness. Charlie, go to her, lad. I've already discussed it with her."

"Is it...this *is* something she will heal from quickly, right, Doctor?"

"I'm afraid not, Son. If it is what I think it is, it could mean a total change for both of you, even something that will effect you both for the rest of your lives."

As Charlie climbed the stairs, Doctor Whittle turned to wink at Mr. and Mrs. Bennetts' smiling faces. "Yes, I figured you'd both know. You should have a wee babe in the house come the New Year or shortly thereafter. Looks like a second generation honeymoon baby! Congratulations, you two." He gave them each a warm hug, then picked up his hat and headed out the door.

Charlie entered the room quietly and found his beautiful wife with tears in her eyes. Crossing the room with great strides, he sat down on the bed beside her.

"Oh, darling, whatever it is, I know the Lord will see us through this!" He held her close, thinking she was sobbing, but he suddenly realized she was shaking with laughter. He held her out at arms length, his fingers gently encircling her upper arms as he studied her tired but beautiful face. "You're *laughing*? Why? What on earth...?"

"Charlie, I'm *expecting*!" She nodded as the light dawned on his face. "We're going to have a *baby*!" They hugged, then Charlie drew back, looking carefully at his wife as though somehow she had just changed. She pulled the blanket down a bit to reveal her still very flat tummy. "Doctor Whittle said he was fairly certain, and I *was* due for my monthly cycle early last week. He said we probably conceived on our honeymoon like your parents did with you!" She knew Charlie was figuring in his head how old the tiny baby was.

"So he's only two weeks old? And we have *how long* to go?"

Carol groaned. "I don't even want to *think* about it, but another eight and a half months actually! Then we will have him...or her...to hold. Oh, Charlie...." He gave her a feather-soft kiss before he placed his hand on her stomach, spreading his fingers wide. He spoke while still looking at her middle.

"Carol, the greatest gifts of my life have been because of you. I may never have gotten saved had you not made me face my need head on. I will treasure how you gave yourself to me in marriage every day of my life. But I never thought...I never hoped...." He leaned forward and kissed her again tenderly.

"Thank you, Charlie. And we need to thank the Lord. *The fruit of the womb is His reward.*" The two bowed in prayer, then waited for the real rejoicing until the doctor called with the positive results some time later. Meanwhile, they ate the impromptu picnic-in-bed Mrs. Bennett had prepared and brought up on a tray.

Mr. Bennett came in from the carriage house just as she was setting their food on the table. "Well, Gramma, what's for dinner?" He found that the appetizer was a big hug and kiss.

༺༻

The next weeks were not easy ones for Carol. She seemed to have twenty-four hour sickness instead of just morning sickness, and she was losing weight instead of gaining it. She stopped wearing her corset, thinking that would help stop the dizziness; but as the weeks went by she actually felt more and more dizzy. Doctor Whittle understood her concern and had her come to his office for an exam, but he said he believed the baby was still doing fine.

"What about the bleeding? I mean, it isn't much, but I didn't think that happened when one was expecting."

"Every pregnancy is somewhat different. Some women have no morning sickness, some like you seem to have day and night sickness. Some women never pass blood until the baby is about to be born, but others have regular cycles through some or all of the pregnancy. Some women only have problems the first three months, some it goes on until the baby is born."

Seeing her reaction, he held up his hand. "Now, don't despair, my dear! We have every reason to believe that this baby will be born perfectly healthy in God's good time. To quote one of the most practical phrases of Scripture, *this too shall pass.* You're barely a month and a half along. If all goes according to the 'norm', you're half-way done with the queasiness and dizziness. I would think by the end of July you should be feeling better, though by that point you may start waddling a bit as you increase in size." He laughed at her facial expression. "Believe me, Carol, Charlie will think you never looked lovelier than when you are great with his child. Now, go home and get your feet up. Take it easy, all right, dear?"

"Yes, sir, and thank you so much. That really calms my heart." Before she turned to go, she smiled again at the Doctor. "And I hear from Celia and Albert that you're going to be a great-grandfather again soon?"

The doctor grinned, nodding. "I'm sure your parents must be thrilled. Two grandchildren in the coming year! What a blessing! Now, off with you. Get some rest!" He turned back to his paperwork, and she kissed him on the top of his balding head before walking out of the office with a smile and a song in her heart.

❧❧

Charlie was watching his wife as she lay there, totally spent after another bout of sickness. Her hair was wet with perspiration, and he went to get a cool, wet cloth to hopefully help ease her discomfort.

"Oh, Charlie, I feel so *miserable*. Have I had a whole day, twenty-four hours together without feeling dreadful?"

He had never heard her sound so down, and it concerned him. "Don't worry, dear, I've not lost faith. I'm just so sick and tired of feeling...sick and tired!" He dampened a washcloth from the sink, bathing her face and neck. "Mm...that feels nice." She lay there looking so fragile, yet the night before she had seemed fine to her young bridegroom. He reached out and touched her hair, lifting it onto the pillow as he cooled the back of her neck. "I think I need to get into the tub and wet myself all over. Do you mind?"

"Of course not," he said, giving her a hand. He noticed from the stains on her shift as he helped her undress that she'd been passing blood again. Calming himself with the words of advice Doctor Whittle had given Carol, he got the water running in the bathtub as she used the commode. In a few minutes she was neck deep in bubbles, Charlie helping her wash her hair.

He reached to grip either side of the tub as he lowered

himself to kiss his sweet-smelling wife. "Call me when you're ready to get out of the tub. I don't want you to fall." He smiled at her raised eyebrow.

When he helped her into her clean night dress, he asked, "May I touch your stomach again?" She nodded, pulling the nightgown down on either side to stretch it across the slight swelling of her middle. Charlie placed his hand over the tiny babe, willing him to feel the love he already felt for the child.

"Oh, little one, we love you so much! We can hardly wait to hold you and kiss your sweet pink cheeks. What color will your hair be? Your eyes? What will you want to be when you grow up? I don't even know what your name will be, because I don't know if you're my son or my daughter! But I love you, wee one! I love you so much." When he looked back up at his wife, she had fallen asleep. With as little noise as possible, he dressed in his nightclothes and joined the two dear ones already in bed.

Chapter Thirty-Two

The Trying of Your Faith

The Bennett House
July 4th, 1890

It had been another long night and queasy morning for Carol, and she and Charlie agreed that she should stay home from church even though it was the Independence Day celebration.

"I surely hope I don't feel this awful the entire pregnancy! I feel achy all over, even my shoulder. And even though I know Doctor Whittle said the blood spotting my shift was normal for some women, it still frightens me a little." She played with the curls at his temple, gazing into his chocolate brown eyes. "I'm not complaining. I'm so happy that we were able to create this baby! It just seems so long right now before he's going to join our little family."

"*He?*" Charlie asked with a raised brow. Carol giggled.

"Or 'she', I know! Now, take your handsome self to church and sing and learn for both of us. Tell me all about it when you get home." She looked so beautiful reclining comfortably on the pillows in their bed.

"I love you, Carolina," he said, leaning to kiss her with all the passion of a newlywed. She responded with all her heart, but when the kiss ended she leaned back on her pillow looking spent from the small exertion. "I'm sorry, Carol! Forgive me, please forgive me."

"There is nothing to forgive, Charlie. I, too, feel a bit short-changed after becoming with child so early on in our marriage. But this child is a blessing from the Lord, and once my body adjusts I should be feeling better very soon. I trust very, *very* soon!"

He kissed her hand, then kissed his finger and touched the tip of her nose. "I won't even talk to a soul after church, just *come straight home* after the last 'amen'. Okay?"

She giggled, then nodded. "Give my love to Celia and Albert!" After agreeing to that last wish, he was gone.

※

Charlie was removing his choir robe and turning in his patriotic sheet music in the choir room when he heard his name called. Turning quickly, he saw Lucas entering, clearly out of breath.

"Mistah Charles, sir, you gots to go home *now*. I rode the General. He's tied up outside. Take him, sir!" He shook Charlie's arm with the last sentence seeing that the young man seemed frozen in place. Leaving his hat, suit coat, and gloves, Charlie fled the room and found the General, galloping at a fearsome pace all the way home.

He could hear Carol as soon as he opened the front door. "Charlie! *Oh, God, help me! Charlie!*" Fear shot through him as he heard Carol's panic and pain-filled voice. Running up the stairs two at a time he froze at what he saw when he reached their bedroom. Jessie was bathing Carol's face and hands in cool water, but her face was pale as the sheets behind her, and her lips were nearly blue! Forcing himself to go forward, he walked woodenly to her side only to find that, mercifully, she had fainted.

"What is happening?" he whispered to Jessie as he cradled his wife's limp form. "When did this start? She was *fine* this morning, just dizzy! *Oh, God, please don't take my wife. Please. Please, Lord.*"

Jessie wasn't in much better shape, her huge eyes reddened with tears and stress. "I done sent Lucas for Doc Whittle 'bout twenty minutes ago. Missy Carol, she was restin' fine, then alluva sudden, she just screamed out like someone had stabbed her!" Jessie started to moan out her heart cries in prayer, the memories were so painful to her. "I know she done lost the baby, but I'm afraid if the good Lord don't help us we's gonna lose her, too."

Beatrix came in then and she did what she could to help. They heard more steps on the stairs and Doctor Whittle came in, assessing the scene and sending Jessie on an errand, kindly keeping her busy as well as getting her out of the way.

Charlie told Doctor Whittle what Jessie had told him. "What went wrong? What happened to cause this?"

"Charlie, from the best I can figure Carol is suffering from a burst fallopian tube. The pregnancy...the baby must have been growing inside one of her fallopian tubes instead of making its way into the uterus. The tube is much too small to maintain a growing fetus, and—"

"She definitely lost the baby, I know that. But...but will Carolina survive?"

Doctor Whittle paused in his work long enough to look into Charlie's eyes. "If God allows, Son. Now pray, and bathe her face and neck in this cool water. We need to make her as comfortable as possible." The room was just shy of sweltering in the July heat, but Charlie was glad the doctor hadn't sent him away nevertheless. He couldn't have left her side; but her face seemed to grow more and more pale as he put the cloth on her cheeks, forehead, neck, and chin.

After what seemed an eternity, Doctor Whittle gave him a word of encouragement. "I think the internal bleeding has lessened. She mustn't be moved or it could start again. Beatrix?" He called the calmer of the servants to help him change Carol's gown and bed linens, carefully rolling the patient on her side. They cut the perspiration-drenched gown off of her, then placed a soft robe beneath her, returning her to her back ever so carefully. After gently pulling her arms through the sleeves and draping the layers across her middle, Charlie thought his wife looked like a beautiful porcelain doll lying there.

Beatrix was carrying the linens and ruined gown out when Mr. and Mrs. Bennett reached the door. Charlie couldn't leave his wife's side; so Doctor Whittle, who had done all he could do, went to talk with them. Mrs. Bennett turned to sob into her husband's shoulder as the doctor explained, having looked beyond the doctor at her precious daughter and son.

※

"Charlie, you need your rest, Son." Mr. Bennett had come in again hours later with his wife to take over watching and waiting by Carol's bedside. Charlie looked nearly as pale as Carol's still motionless form.

"I...I can't. I'm sorry, I just can't leave. Could you have someone bring up a cot that I could sleep on, so I can be right here when she wakes up?"

"Of course." Mr. Bennett turned to do Charlie's bidding, but Mrs. Bennett walked over and began rubbing Charlie's stress-cramped back and shoulders.

"Charlie?" His response was a while in coming, but he replied. "Sitting here grieving is not going to bring her out of this deep, deep darkness she's passing through. May we sing to her? If you don't think you can do it, I will sing alone; but I just know the sound of your voice would strengthen her."

Charlie smiled his boyish smile at his mother, her words of wisdom filling him with hope and a renewed strength. He began with *What a Friend We Have in Jesus*; and although his mother tried to sing with him, after the first stanza she just went to her knees and continued her prayer vigil as Charlie sang verse after verse of favorite hymns.

The cot was made next to the bed. After singing for nearly two hours, Charlie helped his mother to her feet and kissed her goodnight. Then he went back and leaned over the bed, his breath moving the curl of hair at her temple as he spoke softly in her ear.

"Carolina, I'll be right here. If you need me, I'm right here next to you." He kissed her cheek, relieved that it still felt cool. Doctor Whittle had warned him of the dangers from a fever, but so far she had remained cool and quiet. "I love you, Carolina. Listen to me. I love you, and I'm praying for you." He could taste the salt tears as he prayed for her, out loud so she could draw strength from the sound of his voice.

When he finished praying, he climbed into the cot and slept. Beatrix watched and prayed from her chair just outside the doorway, a tiny smile lighting her face as she heard her sweet Mister Charles snoring softly.

Chapter Thirty-Three

Recovery

Uncertain what had caused him to awaken, Charlie sat up quickly in the cot when he remembered the events of the previous day. Jessie was spooning warm broth into Carol's mouth, and she was taking it gladly. As soon as Charlie saw her eyes were open, he rose, walking to her side. Jessie handed him the cup of broth and made her way from the room without a sound.

"Hello, darling." She tried to raise her arms to embrace him, but she was much too weak. He carefully rested on the bed beside her, holding her close to his heart and petting her hair.

"Oh, Charlie, the baby is...gone...isn't he?" Not knowing what she could take, but unable to lie to her, he nodded silently. She cried into his shirt front, grieving their loss. Drawing her closer, he spoke to her gently.

"Carolina, he is in heaven now with Jesus. I know it. We'll meet him someday. But for now, I need to help you get well again."

Her voice was weak as a child's as she asked, "Was I very sick, Charlie?" She didn't seem to remember the agony, and he was glad.

"Yes, my love. Very sick. But the Lord spared you, and I will thank Him for that for the rest of my life." He wondered for a moment if she had fallen asleep, but then she spoke with that weak, breathless voice again.

"Did you sing to me, Charlie? I...I thought I heard you

singing, and then the man came in...the man in white. He said he was here to...to take our baby...Home...." The last was said on a sigh, and then she was asleep.

Charlie held her for some time, tears falling freely as he thanked God that it wasn't Carol's time to be taken Home. He laid her back down on the pillows, pulling her robe more securely about her before kissing her sleeping lips.

※

When Doc Whittle arrived mid-morning, Carol was just waking up again. He went in and examined her, then came down to talk with the family while Jessie helped her dress in a nightgown, braiding her hair for her.

"She is in a very precarious condition right now. Until she is fully healed, any strain made in her abdominal cavity could cause the bleeding to start again. Think of it as a scab that you cannot see, on a very deep wound. She is going to have to be treated like an invalid for a while until I can give her a clean bill of health." He looked at Charlie then, making sure the newlywed knew how serious her condition was. "Charlie, you're going to have to wait a good while, maybe months, before the two of you can have relations again. Even then, if she becomes pregnant again too soon it could very well prove fatal. Forgive my bluntness—"

"There is nothing to forgive, sir. Thank you for speaking freely. I'm more than willing to wait. I...I have wondered more than once in the past several hours if she would still be here, sir. Do you think she will ever fully recover? Ever be able to have another child?"

Doctor Whittle pushed his glasses high on his head as he pondered what to say. "I really don't know, Son. She has been through a lot, but some women who have gone through this have gone on to bear children. Some have not for whatever reason. I think as with everything it is best to just wait on the Lord...place this matter entirely in His hands." Dr. Whittle put his hand on Charlie's shoulder. "You are a very young man in the Lord to be going through this kind of trial, but God is faithful, Charlie. He won't give you more than you can bear according to I Corinthians

10:13. Can you trust Him with your wife's life?"

"Yes, sir."

"All right then." That settled he went on to discuss how to care for Carol. "I've already gone over much of this with Jessie and Beatrix, as they were asking if they could help her into her night clothes. Here is some medication for the pain, and it should make her drowsy. Make sure she gets plenty to drink. She needs to replace that blood...clear liquids, maybe fruit juices, apple or pear would be good. Try preparing her some beef or chicken broth as well." He stood then, shaking their hands one by one. "God be with you, dear friends."

Charlie looked over at his parents after he walked Doctor Whittle to the door. Their faces were still masks of worry. He went over and hugged them both, then shared some of his heart.

"I meant what I said to Dr. Whittle. I honestly didn't know if she.... She was so pale, and her voice when I came in from church...." Charlie shook his head to distance himself from the memories. "But the Lord spared her. I don't know why He did, but I'm so very grateful." He paused a moment, then went on to say, "And thank you both for praying, not just now, but all my life. God has heard and answered with so many blessings. The fact that Carolina Bennett is alive is one more beautiful blessing, and I know He heard the prayers of you and Jessie and Beatrix and...."

They all three hugged again, then prayed for their dear Carol before Charlie returned upstairs. His wife was propped up in bed again, Jessie holding the cup for her to drink some water when he entered.

"Oh, Charlie, there you are. Come, talk to me so this woman will stop trying to drown me with chicken bouillon and water!" Both Charlie and Jessie were so glad to hear Carol laugh that they exchanged a grin as the faithful servant handed the cup to Charlie.

"Good luck to ya, Mistah Charles. She's bein' so persnickety I can hardly bear the sight of her." She turned around and winked at her Missy Carol before she stepped out and closed the door.

"You're looking better even than this morning, Carolina. How are you feeling?"

Carol sighed. "Weak as a kitten, I'm afraid. I already feel

sleepy again. I know you're not tired, but can you just climb in here and hold me until I fall asleep?" Charlie kicked his shoes off and climbed in so cautiously that Carol giggled. "I'm not asleep *yet*, Charlie! You needn't fear waking me." He leaned on one arm as he stroked her cheek, pulling her braid over her shoulder gently. She snuggled in to his side, breathing a deep sigh as she smelled his aftershave. "I love you, Charlie."

"I love you, Carolina." He looked down to see she had fallen asleep, but he just held her close and kept talking quietly. "I love you more than I've ever loved anyone in my life. I love you enough to *give* my life if that is what it takes." He stroked her back, her neck, her hair. "I love you enough to say 'no' to my own physical desires for however long it takes until you are well again. I love you enough that, even if the Lord never blesses us with another child, I shall be perfectly content."

Charlie had to consciously calm the beating of his heart as he held her so close, knowing it would be a long time indeed before he could satisfy the physical longing to be with her as man and wife. *"Dear Lord, give me strength...and wisdom and patience in this."* He lay his head on the pillows then, just listening to her steady breathing as he prayed, at some point falling into a sweet sleep, his wife in his arms.

&

Carol continued to improve, seeming to be almost back to normal by the middle of July. She asked so sweetly if Charlie could carry her downstairs to the sitting room. "I love our bedroom, but if I see the same four walls another entire day, I'll scream." She said this with a drippy-sweet Southern drawl, sending Charlie into gales of laughter.

"I sometimes forget that you are from the deep south, my dear! You are almost *too* good at that accent!" When he came to the bedside to gather her up in his arms, she reached out and drew his head down, kissing him hungrily. It was all Charlie could do not to respond in kind, but he took her hands from around his neck, sitting down beside her. "Oh, Carolina, please don't cry...."

"Charlie, what is it? Why don't you kiss me? This past week

you've treated me like your sister instead of your wife of three short months."

"Actually, three months, two days, and...." He smiled guiltily at her scowling face. "I know, this time the accuracy is not appreciated. Carol, I...I should have explained before, but—"

"But *what*? Am I no longer attractive to you that you...that you don't—" He reached his hand out to touch her lips, effectively halting her from saying more.

"Carol, do you know that what happened that Sunday could have killed you? Do you know that you were very close to leaving me?" Carol shook her head, then the tears began anew as she saw his filling with tears. "Doctor Whittle told me very specifically that we were not to...to have husband and wife relations again until he gave you a clean bill of health. He said it could very well be months. *Months*, darling, not days amounting to a week or two." He wiped the tears from her cheek, then took her hand. "Believe me, my love, watching you suffer was enough to show me the importance of controlling my desires."

Her eyes slid shut as she realized how strong he had had to be. "Oh, Charlie, I'm so sorry. I was so confused, and I just missed...well, after throwing myself at you as I just did, I'm sure you understand." She looked down at her hands folded in her lap. "I guess we'll just have to pretend we're courting again, hmm?"

"That's a very good way of looking at it. Yes, we're back to courting. This will be good for us I think!" He reached out and took her hand, bending over it gallantly and placing an affectionate kiss there. "May I escort you down to the sitting room, my love?"

Giggling at how he was making this almost fun, she put her arms around him, and he lifted her gently. "You've lost a good deal of weight, Carolina." His heart pounded as he judged the difference between her current weight and her weight when he picked her up on their honeymoon.

"Yes, I'm not surprised. I had already lost weight during the first weeks of pregnancy, and now.... I haven't had much appetite even when I was allowed to go back on solids. I'm sorry."

"Sorry for what?" he asked as he slowly navigated the stairs. Mrs. Bennett was at the bottom of the stairs watching her loved ones' careful descent.

"Sorry that you're stuck with a skinny wife for a while."

"What are you two talking about?" Mrs. Bennett smiled as Charlie and Carol exchanged glances.

Charlie waited until Carol was settled on the davenport, pillows behind her and an afghan over her legs, before answering his mother. "We were discussing how I've been seeing less and less of her these days...she's dwindling down to nothing. I think it's time to put the challenge to Venetia and Jessie to fatten my girl up some."

Laura had noticed Carol's weight loss as well. "She may need some sunshine, too, Charles. Maybe if she does well with this little excursion today, tomorrow she can go out on the veranda. Carol, dear, do you feel up to some company for lunch?"

"Oh, that would be wonderful! Who?"

"Albert and Celia are coming. I invited them yesterday."

"Oh, Mother, thank you so much! I can hardly wait to see them." She remembered then that Celia, too, had become pregnant right away, and she would be about three months along now. Charlie and his mother saw her thoughtful look, exchanging glances. Carol went on, "No, don't worry. I do not for an instant begrudge them their healthy pregnancy! Not for even a fraction of a moment." Looking at Charlie's mother she asked softly, "Is that why she hasn't come before now, do you think?"

"It's possible, dear. She may very well have thought that." Hearing a carriage coming up the drive, Mrs. Bennett stood. "That's probably them. Are you ready?"

Pinching her cheeks for color and arranging her afghan a bit, she nodded, smiling a brilliant smile at her mother-in-law. Laura came over and kissed her daughter before walking to the door.

When Carol saw the hesitation in Celia's approach, it wrenched her heart. "Oh, Celia!" The two embraced as the men shook hands then took a seat without a word. Wiping one another's tears, the sisters seemed to talk nonstop for minutes before acknowledging the men's presence. It wasn't until Mrs. Bennett came in with trays of sandwiches and pickles and fruit that they realized.

Charlie smiled broadly while asking, "Shall I pray for the

food, and then you two may resume?" They giggled like school girls, then closed their eyes in prayer. *"Dear Father God, I thank You that You've healed my wife so that she could come downstairs today. I pray that You would heal her completely in Your perfect time. Please bless this food to our bodies' strengthening and nourishment, and bless our fellowship with our brother and sister. In Jesus' name, amen."*

Mr. Bennett had slipped in from his office during the prayer, and he grinned as Charlie heaped a plate with sandwiches, then took them to Carol.

Pulling a footstool beside her, he held the plate, explaining it was for both of them. She took a bite of the cucumber and cream cheese sandwich first, finishing the quartered piece off in three bites. Charlie grinned and handed her an appealingly bright orange carrot stick.

"In case you didn't notice, I've lost weight. Charlie is trying to fatten me up!"

Albert grinned at his wife. "Celia's been taking this 'eating for two' thing quite seriously, but—" He realized his error too late, and it nearly took his breath away when he saw Carol's initial reaction. "I'm so sorry."

"No...no, don't feel bad." Smiling at her brother-in-law, she went on. "I think it would be good to *talk* about this together with you and Celia. May we?" Both of them nodded, setting their plates aside.

"I...I don't know why I lost our baby. I mean, I've heard all the medical terminology, but I don't know *why*. I do know that the Lord allowed it, and that must suffice. But please, *please* don't think for a moment that I am any less happy for you than I would have been had that Sunday never happened."

Charlie expected tears, but there wasn't so much as a hint of them in his wife's voice and eyes. He closed his eyes and sighed; then after kissing her on the cheek, he, Albert, and Mr. Bennett left together while the ladies remained in the sitting room with Carolina.

"Oh, Sister, I've been praying and praying for you...for your healing both physical and emotional. I'm so glad that the Lord has given you such strength." She picked up her plate and began eating again. "Don't make me eat alone, you two! Albert and Charlie stuffed their pockets before leaving, but there is still plenty for us."

Mrs. Bennett laughed, picking her plate back up. "Did they *really* squirrel away food in their pockets?"

"Charlie did that at the wedding reception, too. Did Albert?"

"He *did*! He started pulling them out of his pockets when we reached the hotel room!" The three of them laughed.

"Celia, have you felt the baby move yet?" Carol asked her sister quietly.

"I don't know, Carrie. I've felt little flutters, like a butterfly. I'll be sure to let you know when the little rascal starts kicking."

Mrs. Bennett sighed. "Oh, I remember those little butterflies! I *do*! That *is* the first movement, Celia, I'm sure of it."

The three sat with their own thoughts a moment before the conversation continued, but there were no more awkward moments the rest of the afternoon. When Albert and Celia left, they each kissed her cheek and told her they were praying for her.

Charlie walked them to the door, waving as they drove away. Carol looked tired when he came back into the sitting room. "You overdid it, didn't you? Are you ready for me to take you up?"

"Yes, please." He gathered her close, kissing her full on the lips before starting up the stairs. "That was very nice! Whatever was it for?"

"Oh, just because I love you." She leaned on his shoulder, then went willingly to bed when they reached their rooms. "Are you going to sleep?"

"I am, whether I want to or not." Rolling over on her side to face him, she said, "Will you join me?" He took off his shoes and socks, then his coat, tie, and shirt.

"Even with the breeze, it's too hot for all of these layers." Backing up to her to "nestle like spoons", he sighed as she put her arm over him, caressing his chest while she snuggled close to his back. It was so much easier to keep his mind off his physical desires when she wasn't touching him, but he wouldn't tell her that for the world. Her hand lay still in sleep after only a few minutes, and Charlie wasn't far behind.

Chapter Thirty-Four

Honest Communication

Jessie tended to Carol's needs right up until her own baby was due in mid-August. Carol was so excited for her friend, and never more so than when she heard from Beatrix that Jessie had been blessed with a girl.

"Oh, how *perfect*! A boy and a girl now. That's every mother's dream!"

Beatrix smiled as she tucked some of her graying hair back under her white kerchief. "Do you think, Missy Carol, that you're feelin' up to visitin' Jessie and the baby? I live real close, walk to work with her most mornin's."

"I'd love to, Beatrix! Do you think Charlie and Lucas could take us tonight when Charlie gets home from work?" Beatrix nodded, smiling in relief that Missy Carol didn't seem to feel any bitterness at all over her own loss and another's blessing.

Charlie hadn't even closed the door before Carol was pleading to go see Jessie and the baby. He laughed, but left his hat on and led her back out to his buggy, which as he suspected Lucas was still standing beside awaiting the decision of whether or not to go visiting. He smiled as he handed Carol in, all the happier as he saw that she was getting some color and weight back. Then the four set off as Beatrix climbed up beside Lucas.

It was nearly sunset when they arrived, and the day old infant was making her voice heard already. Carol smiled as she walked arm in arm with Charlie up the path to her friend's grey clapboard cottage. The green shutters and door gave it such a neat and homey appearance that Carol couldn't help but know it was Jessie's home. The small flower gardens on either side of the front steps were tended to perfection, and Carol wondered how Jessie found the energy to weed and tend and do housework after taking care of Charlie's family all day six days a week.

The door opened onto the tiniest of living rooms, a table with a small bouquet of wildflowers sitting in the corner. Beatrix peeked in a door off the living room, then motioned for Charlie and Carol to come in.

The precious baby was nursing, discreetly covered with a rose-colored blanket. Jessie beamed as Carol came forward to gaze at the tiniest toes she'd ever seen. "Oh, Jessie, she's *perfect*! What did you name her?'

"That's the bes' part. Her name is 'Jasmine Carolina', for my favorite flower and my favorite sister."

Charlie reached a finger out to touch the tiny foot, amazed at its perfection. "I'm heading out to chat with the men folk. George just got home from work. But congratulations, Jessie. We're so happy for you." He moved a chair beside the bed for Carol, and she sat down comfortably close.

"Thank you, Jessie, for naming her partly after me! I am honored." Jessie smiled, her eyes glistening with tears.

"My sweet, sweet Missy Carol, I'd give anything to see you holdin' your precious baby in your arms. It's gonna happen, you mark my words. I'm guessin' before this time next year, your arms will be cradlin' your own child." She peeked under the blanket and had to wiggle the baby a bit to wake her back up, then she lifted her to her shoulder and gently patted her tiny back. "I still pray every day for the good Lord to bless you, and I *know* He's goin' to answer those prayers in His own good time." Little Jasmine made the tiniest sound that must have been a burp, and Jessie settled her down to nurse some more.

"Oh, Jessie, I wish I had your faith!" The tears came in a torrent then as she shared her heart. "I've tried to be so strong for Charlie...I know he's been so worried! But, Jessie, sometimes I wake up in the morning still thinking the baby's there, that I'll still be giving birth in January. Then it all comes back, hurting like a fresh wound." Jessie patted her hand, rocking the baby in her arms as though it would somehow comfort her friend.

"Can I be your big sister for a second?" When she saw Carol's nod, she went on. "You need to talk with Charlie. He's there to share your burdens with you. You can't bear this alone, and you shouldn't even be tryin' to. He'll turn you to Scripture, you know he will! And you'll both be comforted with the Lord's own comfort then. Do you hear me?"

Carol lifted her eyes to her friend, her smile a shadow of the joyful Missy Carol Jessie longed to see again. "You know I'm right, don't you?" This brought on more of a smile, and by the time her friend left she looked content.

❧❦

"Charlie, I have a confession to make." Charlie put down the periodical he was reading in bed and looked at his wife.

"And what heinous sin have you committed lately?" His smile faded as he saw the seriousness of her expression.

"I...I haven't been completely honest with you, and that's wrong of me. You see, losing our baby, it's been more difficult than I've let on. I wanted to be strong...." She began to sob as Charlie wrapped his strong arms around her, sheltering her against his chest.

"Oh, Carolina, you're such a rotten liar." He said it so softly and gently that she thought she'd misunderstood. She drew back and looked at him, seeing his smile as he pulled her back down to his chest. "Of course I knew you were not sharing your feelings with me. Darling, no one could go through what you've been through and come out completely unscathed, Christian or otherwise. I've been praying that you would open up to me. Thank you."

Charlie held her close until the tears stopped, then he cradled her in his arms where he could look into her face. "And he was 'our' baby. Although I haven't suffered physically as you have, I've grieved over losing him, too, my love. And don't think this is 'it' with the grieving either. When the memories flood in, *please* talk to me. I'm here, just waiting to listen, to hold you, to pray with you."

"I'm sorry. I wasn't even thinking of you, of your grieving. And I know seeing me in pain.... I just didn't want to become, I don't know, *morose* about everything...dwelling on the 'what ifs' instead of being content." She reached up and touched his face, fascinated by the roughness of his whiskers. "Charlie, does it...has it occurred to you that we thought *you'd* be the one who couldn't have children, and now *I'm* the one having problems?"

"Actually, that has helped in a way. I just try to think of all the comforting things you would say and do if the table were still turned." He ran the back of his fingers down her cheek. "I'm so sorry it had to be you. I've prepared all my adult life to not be able to have children. You had no warning. I don't understand, but I *do* know that God is still in control." He saw the shadow of doubt in her expression, reassuring her quickly. "Just as He was in control all the years Hannah in the Bible prayed for a child. One day, the Lord may bless us with another child, perhaps several children. But if He doesn't, we must take it as from His hand. Can you do that? Can you trust Him with your heart's desire for a child?"

Once again, her husband's spiritual maturity amazed her. "Yes, Charlie," was all she could say, but that sufficed.

"*Good.* Now, roll over and go to sleep so we can get some rest. I'm taking you to Dr. Whittle in the morning to see if we can get that 'clean bill of health'." Carol giggled, but couldn't resist giving her husband a thorough kiss goodnight.

"I love you, Mr. Bennett!"

Reaching to turn down the lamp, he whispered, "And I love you, Mrs. Bennett. More and more every day. Sweet dreams."

※

Carol wanted to do something extra special for Charlie's twenty-third birthday. She talked with Celia after church two Sundays before his birthday, which fell on a Wednesday.

"Celia, I just don't know what to do! I want to surprise him, but with *what*?"

"Well, here's a thought. Mother just sent the photographs we had taken at the wedding, one of the two of us, one of the two of you. I think they kept the one of the four of us together. Maybe you could have one or two of those framed?" She knew from her sister's expression that she liked the idea. "How about we have you two over for dinner, and...." The conversation turned to a whisper as the two schemed. When their husbands walked up, they hushed so quickly that the men exchanged a glance and laughed.

"What say, Albert, do you suppose they might be up to something?"

"Those two? Noooo...." Albert raised a brow at his wife, taking her arm to walk home, which was only blocks away from the church. "Goodbye, Charles...Carolina!" They looked the picture of happiness strolling down the sidewalk arm in arm, her parasol protecting them from the Indian Summer sun. Celia was five months along; and with her slightly shorter frame she was beginning to show her condition through her choir robes, causing her to leave the choir until after the baby came.

Charlie took his wife's arm then, escorting her to the family carriage. "Did you know that Albert is taking evening classes?"

"Is he really? What for? I thought he already had his degree."

"He's taking Bible courses, Carolina. He's studying for the ministry. Yes, I know; I'm excited for them, too!"

"Did he talk to you about whether he's interested in the pastorate or missions?"

"He doesn't know which the Lord would have him to do, so he's training for both fields. I...I wouldn't mind doing the same just to learn more about the Bible. I've never felt a definite *call* to the ministry *per se*, but it never hurts to be ready if the call should come." He looked over to his wife, seeing the wide-eyed expression on her face. "You will be the first to know if He does call me to the ministry, Carolina, don't worry!"

They climbed into the carriage, his parents waiting patiently but with the windows down for ventilation. "This heat is getting to me," Mr. Bennett said waving his hat as a fan. Mrs. Bennett had her fan out as well and began fanning them both. "Thank you, dear. I just need to get home and take a nice cool bath."

"And miss lunch?" Carol couldn't resist, and Mr. Bennett

laughed.

"Okay, eat a light lunch *first,* then take a cool bath!" The light lunch actually sounded nice to all four of them, so when the boys were putting the horse and carriage to rights, Carol and Mrs. Bennett made cold fruit soup, butter crackers, and iced tea, setting a small table out on the veranda.

The four of them immensely enjoyed the luncheon, and true to his word Mr. Bennett retired immediately for his bath. Mrs. Bennett, Charlie, and Carol made short work of the cleanup, then all three went upstairs for a quiet afternoon.

"Charlie?" She had waited until they were both comfortably ensconced in cool sheets and bedclothes before speaking, and Charlie was already asleep. He rolled over when she called his name though, looking at her with sleepy eyes. "I'm sorry, I woke you. I just wanted to talk with you about something."

"Feel free," he said, scooting until he was perpendicular to her, his head resting in her lap. He reached up and touched her cheek to encourage her to go on.

"But you were already asleep!"

"Well, I'm not now though! I'm tired and need to get some rest before work tomorrow, but if something is on your heart, let's talk. The Lord's timing is always perfect."

"Yes, it is, isn't it?" she said with such an adorable grin that Charlie couldn't resist pulling her head down for a kiss. "Charlie, I know that we were both disappointed when Dr. Whittle cautioned us at my appointment in August, but he was able to fit me in for an appointment yesterday afternoon...."

"And?"

"And, how shall I put it? Our license has been renewed!" He sat up on his knees in the bed just staring at his wife. "Please tell me you're awake now...." He needed no words to tell her just how awake, and in love, he was.

❧❧

Carol took the photographs to be framed, choosing a wide, ornately carved mahogany frame she knew would look perfect in their bedroom. She got it to Celia the day before the party, replacing a painting that had a place of prominence in their diminutive living room.

"Perfect! If he doesn't notice this, I'll be extremely surprised!" She sat down on the sofa across from it, and Celia joined her. "You're looking well, Celia. How are you feeling?"

"*Big*. I'm definitely feeling big!" The two laughed together as Celia smoothed her skirts across her expanding middle. "I'm sure when your time comes again you'll not get this big, being so much taller. I already feel short of breath at times, the little bugger seems to stretch to my heart some days! Oh, here...." She reached out for her sister's hand, placing it just in time for a kick and roll from her niece or nephew.

Carol's eyes grew enormous with wonder. "Is that terribly uncomfortable?" she asked, her hand still feeling definite movement.

"Well, thankfully baby seems to have my time clock, sleeping when I do and exercising mostly when I'm awake. I'm glad of it, believe me!" She put her hand over her sister's as it still rested on the baby. "I know it isn't the same, but I want to share all I can with you. If you wish, I'd like for you to come to the delivery. Do you think you will want to?"

Carol leaned for a hug, and the baby kicked her, turning her tears to a giggle. "That little stinker!" she said, wiping her tears with the back of her hand. "Your Auntie Carrie *will* be there when you're born, even if you decide to arrive in the middle of a blizzard!"

Celia brushed aside a few tears before suggesting that they visit the nursery, and the two went arm in arm to the rear of the cottage. It was a tiny room, but sunny, with a window to both the side and rear of the house. She had decorated all in white cotton and eyelet, then showed her sister the two spools of satin ribbon, one mauve, one a muted medium blue.

"For trim once we know if we should use pink or blue!"

"That is a *lovely* idea! And may I make a picture to hang in here? I'll use both colors just in case."

"Oh, yes! That will look so nice...right here, I think," she said excitedly, pointing to an empty space on the wall. They went to the chest then and looked at the few tiny articles already stored there. Celia held one up to her tummy asking, "Do you think it will fit?" She had one tiny blue gown with a bonnet and the tiniest booties Carol or Celia had ever seen.

"How beautiful! And if it's a girl, she will *need* a nice warm dress for her January birth day. Did you crotchet this?"

"Yes, I did." She handled the little gown lovingly. "I worked on it while you were recovering. Every stitch was a prayer made for your healing, and for the Lord to bless *you* one day with another child."

"Thank you for that...for saying 'another'. I fear sometimes that Charlie and I are the only ones who think of my miscarriage as the loss of a child. Though our next child will be our firstborn, he or she will be told when they are old enough that they have an older sibling in heaven."

"That's as it should be. I'm just thankful every day that we didn't lose you, too."

"Yes," Carol said, folding the little gown carefully and placing it back in the chest. "Charlie said how serious I was for a while there."

"His parents got word to Albert and me that very afternoon, but Albert thought it might be too much for me to visit. I wrote Momma and Poppa right away though."

"They told me when they telephoned. It is good to know that you were praying from day one though." She stood to her feet, then helped her wobbling sister back up. "We're going to visit Aunt Lavinia this evening. She has been such a dear, coming over to read to me, watch me draw, listen to me play the piano. I know she's lonely for Uncle Wesley. I'm so glad that she was saved that Sunday last spring."

"Are you going over there from here?"

"Yes, I believe Charlie is dropping Albert off from work and taking us both there."

Celia looked at the watch attached to a brooch on her bodice. "That's in about half an hour if you can wait that long for Mr. Wonderful!"

"*You're* one to talk! I had to wait *how long* for him? And how long did you have to wait for Albert? He was hooked from your first date!"

"Yes, the Bank picnic, remember? Oh, how you probably wish you could forget."

The two returned to the sitting room arm in arm. "No, not really. I look back on it and thank God for His giving me strength to say 'no' to Charlie's proposal. Had I not, he may never have seen his need for Jesus as his Saviour! He was so independent...so in control. Always planning. Everything fit like puzzle pieces, and when I told him I couldn't marry him, his life's plan seemed to crumble. Remember when Albert and I saw him at the park last autumn? Oh, Celia, he was so eaten up with bitterness. You wouldn't have even recognized him. And now.... He's truly the spiritual leader of our home. I wondered how that would work, with his being such a recently saved Christian. But his faith is so strong."

Celia smiled her sweet, contented smile. "I'm so happy for you and Charlie, Carol. So very happy that God has blessed you both so much!"

When the men came to the door after work, both wives were eager to have time alone with their God-given husbands. Carol hugged her sister, patted her niece or nephew, and left with Charlie. He walked her to the buggy, handing her in, then he climbed in beside her and clicked to the General. "I'm glad to see you, too; but why the sudden need to leave?"

Carol cuddled a little closer, enjoying the cool evening. "Oh, we were talking about our wonderful husbands, and before I knew it, you were standing there looking so handsome that I wanted to be alone with you!" She giggled as he sat up straight and tall with pride. "Now don't go getting cocky! I also bragged on your spiritual maturity!"

Carol watched Charlie as he drove, both hands holding the reins loosely, but with constant attention to the General's moods and environment. "God's guiding us through life is sort of like you guiding the General through traffic, you know it? Sometimes He has to keep a tight rein when we're going through distractions...trials. Sometimes He merely holds the reins loosely, allowing us to keep doing what's right, but still He is there in control, watching."

"But the Lord allows us to have our head...to make wrong decisions as well as right. It's then that I wish our relationship were more like mine and the General's...that He would just get me back on the right path with a yank and a word of rebuke instead of my having to muddle my way through and come back to Him with the mess I've made."

"But then we wouldn't have a free will, would we? We'd just be puppets. And for whatever reason, He wants us to come to Him willingly."

"To come to Him and to obey Him *choosing* to do so...out of a heart of love instead of a heart of fear. *'If you love Me, keep My commandments'*.... Not for salvation, for we are saved through grace, not works. But in our daily walk with the Lord after salvation, we can show our love for Him by obeying His Word."

"That's how we want children to obey, too, isn't it?"

"Yes. Just as He wants His children to obey out of a heart of love, we want ours to. There seem to be stages, like at first we obey for fear of punishment, staying in the 'boundaries'. As we grow up, we obey sometimes only with desire for reward for our good behavior. It's a selfish thing, but something every child, physical or spiritual, seems to go through. Then we learn to obey out of love for the figure in authority. That is what God wants, that mature obedience out of a heart of love for Him. Yes, He is worthy to be feared. Yes, He promises reward for our obedience. But to show our love by doing what is pleasing in His sight...."

"That's true love." He stopped the carriage in Aunt Lavinia's driveway, every window glowing with welcome.

"What a beautiful home!"

Charlie hopped down and looped the lead rope around the hitching post, then helped Carol down, walking with her to the door. His parents were already there, sitting in the parlor with Lavinia when her butler showed them in. She welcomed them with warm hugs, then the five of them went in to dinner.

The dining room of the Sutherland mansion was truly beautiful, with three gaslight chandeliers and a table that could seat thirty comfortably. Lavinia had the best china, silver, and crystal laid out, and the curtains were opened looking out on her rose gardens, the walkway lit with lanterns every so many steps.

Before the first course arrived, Aunt Lavinia asked Charlie to pray. When he finished, Lavinia reached out and grasped his hand, then the meal commenced. Plate after plate of beautifully presented delicious food was brought out and placed before them. Carol felt a bit overwhelmed at the extravagance of it all, but other than being a little quiet she enjoyed the meal immensely.

After dessert and coffee were cleared away, Aunt Lavinia rose, took Charlie's offered arm, and began a tour of the house. Charlie hadn't seen all the rooms even as a child. His Uncle Wesley had been of the opinion "Children should be neither seen nor heard", so other than the playroom as a child and the parlor and dining room as an adult, this tour was all new to him as well.

Carol couldn't believe the number of rooms on the second floor, and then Aunt Lavinia told them of the rooms on the third floor, including a large nursery and the playroom Charlie remembered from his childhood. When they returned to the first floor and sat down in the parlor again, Charlie noticed that his parents had said hardly a word at dinner or on the tour.

"Charlie, my son Terrance and his wife have asked me to come out to Saint Louis to live with them. If I do move, I will sell this house, but I would very much like to keep the property in the family. Would you be interested in living here, Charlie? Carolina? I can offer it to you at a more than reasonable amount. I only wish to take things of great sentimental value, and the rest can remain here for your use." She looked from one to the other, seeing the shock on both of their faces. "I only ask for enough to move my things to Saint Louis. Terrance doesn't want the house, and there are no more relatives on my husband's side to offer it to." After a brief pause, she asked, "Well, do you think you could call this 'home'?"

Charlie looked from his parents to his wife, then back to Aunt Lavinia. "I...I'm honored, indeed, *flabbergasted* at the offer, Aunt Lavinia! I will need to talk this over with Carol...and the Lord...." He ran his fingers through his hair, then stood, reaching his aunt's side in two strides. Engulfing her in a tremendous hug, he thanked her softly, then excused himself and Carol for the evening.

The two were silent all the way home, both deep in thought. Lucas even noticed how distracted they both were when he greeted them, letting them into the house before sending for the stable boy. "Wonder what's got them two so discombobulated?" he mumbled, taking his position to wait for the older Mr. and Mrs. Bennett's return.

Chapter Thirty-Five

Happy Birthday, Charlie

Charlie and Carol dressed in their nightclothes in silence then climbed into bed, both speaking at once. Carol giggled, "Please, you first!"

"I don't know what to say, what to *think*! I never even thought about the possibility of the Sutherland Mansion ever being ours. I guess it makes sense with Terrance moving out west, but even so...."

"I think we both prayed all the way home. Do you have the peace about it I have?"

"*Yes*, like the Lord wants us to use the house for Him somehow."

Carol pulled her knees to her chest, wrapping her arms about them and resting her chin on top. "We don't know if we'll ever be able to have another child, Charlie. Do you think that the Lord could use that big house for a Christian orphanage or shelter for children and mothers?"

"I...I just don't know, Carol. That same thought occurred to me, but it takes a lot of money to finance a venture of that nature, not just at first, but to keep it up. But am I right to assume that you join me in thinking the house is meant for us?"

"Yes, Charlie. I really have peace about it. I'll tell you though if I have any nightmares about houses with endless halls that I can never find my way out of!" Charlie laughed. He began rubbing Carol's back for her, then stopped too soon for her liking.

"Charlie! Please don't just stop after five seconds!" He began again, giving her a very thorough backrub as they continued discussing the house.

"My arms are tired, may I stop now?" he asked in mock exhaustion some time later.

Carol stretched then wrapped her arms around her husband. "I had a wonderful time with Celia today. She showed me the baby's nursery. It's so cute and bright and cheerful! Do you think they'll have a boy or a girl?"

"Yes." Carol poked him playfully in the ribs, but he was already relaxing for the evening and hardly responded. "If I were to guess, I would say a girl. I just picture them with a little blonde-haired, blue-eyed girl for some reason. You?"

"I really don't know, but I'll say 'boy' just for competition's sake!" She lowered the wick of the lamp on her side of the bed, then reached across Charlie, turning down his lamp before he wrapped his arms around her, pinning her to his chest with a low chuckle.

"You're appetite's almost back to normal. You're starting to feel like my wife again. I must say that skinny, pitiful urchin was rather lovable, too; but I much prefer you with curves."

"Charlie...."

"Yes?" he replied after her long pause.

"Do you think I'm pretty?"

"Sometimes." He felt her stiffen, continuing quickly. "And sometimes beautiful. Sometimes cute, sometimes adorable...." She gave him a warm, lingering kiss, thoroughly waking Charlie. "Why do you ask?" he asked somewhat breathlessly.

"Well, I don't *think* you think I think this way, but I didn't want our love-making to be...goal-oriented...more specifically, *baby*-oriented. I want to enjoy every moment without an all-consuming hope that it will end in pregnancy. Yet, I still want very much to have another baby, Charlie."

Charlie framed her face with his hands, looking deeply into the sparkles he knew were her eyes even in the darkness of their room. After many moments, he pulled her gently down, her cheek resting on his chest. "What does my heart tell you?"

She nestled until she could hear the steady "thump-thump" of her husband's heart. "It tells me that...you love me."

"And that I love loving you. And that I take pleasure in making love to you...that I would love to give you another baby. It all goes together, don't you see? This is a wonderful way to express our God-given love, to give our spouse pleasure but at the same time, if the Lord wills, to give one another the gift of parenthood."

She lifted her head to look at her husband. "Oh, Charlie, that is beautiful. *Yes*, that is exactly what I needed to hear." She kissed him again, then whispered in his ear, "Are you sleepy?"

"That is exactly what I wanted to hear. No, my love. I am decidedly *not* sleepy...."

❦

The hall was hazy, and somehow Carol knew she was dreaming about the Sutherland Mansion. She walked up and down the hallway, trying every door; but they were all locked. When she reached the last door, there was a crib, and moonlight was streaming in through the open window. She walked to the crib, and a tiny miniature of Celia was there crying. Carol reached down to pick her up, to rock her and console her, but she couldn't seem to get to her. She began singing to the baby then, a silly song from their childhood, then Charlie came into the misty nursery and began gently shaking her by the shoulders. She woke, Charlie's face inches from her own, gently shaking her by the shoulders to wake her.

"Darling, you were dreaming. Are you okay?"

"It was so real...and rather disturbing. I'm sorry I woke you. Can you roll over so I can snuggle up behind you?" Charlie sleepily did as he was requested, finding sleep in moments. Carol lay till the first light of dawn was creeping in at the windows, praying for her sister and the baby in Celia's womb.

❦

"Carolina, I'm sorry to awaken you twice in one morning, but I've got to go to work."

Carol moaned. "I'm so sorry! Did you get breakfast?" She looked at her clean-shaven husband in his work clothes, noticing not for the first time what an attractive husband she'd been blessed with. "You look handsome, Charles Bennett."

Charlie gave a crooked grin, bending to kiss her cheek. "I shall take that very nice compliment as my first birthday gift from you." Knowing the reaction he'd receive, he helped his hurrying wife out of bed.

"Oh *no*! I wanted to give you your birthday present this morning!" She pilfered about her top dresser drawer looking for the handsome pen set she'd found as a distraction from the real gift of the framed wedding photograph. Charlie remained seated on the bed, his expression for all the world like that of a honor graduate from the school of innocence.

"Then am I to assume the wedding portrait hanging in Albert and Celia's living room isn't my main gift?"

"*Charles Bennett*!" She rushed at him, knocking him into the mattress as he let loose with gales of laughter. He looked up at her with his most shamefaced expression, receiving undeserved forgiveness right away.

"Forgive me? I caught sight of it yesterday when I dropped off Albert." Stretching to kiss the tip of her nose, he added, "Now may I get up? You're mussing my new tie from Father and Mother!"

She looked down at the gift, a very handsome dark blue tie with his pearl tie pin neatly in place. "How handsome," she said, pulling herself to a standing position and offering Charlie a hand up. His arms went around her when he stood to his feet.

"I rather like you giving goodbye hugs in your shift, my dear." She pulled his head down, slowly kissing him again. She finished with a lopsided grin.

"*That* was your main gift, Mr. Bennett! Now off to work with you before...." He stopped her from saying more by giving her a quick kiss and final hug, then he headed to the door.

"We're still going to Albert and Celia's house for dinner, yes?"

"Yes, but do you think it would be lying for you to try to *act* surprised? Celia did a lot to help me get everything arranged."

"Would you *want* me to be a good actor?" Carol smiled repentantly, shaking her head 'no'. "Just as I thought. Now come give me one more kiss. The other ones wore off already." Nearly skipping across the room and into her husband's arms, Carol gave him another kiss goodbye, then sent him on his way to work.

※※

The entire month of October was spent finalizing the sale of the Sutherland Mansion and helping Aunt Lavinia prepare for her move west. The day of the closing finally arrived, and the twenty-fifth of October would forever be remembered as the day the Sutherland Mansion became *home*.

As they gathered their belongings to leave the attorney's office, Lavinia asked sweetly, "Can you please come see me off at the depot? I know my dear sister and your father are coming, but...."

"Of course, Aunt Lavinia. We were already planning on it." When they arrived at the train depot Mr. and Mrs. Bennett were already there waiting.

Lavinia walked along between her sister and Carol, then freed her arm from Carol's as the tears began to flow. "I promised myself I wouldn't cry." She sniffled with a very crooked grin on her well-powdered face. "You are all *so* dear to me."

Charlie spoke up. "You'll be back to Baltimore to visit us, I trust. And of course we'll always have a room prepared for you." He kissed his aunt's tear-stained cheek as the conductor called out his final call.

"I'll be back, dear ones! I love you all!" With quick hugs and a swirl of furs and diamonds, Aunt Lavinia left her Baltimore family for her loved ones in Saint Louis. The four waved until the train disappeared from view, then walked quietly back to their carriages.

"Son, did you want to come back to the house, or are you heading—"

"Home?" Charlie finished with a grin. "Yes, sir, we're going home first, then going back to *your* home later to finish packing the last of our things. We hope to stay at our house tonight if we can move everything over that quickly."

"All right then. We'll see you in a few hours?"

"Yes, sir. Goodbye until then!" Looking to Aunt Lavinia's chauffeur he called, "Home please, James!" Charlie waved his hat as he climbed into the carriage beside his wife, his eyes alight with excitement. "Can you believe it? We're going *home*...to our own home."

"And a more beautiful home I could not have imagined. Yes, I know! What of the servants, Charlie? Did you discuss them with Aunt Lavinia?"

"I did. She said that Uncle Wesley's will left enough to their butler, Johnson, for him to retire. Their cook was his wife, and she is likewise retiring, though she has trained another girl to take her place Aunt Lavinia said. Lucas has a nephew that is looking for a position, and he'll be coming by my office at the bank tomorrow afternoon for an interview. Lucas highly recommended him. So we'll only have four servants: James will work with the carriage house and gardens, the cook, the butler, and a maid."

He was glad that Carol was so distracted with the sights they were passing that she didn't ask about the maid. They pulled into their drive a short time later, and James was down in a trice lowering the steps and opening the door.

"Thank you, James. You may leave for the day once you've finished with the carriage. Thank you so much."

Charlie watched as the tall, silent gentleman climbed back up and drove the carriage to the carriage house. He turned to his wife then, scooping her up in his arms and entering the front door with much ado and giggling.

"Welcome home, Carolina."

༺༻

They chose the same room for the master bedroom as Lavinia and Wesley had chosen, and after carrying his wife upstairs and setting her down gently, he fell into bed most ungracefully.

"I wouldn't advise your attempting to carry me up all those stairs ever again, Charlie Bennett!" She removed her hat and placed it on the dresser, then removed her jacket. Charlie rolled over on the bed and looked at his wife affectionately.

"You look like a school marm with that white blouse and dark skirt. Take your hair down, would you please?" She undid the chignon, her hair falling free to her waist. "I never tire of seeing your hair down." He patted the mattress. "Come. See if you can find me in this humongous bed of ours!"

∽ℰ∾

After several hours of thoroughly enjoying one another's company in their new house, the two freshened up to go to the Bennett House. Charlie was already waiting downstairs, and Carol was braiding her hair to put it in a bun when there came a knock on the door.

"You mind if I do your hair, Missy Carol?" Carol was in Jessie's arms in seconds.

"Oh, *please* tell me that somehow Charlie worked a miracle and got you to come with us!" All Jessie could do was nod and hug her dear friend again tightly. She walked her back to the dressing table and began her magic on Carol's coiffeur.

"My sister has worked here for Mrs. Lavinia for years. I...I guess it was nervy after all the years I've been with Mr. and Mrs. Bennett, but I asks 'em last week if my sister an' I could switch jobs. They thought it was a wonderful idea, too!"

"Can you *believe* this place? I try not to think too much about the size of it, or I'm not quite certain I wouldn't soon be overwhelmed!" She looked from the velvet curtains at the windows to the mahogany canopy bed. "How will we ever keep up with it all?"

"I've two strong arms, and so've you. The cooks young, and I know she can manage the kitchen pretty much by herself 'cept for special occasions. We all done talked it out, 'cept for the butler, who we haven't met yet. James and Liza are thrilled to have some young folk in the house!"

Jessie gave Carol's hair a final pat, then looked at her friend's reflected eyes in the mirror. "Missy Carol, are you 'spectin'?" It took a moment to interpret, but thankfully Carol blushed instead of blanching.

"No, I...I'm sure I'm not. My cycles haven't been normal since I lost the baby in July. In fact, I haven't had a cycle since August." She looked down to her waist, then back at her friend's reflection. "No, I feel too good to be pregnant again, Jessie. But whatever made you ask?"

"Oh, just wonderin' if the Lord had answered my prayers yet, Missy. Now, you look pretty 'nuff for dinner with them good folks of yours. You go have a good time!" The friends embraced, then Carol walked downstairs to join her husband before the two headed out for the walk to his parents' home.

Jessie finished tidying up the master suite before she dropped to her knees beside the bed, looking up far beyond the ceiling as she prayed. *"Oh, Father God, bless these two with a youngin' if You haven't already! Please, in Jesus' name, give them the desire of their hearts."*

Chapter Thirty-Six

Giving Thanks

Charlie and Carol had invited Albert and Celia to visit several times, but with Albert's night school and the men's job schedules, it never seemed to work out. Finally they decided to have Thanksgiving dinner together, Albert and Celia and Mr. and Mrs. Bennett all agreeing to come.

Celia was astounded as she entered the house, her eyes going from one thing of beauty to another. Charlie and Carol exchanged a glance though when they saw her face, which looked round as the full moon and nearly as pale. The smile she gave them seemed totally serene as they all went to the parlor to talk a while before dinner.

Celia chuckled. "I'm glad there are some straight back chairs. Sometimes I feel like I'll never be able to climb out of the sofa when I sink into the pillows lately."

"How are you feeling, Celia?" Charlie asked, coming to sit beside his wife on the settee.

"Well, better than I *look*, that's for certain!" she laughed a bit, but sounded out of breath. "I...I feel pretty well...a little dizzy sometimes, but shortness of breath is normal when one has a baby sitting on one's lungs. Albert got me new shoes. My ankles were too swollen to fit in my others, even unlaced."

Mrs. Bennett looked very concerned, but rather than embarrass the other guests at the holiday dinner, she said a silent prayer and tried to move the subject to more comfortable ground.

"How are things working out with Lucas' nephew, Charles?"

"Splendidly! Mason is an absolute gem," Charlie began, leaning forward to share. Before much longer, the six were called to dinner. If the entry and parlor didn't overwhelm them, the dining room certainly did. Turning to Albert he said, "I think this table was what clued us in on the house serving well as a school or orphanage. We could seat a whole house full at this table!"

"I think that sounds wonderful!" Albert said, taking his wife's hand. Celia had taken to wearing her wedding ring on her little finger, but even that looked uncomfortably tight. "Did you know of their plans, Celia?"

"Yes, yes I think I remember your telling me." She arranged her napkin over her ample tummy, then the six joined hands for the blessing.

⋆⋄⋆

"That was as delicious a Thanksgiving dinner as ever I've had!" Mr. Bennett pushed his chair out a little way from the table, wiping his mouth with his napkin and placing it beside his empty dessert plate. "Now, you are the head of this home, Charlie. Are you going to continue the 'giving thanks' tradition of your childhood?"

Charlie began, then turned to his mother, going all the way around the room until they reached Carol. With tears of happiness in her eyes she looked at each loved one there. "I'm thankful for each of you dear ones, for your being here to celebrate our giving thanks to God as a nation, and as a family. I thank God for our beautiful house, which I trust one day we will be able to use to serve Him. And I thank Him that He is blessing me with a healthy pregnancy." Tears ran down her smiling cheeks as the Bennetts, Celia, and Albert all stood and came to her side, hugging her, crying, and praising God.

Charlie sat at the head of the table, his hands folded and his index fingers extended, touching his chin, just watching his wife. It had taken everything in him not to give thanks for the baby, but he wanted Carol to have the honor of sharing their news with the rest of the family.

The group walked to the parlor again for coffee, and of

course the conversation centered on the coming babies.

"How far along are you? Did you just find out? You *must* have, for there's no way you could have kept this a secret long!" Mrs. Bennett sat holding her daughter's hand, making an effort to wait patiently for answers.

"We *did* just find out, but I'm actually two and a half months along already! I was thinking my body was still messed up, but I felt too *good*, too healthy to be pregnant. I still don't *feel* pregnant, but Dr. Whittle confirmed that I am this week!"

"So the baby is due—" Albert didn't get a chance to do the ciphering.

"In June. I'm glad Carol won't have to endure the hot summer months." Charlie beamed at his wife, his whole countenance filled with love. Had she not been surrounded on either side by her sister and his mother, he could not have kept his distance.

"Have you told Momma and Poppa yet, Carrie?"

"Yes, Sister, I wrote them after we got the results from Doctor Whittle. I expect to hear from them any day, but remember they're coming for Christmas!"

"Oh yes! They'll be able to see two expecting daughters! And how are things coming along between Merrie and Caleb?" Carol turned to be sure her husband had heard Celia's question. His chin hitting his chest was her answer.

"You're kidding, right?"

"No, Charlie. They've been writing all summer, and Caleb declared his intentions and asked Mr. Atkins' permission earlier this month to marry Meredith!" Carol looked so smug he wanted to kiss her.

"Oh, *great*. Carol's first attempt at matchmaking is an unqualified success. There'll be no living with her now!" The whole room laughed together, then spoke of the details of Caleb and Merrie's upcoming marriage in the spring.

"Well, you'll look wonderful, Sister, with a three month old baby in your once-again-visible lap! I on the other hand will look like—"

"The most beautiful woman in the room." This time Charlie did have to sit by his wife, and his mother graciously stood to give him her place at Carol's side. He kissed her hand, then continued holding it. Albert stood then, seeing how tired his wife was looking, though he knew she would want to stay through supper if she could.

"I think we need to be leaving. Celia, you're not looking well." That was putting it mildly, especially beside her sister's radiant beauty.

"Do you need to lie down?" Charlie asked quietly. "You're most welcome to rest in any of the guest rooms. Please, I think that would be good for all of us, then we'll come back together for some music and games this evening. Would that be okay?"

Both couples agreed, and the six made their way to the second floor, though slowly for Celia's sake. They took her to a beautiful room decorated in turquoise and peach, and Carol stayed behind to see her sister comfortably in bed while Charlie showed his parents to another room.

"Celia, I'm worried. You're so puffy, and—"

"But I'll be *fine*, Carrie. Really." Carol helped remove Celia's shoes, looking at Albert when she saw just how swollen her sister's feet and ankles were. Celia was looking around the room. "What a beautiful room this is. I love the colors, and the view of the trees is so restful." She slipped under the counterpane and was asleep almost immediately; and after kissing his sleeping wife's cheek, Albert walked Carol to the door.

"We have been going to see my grandfather every month; but since we're nearing the due date in January, I may try to get her in earlier in December. I want to know she is well for when your parents are here at Christmas. Your mother is planning to stay from Christmas until after the baby's birth."

"Please let me know if there is anything we can do to make her more comfortable, Albert. I mean it, *anything*. If you'd feel better with me at the house when you're at classes at night, just say the word. We'll be there."

"Thank you, Carol. I...I don't have to tell you how much that means to me. This is very frightening for me, though I haven't let on to Celia."

"Albert, when is the last time your grandfather *saw* Celia, not just professionally, but the last time they were in each other's presence?"

"She's not been feeling well for a couple of weeks actually, so she hasn't made it to church even since shortly after her last appointment on the third come to think of it."

Carol closed her eyes tightly for a moment, then took Albert's hand. "Call him tomorrow. Promise me." After a quick nod, Albert returned to his sleeping wife, watching in prayer.

❧✦

Albert called Carol and Charlie from his grandfather's office. Carol could tell from her husband's grave expression that all was not well. "Charlie? Do you...do you think Carol can handle this in her condition?"

"She couldn't handle *not* being there. Have you contacted Mr. and Mrs. Montague? They need to be told right away." At that comment, Carol found a nearby chair her legs began shaking so badly. Charlie hung up the receiver, turning to kneel beside his wife.

"Carolina, Celia is very ill. Albert said she has something called toxemia. Doc Whittle says that he thinks they caught it in time to save both her and the baby, but we still need to ask God to have His hand on them both." Dropping to her knees beside her husband, Carol prayed for her sister, her niece or nephew, and for her brother-in-law, whom she knew would be suffering acutely as well. Charlie prayed next, a prayer so succinct that Carol knew he had *'obtained mercy and found grace to help in time of need'*.

The two gathered their things in silence after asking their butler to tell James they needed the buggy as soon as possible. James had the General harnessed and ready to go when the two stepped out into the November sunshine.

"Where are they, at home or still at the doctor's office?"

"Doc sent them home and put her on strict bed rest. He said if her blood pressure is not decidedly improved in twenty-four hours, he'll have to have her admitted to the hospital."

Charlie wished with all his heart he could drive and hold his wife at the same time, but he needed both hands to guide the General through the Friday morning traffic. Sensing his thoughts,

Carol put her hand in the crook of his elbow, leaning on his shoulder in prayer. When they reached the cottage, Carol was out of the buggy before Charlie had finished tying up the reins to the hitching post. He caught up with her before she reached the door.

"Knock quietly, then go in." They entered, sensing the seriousness of the situation in the very atmosphere of the usually comfortable house.

"Carrie?" Celia had heard them come in, and Albert came to stand in the bedroom doorway, allowing Carol to pass by to her sister while he went in the living room to talk with Charlie. Carol was frightened at what she saw, her sister's face even more swollen than it had been just yesterday.

"You can't hide your concern, Sister, so don't bother trying. I know it's bad. I've known for days."

"Why didn't you *say* something then, dearest?" Carol couldn't stop the tear that escaped, wiping it away almost angrily.

"Oh, Carrie, Albert only has two weeks left of his first semester of classes! I didn't want to burden him with my uneasiness. I...I didn't think it was as serious a condition as we found out today it is. I'm scared, Carrie. Not just for me, but for the baby."

"I know." She wiped her sister's tears away with her handkerchief, then stood to her feet. "What can I do? Would a back rub or a foot rub help? Momma always said that'd cure what ails you."

Encouraged by her sister's smile, she got some cool water and poured it on a cloth at the dry sink. "Would some cool air feel good to you?" It was rather stuffy in the room with direct sunlight coming in at the windows. At Celia's nod, Carol opened the windows just enough to relieve the oppressiveness in the room, then sealed them up again to prevent a chill. She walked back to her sister, lifting the sheet to find her sister's swollen feet and bathing them with the cloth. "Talk to me, Celia. Tell me what you're thinking."

"I'll tell you sometime...later." Her voice was so weak that Carol knew she was moments from sleep, so she started humming a favorite hymn as she continued massaging Celia's feet, ankles, and calves.

The men in the living room sat in silence for several minutes before Charlie realized Albert may be in shock. "Albert? They're in God's hands. He's the Great Physician, don't forget." His brother began to sob, trying to stifle the noise so the women couldn't hear. Charlie threw his arms around him, still not knowing how bad a condition Celia was in.

After a short time, Albert regained his composure, dropping onto the sofa, his face in his hands. His voice sounded completely lifeless when he began talking. "Grandfather said the best line of defense is to try lowering her blood pressure through complete bed rest. In many cases, blood pressure returns to normal just with this treatment. I think I told you, he said if she wasn't decidedly improved by this time tomorrow he would have her admitted to the hospital. The goal seems to be to allow the pregnancy to continue until the baby is old enough to be born. But if Celia's blood pressure can't be reduced, he said he may have to deliver the baby by caesarean section." He looked up at his friend, tears falling unheeded. "Charlie, he said that her body is shutting down, trying to protect the baby."

"I think the best thing we can do is the *only* thing we can do...*pray*."

Albert went on as if he hadn't heard Charlie speak. "She...she told me that if she...doesn't make it, she wants me to go on with my work...with the ministry. She wants me to give the baby to you and Carol to raise...in place of the one...the one she'd be taking care of in heaven." His sorrow poured forth in great gulps, Charlie holding him in a bear hug as he cried his heart sore.

"Albert, listen to me." Charlie felt a total calmness as he spoke to his brother-in-law. Waiting until he had eye contact, he went on. "Where there is life, there is hope. Those Montagues are a hardy lot, and they're all God's children. Rest in that. Cling to the knowledge that the Almighty, the omnipotent Creator of the Universe is the One in control here, and that He loves Celia and your baby even more than you do. He will do what is best. Personally, I'm going to pray that He brings them both through this. He tells us sometimes we don't receive our heart desires because we don't ask. Well, I won't be accused of not asking for a miracle." He saw the spark of life in Albert's eyes, adding,

"And I don't think you'll *have not because ye ask not* either."

The two were deep in prayer when Carol came in a short while later, so she went to the kitchen to prepare something for lunch for them all.

Chapter Thirty-Seven

Blessing Upon Blessing

Doctor Whittle was at the cottage before lunch the next day, true to his word. Albert waited with Charlie in the sitting room while Carol stayed with Celia. Mr. and Mrs. Montague had taken a train north that morning, and Charlie had agreed to pick them up from the depot upon their arrival.

"Charlie," Albert said calmly, "I want to thank you for all you did yesterday." He wanted to go on, but that alone seemed to say everything.

Charlie smiled. "God's grace is sufficient, isn't it? *His strength is made perfect in weakness.* Sometimes we just need a little reminding." Carol walked in quietly, sitting down beside her husband.

"Doctor Whittle didn't say much, but if I were to guess I would say he was pleased with her progress. He said he'd be right out." The little group waited silently, but as soon as his grandfather's step was heard on the wooden floor of the hallway, Albert rose quickly to his feet.

"She does seem to have stabilized. The baby's heartbeat is still strong, and Celia seems much more relaxed than yesterday." He looked at Carol before adding, "She said you'd been singing to her, Mrs. Bennett. That's good. I believe it calmed your sister considerably, and for all we know unborn children can hear music from the womb at this point in the pregnancy."

Charlie put his arm around his wife, giving her a half-hug as the doctor went on. "Albert, we're going to hold off delivering the child until we reach the thirty-fifth week point. I'll be by every day, but if she begins having nosebleeds, feels dizzy, complains of pain in her head, or anything else you feel is unusual, call me *immediately*."

His professional demeanor fell away then, and he hugged his grandson, so like him in coloring and build. "I know you've all been praying. That is blatantly evident. I...I want to encourage you, but we're not out of the woods yet by any means. Just keep the faith.

"Carol, take care of yourself, dear. I know you feel well with this pregnancy, but none of us are invincible. Charlie, I don't think I need to tell you, do I?" He saw Charlie shake his head. "Okay now, back to work! Celia needs some fresh fruit for lunch, and maybe some tea. I'm headed home now, but again, call me if there seems to be a problem, however minor."

The three young people saw him out, then Carol and Charlie headed to the kitchen while Albert went in to be with Celia. Carol nearly wept for joy when she heard Albert's voice raised in song.

"Oh, Charlie!" She stopped slicing pears and apples long enough to put the knife down and give her husband the hug they both needed. Charlie still enjoyed just holding his wife, and she stood in his embrace for nearly a minute before she felt a tiny movement. "Charlie, I felt the baby move! The little butterfly movements Mother and Celia mentioned!" She hugged her husband all the tighter, then drew away, finding his hand reaching out to touch her middle.

He bent over until his mouth was mere inches from the slight roundness that indicated the baby's residence. "Little one, we love you!" Then he kissed Carol's tummy and stood.

"Umm, Charlie?"

"Yes?"

Pointing to her smiling mouth, she said simply, "You missed."

※

Mrs. Bennett brought by some food, some loaves of bread and cheese and a basket of fruit. When Charlie got back from the depot with his in-laws, he found his mother working in the tiny kitchen of the cottage.

"You look lovely today, Mother. You must be feeling well." He kissed his mother's cheek as she stood there peeling one of the apples at the sink.

"Are William and Emily here?"

"Yes, and of course they headed straight in to see Celia. Albert and Carolina are in there with them, too." He watched as his mother wiped her hands on her apron. "I meant what I said, you really do look extra beautiful this afternoon. Radiant, like...." He stopped mid-sentence, looking at his mother's grinning face.

"I would have liked to have shared this with you and Carol at once, but...you're going to be a big brother again, Charles!" Charlie embraced his mother, but a moment of worry found its way to his heart. "I know what you're thinking, but I feel *fine*, like I did when I carried you...and Lizzy. If the Lord allows, you will have a brother or sister by the end of next summer!" She couldn't help giggling.

"Mother, what are you laughing about?" Carol had come to the kitchen door, smiling at her mother-in-law and husband as they stood chortling like children.

"Carolina, I'm going to be a father in June and a big brother again in August!" It took a moment for his message to sink in, then Carol let out a small squeal and ran to join the giggling, hugging group.

Carol walked her mother over to take a seat at the kitchen table while Charlie finished preparing the fruit. "Oh, Mother, I'm *so* happy for you! What did Father say?"

"Oh, he was concerned at first, as was Charlie's initial reaction; but then he was proud as a peacock! He's already begun plans to make Charlie's old room back into a nursery."

"I don't know, Carol, you might better send *your* mother back home. There seems to be something in the water here in Baltimore!" The three laughed, then Charlie came and stood by his wife and mother and prayed a sweet prayer of blessing over them and the children they carried.

After he said 'amen', Carol noticed a tell-tale mistiness to his eyes. "Father, Albert, and I will be able to empathize with one another with all these emotional women around us!" He laughed to cover his own emotional moment while Carol and Laura Bennett rose to put the finishing touches on the tray of refreshments.

※※

Mr. and Mrs. Montague prayed with their daughter and son-in-law, once again giving the whole situation to the Lord. Albert was so thankful that the Lord had blessed him with Christian in-laws, their strength during this trial was such a blessing. When Mr. Montague and Albert made their way to the living room, Charlie was just bringing in the refreshments.

"This is perfect, Charlie. Please thank your mother for me."

"She hasn't left yet. She's still in the kitchen with Carol. I think they'll take Celia and Mother Montague their refreshment in Celia's room. I'm sure she's enjoying the company." Charlie grinned into his cup of tea, then willingly joined in with the fellowship.

Mrs. Montague was brushing Celia's hair when Carol and Laura Bennett came in with a tray of food and beverages for the four of them. "Hello, Laura! How are you, dear?"

"I'm pregnant. And you?" Mrs. Montague and Celia both turned their heads so quickly that Mrs. Bennett and Carol burst out laughing.

"No, *I'm* not," Mrs. Montague said with a deeply dimpled grin. "But I'm fine!" She walked over to give Laura a hug, then finished up Celia's hair with a braid and a bow, helping her to a comfortable sitting position so she could eat as well.

Celia gave thanks for the food for them all, then started right in on the fruit salad. "Thank you so much for bringing this over, Mrs. Bennett! I really was starving, though I don't at all look it." She giggled, and her mother reached over from her chair by the bed and placed her hand on Celia's very swollen middle.

"You need your strength, dear. Let someone know whenever you're hungry or thirsty." She chuckled to herself before adding, "Your Grandmother Montague used to say that when I craved something during pregnancy, the baby salivated until I quenched that craving by eating whatever it was I was hungry for!"

"Oh how *funny!*" All three pregnant women mentally took note to try that on their husbands though. "Emily, how was your trip up here?"

The four went on talking until Celia was finished eating and looked drowsy. With tender kisses they left the room and joined Charlie, Albert, and Mr. Montague in the living room.

"Well, dear, we'll be staying at Carol and Charlie's new home. Shall we head over and give Albert and Celia some time alone?" Looking at his younger son-in-law, he added, "Of course, you know we'll be here morning, noon, and night until the baby is safely ensconced in that nursery!"

Albert laughed. "Yes, sir! And you have no idea how thankful I am for a little more male companionship. Mrs. Bennett, do bring your husband next time if he can get away. I'm sure he would enjoy the fellowship as well."

The group left, the four headed for the Sutherland Mansion and Mrs. Bennett headed home. Albert went back to lie beside his wife and soon-to-be-born child.

❧❧

Celia had felt a few weak labor pains, but as morning dawned on the seventh of December, they became breathtakingly sharp. After the first had passed, she rang the little bell Mrs. Bennett had loaned her. Albert came in with a grin and a tempting breakfast, only to put the tray down immediately.

"Albert, I think the baby is coming." He ran for the door, then returned to kiss his wife.

"I won't be long." He ran the two blocks to a little grocery store, the proprietor of which he knew lived on the second floor. He asked to use their telephone and called his grandfather, then Charlie and Carol and his in-laws, who were staying with them.

When he got back to the house not ten minutes after he'd first left, Celia was in the middle of another hard contraction. Albert never faltered, walking quickly to her side, then going to get a cool cloth to bathe her face with when the contraction passed.

"They're coming, dearest." He tried to keep his voice calm, but her eyes showed her fear. She began shaking, trembling so violently that Albert put his arms around her to keep her on the bed. When he saw her eyes roll back in her head as she went stiff, then limp, he feared they would be too late, crying out to God once more to spare his wife and child. He felt for her pulse, then saw the rise and fall of her chest and knew she was still with him. The minutes it took for his grandfather to arrive were the longest in his young life.

After a quick conference with Albert and a preliminary examination, Doctor Whittle spoke to his grandson even as he prepared for surgery.

"Albert, I'm going to need hot water and lots of towels. I need you to sanitize the room as best you can. Open the windows a crack; the cold air will help."

Albert went about quickly doing as the doctor ordered. When he returned with the scalding hot water in a basin, Doctor Whittle had prepared for an immediate caesarean, rolling her shift back and about to begin the incision. "Son, we've got to take the baby right away, before it moves into the birth canal with the contractions." He handed Albert a wad of gauze. "Hold this over her mouth and nose. I don't think she'll come to, but just in case, this is ether."

It only seemed like moments later when Albert heard the sound of a tiny baby's cry. He left the gauze in place over his wife's mouth and nose, then reached for the bundle of squalling child as Doctor Whittle continued working.

"It's a *girl*, Celia! God has given us a sweet baby girl!" He worked diligently to clean the baby up, feeling like his hands were the size of a giant's as he tried to work with the tiny kicking form of his daughter. He carried her to the nursery in a soft, warm towel. Placing her down for a moment in the crib he searched for a comfortable gown for her. He heard someone at the front door then, and as he finished dressing his daughter he went to meet the family before returning to his wife's bedside.

Carol was holding the baby, the whole group looking at the tiny child. The baby had stopped crying, and was looking around with the biggest eyes any of them had ever seen on a newborn. Carol stooped to kiss her niece, then turned to her father.

"Here, Grampa. Gramma and I need to go see if we can be of

service in the delivery room."

⚜

It was some hours later before Doctor Whittle stood and looked around the room. The team had done an excellent job, sometimes doing the tasks that needed to be done before he even asked. Celia was stitched up and resting quietly, but she still had not regained consciousness. The doctor took his grandson out of the room a moment to discuss the situation.

"I will not pretend to tell you that all is well yet, my boy. I believe Celia suffered a seizure from what you described. Her blood pressure must have spiked when the contractions began. If she went into ecclampsia, she could remain unconscious for a matter of days; so we need to prepare, find milk for the baby until Celia is well enough to nurse her."

"We...we could still lose her, couldn't we, sir?"

Before Doctor Whittle could frame a reply, the two men heard a commotion in the bedroom. They entered to find Carol bending over her sister's bed crying; but when she turned to look at Albert, he saw her smile, then saw his wife's eyes open. The other ladies left the room as Doctor Whittle examined Celia. Albert knelt beside his wife, telling her softly of their beautiful baby girl.

When Carol went to the sitting room, she found her niece in Charlie's arms, slurping for all she was worth on the tip of his pinky. He knew from his wife's smiling face that it was time to take her to her mother. "Okay, little one, time for the real thing!" He kissed her smooth little head before giving her to his wife, who was looking at him with such love that he stood up and walked with her into the hallway for a kiss. "Look at her, Carol. She's perfect, so pink and wide-eyed! And I was right, right down to her pretty blue eyes!"

"All babies start out with blue eyes actually; but I think they may just stay that color." Her little bow-shaped mouth was working a mile a minute, and Carol took her in quickly, kissing her sister and walking out, closing the door behind herself and Doctor Whittle, who was exiting also.

Albert lay on his side beside his wife and their sleeping daughter. "She has my appetite," he said softly, touching the tiny cheek. Celia watched her husband as he caressed their tiny child. Nursing had come easier than she had expected, especially after Doctor Whittle's detailed instruction for holding the baby so as not to disturb the stitches in her own abdomen. The baby had nursed for nearly half an hour, with only time for the smallest hint of a burp in between.

"What shall we name her?"

"*Rachel*. Our wee little lamb." As if on cue, Rachel gave a great yawn, wiggling a bit to find her comfortable position, then going back to sleep.

"Do you hear that, little one?" he asked in a sweet sing-songy voice that made Celia giggle. "You're named after a lady of the Bible!" He looked into his wife's face then, noticing that she was looking at him instead of little Rachel. "I love you, Celia Whittle." He leaned carefully over the baby, kissing his wife tenderly. "Do you want me to try putting Rachel in her crib?"

"Yes, that would be fine. I...I feel very achy and tired." She still lay on her side, running a weary finger along Rachel's tiny pink arm.

"That is totally understandable. Let me see if I can't get her to sleep for a while, though I know there are four or five pair of arms out there just waiting for a chance to hold our little girl."

He scooped her up like a natural, turning her around for her mother to have one last peek, then took her out of the room. All talking ceased as he walked the few steps from the hall to the sitting room, and Carol was on her feet waiting as he entered.

"She's fine! They're both fine, thanks be to God!" Albert turned to his grandfather then, handing the tiny bundle to her deliverer. None of them had ever seen Doctor Whittle cry before, but tears rained down his cheeks as he looked into the perfect face of his great-granddaughter.

Chapter Thirty-Eight

God's Gift

Celia said she wanted to go to Charlie and Carol's home for Christmas dinner, and no one would say her nay once Grampa Whittle decided to oversee his granddaughter-in-law for the day. Merrie was helping by staying with Albert and Celia in the upstairs bedroom. Caleb was staying with his parents at Charlie and Carol's, though they only saw him there when Merrie Atkins was nearby.

When Albert, Celia, and baby Rachel came into the mansion, all eyes were temporarily turned away from the beautiful nativity scene Charlie was showing everyone. He had found it in the attic with the other Christmas decorations, but no one could recall its ever being used, even Mrs. Bennett who had been to her sister's house every Christmas for many years.

Coming forward to greet her guests, Carol put a guiding arm around her sister, walking her to the most comfortable chair in the parlor. "Oh, Carrie, thank you. Would you like to hold Rachel?"

"I know I just held her yesterday, but my arms are simply *aching* to hold her again!" Rachel was wide awake, and she stared up into her Auntie Carrie's eyes. "Oh! She's wearing her prayer gown!" Carol caught a glimpse of the tiny blue gown Celia had told her she'd crocheted. The blue of the yarn matched the blue of Rachel's eyes to perfection, and Charlie came by then to watch his wife with the baby.

"You know," Carol told her husband quietly as the others

mingled, "I still haven't cried over this precious baby. I thought maybe—"

"No, she's too wonderful a gift for even the tiniest bittersweet thought, isn't she? And God has also given us the gift of another child, plus I was born into His family this year as well." He could see a definite roundness to his wife's stomach as she placed Rachel high on her chest, and the sight filled him with joy. "Just six more months, and we get to hold our baby, 'Lord willing!'"

He kissed his wife's cheek, but she moved to get a *real* kiss, then looked up over her head. Charlie followed her glance, seeing a tiny sprig of mistletoe in the holly garland that lined the archway. "You'd better not let Caleb see that!" he said with a chuckle, kissing her again before joining the rest of the group.

"May I have your attention, please?" Albert stood between his wife and the large mantle, which held the nativity set. "Charlie gave me permission to speak to you all, kind of my guinea pigs for my first small address!" A wave of quiet laughter went around the room as everyone found a seat. "I just want to read a portion of Scripture, and then much like Thanksgiving, go around the room giving thanks for some of the wonderful gifts God has blessed us with this year.

"I'm reading from the Gospel according to Matthew, chapter one and verses eighteen through twenty-five.

> 18. *Now the birth of Jesus Christ was on this wise: When as His mother Mary was espoused to Joseph, before they came together, she was found with child of the Holy Ghost.*
> 19. *Then Joseph her husband, being a just man, and not willing to make her a public example, was minded to put her away privily.*
> 20. *But while he thought on these things, behold, the angel of the LORD appeared unto him in a dream, saying, Joseph, thou son of David, fear not to take unto thee Mary thy wife: for that which is conceived in her is of the Holy Ghost.*
> 21. *And she shall bring forth a son, and thou shalt call*

> *His name JESUS: for He shall save His people from their sins.*
> 22. *Now all this was done, that it might be fulfilled which was spoken of the Lord by the prophet, saying,*
> 23. *Behold, a virgin shall be with child, and shall bring forth a son, and they shall call His name Emmanuel, which being interpreted is, God with us.*
> 24. *Then Joseph being raised from sleep did as the angel of the Lord had bidden him, and took unto him his wife:*
> 25. *And knew her not till she had brought forth her firstborn son: and he called His name JESUS.*

"I know that all of us are thinking about babies this Holy Day, are we not? And each baby here is a gift from God...the Bible calls them *'His reward'*. But these babies, both here bodily and those to be born this summer, are not *the* gift...the gift of God mentioned in Romans. *The gift of God is eternal life, through Jesus Christ our Lord.* This Baby," he said, picking up the delicate piece of sculptured marble, "The holy Babe this piece of artwork represents is *the* gift. The *unspeakable* gift that we are to thank the Father for! And not just the baby Jesus, but the *adult* Jesus, Who so willingly gave His life that we may have eternal life in Him."

He turned to his friend and brother Charlie. "You received that gift this past spring, didn't you?" Charlie nodded mutely, a lump in his throat as he remembered the day as if it were yesterday. "Each adult in this room has at one point received this unspeakable gift...we have received Jesus Christ as our Saviour! I want to focus on that Gift today, and on giving thanks for Him and what He has done in our lives."

He closed his Bible, caressing it and bringing it close to his chest. "This Bible is God's Word. Jesus is the Living Word. Whenever I feel the desire to draw close to my Saviour, I do so by getting to know Him through reading my Bible. He tells us that if we love Him, we will show Him our love by seeking to keep the commandments given us in the Word. Not for our salvation, but for love of our Lord.

"I will give thanks first. I'm thankful for baby Jesus, God incarnate. Celia?"

"I'm thankful for eternal life He gives, and for the life of our Rachel."

"I'm thankful for victorious life in Christ, and for the lives of my dear sisters." Caleb looked at Celia and Carol, then to Merrie to share next.

"I'm thankful that our Saviour is still very much alive...daily interceding on our behalf."

"I'm thankful for the two sons-in-law, granddaughter, and soon-to-be daughter-in-law God added to our lives this year. Poppa?"

"Well, you *took* mine, Momma!" Everyone laughed, then he went on. "I'm thankful that all three of our sons have a boldness to share this lively Gospel with others."

"I'm thankful for the four generations in this room, and for the blessing it has been to help two of those generations into the world."

Mrs. Bennett reached out and grasped Doctor Whittle's hand in loving appreciation. "I'm thankful for all our family, not just by birth or by marriage, but by *new* birth."

"I'm thankful for God's blessing Laura and me with another child as well as with a grandchild."

"I'm thankful for God's giving me new life in Christ this spring, for His sparing my wife's life this summer, and for both of our babies, in heaven and soon to come."

"I'm thankful...." Carol paused, the whole room feeling hugged close with her glance. "I'm thankful for an accident that happened two years ago. An accident that brought us all together. An accident that was really no accident at all."

Epilogue

Doctor Whittle was meticulously packing his instruments in his doctor bag as the nurse finished cleaning up the baby. She handed the doctor the newly-delivered infant wrapped in a soft blanket. Carrying the tiny, wiggling form carefully to her mother, he said with a face wreathed in smiles, "Here is your daughter, Mrs. Bennett."

Though totally exhausted from childbirth, the moment she heard the sound of her sweet baby's cry, Laura Bennett's arms reached out. Her husband came to her side as she held their beautiful child, and the doctor and nurse slipped quietly out of the room, closing the door silently behind them.

"Oh, Laura, *look* at her!" He touched the tiny curl on her forehead. "Curly hair like Charlie and Lizzy. Is your heart still set on the name we chose?"

"Definitely." She passed the precious bundle to her husband ever so gently. "Benjamin Bennett, meet your daughter, Miss Abigail Jayne Bennett." While Ben held his daughter for the first time, there came a knock on the door. "Come in!"

Charlie, Carol, and baby Chandler came in to see how mother and baby were doing. "Well? Does our son have a new auntie or an uncle?"

"An aunt!" Mrs. Bennett beamed as her eyes hardly left her husband and baby girl, but when Chandler Michael caught sight of his grandmum and began to coo and gurgle his greetings, her attention turned quickly enough. Wiggling her fingers, she reached for him. "Chandler, you have an auntie who is nearly three months younger than you are! What fun you will have growing up together, dearest!" The child's reddish-brown curls and dimpled cheeks were his mother's, but the smiling eyes that looked back at Mrs. Bennett were so like Charlie's. Though still blue, they already seemed to be changing; and Mrs. Bennett couldn't help but think how handsome he'd be with brown eyes like his father.

Abigail chose that moment to cry, indignant that she hadn't been fed yet. Chandler began to fuss in empathy, and Carol took him quickly and petted him until he quieted down. "We just wanted to be the first to meet the baby. She's *beautiful*, Mother." Remembering Charlie's description of his sister Lizzy, she wondered just how much Abigail would look like her. She knew Mrs. Bennett must've been having similar thoughts from her next comments.

"I remember when I found out I was expecting Lizzy, I wondered if I would have room in my heart for another child. I loved Charlie so much, and I just couldn't imagine.... Now with a third child to love, I know that our capacity for love is elastic...it expands with the need." She took Abigail from her husband, then smiled a glowing smile at her son and daughter-in-law and grandson. "Thank you so much for coming. God has been so good to us."

Charlie stooped to kiss his mother and newborn sister, then with loving farewells he guided Carol and Chandler back to the carriage. As they rode back to their home, Charlie placed his arm around his wife, their sleeping son in her arms. "Yes, God has been very, *very* good to us. Always."

My Refuge

The Bennett Vignettes continue.
The year is 1912, and "progress" is a small word
for what is happening in the world.
The realms of technology and finance are
ever advancing with man's
knowledge and ingenuity.
Progress is not appropriate terminology however
for what is happening to the world's
moral and spiritual condition.

A.J. Bennett is a young entrepreneur.
The financial industrialists of Baltimore
have begun to see A.J. as being synonymous with
leadership, *industrialism*, and *capitalism*.
But A.J. has troubles of her own.
As a young woman in a man's world,
she is fast becoming callous to the things that truly
matter in life—to love, friendship, and God.

Follow the story of Abigail Jayne Bennett
and the rest of the Bennetts' friends and family
as they learn the vital importance of
Biblical priorities:
faith, family, and forgiveness.

*God is our refuge and strength,
a very present help in trouble.
Psalm 46:1*

Printed in the United States
62556LVS00003B/154-198